PENGUIN

ALL IS B

Jean Arasanayagam is a Sri Lan   ____. Burgher
origin. She attended a private Methodist Missionary School, is a
graduate of the University of Ceylon and obtained an M.Litt in
Literary Linguistics from the University of Stratchlyde, Glasgow.
She was an Hon. Fellow in the Creative Activities of the
International Writing Programme at the University of Iowa in
1990. In 1994 she was International Writer-in-Residence in the
South West (U.K.) and was Visiting Fellow at Exeter University
in the Faculty of Arts. Her work has been published widely in
Sri Lanka and abroad.

She is married to Thiagarajah Arasanayagam, writer, painter and
playwright, and has two daughters who are themselves writers.
She lives in Kandy but has travelled extensively in the United
Kingdom, the United States, Europe and India.

All is Burning

JEAN ARASANAYAGAM

PENGUIN BOOKS

Penguin Books India (P) Ltd., 11 Community Centre, Panchsheel Park,
New Delhi 110 017, India
Penguin Books Ltd., 80 Strand, London WC2R 0RL, UK
Penguin Putnam Inc., 375 Hudson Street, New York, NY 10014, USA
Penguin Books Australia Ltd., 250 Camberwell Road, Camberwell,
Victoria 3124, Australia
Penguin Books Canada Ltd., 10 Alcorn Avenue, Suite 300, Toronto,
Ontario M4V 3B2, Canada
Penguin Books (NZ) Ltd., Cnr Rosedale and Airborne Roads, Albany, Auckland,
New Zealand
Penguin Books (South Africa) (Pty) Ltd., 24 Sturdee Avenue, Rosebank 2196,
South Africa

First published by Penguin Books India 1995

Copyright © Jean Arasanayagam 1995

10 9 8 7 6 5 4

Typeset in Palatino by FOLIO, New Delhi

The author and publishers would like to acknowledge the following magazines
in which some of these stories first appeared :
Kunapipi, ed. Anna Rutherford, University of Aarhus Denmark in which 'I am
an Innocent Man' first appeared ; *Kenyon Review,* Gambier, Ohio, in which 'Fire
in the Village' first appeared : *WERC*, Women's Education and Research Centre,
Sri Lanka, where 'Fragments from a Journey' was first used.

Made and printed in India by Swapna Printing Works Pvt. Ltd.

To my daughters
Parvathi and Dewasundari
Continuing sources of inspiration and support

Thus have I heard, The Blessed One was once living at Gayastsa in Gaya with a thousand bhikkus. There he addressed the bhikkhus.

'Bhikkhus, all is burning. And what is the all that is burning?

'Bhikkhus, the eye is burning, visible forms are burning, visual consciousness is burning, visual impression is burning, also whatever sensation, pleasant or painful or neither-painful-nor-pleasant, arises on account of the visual impression, that too is burning. Burning with what? Burning with the fire of lust, with the fire of hate, with the fire of delusion; I say it is burning with birth, ageing and death, with sorrows, with lamentations, with pains, with griefs, with despairs.

The Fire Sermon of the Buddha
(Adittapariyaya–sutta)

Here too, the night is dark, thunder-black, as the fire
In the village spreads, it's best to escape while you can,
Take to the forest, mats rolled up on the head,
Children tucked under the arms, no time to cook
The evening meal, just milk in the breast, the morning's
Rice wrapped up in a plantain leaf, to lie awake
Watching alert for the sound of gunshot and wailing
Cries, the moon wounded, the clouds bleeding . . .

Excerpt from *Fire in the Village*

Contents

The Journey

Two . . . THREE . . . FIVE . . . eight . . . twelve . . .
sixteen . . . . Always the counting. Numbers. Under
the breath. In soft, sibilant whispers. There must be
no slip in their precise numbering. But we had
names. Must we forget them now? Names that were
known among friends. Parents. Loved ones. In which
country? One that seems so distant now. The one we
have left behind. Home: hills, fields, valleys; rivers,
jungles, habitations; trees, flowers and fruit. They

pass through my mind like those Jataka tales unfolding in the temple murals of my country. Tales of the several lives of the Bodhisattvas. The striving of The One to reach Enlightenment, become a Buddha. But first to reach the highest state of perfection. Until then he is on the road to Enlightenment and on that road which he travels through successive births, he will live and speak with all beings—animals, birds, humans. That journey of his, that Road to Perfection . . . . And ours? We are travelling on many unknown roads. Taking unfamiliar routes through alien terrain, crossing frontiers and borders. On and on we travel. To reach what destination and why?

The guide knows where we are being taken. We must trust him absolutely. We are walking through a forest. There are no tracks. The trees are silent and watchful sentinels. Yet they offer us protection too. Oak. Birch. Beech. Pines. The snow piles up silently. Our boots sink deep as we step cautiously through it. We cannot afford to flounder. Or delay. In the darkness we have to keep together. By instinct. Animal instinct. If we veer off the track we will be lost. Losing our way will mean that we can never make it to our destination. There's a woman among us, with her young son. That makes sixteen of us altogether (asylum seekers, refugees—call us what you like). Seventeen with the guide. The guides change from time to time and place to place. No names. Just gestures to follow them. Trust. Absolute trust.

The woman doesn't ask to be treated in any special way. Bears everything silently. But she is always watchful and alert where the boy is concerned. She's prepared for any hardship. Tough woman. Only tender towards the child, but doesn't cosset him too much. I'm the only Sinhala male in this group. The others are Tamils, from the North of the country which we have left. And the guides? Who knows? They change. German? Russian? Swiss? Jewish? No one questions. No one asks with easy and casual familiarity, 'Hey, what's your name? Where are you from? A family? Children? Have you ever travelled before? Visited my country?' No, no. No time for questions, for entry through the slightest aperture into any life other than one's own. Danger lies in too much knowledge. We do not share information about each others lives. We have learned to store away all facts that are useful to us. When the time comes we will unearth that store. Moreover, identity isn't important here, at this juncture. Identity is still the burning question of the day in our part of the world; identity that separates and divides. But here we are one, because we share this journey and all its travails. We eat the same food. Bread, cheese, apples. We quench our thirst from the same flask of water. No one makes me feel that I am not one of them. It would have been easy for them to have done so.

We maintain silence most of the time. I have no one to talk to in my own language at any rate. Nor can we speak in each other's language. We use signs to communicate with each other when the necessity arises. What keeps us together, keeps us going in a landscape that has no recognizable signpost or landmark is just one purpose and that is to reach Berlin. To disappear there or to seek, through legal means, political asylum. The question of maintaining an individual identity will come later.

Two routes lead to Berlin. One through France, the other through Russia. We have taken the route through Russia.

We continue to move stealthily. Fear. It is perpetually with us. We need physical and mental stamina too. We must be strong in body, mind and will. No sign of weakness must be shown, or we might be left behind. We must not impede the rest of the group. We must move together. I am reminded of the stories about the plantation workers who were brought to our island two hundred years or more ago. Brought from south India in their hundreds in ships. Disembarking at Talaimannar, they made the long trek from the north, through thick, animal-infested jungles, to the central highlands to work on the tea estates. So many died on the way of cholera, dysentery, malaria. Many were left behind to be attacked by wild bear and leopards or to grow weaker and weaker and die, leaving their skeletons as new landmarks on that terrifying journey. And of those who reached the central highlands, many hundreds died of fever, chills, pneumonia in those mist-veiled mountains. Always the weak have had to succumb . . . . No, we must keep up our strength. There is no letting go even for a moment. And always to remember that we are a group. Numbers. Each of us is a number. The numerals reverberate in our minds: sixteen of us, seventeen with the guide. No one should go missing.

Our dependence on the guide is total. This is unknown country to us. We are not human beings to them. With names. Personal lives. Habits. Feelings or emotions. When we are handed over at the border for the next stage of the journey to the next guide or agent, we are 'dollars'. We bear with the irony. We're not people, we're money to them. We provide employment to them. They take risks too. We understand that. Dollars. Money. What do they care about the politics of our individual countries? About war and violence. Conflict. Ethnicity. Massacres and assassinations. Revolutions. Human rights violations. Disappearances, torture, death. Though it's nothing new to anyone, really. The soldier justifies his rape of women in war. He asserts the triumph of the victor. He has to let off the tensions and the horrors of the battlefield, has to have his booty. The map of Europe has been changed often enough and is still changing. People are reclaiming the territory that once belonged to them before the invasions and conquests of historical eras and epochs. The changing of borders and frontiers leads to extensions of power. And now, ethnic cleansing, so that the reclaimed territory rests on a foundation of skeletal remains: bones that branch out like a subterranean forest, the flesh nourishing the soil yet its poisons creeping through the still veins to create a monstrous foliage. We know the histories of all these worlds. They haven't had time to learn ours. Our wars, our revolutions, our conflicts, our displacements, are important only to ourselves. We become refugees, asylum seekers. Their laws restrict our entry into their countries. Yet there are people who help us to bend these laws. They've got to eat too, haven't they? We serve their purpose. They serve ours. When we reach a destination, the desired one, we can't expect a friendly welcome. Although looking back on our own history, didn't we open our doors to the invader? Didn't we even adopt the colonizers' way of life? Change our language, our religion, our culture? Didn't Kuveni herself take Vijaya for a lover?

To reach Europe we had to pay thousands of dollars. Somehow we made it. To Russia. We reached there by Aeroflot. Not as tourists, of course! No one questioned our identities. We had passports and visas we had purchased at a price. And hard currency in our pockets. That would help us through part of the journey. In Moscow we were all put in one room. It was winter. There was no heating. We were grateful for the warmth of each other's bodies. The comfort of each others breath. Our being together. We had glimpsed streets white with snow piled high, snow crisp like mounds of freshly laundered linen. We still did not have the freedom to tread those streets.

The woman and child were cold. I saw her remove her fur-lined jerkin and wrap it about his shoulders. I had a warm woollen muffler. I unwound it from my neck and held it out to her. 'For him,' I gestured wordlessly. She looked at me, uncertainly, almost unbelievingly, took it, gave me a tentative smile. Why had I done this? I was thinking of my *malli*, my youngest brother, I suppose . . . . It wasn't gratitude I wanted, or even friendship. Just a little human feeling. We weren't divided in this country according to our racial or ethnic groups. We hadn't brought our weapons, our arms to this country. We didn't bear labels here—terrorists, militants, subversives, misguided youths . . . . Those identities had been left behind. We had a different mission here. The journey. The pilgrimage. We weren't a warring people here.

The others talk to each other. In whispers. But in very few words, and in their own language. I wish I could join in. I feel lonely sometimes but most of the time I am not. I think of the next stage of the journey. I've reached so far, but then, what happens next? I count the dollars in my wallet, open my travelling bag, touch my warm clothes. I have my passport with me and a photograph or two of my family. No letters; I have no address as yet. It is best this way. I don't want to reveal my whereabouts to anyone. We travel incognito. No longer in touch with the outer world.

I wonder what's happening at home. When I was there I sometimes felt I would like to join the Security Forces. Ideas of courage, of patriotism spurred me on but I had seen too many young friends missing in action, or blinded or crippled for life . . . when they had hardly begun their journey. Landmines. Ambushes. Dying in action. Dying for the Motherland. Too few people caring anyway. Each in his own way dividing the country further. And would any of us want to return? But this is no place to talk politics. Though why should I, who has not suffered in any way through displacement, loss, bereavement want to leave my comfortable home? Why should I be with this group that I would have had nothing to do with in my own country, with whom I have nothing in common, neither language nor culture nor tradition?

I have my own reasons for making this decision to leave home. I'm not like these people. They have other reasons; so many things to escape from. The long and protracted war that has been going on for ten years and more. Armies of occupation in their soil. Their sons, and daughters too, martial women who have their own regiments, have gone against all the traditions of their society, joining the militant movements. Fighting for a cause. Families broken up. For them, seeking political asylum is often a matter of life and death. Am I, belonging to another ethnic group, the majority group in the country, am I too responsible for making them refugees? No. I'm not guilty. I'm really a peaceful kind of person. I have been more or less privileged all my life. I've had a good life. My father is a businessman, he has wealth. So I've always had what I've wanted. I was educated in a good private school too. Maybe life was too easy for me. I didn't join the revolution like many of my friends did. I had no interest in destabilizing the State. I was not one of those who were socially deprived by caste, a feudal power structure, or lack of wealth. I had no social conscience either. I didn't rave and rant against the exploitation of my own people by multinational and vested interests. I had no purpose in life. So many of my friends had disappeared, died or been detained in camps during the revolution that my father was only too happy to give his consent for me to go abroad. He had enough money to give my sisters in marriage. Besides, I didn't have a profession or a career. I wanted a change, some adventure. I wanted to make a journey that would change my life. I wanted to venture into an unknown country; make my own predictions and decisions, question the revelations that would confront me at the end of this long saga.

I was as yet unenlightened in many ways. For one thing, in my own land would I ever have undertaken a journey with people who were not of my own kind? We had looked upon each other as strangers, even enemies, dangerous to the unity of our motherland. To me they were people who were trying to divide the country, claim territory for themselves. We too had moved into their traditional homelands, changed the demographic map. Each ethnic group had accused the other of untold crimes. Was I joining a band of pilgrims disguised as asylum seekers? Was I innocent enough to think that in the new country I would find enlightenment which would release me from all suffering, *dukkha*? I . . .? Taking the path of the Bodhisattva, is it also the route of the asylum seeker, the refugee? Is the shedding of an identity also the path to enlightenment, if that identity is part of an existence that entails hatred, enmity, violence? With these people that I am travelling with, there are no such feelings. We do not look upon each other as brothers, nor do we look upon each other as enemies. We can learn a lot about survival from each other. Even without a shared language. The guide knows the route, that's all we need to know.

And yet sometimes I feel unsure and afraid. Who will meet me at the end of this journey? One thing, however, we are well fed here. They bring us plenty of food. Pans of steaming hot, boiled vegetables and soup. Cabbage. Cauliflower. Rye bread. Black bread. Borscht. Nothing spicy, but the food fills that pit in the stomach. We eat, then sit on our haunches, stand around, smoke cigarettes, wait. Wait until it is time to get the OK to move on. To leave this temporary shelter, take the lorry or truck or container to the next assignment.

In Moscow too we had waited. We could see nothing of the city. We were not there for sightseeing anyway. No strolling along the streets or sitting in restaurants drinking vodka. I would have liked to see the Kremlin or shop in their markets. Taste caviar perhaps. All we heard was news of the White House being under siege, of the deaths, the surrender, the trials and imprisonment of the leaders. The epochs we moved through were historical. We were part of it all, caught up in that turbulent stream of events.

Yes, we continued to wait. On the way we had learned yet another lesson: Patience. Nothing would move until the right time approached. I knew there were risks. We had always to be hidden. Once, a man's body had been found wedged into the compartment of an air-conditioning unit in a container. Suffocated. Chilled to death. What a slow, long drawn out and agonizing end. And those three men, my own kind, who were flung out of the truck they had been loaded into on a journey similar to ours in some part of Germany. It was winter. They had smuggled themselves into a truck among crates and packages and when they were discovered they were scarcely breathing. They were hardly thought to be human, to have breath. No one investigated closely. They were left in the frozen ice and snow, still half alive, crushed by the weight of the crates, to die by the wayside. Slaughtered animals. All they needed was to be suspended from meat hooks.

When the call finally came we were asked to get into the back of a huge container truck. It was already packed with heavy wooden crates. We could neither sit nor stand upright. We had to lie one on top of the other the way firewood is loaded in our country. The journey lasted for so many hours. We travelled hundreds of kilometres. We were conscious of the bodies beneath ours, their breathing almost imperceptible, trying to be as still as possible so as not to cause the other discomfort. Layers of bodies. Orders were tersely barked at us:

'Head down! Lie down. Flat! Flat! No moving. Still! You can die.'

The container moved swiftly on a silent empty highway. Suddenly it lurched. Came to a halt. The doors of vehicles slammed shut. Footsteps sounded on the hard asphalt. Our bodies tensed. Grew chill. Petrified. Flashlights bathed the container in harsh white-green flares. Voices, many voices, high-pitched, interrogative, assailed the man at the wheel and the guide Their voices had already warned us: *'Polizei! Polizei!'*

My heart thudded against my breast. Fear. Fear of being discovered. Arrested. Put in police cells. Deported.

'What are you carrying?'

The voices of the driver and the guide answered calmly and matter-of-factly, 'Wine. Here, have cigarettes.'

'Cold. Cold tonight. Well below zero. Not good for asylum seekers . . . contraband goods. This is the route they always take.'

'Not us. We don't carry them. Flooding into Berlin from everywhere . . . creating problems'.

'How many kilometres to go yet?'

'We travel tonight and tomorrow. Then we deliver our beer and wine. Everybody's thirst quenched!'

We heard them walk around the container truck. Boots clicked on the asphalt. How long since we had ceased to breathe? I stifled a cough. The order was finally given for the vehicle to proceed.

'OK. Go'.

We drove fast, it seemed for several hours. The vehicle stopped. The guide came round to the back. There was a slight gap among the crates for us to move out.

'Get off. Quick!'

We stopped at the edge of a vast forest filled with fir trees. It was freezing outside. Our sweat chilled in no time. The trees stood still. So silent. Great giant crosses. Black. The snow glittered on branches with touches of silvery frost. Our blood was an icy current in the veins. The guide led us into the heart of the forest. He would remain with us. The container would proceed on its journey.

There are no discernible pathways here. Only white blankets of snow. And silence. We are at the mercy of this stranger, this unknown man. We have learned to trust these guides. It's better that they are impersonal. Then there are no loves, no hates. Once more the counting begins. One . . . three . . . six . . . seven . . . ten . . . twelve . . . fifteen . . . sixteen . . .

'Go. Go,' He urges. 'Quickly. No delays. Understand? Quick. No delay. Before light comes.'

We feel dwarfed by the trees. So small. So human. So puny and insignificant. We look at our guide. What do we do next? We know he must have a new set of plans.

'Take only what you need.'

Some begin to unzip their travelling bags and rapidly dress themselves in as many suits as they can. Three pairs of trousers. Shirts. Coats. Socks. But of course only one pair of boots.

'No more bags. No more carrying anything with you.'

Discard all the things we had thought so necessary for survival? Passports. Cameras. Clothes. Personal possessions. Now the time has come for us to assess their importance.

'Throw away your documents. Tear them into little pieces. Your passports, letters, diaries, photographs, everything.'

Those passports and visas had cost us thousands, no, lakhs and lakhs of rupees. Well, they seem to have served their purpose. We don't need them anymore. I begin to tear up everything meticulously. It's my past life I'm tearing up. I am aware of that.

'From now on, no identity. No identity. You understand that? From now on, no names. Nothing.'

No names. No identities. On no man's land. In a sense the load grows lighter. I begin to experience a new kind of freedom. Heady. Yes, its heady as if I've drunk a lot—champagne, now that I'm in Europe—

for celebration. Celebration of some kind of victory. I look at the woman, the child. It's so cold. Freezing. She keeps the boy close to her all the time. There is a deep, wordless communion between them. A bonding that no one can share. She smooths the thickly knitted pullover on his chest. It's grey in colour. Drab. The clothes we wear are all drab and anonymous. His eyes look trustingly into his mother's. She will protect him with her life. She is strong. Asks for no special treatment at any time. Eats what is given her. Drinks what is given her. But first sees that her son is fed and his thirst quenched. She walks the long distances without complaint. The boy too. His body still trembles, perhaps more with the tension and exhaustion than with the cold. I have one jerkin too many. I hold it out to him.

'*Malli*,' I say hesitantly. 'Take. *Méka gandé*. For you.'

He looks at me. Points to my shoulders, my chest.

'No, no. It's OK. I'm fine. Not cold. Not cold.'

He reminds me so much of my *malli*. *Malli* must be playing cricket with his friends at this moment. Waiting for a letter from his *loku aiya*. From me. Waiting to show off the stamps and boast about me.

'*Loku aiya* is in Germany. He'll send me a new video camera soon.'

The boy's thin shoulders are covered with my jerkin. They stop shaking. He looks at me as if at an elder brother. What is there to divide us at this moment? Nothing. Even lack of a shared language is no barrier to our communication.

'Now we go. To Border.'

Very little is spoken. We conserve our energy. Our voices will give us away if there are any guards searching the forest for people like us. The *polizei* are on the alert constantly. All of us begin walking

13

together, shambling along. Our names, our identities relinquished. I can take on any name now. Gerhard. Or Pieter. Or Samson. No, no; Dollar—that's my new name. Dollar. The agents never have names. The guides never have names. And we are thought of only in terms of dollars. The counting begins again—one . . . five . . . eight . . . ten . . . fourteen . . . sixteen . . .

Each one is concerned about himself but is aware of the others too. We will not abandon the weak. There is an unspoken bond between us now. I'm not one of them but it no longer matters. It will never matter again.

Our dangers have been mutual. When it's a matter of survival the politics of a country left so far behind do not get first priority. If there's no food, we all go hungry. If there is food, we eat. We share out equally. I keep the apple I am given in my pocket for the boy. I silently hand it over to him as we walk. My *malli* loves apples, the red ones. I'll see plenty of apple orchards, I'm sure, laden with fruit of bright colours—russet, yellowy-pink, green—when winter is past, when I'm settled somewhere in Germany. If I reach my destination safely, that is. The boy takes a bite and offers the fruit to his mother. She smiles. Shakes her head.

'You eat,' she tells him in their language. They smile at each other. At home, the militants, the 'Boys', bite on cyanide tablets when they're arrested. I'm glad he won't have to do that here. I've grown too fond of him. He's become my *malli*.

We come out of the forest. The timing is perfect. There's a truck waiting on the side of the road. We get in. 'Quick. Quick,' the guide orders.

We begin our journey again. To the border. The German border.

At the border the truck stops. It's instantly surrounded by border guards with their loaded weapons. Our hearts are quaking. We're hiding behind the crates with their frozen carcasses of sheep and cattle.

'What are you carrying?'

'Frozen meat.'

'OK, proceed.'

We scarcely breathe. The boy shows no fear. Even at a tender age the young ones know how to handle firearms, set off landmines. They're not weak by any means. I'm not sentimental or homesick or anything. It's just that *malli* keeps coming into my mind. He knows where I'm going. To Europe. To Germany. To become rich. Get a job, gain wealth. I know he looks forward to letters, photographs, gifts from a foreign city. He's likely to boast and I'm sure he does, about me, to is friends.

'*Loku aiya* is in abroad. In Germany. Look, he has sent me this shirt and this watch and money, too, German Marks to buy a new cricket bat . . . . He's promised to send me lots of things . . .'

He will never know the realities we have to face. The fear, tension, terror. The humiliation. But we can't complain. We asked for it, didn't we? This journey. And at the end of it . . . what kind of enlightenment? Will we find it in a cell when we're arrested and locked up? And even if we manage to find safe passage, what about the attacks of the neo-Nazis we'll have to face? There was the case of two youths, neo-Nazis, who were responsible for killing a Turkish woman and two of her grand daughters by fire bombing their house in Mölln. Yes, we'll have to face the neo-Nazis too. They are the same although they have other names. Skinheads and Rightists. Everywhere the minorities will face such dangers.

Ironically enough, I'll become the minority here, in this country. Not only will I have to relinquish my identity but also the power attached to it in my own country. We are newcomers here; the Turkish woman Bahide Arslan and her grand daughters Geliz and Ayse, two little girls, were long established residents— yet their houses had been torched. Reminds me of what happened in our island in '83. The torching of the houses and the business places, the killings. History will always question these facts. My parents gave shelter to Tamil families during that time. I understood their fear. Is that the fear I must now feel?

Once more we get off the truck. We have to cross a field. We crawl through mud and slush. We're caked with it. Our clothes stiffen and grate against the skin. When was the last time we had a good wash? A hot bath? It seems like ages and ages ago. We reach a township. Turkish music comes from the cafés. We see people drinking foaming beer, eating off steaming platters of food. A cooked meal. Cups of hot coffee.

Where to wash off the mud and slush? There's a fountain in the heart of the city. We wash ourselves thoroughly in it. The water is icy but fresh.

The guide leaves us.

'Another guide will come to lead you,' he says and disappears.

We're alone. Abandoned. He never turns up. We move out of the city, walk endlessly along a gravel road. No one to be seen. No dwellings. No habitations. Walking into the countryside, only the woods on either side. Silent trees. No birdsong. Scrunch of gravel underfoot.

Suddenly patrol cars drive up.

'Police, police,' someone calls out.

No escape for us.

'Aliens. Aliens. Asylum seekers.' We understand what they are saying.

'Passports. Show. Where passports?'

We have no identities any longer.

'Inside. Inside. Get in.'

Car doors open and we're bundled in. Doors slam shut. We're driven off. Taken into the city. Berlin—we're here at last.

We reach the Police Station. They take us in and lock us up in cells. I can see the police officers seated round their desks laughing, talking, smoking. Have to think fast. Really fast. I remember the telephone number of the original agent. It's in my mind, flashes across my memory. I make signs to the police officers. I somehow get the message across to them.

'Embassy. Sri Lanka. Embassy. We go . . . there. Country embassy. Go back . . . country . . . home. Home. Get taxi. Here, hundred dollars I have. I pay . . . for all. All of us. Others have money also. We pay taxi.'

It is my plan of escape. They are convinced, only too happy to get rid of the burden.

I first go to a phone booth. I repeat the number which I've carried in my head. Establish contact with the original agent.

Instructions are given.

'Wait at the railway station. I will send someone else.'

Another guide arrives and we prepare for the next lap. The last lap of our journey. We look at him silently. We have got to trust him.

We pile into the taxi the policemen have arranged. Halfway, we tell the driver, 'Look. Money. Dollars. Dollars. Free us. Let us go free. Free.'

The driver accepts the money. We are several

kilometres away from the city. He counts the notes before tucking them away in his wallet. Then he opens the doors of the taxi. We get off. We stand in the middle of nowhere. We have to make a split second decision. From this point onwards we will walk back with the guide, to the city. Past the wood. Oak. Birch. Fir trees. Ancient woods. Fugitives can hide here but for how long? And food? From where? We have nothing. Better walk on. A motley group of us. Hope no police patrol cars come upon us again. We reach Berlin and enter through the Brandenburg Gate.

We enter the Unter de Linde. We see parts of the old city which still remain left over from the bombings of the Second World War. There's no East, no West any longer. No Wall. We see trams. Cars. Innumerable cars. Volkswagens. They remind me of home. The trams belong to East Germany. Police cars stop at the pedestrian crossing. There are little green men with hats in them. That again is part of East Germany. The green men without hats belong to the West. Berlin has known defeat. The defeat of two World Wars. It's a city that seems to be seeking a new identity, one made up of many nationalities and races, not just pure Aryan alone. For us too it will provide a new identity. We see bulldozers flattening out the past; cranes, cement mixers. We also see the new synagogues like monuments to change. Do the Jews still face persecution, I wonder? No, they are strong now. No longer the victims of the holocaust. It is a past they will carry with them, but the new breed of Jews will be different. I am told that the survivors used to visit clinics in Israel to have the tattoos of the concentration camps removed. The numbers. They did not want that identity any longer. It was unacceptable to the new race of Jews who wanted to be identified with their blond, blue-eyed Aryan counterparts.

We pass huge apartment blocks with murals in brilliant colours on the walls. Graffiti too. I am reminded of the graffiti on facades of buildings and on walls in my own country during the revolution of 1989 and the 1990s. The bold, eye-stabbing red and black announcements, messages, statements of the subversives. The country was in flames. What graffiti will we discover about ourselves here in time to come? When will we be free to go undetected on these cobbled streets where no one will ask to see our identity cards? Can we find employment here? It will be difficult, I know. There's an influx of East Berliners here and asylum seekers of all races. Not safe either, at anytime, with the neo-Nazis. Apartment houses, refugee centres set on fire; the exiles beaten up, killed.

Plenty of people like us on the streets. Africans, Turks, Sri Lankans, Indians, East Europeans. But we don't talk. As soon as we spot a telephone booth, the Tamils go directly towards it. They have all their phone numbers in memory. Before long, taxis and cars arrive and one by one they are whisked away. Only the woman, the boy and myself are left behind. I have nowhere to go. No contacts either. She gestures to me, points to the two of them, as if to say, 'Join us, be with us. You can come where we go.'

Why this invitation? Because of the occasional kindness I showed her along the way? No one thought either of us traitors for talking to or helping each other. No suspicious looks or fear of me being an informer. We will never know each other's names, yet I've got to trust myself to her. The last guide we were to have has left us. His responsibility to us is over. We are now on our own. I am fortunate that this woman has decided to befriend me. Does she see me as a brother or as her young son grown up? Does she think me another political asylum seeker, one who has escaped the detention camps after the revolution? What about her husband? Probably here already in Germany. Must have arrived earlier, prepared the way for her, sent her money to get across. What a reunion they will all have. But what about me? I know the realities. Just as much as the others do. The safe houses. Old dilapidated buildings. Bullet holes still pock mark some of the walls. Peeling plaster. Endless spiral stairways. Bunks. Blankets hanging as room dividers. Rooms full of immigrants. Refugees. See them passing by. Some of them look as if they've assimilated the new culture. We're not wanted here. We'll have to be illegal workers and merge among the others. Don't want to be noticed.

The woman, the boy and I get into a taxi. The woman speaks one word:

'Saarbrucken'

We travel a thousand kilometres away from Berlin. We arrive at the address she gave. On her arrival she and her son are greeted and welcomed by their own people. As soon as they see me they decide that I should be among my own. How can they be responsible for me?

Again, numbers. They make calls. My people arrive in a taxi. The first question they ask, is, '*Machan*, how did you get here?' They sound incredulous.

I am handed over to them. I feel at home in their presence. They give me a cup of tea, some food. I have a hot bath and change my clothes. They are generous. My beard has grown and I look different. My eyes have a more worldly look, my recent experiences, the risks, tensions and dangers, mirrored in them. My journey has been no ordinary one. It is not a mere adventure story. I have made my pilgrimage on this road. But this pilgrimage, this journey has not yet ended.

The red tape involved in granting asylum must now begin. I am taken to the place where I have to register myself. Official matters. I have to give all the details about myself. Then the trial will begin. I want to stay here. I don't want to be deported. But I am not a political asylum seeker. What legitimate reason then do I have to remain here?

What can I say?

The truth?

I Am an Innocent Man

I OFTEN CYCLED past the prawn farms with a friend on our way to the school where I teach. There are great ponds on acres and acres of land in this coastal village in the Eastern part of the island. On these lonely roads, in their deep silence, grew my awareness of the life that was evolving in the ponds as the crustacea emerged from the spawn, creating concentric ripples as they swam beneath the water's surface. A subtle movement seemed to stir the expanse of water, breaking the slivers of light, scattering them on the ponds. I was not able to observe these forms of life minutely but there was this feeling that the ponds were seething, alive, and that the prawns were trapped in their aquatic prisons from which they could not escape until they grew large enough to be caught, netted, packed and sent away to titillate the appetites of the wealthy gourmets who could afford them.

The great expanses of water reflected the stark white light of these arid regions; silvery, sky-reflecting mirrors that trapped the clouds. Light and dark changed the images that floated on the surface. At night, the moon, stirred by the wind, shivered fragmented like the segmented petals of a waterplant. It was on moonless nights that the prawn stealers came to the farms. They crept through the land in stealth, defying the guards, to net the prawns, at the terrible cost of being caught, beaten up, even killed.

To me, the prawns appeared to have an even greater price than that placed on human life. They were being reared for profit. Foreign investors had put a great deal of money into this venture and the prawn farms had to yield a good harvest. The crustacea had first to grow, after which their globules of luscious flesh were carefully packed for export abroad. Sometimes the horrible image of death appeared in my mind—the opaque covering on the prawns like the polythene shrouds which hide the remains of those killed in battle, or in land mine explosions. Those who ate them would not have such disturbing reflections.

The process took time. The prawn ponds were carefully tended. First, the spawn was put in and from the fertilized eggs, the nauplii emerged. These metamorphosed into protozoa which developed antennae, eyes and thoracic limbs—all the while growing and multiplying in their aquatic environments, keeping the workers on the farms fully occupied. The prawn farms provided employment to the villagers, many of them young boys. There were the older, familied men, too, who worked there. The tending of the prawn ponds, the netting and packaging for sending abroad were the tasks that engaged them. Before the prawn farms were begun, the villagers cultivated their paddy fields and cleared the jungle for their *chenas*. They had herds of cattle and buffalo which they milked to fill their curd pots. At night the animals would be driven into the jungle and then herded out the next morning.

But the jungles had changed now. This territory was ravaged by fighting between the guerrillas and the security forces. But so was territory elsewhere. It was always the innocent villagers who came under attack. The jungles became a place where they would seek shelter, fleeing from massacres or reprisals. This happened with all the communities that were embroiled in these violent events. The villagers would carry their few precious possessions with them and find refuge deep within the jungle, even at the risk of being attacked by wild beasts or bitten by snakes. Many of them died of snake bite but they still fled there at night. There were the sudden attacks, the brutal massacres, huts that went up in flames, the devastation of human habitations where the land was soon overtaken by the thrusting growth of the jungle while the people, displaced, had to move from refuge to refuge, from village to jungle to camps. Within the jungle there existed other networks of communication too. This was where the guerrillas operated from. They had their underground hospitals and storehouses for arms, ammunition, food.

Among the villagers, who in the midst of violence carried on their peacetime occupations and worked on the prawn farms, there were others who had no employment. The prawn ponds were a great temptation to them. Not that it would have mattered if a few prawns were taken, whether to be sold or eaten by the villagers; yet every prawn in these ponds seemed to have a price on it. For, these acres, which had once belonged to no one, were now in the hands of the foreign investors, those nameless people whose presence was only felt as a power that existed beyond this coastal village. The land was now private property, enclosed and fenced in. No trespassers, and the trespassers would be the villagers themselves, were allowed in. But there was interference from certain other groups that had interests in this territory. Some of the guerrillas operated in the vicinity. Not only were the different guerrilla groups waging war with the State troops, they were in conflict with each other too. On the one hand the guerrillas had their advantages, on the other they were disadvantaged. They lacked air power, but they could depend on their knowledge of the terrain, their being part of the community and their ability, with a small band of fighters, to contain a large number of their enemy. But their tactics also involved the civilians who were often caught in the cross fire. The guerrillas managed to slip away, vanish into thin air as it were, while the villagers were caught, rounded up and made to pay the penalty.

On several occasions, one particular guerrilla group would break into the prawn farms. It became a nuisance and an inconvenience to the foreign investors. All they were concerned about were their profits, not the political ideologies of a particular group. They wanted their prawn farms protected from any marauder, it did not matter who.

One of the most powerful guerrilla groups offered protection. Their offer was accepted and a large sum of money was paid which went to their cause. They would guard the prawn ponds and prevent the prawns being stolen. This guerrilla group was very efficient at its job but they had to be ruthless when

it came to keeping out the prawn stealers, even if
they were their own people, the people from the
village. As I said, they were very conscientious. They
mounted guard at night but this did nothing to deter
the villagers who came in by stealth. One of them
was caught and warned. He came again. This time
he was beaten up severely. The final time arrived
when he was caught yet again. This time he was
killed. The victim's wife wrote to the army command
complaining that there were terrorists operating on
the prawn farms and that they had killed her
husband. Because of this it was now only a matter of
time before the State troops moved in with their
commando units. This was war. The policies on both
sides allowed for no compromise. If any terrorist
was caught he would be given short shrift. There
would be no give and take on either side.
Extermination would take place. Where the guerrillas
were concerned, this often constituted a problem.
They moved freely among the people and did not
always wear uniforms. This meant that any young or
even middle-aged male was suspect.

Often the foreign investors were seen with their
uniformed guerrilla guards, posing for photographs.
No one could be absolutely certain whether they had
any political interests in these areas. They simply
came and went. They pursued their other lives. The
guerrillas remained. So did the villagers. In a situation
as volatile as this, there is room for underhand
goings-on. Collaborators, quislings, informers and
traitors—those hooded people—will always be there.
Sometimes out of fear, sometimes compulsion,
sometimes for thirty pieces of silver. The traitors, if
they were caught, were made to pay with their lives.
There were 'kangaroo courts', summary executions,
lamp post killings.

Yet another man who was in the habit of stealing prawns was caught by the guerrilla group. He was a strong, fearless man. The guerrillas beat him up badly. He warned them and said, 'Finish me off now because if I escape I will revenge myself on you.' But they did not kill him. They bound him up tightly and left him in a room. Meanwhile they relaxed in that man's house and watched television. There appears to have been a certain naïvete in their actions, a naïvete which lay in their confidence in their own power. The man managed to free himself and crawl out into the dark, carrying information to the army headquarters. Everything led to a confrontation with the guerrillas at the prawn farm.

And where do I fit in? I am an innocent man. The school teacher, respected by all in the village. Not only am I not a killer, I also stay out of trouble. I play safe. But do not be mistaken. I am not a weak man. I am very strong inside. I can look after myself, handle firearms. I learnt how to use a gun from my father who was a farmer and had to protect his crops from marauding animals. I know how to handle an AK-47 too, although I have not yet learned how to handle the more sophisticated weapons. And I am very particular about my appearance. I always take pains to appear clean and tidy, so that people may always have a good impression of me. I do not want anyone to think that I am a terrorist, or a militant, or a guerrilla, or one of 'the Boys'. The image I have always wanted to project is that of an innocent man. My face is clean shaven, my cheeks smooth. My clothes always immaculate. I dress in spotless white clothes, freshly washed and ironed—white veshti, white shirt of crisp white cotton. I am careful not to show hostility or aggression towards anyone and I have practiced, through yogic exercises, the sending out of friendly rays from my inner being so as to counter any hostility towards me. I sometimes think I see a radiance surrounding myself. I feel I am wrapped in a shining, protective light which protects me from all evil forces. I have a great sense of responsibility towards the children I teach, both boys and girls, and I do a lot of social service among the people. I record the songs of the old men of the village on my cassettes so that they will be remembered for all time—a man's life span cannot be predicted. No, especially not in these times.

My life goes on, day in, day out, at its usual, regular pace, for I allow very little to disturb me. Every day, I cycle past the mangroves on the road to my school. The mangroves flourish and grow dense and dark, a thick screen of leaves and succulent stems swollen with water. Their aerial roots grow and spread above the surface of the lagoon as if struggling to reach the light and breathe the air. A wild tangle of thick, rope-like roots traps the sediment that flows from the water. The roots stand out of the stiff mud banks like fortress walls. Colonies of trees grow out of these embankments. Symbiotic forms of life thrive in this environment. Tiny fish and molluscs thickly seed the water. Small armoured steel-grey crabs scuttle about in the rich mud. And in turn, all ·these forms of life are prey to water snakes and iguanas. The landscape will never change on these lonely roads but people have begun to change. Sometimes need impels a man to risk his life to carry away the prawns in stealth from the ponds, prawns which he used to take freely from the lagoons in the past. No man is safe anywhere any longer, not even in his own territory. Although I am an innocent man I too must learn that fear and danger can touch me as well. I must begin to prepare myself. Death lies within the jungle and outside it—anywhere, on the road or even in my classroom. Meeting death is not like meeting a friendly stranger. I know this now ...

This time when the rains came, for twelve days it rained continuously, drenching the earth. The vegetation sprang up fresh and green, the roads flowed with rivulets of muddy water. As the rains ceased I felt a change in the air, a change in my own life. The nights were clear and chill. Stars shone with a knife-sharp brilliance in the sky. But there was an ominous feeling that made my blood run cold in my veins. My ears were alert to stray rumours. The time was ideal for military operations to begin. There was news in the air that supplies of diesel and petrol were being brought in. The grapevine buzzed.

On that particular day, that fateful day in my life, I woke up early, at four a.m. I was staying over in the school premises during that time. I went to the well to have my bath as was my habit. In the middle of my bath I heard the sound of helicopters in the air but I did not pay much heed at that moment. Suddenly a pick-up appeared, driving at furious speed towards the village where the prawn farm was. The alarm had been given that the attack was to take place there that morning. There were guerrillas in the pick-up. They were armed.

The sound of the helicopters grew louder, a curious chugging sound which increased as they came nearer. I stood at the well, looking skywards, the water still streaming down my body. The helicopters were flying low. This was unusual. Then I saw them preparing to land on the vacant site which was the playground of the school. Men in camouflage uniform were disembarking from the helicopters. Some of the guerrillas had already jumped off the pick-up and taken cover beside the school buildings. They started shooting—they were just three or four young men. The men from the helicopters began to return fire. One of the guerrillas climbed a tree and took sniper shots at the men. I stood petrified. I couldn't move. The folds of my thin veshti were wet and clinging to my loins. I felt myself apart from all that was taking place. Detached, because I was not part of what was going on, uninvolved, yet, by virtue of being a spectator, in some way involved. I could feel everything that was happening move within my body, my limbs. Fear laid a lash on my tongue. I could not even cry out. The dawn had suddenly darkened. The sniper on the tree had the advantage. Three officers fell. Another of their men. Then one of the *drohi*, the informers. The commando unit had been taken completely unawares. I stared death in the face.

The pick-up drove away with the guerrillas. They laid a mine on the way to the farm. A truck with the security forces was following the helicopter trail. Suddenly there was a tremendous sound, a reverberating explosion as the mine went off and the truck with the army men was blown to bits. I heard later that ten men had lost their lives. Others had reached the farm before the mine was laid. The fighting then began. The sounds of shooting, blasting, explosions travelled through the flat terrain of the countryside. There was bitter fighting between the forces and the guerrillas who defended the place. What, or whom were they defending? The vested interests of the foreigners or their own position? But the guerrillas never remain long in a vulnerable position. They don't get caught. They slip away. They vanish. There are always others who invariably suffer in the crossfire. The foreign investor was out of the country at this time. He was safe. But the matter did not end there once the guerrillas had escaped and the battle had abated. The others who were left, the unarmed, were rounded up. All the males at the prawn farm above the age of fifteen, ranging from forty to fifty men, were lined up and shot. The rest were taken behind a temple and clubbed to death. Eighty-seven of them died. One expects no mercy during these times. One shows no mercy either. There is a war on. An unending war. These are the consequences of war. As I said before, it is the civilians who suffer, especially the males. They are all suspected terrorists. Many more were rounded up from the cluster of eleven villages and killed. The wind travelled towards other villages bearing the odour of blood. Later on a tractor was seen being driven towards the farm to take the bodies for mass burial. The roads were clogged with mud and this impeded the operation. It was a time of crisis and as they had done before, the villagers, with mats, pots of water, some food and a few of their precious belongings, took refuge in the jungles at night. In spite of the snakes and death from their venom, they preferred this uncertain safety.

But what about myself and my responsibilities towards my children? I dried my body and put on my clothes. I waited for my students to arrive. At about 6.30 the children came running to the school. It was very early, too early for lessons to begin, but they were searching for a safe place, away from the shooting. I put them into two classrooms—the school buildings were in different blocks—and shut the doors. I tried to lock them but the locks wouldn't work. I tried to calm them. 'Don't move,' I said. They were in a state of terror. They would be safe here for the moment. The messages would come later. Messages that are always brought by the women. They go from place to place on their secret missions, searching for food, searching for bodies. They also search for their sons; they wait by the camps to get a glimpse of them peering though a grill or a half shut door. They wait, they are patient. They came that day, just as I had expected—the grandmothers, at about 1.30 in the afternoon, in search of their grandchildren, anxious because they had not returned home for the midday meal. The battle had been raging and the sound of shots had warned the villagers of the attack. Now the search operations would continue. The helicopters were flying over the school; bullets were whizzing all over the place. The grandmothers stood petrified, like logs; they couldn't move. The children could not be kept inside anymore. They came running out to meet the grandmothers. The helicopters flew low and splattered the building haphazardly with bullets. Two bullets whizzed past the children.

No one was hit or wounded here. The children looked up fearfully at the bullets that were being sprayed from the helicopters. They didn't dare run back to the buildings for shelter so they cowered beside the walls. When the shooting ceased they were led away, back to their homes. I remained behind.

When there is trouble the boutiques and shops pull down their shutters. I was able to get only a packet of biscuits from a boutique close by. I had no other food. I waited in the school. I didn't want to move out. I closed the door behind me and watched through a keyhole. I heard the tramp of boots, the sound of voices. I saw the soldiers walking past, peering into the school premises. They were watchful, alert. They came to the gate. I was afraid that they would open it and walk in, but the buildings looked empty, silent, abandoned. If they had come inside and found me I would have been suspected of being a terrorist. There would have been no time to answer questions. I would have been shot.

It seemed like hours to me. I was kneeling by the door, I could see them passing. My state of mind was such that I imagined they could see me. But it was only I who could see them. They moved past and away. I began to breathe again after they had left but I knew that it would not end there. The mopping-up operations were on. The existence of the school teacher was known and the next day a woman came to the school bringing a message that I had been summoned to the army headquarters. I had to go, but I was afraid, afraid more than anything else of interrogation. The interrogators, I knew, were very skilled at their task. Clever. They were trained for this. I had only one hope. I told the woman to carry a message for me. I had a friend, the Superintendent of Police. He was from the south. We often met and spoke. We could communicate in English and Sinhala. I had only him to rely on, he would know that I was an innocent man. But I was innocent only because I did not carry firearms. Whoever has witnessed death as I have seen it, men falling, hit by bullets, dying under a clear sky, not knowing sometimes from what direction they were fired upon, could not think himself to be innocent. Nor could I do anything about the killings on either side. It made me feel guilty, as if I had been a participant in all that had happened. I had knowledge, I was a witness; I could not claim to be innocent.

I could no longer ride my bicycle along the roads past the prawn farms watching the great ponds, with their water mirrors reflecting clouds, stirred by the swimming of the crustacea beneath their surface.

What was the use of hiding in the jungles at night? That could only be a temporary refuge. There were worse risks there—the danger of being spotted by soldiers in the low-flying helicopters or being bitten by venomous reptiles which abound in the thickets. Moreover the Special Task Force, the commando group, had armoured vehicles that could go through the jungles. I preferred to stay outside the jungle. I was no terrorist. So why should I have had to hide? I did not like to listen to the stories that the guerrillas came and told me about their exploits. Killing is nothing to boast of, but those people had lost their humanity, so they boasted. I always felt that innocence would be my best protection.

I had to answer the summons and go to the army headquarters but, as I've said, there was fear and trepidation in my heart. The road was lonely, not a single other person walked along it except for myself and the woman who had brought the message. My shadow appeared to extend and diminish, extend and diminish. At moments I even lost consciousness of its shape and form. My ears were buzzing. There were voices, confused voices, intermingled with the whirring insect sounds that emerged from the jungle. The interrogation had already begun in my mind. I was rehearsing the questions I would be asked, interrogating myself. It was a preparation for what I would have to face. I reached the *kade*. The soldiers were standing around with their guns. Their expressions changed when they saw me. Their faces were hostile. I was on the other side as far as they were concerned, a terrorist. I looked closely at their faces to see whether I could recognize any of them. My students used to describe them to me, faces without names, yet by studying their expressions you could sometimes discern what their natures might be. Their faces were young, as young as those of my students, but we looked at each other across tremendous, insurmountable barriers. One face struck me. It belonged to a short, squat-looking soldier. He had a look of aggression on his face. He watched me warily. I would have to be careful of him. Those men must have wondered at me, silently forming their own ideas about me. I felt I could read their minds:

'He is one them. How did he escape? These terrorists are elusive. He must have slipped out of our hands. They vanish, then they appear. They lay mines. They take sniper shots at our men. How did he alone escape from the prawn farm?'

Fear gripped me. I tried to calm myself, control the trembling in my hands. I was helped by the fact that I had practised yoga. From my inner consciousness I was sending out friendly rays, but the hostile expressions did not change. I tried to still the thudding of my heart. It sounded thunderous in my ears. Had one of them placed a hand against my heart, he would have felt its rapid beat. This was a way they had of testing you, testing to see whether you were a terrorist. I was afraid of two things—of being interrogated, and of being shot. I tried sending out rays of friendliness towards the interrogators. I always wanted to have good thoughts towards everybody. I did not want anyone to feel that I was a terrorist. But at that very moment, when I was fearing for my life, a police jeep drew up. My friend, the Superintendent, was in it. I felt as if scooping out a hollow in the desert I had discovered water to quench my thirst. I bathed my face in this sense of comfort. It felt like cool water against my parched lips and throat. The Superintendent greeted me in a friendly manner, 'Ah, Das, what are you doing here?

Where have you been all this time?' I was still very conscious of the expressions of the soldiers around me. Now they began to change, ever so slightly, like a shifting breeze, like the ripples in the ponds growing wider with the movement of the crustacea beneath the surface.

There was silence now that the gun shots had ceased. For some reason, perhaps only to cope with the fear, I started thinking of the prawn farms. No one would come to net the prawns for a long time now and they would grow and procreate in their underwater world undisturbed by any marauders. They would crowd the ponds and jostle each other as their numbers grew and soon, perhaps, they too would begin to war against one another and turn cannibalistic as the space that contained them became smaller. Then, the prawn ponds too would begin to smell of death like the landscape around them. Death has an odour and the wind carries it in waves from village to village. It would not be easy moving the bodies that lay strewn about because the roads were clogged with mud after the recent rains. The flies would be buzzing about them. The guerrillas meanwhile would have slipped away, vanished into the jungle, disappeared along the pathways and tracks that only they are aware of. And who knew how long it would take for some of those shot to die; death does not always happen instantly. But it was only a matter of time and then the women would go out. They would follow perhaps the odour of death and find the bodies, identify them, carry the news back. The death couriers.

'Look, I'll try to get you transport in one of the helicopters but at the moment it is difficult. I had hardly sitting space myself,' said my friend the Superintendent.

He drove off and I realized that I would have to go and wait in the camp. I had to be patient. It would take time. The press and TV crews were using the helicopters and the search operations were still continuing. I had to have faith in my friend. I was a survivor in the eyes of the others. A survivor and a terrorist. How had I managed to escape?—was the thought uppermost in their minds. I was still not safe.

In the camp the soldiers were young boys, younger than myself. They were almost like my students. I did not want them to be the first to begin asking me questions. I would have preferred to be the one asking questions. We got talking. The soldiers were curious but wary. They wanted to know about the massacre on the prawn farm. They wanted to know how much I knew, how many deaths had taken place. They knew how many of their own men had been killed preparatory to the operation. They asked me how many had been blasted in the land mine explosion. I could not tell them all I knew. My safety lay in concealment. I had to pretend that I did not know much. I did not tell them the exact number of the dead. I said that only a few had died, five or six. I concealed my true self like a wily prawn that goes deep into the pond to escape being netted, settling ·itself in the silt, not letting its antennae appear above the surface of the water. I felt myself metamorphose into one of those crustacea. I felt so much safer then in my mind. My human role could only have spelt vulnerability.

I was an innocent man. My hands had never tied the fuse wires in a land mine, nor did I boast like the others of the killings that were so easily performed. I was not one of them, the death searchers, who moved in and out of jungles, hopping like jungle

ticks from one pelt to another, following blood trails.
Now, even here in this camp, I felt I had to create
my own prawn pond, change my shape and form
until it was safe to assume my human lineaments
again. I had learnt much from those bicycle rides on
those lonely roads. I was careful not to create enemies.
I moved like a tiny land crab scuttling about the
mangroves, cautiously, so that no bird would swoop
down on me from the air. The soldiers were not sure
of me at all. Even at this point they would keep me
back for interrogation. They were very skilled in this
art. I could perhaps not match their subtlety. I was
still in a very delicate position. No one knew who I
really was. And the other prisoners might have
thought me an informer, a traitor, one of the *drohis*.

'How many died at the prawn farm?' the young
soldiers asked.

'Only about five or six,' I answered. They must
not know how much I knew.

'We feel sorry for the poor people who died,' one
soldier said. 'But how are we to know who is a
terrorist and who isn't?' said another. 'They mingle
with the people, with the civilians, and we cannot
question each one of them individually. It is either
them or ourselves. But in war who has time for pity?
We see our men blown up in landmines. The flesh
has to be scraped off the Claymores. They are shot
by snipers. Reprisals and massacres take place—are
these happenings not inevitable in a time of war?
Killings will go on. The civilians will always suffer.
They have to bear the brunt of the killings. Sometimes
they, too, are caught in a situation from which they
cannot escape. They cannot betray their own boys.
They are caught in the crossfire. If there is a landmine
explosion the security forces have to search for the
guerrillas, but who can get hold of a guerrilla? He

knows the terrain so much better than we do and he can disappear. So it's the civilian who is left—any male above a certain age is suspect, so they must pay. Death comes out of the jungle, it happens on the open road. Are we not all expecting death at any moment?'

Questions for which I had to find my own answers tortured my mind: 'This is a time of war. Of course we have become used to the new conditions. Each man has his pre-arranged role to play. When the guerrillas ask the villagers to provide food for them, they do it. After all, the guerrillas do not have time to till the soil or gather harvests. In turn they protect the villagers in whatever way they can with their arms. The women have to search for food. They move freely about on the roads so they can bring back news or carry news. Then there are those, the men, who use their own weapons. One does not always find loyalty. There is plenty of betrayal too. Betrayal means arrest, torture and death. Those who betray are also terrorists. And if you, in these circumstances, cannot speak the truth, aren't you betraying yourself too? And is it worth paying the price for safety when you see so many dying on both sides, often people who are unable to defend themselves? Yes, on all sides. Among all communities. Children who have lost their parents. Parents who have lost their children, husbands their wives and wives their husbands. They have no homes. They have no hope. They are haunted by the sights they have witnessed. No hope . . .'

In the past the villagers used the jungle for their cultivation. They still do. They cut down the trees, they clear the land, burn the scrub and plant their chillies and vegetables and grains. They set up watch huts to protect their crops from the animals, wild boar and elephant—in the past those were the only marauders. Their herds of cattle were driven into the jungle at night. In the mornings the herds came out and were milked. The milk was made into curd—there was time for it to settle and grow firm. Now, often, the everyday things of life cannot go on. There are curfews that disrupt life and people have often to abandon their homes. Now humans themselves herd in the jungles. There are deadly poisonous reptiles in the thickets, but perhaps the villagers prefer to have at least this choice, to choose the freedom to die in whichever way they want. I never joined the villagers who called me to spend the nights in the jungle. I preferred to remain in a silent and deserted schoolroom. Though I did not know how much longer I, too, could remain safe. Killing has become a legitimate pastime. At any time, at any point in the road, a land mine could explode. A party of villagers might be travelling in a vehicle, a bus, truck, lorry, van, and they could be blown to smithereens. Not only men, not only army personnel, but women and children too. They may have been going to the market to buy their provisions. People, often innocent people, are dragged out of buses and shot. Massacres, reprisals, horror and violence. Men open fire on those who are praying in mosques, in churches, in temples and refugee camps. And so it goes on, on all sides, among all communities. No mercy, no pity is shown on any side . . . . And I myself, did I go up to those who had fallen when they got out of their helicopter, touch a still warm brow and utter one word of comfort? I thought I had no enemy. Then whom did I call my friend?

We are all trapped in our different camps. We have to devise our own weapons for protection if we do not carry AK-47s or T-56s or grenades. The silent men are trapped in their hoods. Their thoughts, too, are bitter if they have lost kith or kin. Or they might do it out of simple greed. I feel pity for those young soldiers who had reminded me of the students I teach. They wear the sacred thread on their wrists for protection. Their faces are often bland, smooth. They, who should have expectations of life, can only have expectations of death. Their hands clasp the guns strongly. That weapon is, after all, their life. We all have to deceive ourselves over and over again for what we do. Or don't do. I could do nothing to stop the killings of those officers or the soldiers or the informer when they got off that helicopter. Am I then guilty too? I was safe, the guerrillas would not have harmed me. No, I cannot say that I had nothing to do with those deaths. They were taken unawares with no chance of defending themselves. True, they shot back, but at whom? At an unseen enemy. My prior knowledge of what was to take place did not stop me from being silent. I witnessed the panorama of death. Where did I belong? My life had become like one of those ancient epic plays, but I was only the observer. I was no hero. Will the rest of my life be like this because I want to protect my innocence? Am I not already besmirched and defiled by being the witness to violence and death?

I waited in the camp until I got a seat in the helicopter that would take me back to Kallady. The chopper, I observed when I got in, was navigated by a foreign pilot. He turned his face away from me. I saw another mercenary too, tall, strong, armed to the teeth. I recognized the countries they belonged to but I kept silent. This was no time for familiarity, for asking questions. In time our own people will also carry arms to other countries to fight for other causes. We accept this fact of history. Identity does not

41

count for a mercenary. He chooses to put it aside, even lose it when he fights for a cause that has no meaning for him.

In the helicopter I was tense all the time. I was flanked by soldiers on either side. A childish thought came to my mind. What if I were secretly pushed out so there would be no trace of me? After all I had been through, was this a game I played with myself to release the fears and pressures that had built up within me?

I was taken back to Kallady camp and interrogated there. They wanted to know all the details of what had taken place, about those violent deaths, the number of deaths, about how much I knew.

'We want to know the truth about how many died,' they said. And I had to pretend that I did not know. The truth, once it was out, would endanger my life. All I wanted was to go back to the people, the villagers, to live among them peacefully. I did not want a lot of possessions or goods or wealth. I wanted to go back and teach in my village, listen to the old men as they cleared their throats and began to sing their folk songs. After they die who will remember these songs? The young have no time to learn them. There will be nothing to remember except the horrors of this eternal war that goes on, day after day after day. The people are tired, tired of war.

I am back in my school now. I have placed my fingers on the bullet holes that pit the walls. Looked out to the field where I saw death. I remember. Perhaps in time I will forget. But—an innocent man?

Elysium

I WAS SIXTEEN. I was in a world that was green, with rills of the purest water and covered with flowers. A tranquil landscape. I sat gazing at it. Colours. Fragrances. Ah, the sensuous feel of flowers touching my skin. And the sound of water sliding over pebbles—very cool, liquidy, like flute notes. Elysium. Paradise. Persephone's heaven for heroes. Isles of the Blest. An apple land, like Avalon and Eden. This was where I could always escape to in between dreams and reality.

Lipovsky. Lipovsky. No, I was never in love with him. I did not allow myself to be attracted to him. What would have been the use? To have given myself, all of myself to a man—and then to have been forgotten? Oh, everybody thought I was beautiful. Schön, Schön, they would murmur, all of them. I was a virgin. It was rare, in that country, to be a virgin at my age.

Did Lipovsky touch me? Yes. Sometimes, when we danced together in that quiet room in his house. Or when we drove out into the woods, travelling along those quiet country roads, not a soul to be seen, only trees on either side.

Lipovsky promised to take me nutting. I imagined myself gathering the nuts. How sweet the flesh would taste once I had cracked open the hard shells. The berries I would crush against my lips and let the juice trickle down, tart, sweet. And drink the pure water that flowed in the little stream green with the shadow of overhanging trees.

Lipovsky would initiate me into the rites of spring. Sometimes he appeared to me to be a god of the woods. Pan. Sometimes I grew afraid; he stood like a satyr in the shadows.

He took me to his home, his bedroom. He put on a record of soft Danubian waltzes and took me in his arms. We danced through the shadows, shadows ourselves.

'Do you like to dance, my little woman?' His voice was tender. I heard it like the distant hiss of waves through a whorled shell.

No, no. Never. Temptation. To be used. To be cast away, forgotten. I was pure. Chaste. I was strong. I did not give in.

The Fantasy in the Forest

My clothes were airy, diaphanous. I stretched out my arms to feel my body—fleshless, an embodiment of light. No female odours breathed from its most secret places, only strange fragrances distilled from flowers, flowers that belonged to Elysium. They were all around me, brilliant flowers, violet, flame, gold, as if painted with the finest brush strokes. The grass was soft underfoot, very springy. Moist, dew-impregnated. And always the music of water from secret streams. Also, birds. These were no migrants that had flown from other countries but birds of the forest, nesting birds. This was the country of my youth. I had this treasure. I had to guard it until he came to me. On his white horse. I saw its white flanks in the water pressing against the green shadows of the overhanging trees. Silvery white, coming towards me. I saw his face, the man who rode the horse. I wanted to interpret that smile as he came closer. I wanted to find that it had some meaning for me. Not irony. No, not on those lips. I traced their curving shape with a half-musing, half-hallucinatory gesture. I stood before him as he climbed down from the stirrup. Where had he come from? I had seen him before, but only half-imagined his face, his expression. Would he ask me for a different consummation? I stood rooted to the earth. I had to speak to him before he vanished, hold him back. I suddenly felt hungry and very thirsty. He pressed me to his breast. I felt very warm. My clothes, light though they were, clung to me, grew heavy. It was cool in the grass where we lay. I looked up at the canopy of leaves above me. The forest stretched beyond into darkness. Large butterflies fluttered about my face—white, with flame-red markings; yellow; orange. Like so many petals falling on my face.

Dreams of the Forest

I was always in the forest. Dark, interweaving branches spread canopies of shade over the little cottage at whose doorway I waited. There was just enough room for me to fit my slender body in, within those narrow walls. I stood at the door and watched the waking forest. The birds were invisible to the eye but I heard them from behind the leaves.

Wild berries like drops of blood were scattered over the bushes. So red. So stark. There were no nuances of shade in that red. And those purply black berries, too, their skins crinkled with ripeness. I was awaiting something. I knew I could not remain confined within that space forever. I watched the path that led from my door. Expectation. Then, walking towards me was a tall bird with long stalky legs. Its wings shone with a golden light reflecting from its plumage. I stretched out my hands to catch it, hold it, but it turned and walked away from me, vanishing into the darkness of the forest.

Lipovsky had come to London from Germany. Karin had told him to help me if ever I were in need. He came to the house where I was living in London, but whatever he had to tell me, or even give me, could not be discussed. I was living with conservative friends, I could not talk freely. I did not go out with him. Also, there had been a bereavement in the family I was with. The house was in mourning.

The gilded bird had vanished and with it all my hopes.

Puberty Rituals

Being prepared for procreation, for motherhood. Strengthening the womb. My mother saw to it that we had plenty of eggs and sesame oil. Varieties of fish rich in oil, like shark, were cooked for us. The bitter margosa leaf was ground on the stone and we were given its acrid juices for cleansing the womb. Fertility was important. To be fertile was auspicious. If barren, you would be left out of all the rituals of marriage. You could never bathe or dress the bride or come before the couple. So I was prepared. Yet, I never married. I always remained chaste. Pure.

At home, during that period of puberty, although we were Christians we observed the ritual taboos of our culture in the North of that Island where I was born. The pillows were sprinkled with water and put out to dry in the hot sun. The dhoby washed all our clothes and we would remain in a separate room and not emerge until the purificatory rites had been carried out. I became aware of the mysteries of creation. It gave me a sense of power in myself as a woman but I knew always, yes, even then, that I must protect myself. Amrita, soma, moon-dew. The mystic birth. But as I grew older and was admired by many, my mother would not allow me to make a choice.

'If you were to marry that man, think of the children you would have.' It was a subtle way of telling me that I too must seek out someone beautiful, a man who would be worthy of me, for I was very special. I felt myself elevated, carried on a cushion through life. My body, my face were delicate. My mother did not want me to know the world yet. She had married, brought forth children, prepared me for marriage and childbirth, and yet she kept me back from marriage. I began to observe closely the faces of saints. Saintly men. Their faces had that look of absolute beauty—Clear, unflawed. They retained all that wisdom, energy, sight, strength and vitality which the Laws of Manu speak of because they did not squander that precious essence, that vital substance within them. If you look at the faces of saints you see that they look forever young, their faces unsullied by all those creases of anxiety that appear on ours . . .

The Dream of the White Horse

My sister and I would watch this young man as he swam every evening in the sea. He would swim out until he reached the rock that jutted out like a pinnacle and touch it. One night I dreamed that I was on the shore. I looked out, waiting, watching expectantly. Out of the spume and spray, a white horse appeared, riding the great foaming waves. It reached the shore and then out of it—for it was like the Trojan horse to me—stepped the figure of Jesus Christ in flowing white garments. The young man whom I had seen swimming in the ocean flung a garland of white jasmines round Christ's neck. I felt that there must be some deep significance in this dream for me, that the sea, the white crested waves, the white horse, the vision of Christ and the young man with his garland of jasmines had a message for me.

Was there already conflict in my mind between the turbulent and elemental forces of nature, over which I could have no control, and my own emotions? There was turmoil within me. I knew I was attracted to that young man swimming out to sea. I would come to this particular place to see him every day. But I knew I should not submit to the temptations of the flesh. The white horse stepped onto the shore; was it not meant for me to ride that white horse? Could I not ask the young man to accompany me? But then, the garland of white jasmines, like a marriage garland, was flung round the neck of Christ and the sensual flesh was stilled by this gesture. The young man had turned away from me. He had rejected the flesh. He had made his choice. I had seen him as Eros. I knew then that the temptation and allure of the flesh was something I would have to relinquish for the moment. What then was I to do? Soon afterwards a message reached me. I was summoned to Germany to work among young Germans, to rehabilitate them. I was to prepare to go first to the University of Heidelberg for a course in German. That was a sign for me. For the moment I must forget the young man and the white horse. Where would I meet them again? At what stage of my life?

Prayers, Dreams and Visions

I remember the mystical dreams of my childhood. I was then five years old. I was lying on the white sands of my village in the North when suddenly the goddess Saraswathi appeared, a towering figure descending from the skies. Wide-eyed I watched her as she floated down in my direction. In her hands she bore silvery shafts of rain which glittered as they caught the light. She alighted on my chest but I did not feel her weight. I felt tiny spears of moisture grazing my skin. I ran inside the house to tell my grandfather. He would interpret this strange dream-vision for me.

'Why didn't you open your mouth?' he said. 'You should have allowed her to spit into it and imbue your utterance with mystical powers, inspire you to write poetry. Remember that woman poet into whose mouth the goddess spat? Ever afterwards every word she uttered was poetry.'

Perhaps it was at this time that I began to write my poems. Poems of birds, of the elements, of the spiritual life. The golden heron stood over me, the silvery fish. I was the carp. His bony beak snapped and jerked to trap me. Even the white-plumaged stork. They were all predators . Lines, phrases from my poetry flashed through my mind. I saw myself as the fish with its instinctual beauty, the carp with 'its lovely eyes and head.' Somewhere I had translated the woman image into that of a fish—merging with the natural world and yet so vulnerable. The predator always ready to snap the wriggling trout with his cloven beak. I was always the fish, caught in those avid beaks, my tender flesh jabbed at, wounded. How strong those beaks were. How could I escape being trapped? In Christ alone I would find the heart of the gentle dove. Peace. Tranquillity. But then the cyclone would engulf me. Storm images would stampede through my mind:

'Whirlwind. The wild rampage. The gale. Rain. Trees torn. Leaves scattered in a violent rage.'

My imagination was inundated with poetry. The turmoil of my passions would start up time and time again.

It was that mystical vision of the goddess which gave me the idea that poetry would leap from my lips. I was thirsty for those pure shafts of rain which she held in her hands and which moistened my parched tongue. My grandfather encouraged me. He too had gone in search of the mystical experience. He had suddenly left his family and disappeared for years and years. He had wandered everywhere. A pilgrim? A swami? When he returned after his years of wandering his appearance had altered. His hair was long. He was dressed in the robes of a sadhu. He had come back to his family. Perhaps now he was at peace with himself. He had lived in the foothills of the Himalayas. The mountains were peaceful, he said, with their silent snows. Your thoughts could reach into pure space like those mountain peaks. Always allow good vibrations to emanate from you, he would say. The good within you will never attract evil forces. One night he had found himself in a wild and lonely place. He slept beneath a tree. When he woke up he found a cobra coiled under his hand. It had not harmed him. He was filled with pure feelings. There was no hatred or animosity towards any living creature after that. He taught me all the mystic sayings of the Vedanta. Every morning I would recite those holy stanzas. I was overwhelmed. My prayers were being answered. I too had spiritual powers now. I prayed for a woman who had not been able to carry a child. She conceived and gave birth to a beautiful baby girl. The parents named her 'Sweetness.' My prayers had been answered.

But I had to remain pure. Perhaps all those mystical visions and dreams had made me feel that I should remain a virgin. Now the time is long past for marriage. My virginity has been like a bird which has ceased to sing. A bird whose feathers have lost their lustrous sheen. When I was in the west I realized how greatly treasured virginity is. The men were always so polite and courteous to me. I once gave a friend of mine a cube of lavender-scented bath salts. She told me that it had lost its fragrance. It crumbled like desiccated limestone in her hot bath. The water became cloudy but there was no fragrance. I had kept it too long in my wardrobe among the silks and jewels I no longer wore. I now belonged to a religious order that frowned on vanity and adornment as sinful.

I watch this treasured gift of my virginity as in a mirror. The mirror is clear. It has an image. It is the face of a beautiful young girl. Her skin like ivory silk, her eyes blue and milky like moonstones. Her hair is lustrous. Ah yes, I will always bear this image in my eyes. Nothing has marred it. I have given my imaginings a shape, a form.

Once more I stand on the shore. The waves of the ocean surge about my feet. The rock that I see beyond is jagged. Like a sharply pointed pinnacle. The surf swathes the rock. The froth shimmers like wedding lace. It conceals the weapon of the rock. The rock is merciless. I know it will never yield even to the rage of the sea. The young man swims out to reach it. Will he return safely?

Again and again I see him fling the garland of jasmines. On whom? On the white horse? On Christ? It was here, here, at this point, that I had the vision and asked to be baptized. Here the young man set out to touch the rock. Here the white horse rose out of the waves. Here he gathered the white jasmines in his hands. Here I, the young virgin, stood.

The call had come for me to reach Germany at the earliest. The summons were urgent. I had no time left to waste. The white horse had wanted to carry me away. I was yet to meet Lipovsky. To know that he would one day marry Karin.

Time the Destroyer

THE HOUSE IS on a hill, hidden behind a thick, wildly overgrown clump of bamboos; a secret place tucked away, concealed in an era long past and never to be retrieved. A dark, lost image pushed behind the eyeballs of memory, its windows shuttered, its doors locked. Human beings had once wanted to live in the safety of its prison. Ghosts now dwell in it. It is now gradually emptying itself of life, now that death has taken away its matriarchal mistress who had woven herself into a web of isolation which she had spun through the long, secret, arid years of her life. Her only son, John, clings on to the sad ghost of a decaying and vestigial youth whose first promise with its brilliant flare of colour had soon begun to blacken round the edges. His sister, Serena, has returned once more from Switzerland, swooping down upon the family home, a mausoleum musty with secrets; her entry a faint disturbance of the almost invisible dust that lies like a blemish on the ancient wood grains and textures.

Serena now has what she has always desired—the house, the entire house to herself. She can move at will through rooms empty of human beings and carry out her austerities and extravagances at will, without the eagle eyes of her mother observing her, resenting her intrusion. The mother with whom she had had so much conflict through the years. Now there is nobody but herself within the house, exploring every nook and cranny of its once closely guarded privacy.

She invites Lydia to tea. Is Lydia her friend? She never utters the word friend, yet year after year she visits Lydia from her trips abroad, wearing the same clothes that she has worn for the last thirty years, her age showing in the gathering strands of grey that first flickered through and then densely covered her dark hair. Her clothes, unvarying in colour and cut: well-worn kurtas and denims, mountain boots, a scarf that holds back her hair—the cossack-like costume she pulled out from the old wardrobe of Time. Plain, colourless, sombre for her role-playing.

'Come to tea,' Serena persuades, 'before everything goes, divided between the family members. I have to make inventories. You must come and see the old photographs, the paintings.'

'What's left of a heritage,' Lydia thinks to herself. 'These people who have built up their histories, layer upon layer. All forgotten. Anonymity replacing the once grand gestures, the lost philanthropy. Histories to be recounted like an ancient seafarer's yarns. An exploration of heredity, even of degeneracy of the blood, the forgotten heirs who open window after window into the past to establish the monumental inscriptions of forgotten epochs. But again, a history that is recent, perhaps two hundred years or so ago. And before that . . . .' The mists are thick and opaque.

'You must read my uncle's sermons,' Serena tells Lydia. 'We can read them together. They've all been neatly tied up and put away by my mother. Oh, how she loved that brother of hers. When you come, I'll show them to you. What shall I do with them? We can decide, can't we?'

Lydia goes to tea. Up the stony path with the charred remains of gigantic bougainvillea bushes. An empty stone pond with a stone frog splayed out above it, hovering like some uneasy spirit over the cracked basin. Lydia knocks on the door. The security man who is guarding the house comes out of his watchtower. A severed trunk of a huge tree stands like a guillotine block at the foot of the high bank which is covered with more black-green bamboos.

Some moments pass. Serena appears at the door which opens, but not fully, to allow Lydia entrance. The security man hovers about, giving her a sense of unease: the suspicion for an outsider, an intruder.

'I was preparing for you. Come in,' Serena says.

Lydia almost wishes she had not come on this visit to sit in this museum of death. She has rarely come here before. The last time was when the matriarch was alive. And also her husband. Lydia and her husband had been invited to their home. Serena had not been present. The old servants had stood around like bodyguards but had appeared to be part of the background, unlike the uniformed security guard who watched for any sign of encroachment, or . . . what? There is constraint in this new atmosphere. She enters the gloom of the shuttered house. Above her head is a ceiling of faded, woven Dumbara mats, their brilliant colours turned a neutral, mushroom tint. Lydia is curious. Someone's Holy of Holies. Serena spreads her ambience around. It is to be a kind of guided tour. Lydia, no voyeur, feels a reluctance to begin this exploration so compulsively planned by Serena. Serena puts the finishing touches to the bowl of ice cream she is making and puts it away in the refrigerator. Every bit of space is now hers. She is the mistress of the house, and the unhappy ghost of her mother begins to edge its way into oblivion.

'My uncle's sermons are all in that chest,' Serena points to a carved piece of craftsmanship wrought out of golden-brown satiny wood. Orientalism. Chinese. The Christian sermons have lain undisturbed for years in old boxes, the pages yellowing with age, proselytizing the minute creatures that feed on paper and text. Preservation. Preservation in the sarcophagus of memory. While the fleshly body was dust, these ghostly emanations remained.

'What shall I do with these sermons?'

'Give them to the Theological College,' says Lydia.

Models of sermons for young students. What do these sermons contain that had spoken of salvation, love, forgiveness to the frail, weak flock he ministered to. Would they, even today, sixty years later, speak with the same chiselled language—that alien, colonial language—to that refined and genteel congregation who sat in high-backed pews surrounded by stained glass windows which burned with brilliant ruby red, gold, blues of cobalt, Prussian, turquoise, azure and viridian; engulfed in that rich and sensuous religiosity, unstiffening momentarily their upright spines, feeling the touch of silk and chiffon, tweed and woollen clothes thrill against the honeyed flesh sated with gilded texts from the St. James version of the Bible . . . . The young priest from his carved pulpit, fresh from one of the English Universities, taking them along the straight and narrow, and even as he grew older and they, his congregation, aged, no hint of chastisement lay its harsh whip against the flesh of the renegade or the penitent.

'The sermons for the Theological College? No, they won't read them. I'll keep them.'

'Why don't you publish them?' Lydia suggests, as if in connivance with that hovering spirit.

'Shall we sit down and read them together one day?'

It is not what Lydia wants to do, share the sadness of those forgotten sermons and think of that ghostly congregation long since mouldering in their cerements. But she is too polite to reject Serena's suggestion—as she is always too polite to reject her suggestions, her offerings of bits of lace and candles, hot bread, yoghurts, oil paints that have dried in their tubes, crayon pencils, the Gauguin print—wild flowers for Lydia who now knows, at long last, what she wants and what she does not want. But she is always too polite, and leaves it at that, for all these are offerings of friendship. Never to be rejected.

'Come, I'll show you the photographs. That's my uncle, the priest.'

A face that is youthful. Handsome. Wearing a dark cassock, he hangs in this portrait gallery on a wall of this gloom-filled house. His eyes gaze out on a celestial world. Waiting for the Messiah. All things moulder in the grave, but those fresh young eyes see beyond this worldly garden. His grandfather had struck it rich when he bought the coffee garden of the last king of Kandy in the mountains of Hanguranketa. The king was captured by the new

colonial masters, the British. He was exiled. The new
colonialism rode in and the Royal coffee gardens
were planted with new seed, new crops that brought
the entrepreneurs from the South untold wealth.
According to the ancients of this island, the wealthiest
man is one who is rich in offspring, friends, cattle,
pearls, money, houses, land. And the new
entrepreneurs set out assiduously to acquire, to
cultivate, the tenets of the ancients. They succeeded.
But for how long? How many generations . . . and
then the weakened blood petered out and flowed
thinly through the arteries of etiolated branches. But
the names entered the annals of a history that was
being re-written—Susew, Jeronis, Jusay. The Lords of
Creation. 'The natives', as their colonial masters
named them.

'That's the uncle, the priest. My mother's brother.
Oh, he was lovely. Whenever he met me he would
say, "Hello miss", as if I were special, grown up, a
young lady.'

'And did he marry?' Lydia asks, peering into an
unshadowed face. 'He could have. He belonged to
the Anglican Church.'

'No, he never married.'

The vows of celibacy were voluntary. Ended up
a bishop in the Anglican hierarchy. Left nothing for
posterity except for a hundred, perhaps hundreds of
sermons preserved carefully within this locked
oriental chest with its fine carving. A carving that
has become nebulous, indecipherable, in its
landlocked territory.

'Oh, all the sermons written from the nineteen
thirties.'

Dead Sea Scrolls. Urn burial.

The natives were proselytized. They prayed. They
preached like their masters in the same carefully-

worded language, devoid of extremes. A pure fountain of crystal words. Clarity without complexity. Innocent naïve theology, for those were the guidelines for the congregation. No steaming, champing controversy.

'My mother loved that brother of hers. She preserved all his notes, the ones he made as a student at Cambridge. And the sermons too, all carefully annotated . . . let me show you—' Serena unlocks the Chinese chest. Flat boxes repose within its recesses. Christian theology to confound the knowledge of Confucius. She opens the boxes with great care. Each sermon is preserved intact. Tied neatly with yarn meant for her weaving. Blue yarn. She, Serena's mother, was dilettantish. She could afford to be. Tried everything—weaving, designing furniture, painting, singing, but nothing left its impact on history. She was a woman of her era where wealth gave her the privileges of living abroad and studying under European masters, then returning to her country, her inherited estates and properties with an English governess for her son. The evidence is there. The documentation. The whole house belongs to Serena's mother. Everything that is here is hers. And her ghost watches the two women, Serena and Lydia.

Each sermon is preserved intact. Tied neatly with yarn meant for the sister's weaving. Blue. A deep royal blue. The dryad looms are now breaking up— left unused for years. Tapestries woven in the past gather dust in some hidden corner of the house.

'My uncle was a young curate in Hampstead. Every sermon he preached in that parish still remains. He returned to the country of his birth. Rose high in the hierarchy of the Anglican Church.'

Serena places the box of sermons in Lydia's hands. She opens it. Yellowing pages like some faded moth.

The writing is meticulous. There is a pattern of thought. Clarity and simplicity, no confusion, no abstruse, complex, mind-confounding theology. Each detail in that fine, almost scholarly script. Recorded history: the church he preached in, the dates, the places, the subject; churches and cathedrals in England—Cirencester—and in his own country where once the coffee gardens had flourished, before they were blighted by the pest that devastated thousands of acres. The cash crops of the new colonial economy ushered in.

'My uncles were in trade,' Serena explains.

A special calling in the Anglican Church for this uncle. His sermons are preached in every Anglican church built by the British missionaries. The Church of St. Paul, St. Michael, St. John, St. Jude, St. James, Holy Trinity. Sermons of half a century ago. Lydia gently takes up one of the sermons and reads:

> Sermon—St. Michael's. Trinity 1, evening—
> the fourteenth of June in the year nineteen
> thirty six.
>
> I am the Living Bread which came down
> from heaven; any man eat of this bread he
> shall live forever, yea, and the bread which
> I shall give is my flesh, for the life of the
> world.
>
> We are in the Octave of the Feast of Corpus
> Christi, the feast of the Body of Christ, the
> Blessed Sacrament. For who among us who
> know and value even in part what the
> Blessed Sacrament means to us, can deny
> our duty to offer our adoration, praise and
> thanksgiving to God for this, His wonderful

gift? In the General Thanksgiving found in our prayer books we thank God 'above all, for the redemption of the world by our Lord, Jesus Christ . . .' It ought, therefore, to occupy the foremost place among the innumerable gifts for which we thank God.

For this Holy Sacrament of the Body and Blood of our Lord is indeed the most precious thing in our lives. It is the centre of all our worship and devotion, the source of all our strength, the fountain of our very life. 'Except ye eat the Flesh of the Son of Man and drink His Blood, ye have no life in you . . .' God, in His holiness, intervening in this world of ours to enlighten, rescue and support us, His creatures, acting wholly in love to bring us to the perfection to which we are made. That perfection is to be found only in our lives in Christ. We cannot achieve it in or by ourselves. This is obvious to us as we look round and see in some places the highest human hopes come crumbling in the dust and in others lives, rich with promise, suddenly cut off in this world. We are made for perfection only in Christ.

How many souls had he saved and brought comfort to? Sorrow, earthly sorrow, had existed in his own family. His great grandfather had died, bitten by a rabid dog. He was a man who had sired fifteen children. Their individual histories, when they grew up were bound to colonialism. They took office under their colonial masters whom they served loyally. Theirs was a family of philanthropists whose wealth enabled them to be munificent and liberal dispensers of charity. They were designated Patriotic Natives under the colonial regime of the British. Yet, that cherished knighthood was never bestowed on that grandfather, that benevolent philanthropist who gave thousands of pounds sterling to charity—hospitals, schools, roads, churches. That knighthood was denied him during the era of the British Governor, Gordon. He, that benevolent native patriot, did not belong to that specially privileged social hierarchy within the country itself. The British Governor could not alienate that section from which the ruling caste was derived. Colonialism had to pander to those who held the regalia, the accoutrements of the hierarchy, born into a life of privilege.

The new entrepreneurs flourished during the period of British colonial rule. 'After 1845, Ceylon was favoured with a succession of enlightened Governors . . . Among them Ward, Robinson, Gregory, Gordon, Ridgeway . . . .' Arrack renters, those engaged in trade and commerce, the philanthropists, the native patriots loyal to king and crown, albeit an alien king and crown, built their magnificent homes, opened up their vast plantations and embarked on an unlimited entrepreneurship. His Royal Highness, the Prince of Wales, on a visit to the Crown Colony, was entertained to a magnificent banquet—to eat off the gold plate that had been specially made for the occasion. The Midas touch—gold plate, cutlery of gold, a glittering array of dishes, a galaxy of jewel-bedecked women . . . no one else was prepared to host the Prince but this one man, the Native Patriot. A century later an austere great grandson preached the sermon on the Living Bread.

'Except ye eat the flesh of the Son of Man, and

drink His Blood, ye have no life in you.'

The walls of Serena's family home are covered with photographs and paintings in oils and water colours. The faces of the past in all their youth and fullness impinge on the weary and ageing faces of the present.

'Look,' says Serena, 'my grandfather and his family. My father's family.' She points at a young boy who looks out of the sepia tint into a brief future. A bright head with dark eyes, sword-thrust eyes look piercingly out of the fading print. 'That was a tragedy; a tragic family. One night my grandfather took that son of his out on a moonlight drive in his racing carriage. They were living in Galle where he was a doctor . . .'

The carriage had raced along as if it were racing to reach the heart of the moon. The horses were swift.

'The son slipped from his seat—it was one of those very small, light carriages. The buckle of his shoe got caught in a wheel. His father did not notice.'

The horses sped into the night. An appointment with death itself. He lifted his whip and spurred on the horses, lightly drawing in their reins. The horses frothed and tossed their manes. They flew into the heart of that white radiance, that desired consummation with Diana, huntress chaste and fair— 'the lunar virgin: Dione, Diana, Nemorensis, goddess of the moon grove.'

'That his son had fallen off the carriage he did not know,' says Serena.

Too late. Too late, that discovery.

'When he came home all hell broke loose. The mother had a nervous breakdown.'

And who picked up that limp body after that

tragic moon-journey to death? Who were those unfortunate searchers sent out to find that body and bring it back to the house to be readied for burial? Who wept over that body? Mourned for a lost son? A grief-stricken father, guilt-ridden? A mother inconsolable in her sorrow? But the tragedy did not end there.

'My grandfather accused his wife of infidelity. He said that she had an affair with another man; which I am sure she didn't,' says Serena 'and then he went away to England, leaving her behind. He took all the children with him. The nanny went with him.'

'And the wife was left behind? She did not protest that her children were taken away? Niobe with all her tears?' asks Lydia. 'To punish her hubris, her love and pride in her children? Nothing could be more cruel. What power husbands had in the past. Was there no one to protect her?'

'She was left behind. Alone. In the end she was helpless. You see, she could do nothing. She could not protest. But he was cruel to her when they were together. One day he took her by her hair—she had long hair—and locked the doors of the cupboard with her hair caught in between.'

Macabre. Gothic horrors.

Gentler, Serena's uncle. Lydia turns to yet another sermon.

The text: 'When we sin and do what we know to be wrong we are breaking God's spiritual laws for our happiness. When we, knowing what will happen, hold our fingers in a flame, the fingers are burnt, the process hurts us and that part of our body is spoilt, it is not what it might have been, healthy and whole, if we hadn't broken the law . . .'

Pre-ordained roles in society: Women. Wives.

Mothers. Mistresses too. Women whom those men had lain with. Procreated. Brought forth offspring. Maligned. Abused. Abandoned.

'She never saw her children again,' says Serena. 'She became so helpless, everything had to be done for her. She had to be washed, bathed, fed.'

A woman bereft. Niobe's tears.

Serena and Lydia remain standing before the family portrait. Serena points to one of the sons sitting at the parental feet. How they posed together in those paterfamilial portraits! As if the strong bonds united them until the parting of death.

'He was brilliant too, that son. He died in the flu epidemic that swept Europe after the First World War.'

How did these patriarchal men continue living with themselves? Were they not tortured by the demons of conscience? Racked with regret? Serena's grandfather—he needed more the Divine than the physician. The ship took him away, far, far from that woman whose hair he had grasped, first wrapped round his hands in love, then clutched in anger; those strands that must have left weals of remembrance in his hands. She could not escape him as perhaps he could not escape her; as he could not escape the Furies who sought their revenge for the slain son. Perhaps his own guilt made him want to flee from her anger, her vengeful thoughts. So he turned upon her before she could destroy him and fled from her presence.

The ship took him far away, far from that woman whose sharp hair left cicatrices, unhealed lesions, in his hands. She retreated into the very recesses of her soul, the remote hinterland of her being, and locked the doors against him, against everyone. No one could ever reach her again. For him, that final going away was a voyage of despair. Of utter loss. He could not, however far his journey took him, escape his conscience. He had to take ultimate responsibility for the death of that son. Yet, out of the wreckage of lives, the survivors would lift themselves up and walk out, stepping over the splintered wood, the debris, the cracked beams and shattered tiles of a once solid structure. Surrounded by phantoms of guilt. Hands bloodied, having touched a mangled corpse. Hair streaming behind, wrapped in veils of cobwebs with the smudgy tears of grief, the dust of the grave caking their cheeks and cracked dry lips seamed with threads of blood. Survivors from what holocaust of the emotions, to live and die, to live and die, and live . . . again, breathing the foul air of putrefying amours.

All that remains: portraits of solid paterfamilias, passions locked within those bosoms that appear chaste, puritanical. Those caches of inhibitions and suppressed feelings.

'And this?' Lydia stands before a bridal photograph. It is sometimes difficult to discern that subtle difference, that gentle shading in mutations of colour, between the past and the present.

'That's myself,' says Serena, 'myself on my wedding day.'

Serena. Young, wistful. Slender as a slivered petal snipped off a hothouse bloom. White lily. So virginal. Hardly any dimension to the flatness of her body. A disembodied spirit.

'Where's the other half then? Your husband?'

Serena laughs lightly. 'My mother cut off his picture.'

'Why?'

'I don't know. She never liked him. He is still afraid that I will become like her. He never comes to this house, not even after her death.'

It had been an arranged marriage. Even copulation had to be decreed by family, by society.

The two women slowly edge themselves along the walls from picture to picture. Portraits—of the maternal grandmother, Lady Jocelyn—with her children arranged about her. Society's theatricality. Tableaux of families.

'Isn't she beautiful?' Serena asks, standing before the photograph.

And of Serena's parents. Wedding photograph. Look closely. The groom wears a tailcoat, white spats and waistcoat, natty pin-striped suit. White silken hose. Patent leather shoes. Which century? Which era? The twenties, thirties? The bride clings to his arm. He is a handsome man. Well turned out. His first born, a son, disappointed him. 'I want to make him a man,' Serena quotes his ghost. 'He caned him four times in his life.' He did not succeed.

John was a changeling. The vine was withered at his birth. 'But he was kind to us, his daughters, my sister and myself.'

Horror stories of John's life: 'He was bullied, beaten, caned. Some marks are still on his wrist.' Who could understand this changeling?

Serena's mother was a strong-minded woman. Upheaval unhinged her and wrought turmoil in her life. The first born, the heir to the heritage, a changeling. No one knew how or why. It was in the blood. The strain of weakness through successive generations of inbreeding, perhaps.

'My mother had an English governess for us, Mrs Larkin. One day my brother asked her, "And how did Mr Larkin ask you to marry him?"' A polite question, but for him, who was never to know that consummation, a dramatic, soul-searching question.

'Oh, we loved her,' recalls Serena. 'We loved Mrs Larkin. You see, we were always alone. We spent so many hours by ourselves. We ate alone too. In the evening my mother would read aloud to us from *The Lives of the Saints*, and I would howl and howl through fear. All those terrible martyrdoms, stonings and torture.'

Serena stands suspended before those portraits of the past. 'My mother,' she muses, 'she was educated in England. She studied painting there. She was taught singing by a very famous singer, Madam Marchesa. Oh, my mother had a clear, beautiful soprano. She had this beautiful song book with oval-shaped illustrations and all those English songs . . .

> *Nymphs and shepherds come away, come away,*
> *Nymphs and shepherds come away, come away,*
> *Come, come, come, come away . . .'*

Lilian's paintings, the paintings of Serena's mother, hang on the wall of the drawing room. A portrait and a still life. Glass. Transparent water jug. A thirst that was never quenched.

Serena points to a chair. European in style, part Renaissance. Seat carved like a bow. A heavy table, almost mediaeval. Belongs to the refectory of a monastery. 'My mother designed furniture.'

The dryad loom sits in a corner. To weave cobwebs. So many women were Penelopes.

A photograph of three beautiful women. The Three Graces. Lydia gazes at those faces, so smooth, so flawless in their beauty. They look Rossetti-ish. Romantic nineteenth century. Pre-Raphaelite beauties. The Lady of Shalott. Shingled heads veiled with sarees. Their faces could belong to any Western woman. They had lost that distinctiveness that belonged to their culture.

'That's the most beautiful one. Beatrice.' Serena indicates one of the Three Graces. 'Men were crazy about her. So many Englishmen wooed her. But it was unheard of at that time to marry out of the inner circle. One Englishman, a planter, came to the house and asked for her hand in marriage. The family would not accept it. She ran away with him to England. They went through all their money and returned to the island. Oh, she was so beautiful.'

'And who is this?' Lydia roams through history, through pictures of this family. They have died, except in these fading visual reminders to posterity. Leaves that have drifted downriver with the strong currents. The detritus of Time.

'That is John, my brother.' Snapshots of the baby in the arms of a buxom English nanny who looked after him for a year. 'Yes, that's the nanny who would allow him to cry at night, cry and cry . . . '

The eldest son. Portraits of his early beauty on all the walls. Childhood, adolescence. That beauty left him long ago. Not a vestige left, only the poverty of a neglected ruin. His profile turned away, away from the rage of life. He cannot peer into the dark chasm of his future. Gazing into the Narcissus-pool of the past. Impeccably dressed in his suit and tie like any young man about town, open-faced, confident.

'Handsome,' Lydia ruminates.

'By that time he was disturbed. He had already been in institutions.' Matter-of-factly stated.

The face is now mutilated by the Furies, those repressed passions of the heart. Regret. His body untouched except for the manipulations of physical needs. Carapace. Catacombed mind. Vaulted death of youth. His longings, his desires unfulfilled. Has never known a woman.

'I want children, I want to marry,' he had told Lydia when he was brought on a visit to her home by Serena.

'Oh no, John,' his sister had said, 'too late, too late.'

He had embraced Lydia warmly on that visit and kissed her cheek. No one to touch or caress him with love. What denial. Cruel. Cruel. 'I want to leave this country,' he had said, 'bury my bones in England.' It is here that his soul will find its comfort.

Sometimes, on those visits, he would be drugged, sedated, a zombie. Lydia preferred him when he talked.

'It disturbs my mother,' Serena says, 'she cannot bear to face the truth.' Anglican conventions of marriage had kept her marriage with her husband going for years and years. Those sterile years.

John is an eroded statue left in an ornamental park. A ruin. A ruin, in a wasteland. Time had, with weatherbeaten hands, scraped off the outer skin of the sculpture, chipped off bit by bit of the marble. He had never known magic, the alchemy of change through love. His mother's hands, so slender, so unused to harsh work, throbbed with pain as they touched him, tried to quieten his turbulence. He was restless and could often become boisterous. Phials of pills were emptied down his throat. The first born. The changeling. One who should have been destined to be part of that tradition created by the Native Patriots; the tradition of wealth, property, trade, perhaps a sinecure in the Church of England; a tradition spawned by those colonial masters. There were vast acres of estates to be looked after. Business. Trade. Commerce. Opportunities for entrepreneurship. A knighthood had been bestowed upon his maternal grandfather. Largesse. Philanthropy. The benevolence and privilege of wealth could have been his. Or he could have entered the Anglican Church; or one of those ancient British universities. No, there was no destiny for him. To look after him, this disruptive element in the smooth silken flow of their days, his parents had to suffer agonies. They had searched for explanations everywhere.

'He was bullied in school. Made fun of, taunted.'

The British public school system perpetuated in those private missionary schools. Great, dedicated principles. Men of learning. Scholars. Yet, beneath all that stern and disciplined existence seethed the turmoil of childish and adolescent emotions. Sometimes whipped into submission, into conformity, mocked at by your own if you were different. John was different. The vine withered. The grapes grew sour.

Another explanation: 'He fell off his cot as a baby,' the father would say.

'Who knows how it happened,' Serena says.

The mother suffered in silence. They drove along the streets in their chauffeur-driven car. He sat beside her at church or at theatrical concerts, variety entertainments. As long as she was alive, he lived too.

His voice drags on and on whenever he speaks of those days. Grows petulant. He remembers an uncle. 'He spoilt me, spoilt me. A corrupt man. He did bad things to me, he taught me dirty things,' he keeps saying. 'I can't marry. It's all dried up now. Dried up now.'

The awakening of sexuality was, to John, corruption. An unnatural act that led ultimately to sterility. It was a despoiling. He was vulnerable, and a beautiful youth. His uncle had inveigled him into a relationship John was powerless to resist. That act of despoliation, of violation had taken place in that holiday home in the hills, set in a garden which proliferated with fruits and flowers. It was the first loss of his virgin innocence in the Garden of Eden. He could not realize that act was inevitable. It had to happen sooner or later, but he blamed his withering away, the drying up of his fluctuant seed, on the pagan act for which there was no retrieval. To whom could he confess? Who would give ear? Too hemmed in by the inhibitions of a stern morality. Did no one have pity on his ruined youth as he plunged, doomed and Icarean, into the pit?

That garden paled and withered and a carefree uncle went away to live his own life after he had pleasured himself with his young nephew. Whistling between his teeth, careless hands thrust into the pockets of his flannel trousers, he had gone his own way blithely, quite unaware of the shambles left behind. Ann Somers, a middle-aged married woman had often spoken with kindness to John, but then she had gone away. Lost to him. Vanished into her own oblivion, in need of compassion herself. Her mind, too, had given way, her home, too, lost, and now there was no one left for John.

'Where is Ann Somers now?' he would inquire wistfully, 'where is she?' But no one put themselves out to trace her.

The citadel is in ruins. Myths lie tumbled about the feet of humans. Adonis wounded by the boar. Narcissus dwindling away. And an ever-elusive Diana, huntress chaste and fair, the pursuer and the pursued. John has been taken to 'Shanthi', a haven for people who need its peace and calm. But he does not fit in. How can he, having been taken away from the mainstream of life long ago. He cannot be singled out for the preferential treatment he thinks is for him.

'They will not speak to him in English,' explains Serena. There is no other language he is more at ease in. 'He asks for a spoon and fork to eat his lunch. "Eat with your fingers," they say.'

'Second to none' is the epithet applied to this family. Second to none—to be conquerors, the colonial masters whose culture and civilization, manners, morals, clothes, religion and language made them the true servants. Knighthoods. Honours bestowed by the king and queen of England.

Lydia remembers a lunch she had been invited to once, long ago, when the parents of Serena and John were alive. They had all been seated formally round the dining table, crisp, starched serviettes unfolded and spread on their laps. The lunch began with a soup. Afterwards there were ripe mangoes for dessert. John was petulant. 'Bring me another knife,' he demanded of a servant who hovered near at hand. Sharp bladed knives were always kept away from him. He used the indigenous word, *motta*. He embarrassed his parents. There was a well-bred silence. So John persisted until another knife was brought him. The use of one's own tongue, one's own language, was not encouraged in that environment. Manners, ritualized, belonged to another era and clime. The family had no language to talk to the servants in.

'My mother never talks to the servants so they blackmail her,' Serena had once said.

Serena remembers other parties. 'My grandparents had such grand parties in that huge house in Alfred Place. The house belonged to an aunt who lived a simple life in Moratuwa. My grandparents did the grand in her house. The aunt's children did not like it. My uncles were wealthy businessmen, they entertained lavishly. Oh, those dinners where they entertained all the Englishmen! There was this enormous table and the most important guest would be served first. Starting from the top right hand corner, coming down to the end and then the next serving would begin from there.'

It must have been terrible to be at the bottom of that table. The lesser beings.

'The table was always beautifully arranged—gleaming cutlery, cut glass, damask. The dinner would begin with a clear soup with a little wedge of custard in the middle. Tiny strips of carrot cut in juliennes would be scattered in it. Then the fish course would follow. Tiny portions, but the plate would be decorated. Then the meat dish, all sliced on a salver, would be taken round and the melt-in-the mouth dessert and wines, red, white, the water, the claret, served.

'For us it was Sunday lunch with yellow rice and roast chicken—lots of plums in the rice. My mother, too, would entertain guests. She would create wonderful table arrangements with fruits and vines. They were my father's friends. Englishmen.'

Now death, bereavement, going away . . . There are no guests at that empty table.

Serena had been insistent that Lydia should come and see the old house. Why? Why? Her mother had lived in this fortress for years shut away with her son John who was progressively becoming more reclusive and secluded from the real world, surrounded by servants, a chauffeur and the attendant who was like a warder. Serena lived for the greater part of her life in Europe, flying in, flying back, a migratory bird who would alight in the sunny garden and pick branches and bunches of flowers and leaves that she would bear to Lydia in her arms as if she were reenacting some ancient rites of the Earth

Mother. She never changed. Her voice reed-like, through which legends of the past whispered. She had rejected feminine fripperies.

'I hated all those beautiful dresses my mother made me wear,' she recollects. Each time Lydia met her she had become more and more austere. 'Why do you wear a hairshirt?' Lydia would ask her.

For years she has not changed the white kurta, the cassock-like shirts. The straight grey hair is always tied back with a scarf to protect it from the dust of the roads. She walks in her heavy mountaineering boots more suited to the Swiss Alps than this country. In wet weather she stuffs the boots with newspaper.

'I cook my own food. Everything together, brown rice and vegetables. I like roast chicken. Just give me a wok and vegetable knife—that's all I need in cooking. My mother loved good food . . . I would not eat with her.'

'Why?' Lydia asks.

'Because the servants put things into it. Into the food.'

Poison? Charms? Evil ingredients to dull the senses with strange opiates?

Serena has found no happiness in living in Europe. 'Europe has been a total sell-out.' But she goes back all the time. When she is here, she walks round the old house, stirring memories out of the dust of ancient possessions—books, photographs, furniture, paintings, a cupboard full of starched linen. She lives in the past. Memories of the family greatness during the colonial era. She holds on to those desiccating memories which compel her to make inventories of the possessions that have now to be divided. Her brother gets one third share which will mean nothing to him. To Serena, too, in a sense. She envisages a museum where the artefacts of her family will be preserved—possessions that she feels fit into the British period of history. No one thinks them important. She documents every detail of her life, of her past. Lydia is the catalyst to all this, but feels that corrosive dust thick on her hands, dust which she must wipe off.

'Why am I drawn into this?' Lydia thinks to herself. Taken into a museum that is a mausoleum. The house of dead memories. Serena now has the house to herself. It is slowly being denuded of all its possessions. But before it becomes finally empty what does she want Lydia to see, to say?

'The truth. Speak the truth,' says Serena. 'Only you will speak the truth.'

Lydia begins to think of her ancestors. Once they too had acres of coffee gardens in Balana. Came into this territory that had held out for so long—held out against the invaders. But, ruthlessly, the invaders had finally come in. The land had been opened up to be gashed and seared like some sacrificial victim. Her people, too, had had wealth. A huge college stood on the land which once belonged to her great grandfather. The gardens had been named after him too—it was on its extensive acres that the young people of that generation would take in the air. Her grandfather had been a scholar of Hebrew, of the Classical languages; her forebears had been educated in a system which belonged to those colonial times, had adapted easily because that was their birthright—the language; the religion too. The coffee land had been devastated during the coffee crisis in 1868 when a fungus began attacking the trees.

(Lewis, one of the British colonial administrators of the time, describes the scene dramatically: 'All around me,' he wrote, 'there seemed to be an air of expectation of disaster . . . . The crisis was acute, the colony was practically in a state of paralysis.')

The land had gone back into the wilderness and back to the villagers to whom it really belonged. No great desires and longings had attached to the possessors of those lands. They had merely moved on to other areas of education and scholarship. Theirs was a vigorous new growth that sprang out of the hybrid seed. It was not a weak plant that diminished with the loss of wealth and power. Their philanthropy lay in the knowledge they imparted to others—they would not let the dust of ancient artefacts choke their speech, or breathe in the past, inhaling it like some malefic vapour spiralling out of urn burial.

What Serena seeks is indeed remembrance, but it is also a subtle assertion of power. Those individual power-packed histories showed a yearning for recognition in society, among the colonial masters. The palatial buildings where play games went on, entertainment, dining, wining, wealth accumulating from tea, from graphite, from arrack, from so much else, are crumbling as all such facades will with time. Serena wants to remind posterity of what once was, in her eyes, monumental. She wants to revive myths and legends and the court of Camelot. But here, the photographs on the walls suddenly change in their aspect. Spectral death leers out of those gentle and ruined faces. Ruined lives.

Serena brings a tray with frothy ice cream for herself and Lydia. And iced ginger ale. The glasses, the ice cream bowls, all repose on a kingfisher-blue woven tray cloth. Woven on the dryad loom. The ice cream tastes of egg. There are no artificial flavours to titillate the tongue.

'Come, let us look at the room,' Serena opens the door of her mother's bedroom.

'Holy of Holies,' says Lydia.

The emptiness and silence of a room bereft of its spirit. The furniture is painted white. With wreaths of flowers and garlands. Nuptial chamber. A place for nymphs to disport themselves in.

'All this furniture belonged to Beatrice long ago. Then my mother inherited it all after her death.'

A single bed against the wall. Solitary. Separate. Covered with a worn blue blanket. Serena's mother lay beneath it often, in the later stages of her life, in great agony. She had cancer. The cancer must have started a long time ago, eating into her slowly. The cancer of her regret. On her mirrored dressing table an old box of Coty's face powder gathers dust. A bottle of Oil of Olay. Tiny perfume bottles. Flower fragrances. Nothing luxurious. Little vanities. There is a wide, locked wardrobe with all her clothes.

'She looked after her things carefully,' remarks Serena.

On the clothes-horse folded garments neatly hang over the rails. Just as if she had carefully kept them for another day, to be worn again. It is several months now since she died.

'She died on the 23rd of October. Three months later, one night, I heard the sound of bitter weeping. Such bitter weeping. It came from her room. After her death my husband went through her handbag and tossed out her diary. It was a record of her intense suffering.'

Serena takes up another of her uncle's sermons and together she and Lydia turn the pages . . . 'Then there are others who are afraid of death because they do not know what lies beyond it. And also because they haven't won forgiveness for all the wrong they have done in their lives and are afraid to face God because they fear judgement . . .'

The rage of a sea of passion stilled, frozen. To whom could the mother cry out? It had begun, this death of the soul, many years before. Those disappointed hopes of a son who was slowly digging their grave. Who could say why or how?

John's body became his own area of exploration. The cicatrices of pain in his mind. And after all that naked brutality, this . . . to become a vegetable; to be bathed, dressed, fed, taken out. In someone else's power. The dominance never ceased. He could not call his soul his own. There grew a bond between the two victims. Mother and son. The two sufferers. The father took to his bed. His protest against a wilful and dominant wife. He retreated into silence.

She was not loved, that mother. Maternalism was her social role. Her whole being was consumed by the sufferings of her son. He hurt her while he was beyond hurt himself. But till the end she thought of him. Three rooms of the house will always be kept for him until he 'passes away'. He has already passed into oblivion.

Serena cares for him. When she returns from abroad she takes him for walks. Sees that he bathes himself. Cooks for him. Brings him on visits to Lydia's home. Life has been denied him, in every sense. This is his tragedy. He is now ageing. Pushed back, deep, into his own history. No monuments. No epistles. No remembrance in the hearts and minds of friends. Lydia remembers having seen him in church in the past. The back of his head well shaped. Slender neck. When he turned his face, the lines seemed to blur and dissolve. There was something not quite right. Years passed and Lydia saw him again. In church with his mother. At classical music concerts with his mother. At the theatre with his mother. She was at once his wardress and his mainstay. They both loved good food. She was, as a result, in the power of her servants.

Serena is suspicious. She trusts no one. 'I am sure the servants put things in her food. One day, before she went off for the day, the woman said, giving me a covered dish, "This is only for your mother. See that she has it."'

Serena complains about the servants. 'I don't want any servants. It's they who brought all the evil into the house. The cockroaches, the dirt, the dust, all the malaise. Greedy, grasping . . . . And my mother was in their power. They stole everything. And even now they come, asking, asking for things, for money. They've forced open the linen cupboard and taken away all the sheets.'

Winding sheets. Mummy shrouds.

Lydia and Serena walk round the gallery. Portraits. Oils. 'That's my mother's grandmother. That's her grandfather. She was young. They married her off to an old man. When he died, she begged and pleaded not to be married off again to the man they had chosen for her. But they did. Another old man.'

Dark oils. Ancestors. The grandmother wears a white kaba-kurutha jacket and skirt, Portuguese style. Western influences had already begun. Later, photographs of women with bobbed hair—nineteen twenties. The deracinated people. British Universities. Oxford. Cambridge. English governesses. Education in England. English manners. Anglicanism. High Church.

Serena's father carried his full suit on a coat hanger along the station platform. He visited Lydia and her husband, brought his own beer and beer mug. Everything packed away in the boot of the car. His own private picnic hampers.

'Look,' Serena says and points to cupboards draped with white cloth. Lifts them and shows shelves with China and porcelain and glass. Lalique ware. Slender green vessels. 'Ode to a Grecian Urn'. Everlasting. Immortal. So much of it has already been taken away—cut glass, crystal, and all her mother's jewels, beautiful garnet necklaces.

More photographs. Serena is seen against snow-covered mountains. Delicate backdrops. Snow maiden. She is now very austere, her clothes in sober colours. No jewels at throat or neck. Heavy shoes.

'I go every morning for Mass,' says Serena. 'I live each day as it comes. I get up at four-thirty every morning to prepare myself for the day.'

On the wall beside the Indian tapestries, is a Byzantine painting of Our Lady, Mary, the Mother of Jesus Christ. The walls leave no space. A Picasso reproduction. Jamini Roy. David Paynter has been removed. The George Keyt too. The eyes are bemused by this visible historical album. This minuscule museum of lives whose relevance to their history will soon be effaced.

'I have my own ideas,' Serena says. 'I want continuity. Things to flow. Things to be as they have always been. My mother was, someone said, a most unpleasant woman. She was alone. She had no friends. She wanted no one in her life. She bullied my father. She did not encourage anyone to visit her.'

They prepare to leave, Serena and Lydia. Lydia takes one last look at the house. She will never return. An embellished shell. A blind man will only touch and feel sharp edges that will hurt.

'I have my ideas. No, no home for the aged. That's what the church wanted.' She gives a tremulous laugh. Like cobwebs, broken. 'How nice it

would be if children from this terrible war could
come here . . . or . . . if I could have a gallery . . .
the Thirties . . .'

'May I close the door?' Serena asks Lydia.

'Yes, I am ready.'

'I'll walk back with you,' Serena says, as if she
does not want the visit to end.

The greater part of the house with its many
windows has already been sealed with white tape. In
this silenced house, dispossessed of its chatelaine
whispers, the past and present settle into a gathering
dust softly, subtly. It is late evening. The hills which
stretch beyond the house and garden begin to darken
with shadows. The security man walks restlessly on
the threshold. He holds in his hands a piece of white
tape for the front door. Lydia and Serena go out into
the garden. Serena points to the enormous severed
trunk of a thick-girthed tree. It had been cut at the
base.

'It fell onto the building and destroyed it.
Deliberate,' Serena says. 'They wanted it to be
destroyed, the servants. Evil. Didn't you see Heen
Menike carrying away the grinding stone? She had
paid for it, she said.'

Soon the house will be emptied. The secrets locked
within its walls.

'I must stay up all night to make inventories.
People want, want, want . . . Marie says, "I want to
buy your house." Out of the question, I tell her.'

Marie is a Joceleyn Nursery girl. She had
emigrated to Canada and made good there. Serena
feels that the bastions of privilege are still
impregnable. Not everyone can aspire to assail them.

Lydia and Serena walk down the drive together.
A large stone-grey cement frog crouches over an
empty pond filled with dry and withered leaves,

never to turn, transformed by love into a fairytale prince. The golden ball which had flashed through those enchanting, fantasy-filled gardens perhaps lay tarnished in the turgid depths of a wounded psyche.

Parts of the garden are scorched. Burnt in patches. The bougainvillea bush crinkled and seared like burnt paper. The dark bamboos stand like grim sentinels behind and before the house.

'Anil, my nephew, is going to cut that ancient clump on the hill and clear the land.'

At the foot of the hill drive, Serena touches the tiny truncated nodes of the bamboos. 'People will kill even the small ones . . . .' she says regretfully. 'I will come back,' she continues. 'I want children here. Orphan children affected by this bitter war, to come and spend holidays. No tourists for me. I won't sell. I won't rent out the house. People will never go. No restaurants. No guest houses. Perhaps for my friends to come and stay.' But where are these friends? Do they want to come and share the memories of ghosts?

Above them, on the hill, lies the hidden citadel. Every orifice, every entrance taped into silence. Imprisoning those myriad voices that will soon whisper into dust, dwindle, leaving those speechless ghosts to the death of perpetual silence.

The Mutants

SHE SWISHED THE water in the bathing tank with the full swirl of her palm, then lifting it lightly with a myriad sparkling droplets catching the sunlight, she let it skim gently over the surface like a dragonfly.

Nanna knew that Zuleika was in a happy mood but she could not allow for the distraction of so heady and bubbly a feeling, temporary and transient, in her granddaughter's mind.

'Zuleika, stop playing with the water and have your bath,' she called from the house.

The water tank was outdoors, filled to the brim. That was where they bathed and washed their clothes. They lived, the old lady with her thin praying mantis body and the grandchild, in a small one-room annexe near the sea. The rent was paid for by one of Nanna's daughters who had married a foreigner and lived abroad. But soon they would have to leave this place because the landlord had decided to put up an extension to the house.

Zuleika wouldn't stop playing with the water. Her eyes were taken up by the silvery swathes, the shimmer of patterns she created. Images: branches swinging with sharp pointed leaves and birds perched on them, their beaks deep in fruit. No one else but she saw the silver forest swaying beneath her hand. She hummed under her breath.

'She loves me.'

That was the thought in her mind.

'There's someone to love me again. Someone has been nice to me. She spoke to me so kindly, that aunty. I may never see her again but today she has made me happy. Nanna says I'm always like this, excited, happy, unable to settle down to anything if someone shows me love. Yes, it's natural. People seldom say they love me. My mother, my father, where are they . . . ?'

Zuleika's father had married thrice. She and her two brothers were the children of the first marriage. He had abandoned them and now he had yet another family to support. She thought of her mother. She too had remarried and had a life of her own with a young child to care for. Her husband was in the States and she lived with her in-laws.

In the past she did so much for us, Zuleika thought. She worked in the Middle-East and sent home money which Father squandered. We had a good life then—clothes, food, toys. We spent a lot of time with our grandparents, aunts and Uncle Jerome in Colombo and in the South. But my parents are no longer together and my brothers and I are separated. We all live in different places. Nanna cannot look after all of us. And the saddest thing is that one of my brothers is lost.

Zuleika thought of her early childhood in the village. The village in the south. Uncle Jerome, tall, tall as one of the coconut trees in the estate, with his long, wavy black hair, like a gypsy with the gleam of freedom and pleasure in his eyes, carrying her high on his shoulder.

'Come, Zuleika, let's go and see my girlfriend,' he said, the huge gold ring flashing in his ear. 'I'm going to get married.' His sisters, Isolde and Karen, laughed.

'He'll never marry.'

'Yes, I will,' he said with a serious look but with laughter behind his eyes. He had walked tall and straight among the coconut trees with their elongated shadows weaving serpentlike at the roots. Perched on his shoulder, she felt she was riding a horse, one of those high stepping white palominos in the story books that Isolde and Karen read to her from.

Uncle Jerome walked on and on but there was no girl friend.

He stopped before one of the coconut palms. It stood separate from the others. It had still to bear its clusters of nuts.

'I just wanted you to see the tree I planted,' he said and laughed and laughed.

'The tree will outlive me,' he said.

No, he wasn't at all sad and he didn't look as if he would die young either. He was so handsome. So very handsome. Olive-skinned, with brilliant dark eyes which changed their colour in the sun, and a mane of wavy hair. He was a model. Clothes sat beautifully on his frame. His stance casual, his stomach flat, his back straight. He had a sensuous, languorous stride on the catwalk. The villagers hated him. He knew it. The village boys now smoked marijuana, pot, heroin. Isolde and Karen smoked too, squatting on their haunches on the earthen floor of the small *kades*. Probably their mother Sonia smoked pot too. They all smoked pot, the whole family. What euphoria it produced. What heavenly forgetfulness being high. That was the other plane of reality they all escaped to. The landscape was not of this world. The colours, unearthly, kaleidoscopic. They floated up to the mountains, bodiless, supported by billowing clouds that carried their bodies in a sensuous drift. The purest ether they breathed in. The aching flesh was cushioned in downy softness as if brushed against by a million feathers. They swam in oceans and never drowned; stepped onto islands where fruits clustered ripely on trees, flowers burgeoning out of their smooth trunks. But they needed so much money to purchase this bliss, this temporary escape.

Prospero's island. Those beguiling airs seducing the senses. And when they returned after a trip it was excruciating. Life was so dull. So drab. The dark cavern with its invisible ceilings and jagged frozen stalactites jabbed the wounded heart. The yawning pits gaped wide open at their feet. They felt fear, fear of falling in, swallowed by flailing dreams. Winged panthers clawed at their throats. But to pay for the paradisal dreams to summon you through trance-like sleep money had to be found. So the big house began to vanish bit by bit. The doors, the windows, the bricks, the tiles, until only a long passage was left. By then Isolde, Karen, Sonia had all gone away, emigrated to Australia. One day, the villagers thrashed Jerome. There was blood all over his body, his hair clotted with blood, his shirt sodden.

'For his evil ways,' Madeleine said. She, who was so tolerant and compassionate.

'The house, the house,' Jerome mourned. 'What am I to do? How can I live? I don't have money. No one supports me. No one gives me money.' So his castle, the citadel, the tower, the turrets dwindled away. He had to sleep on a mat. There was no furniture left, he had sold it bit by bit. His nephew Denham slept on a plank supported by bricks. He studied by the light of a bottle lamp. Sometimes in sleep his body would slip into a deep furrow in the earthen floor.

And Jerome, with his beautiful, powerful stallion-like body, going without food, without any comforts. Without any money What a family he had belonged to. They had been so wealthy. You had only to mention the name, so well known in the whole country. They spent lavishly, had flashy cars— Citroens, Rolls, Mercedes, antique cars.

Raphael, da Vinci and Michaelangelo—Zuleika's Narrative

Oh, if only my father were here again. Where is he? And my little brother? Everybody says, 'We don't know where he is.' Why was he allowed to disappear? He was being abused by the people he was living with, Aunty Madeleine says. She uses a certain word when she talks of him to others . . . 'Those men are paedophiles,' she says. It's only Nanna I have now. Where are those parents of mine? I don't even have their addresses. I can't reach them in a time of emergency. They too have disappeared.

My mother. My father. How could they allow my brother to get lost, to vanish, never to be found again? And if he were found would he want to return to us? Return to whom? No, there's no one to return to, only Nanna and myself. Aunty Madeleine says he has plenty of food, drinks and drugs. He has to offer his body too, she says. Aunty Madeleine belongs to the Seventh Day Adventist Church and she's always trying to help someone. She wanted to save my brother, take him away to Canada. He was on the streets. 'Selling his backside on the street,' Aunty Madeleine said. She couldn't save him because he had disappeared. He'll never return. Who knows what will happen to him, to my brother. Will I ever see him again? And my other brother, staying with friends. But he hasn't enough to eat, he goes hungry, I know. My mother comes to visit Nanna. She says 'Hello' to me. That's all. She doesn't make me feel I am her daughter. She never shows me love. She talks endlessly to Nanna. About her own problems, I suppose. Her new husband is in America. She lives with her new in-laws. She has a child. She doesn't want them to know that she has a family already. They are supposed to be a very conservative family and would not want to have a daughter-in-law who is divorced or abandoned. She has to conceal everything, her family, us three children, her past.

Sometimes she gives Nanna a hundred rupees. Then she goes away. The two of us, Nanna and I, are alone. Nanna keeps our little room so neat and tidy. I am free. I go where I like. I have friends. I visit the two girls who are doing gem cutting. They live in the house of the gem cutting *mudalali*. They cook their own food, delicious curries which they share with me. Then there's the Scherezade toffee lady. I visit her too and somehow a sweet comes into my hands. They are very polite to me, open the door, say, 'Come in, take a seat.' The children give me the toys they are tired of. Then I play on the sea shore. I can defend myself against the rough boys. There was one who used to trip me. I hit back.

I miss Isolde, Karen, my grandmother, my grandfather. I miss them so much. My grandfather is dead. All the others have gone to Australia. I miss the big house on the coconut estate and Aunty Elizabeth and Debbie. I remember the night Elizabeth had that heart attack. Oh, she was beautiful to the end. She drank. She smoked. Her last words were, 'Don't drink, don't smoke.' Her daughter Debbie lives close by. Nanna goes to visit her. I go too. She drinks and smokes too.

Now I have my Ninja turtles. They will protect me from all danger. If only my father would return to me. Why has he gone away leaving us to fend for ourselves? I remember the days he used to come visiting us. How I would run to him and jump onto his lap. He would carry me on his shoulders to the swimming pool. I'll tell everyone stories about him then they won't pity me for not having a father. I'll impress them with the image of my father as a racing car motorist and of my grandfather with his collection of antique cars—Mercedes, Rolls, Citroens. They were wealthy men. They were the biggest funeral undertakers in the country. And now I live with Nanna, my mother's mother, in this little room. She's all I have.

Aunty Madeleine tried to help me, to pay for my education in a school where there would be discipline, community living in a religious atmosphere, but it would be far away from home, far away from the city with its people, its excitement, where I had the freedom to run out and play whenever I liked. How could I tell Aunty that I didn't want to be separated from my grandmother, my Nanna. I could only bow my head and be silent. When she said things like,

'Now don't run away from school. It's your final chance,' I felt panicky. When would I ever see Nanna again if I went away? She couldn't afford to visit me. I knew what it would be like. I had to plan my escape already.

We travelled up to Kandy from Colombo. Aunty Madeleine brought us to a house with a big garden full of plants and fruit trees—guava, jambu, mangoes, pomegranate. The bird bath was beside the clove tree. It was full of birds—mynahs, sparrows, konde kurullas. The house was full of books, comfortable chairs, sofas with plump cushions. There were showers and hot food. The aunty there, Aunty Lorraine, was very kind. She looked at me in a special way, as if she had taken a liking to me. There was sympathy in her eyes. 'Are you sure you're doing the right thing?' she asked Aunty Madeleine. 'You think she'll be happy away from her Nanna? It's a very remote place, winding roads that take you into the very heart of the countryside. It was once a vast estate with a large estate bungalow. It now belongs to your religious group, the Seventh Day Adventists. I know you have a lot of faith in the way of life that is followed there but Zuleika—I don't really know how she'll fit into the special kinds of discipline there . . . . Zuleika, why don't you go out to the garden and pick whatever fruit you like? The guavas are ripe, and the jambus,' Aunty Lorraine said, turning towards me.

'So many birds, Aunty. Where do they come from?'

'They're displaced. Most of the trees have been cut down for the new houses that are coming up. Sometimes we find reptiles in the garden and one night an owl flew in. Perhaps it had escaped from the pet shop next door. It was hurt. Its wing had been injured.'

'Didn't you want to take it and look after it?' I asked.

'No, owls don't belong in houses. They're night birds. They must be free to hunt small animals and rodents, find a perch on the branch of a tree. No, they don't belong in houses.'

I liked owls. I would like to have a garden full of birds, all kinds of birds. At night I would like to feel that there is an owl perched outside the window of my room. The owl, Nanna would tell me, was a bird of wisdom and it was a night bird. It would be awake while I was asleep.

I went to the garden and stood at the gate. I liked to watch people walking along the main road, talking, going in their cars, and the place I would have to go to the next day would be so far away . . . .

I felt so clean after my shower. Aunty gave me some pretty clothes, a cream blouse, delicately embroidered, of Chinese silk and a shirt but I preferred my own shorts and shirts. I liked to look like a tom-boy. The food was brought to the table in a big shiny wok—noodles with vegetables, mushrooms, prawns, sauces and hot fish curry in big chunks. There were sausages too which I loved and then ripe mangoes after dinner and a cup of milk before bed. The next day after breakfast, the journey would begin. I slept close to Nanna that night, sharing the same mattress. Aunty Madeleine slept on the big four poster. I felt cozy. Protected.

We set out on our journey in a three-wheeler the next day. It was so far away, beyond winding roads, acres of land cultivated with vegetables, hills covered with tea gardens in the distance. I did not want to come here. So far away from the sea. The school was in an estate, I knew, I couldn't run away and play with my friends anymore. There would be all those rules. I wouldn't have my Ninja turtles to speak to. I couldn't roam about the lane or go to Aunt Debbie's; Aunty Debbie with her knee-length hair, sometimes so kind, welcoming Nanna and myself, saying, 'You come and stay with me', at others shouting, angry, drunk. She even chased her father away when she was in that mood.

Uncle Mac, her father, is now a sadhu. His hair is long, he wears saffron robes. He told me he once had a vision on the beach, a vision of St. Rita. Uncle Mac had led an adventurous life. He had been an underwater diver and he needed to go deep down into the bottom of the oceans to search for ship wrecks and to bring up coins and pewter. He always smoked, marijuana, heroin. He had three children. He and beautiful Aunty Elizabeth drifted apart. Now he's in saffron robes, living in an ashram where he has gone in search of peace. He doesn't go diving any more. And his daughter Debbie, what's her life? Living in this house with her young son, nine years old. He doesn't go to school. His father was Japanese. He left Debbie because she was impossible to live with. She never cooks, just eats rice packets, and her son makes Maggi noodles soup for himself. He does everything for his mother, sweeps and arranges the house, tidies the beds, sweeps the garden. Oh, I'll miss him, playing with him. I know. I know in my heart of hearts that I'll never live here in this school.

I can't do without Raphael, Michaelangelo, Leonardo da Vinci. They are there in my little room which I share with Nanna. My Ninjas will protect me even when sometimes we have to starve. Nanna gives a little tuition in English. She's had a hard life too. Look how thin she is. Her body caves in, seems hollow, bent like a slender wand. How long will she last? I know what her life was like. I heard her telling Aunty Lorraine. She lived in a convent for sixteen years with her two daughters, one of them my mother, to escape from my granddaddy who was an alcoholic and beat her up . . .

They tell me I can learn, I can pass exams, and there's an American lady who they say will take the promising ones to the States.

I liked the American lady when I met her at the school. I had been there a few days when she took me to her home and gave me biscuits and tea. While I sat in her drawing room I began to imagine all kinds of things . . . . The room became a forest. There were no walls any more. I felt trapped like a rodent. I felt myself surrounded by owls. Stuffed owls, pictures of owls. Clocks, ornaments, everything became owls. I thought I saw an owl flying about the room. I knew then I had to escape. I could not live in this forest where these predators roamed. I had to run away from the owls. The American lady, the missionary, and her husband stood before me, no longer human. They were owls. They would swoop down on me and . . . I felt so small, so helpless.

The next morning I woke up early, before 4.30 a.m. and slipped out with the help of one of my sympathetic new friends. I took a bus and came to Kandy. I got off near the lake and walked and walked with my bags until I reached the house with the kind Aunty. I opened the gate. She sat reading on the verandah, looked up and smiled at me. 'Come in. Sit down . . . did you run away? Yes? Don't worry, you're safe now.' She gave me tea and biscuits. I didn't tell her the truth. I didn't know why. She would have understood but I am afraid to tell the truth to people. They don't usually believe the truth. I can't tell them I was homesick. That I missed my freedom, missed Nanna, missed the excitement in Colombo of my life with Nanna, Debbie, her son.

Getting up at 4.30 a.m. every morning, worship in the morning, worship at night again, vegetarian food, tasks, carrying bricks and stones. I had to weave tales to convince her that life was horrible there. I began . . . nothing to eat, a cane, boys afraid to speak, their hands fluttering like rags, weals and marks on their legs . . . no time to bathe . . . . Her eyes opened wide. I wanted sympathy. I wanted her love, her attention. She grew angry that I had been subjected to all this. I went on and on, I couldn't stop myself. Why? It wasn't like that at all, yet . . . I didn't want her to send me back ever, ever again. This Aunty would protect me until I was back again in my little room with Raphael, da Vinci and Michaelangelo. Of course I didn't tell Aunty the Ninja turtles existed only in my imagination. They were so real to me. Thinking about them alone brought me so much comfort.

I had to create a picture of a strange house which was full of owls. I described as vividly as possible paintings of owls, carved owls, stuffed owls, and I even made Aunty believe that a real owl flew across the room in my presence and perched on the branch of a big candelabra. Yes, I really had to make her believe—she who was a stranger, a new person into whose life I had entered. I had to make myself interesting. She had to see me as someone who was special. I could even make her feel that those people I would have to live with were strange, even sinister. Then she would think, how can this young girl live in that desolate place with its dry swimming pool, its remoteness from the city, its broken down pop corn machine and bakery which no longer baked rich, crusty loaves of bread. And why, she would question, were there no kingfishers or golden orioles? Why only these night creatures with their staring yellow eyes, their avid beaks pecking at their prey. Would I change into a mutant too? Would I be able to struggle out of those snares? Would I be trapped in this wilderness? Would I become the rodent? Or the owl?

I smiled a secret smile to myself when I heard Aunty say: 'Stay here, I'll phone Nanna and Aunty Madeleine. You're sure then that you don't want to go back?' I knew then that I had won. I had escaped. I could continue creating my fantasies. The Ninja turtles had come to my rescue again. Those mutants who were strong, much stronger than the owls. My fantasy protectors.

Man Without a Mask

All tremble at weapons; all fear death. Comparing others with oneself, one should not slay, nor cause to slay.

—The Dhammapada

We travel in two Pajeros. The shutters are up so we cannot feel the cool night air. But the Pajero is well equipped with air-conditioning and turbo coolers and we do not feel any discomfort. The roads, at this hour, are quiet and deserted; we travel swiftly and smoothly along the tarred carpet. Our destination is fifty miles away from the city. At a certain point, we have to branch off the main road and take the turning which leads to the village where this man lives in his ancestral house. It lies in the midst of a vast coconut estate. Family property.

I have the necessary information about him. I know his name, although I have never seen him before. I'm not interested in his private life or his personal habits nor in his virtues or vices. Morality does not come into this business. I have no feelings towards him. My detachment enables me to achieve my purpose each time. Emotions do not play a part in my job. I'm a professional. I pride myself on my impersonal attitude towards my goal. An iron will. A one track mind and a crack shot. No clumsy fumbling ever mars my work. I don't leave a man to bleed to death. Like a good sportsman I finish him off before I leave. Plenty of others to hunt out in this human jungle. I'm a hunter. Not a predator.

I have cultivated a personality of my own. One that I have created gradually over the years. I may have been born with human traits that society values but I realized they would have hindered me along the way. What I was in the womb or in the cradle is not what I am now. I'm known as a man who can be trusted implicitly with a job of this nature. That's enough for me. They all seek me out, so I can name my price. And I don't go in for small fry. My reputation would lose its lustre if I were to do so. I am a man of few words. I don't speak much. To whom could I speak? I have no woman in my life. No children. My weapon speaks for me. I have confidence in my skills. My hand must be steady. There must not be the slightest tremor in my fingers. My eyes possess a steady, unwavering gaze. They transfix the object before I take aim. I don't hold dialogue with those whom I've got to get rid of. No negotiation takes place. It would give them time for retaliation. Moreover, whatever they say will not, cannot, move me to change my purpose. Besides, I don't want bodyguards overpowering me, although most often they haven't a chance. They themselves do not escape. It's a sacrifice they are compelled to make. They have to take chances. How many assassins, how many hit-men get caught anyway? Better die than get caught. We know what happens. Limbs broken. Bastinadoed. Torture and interrogation go hand in hand. There's no chance of escape. And does the right man pay the price? There are so many underlings. Substratas, subversive layers, like the shifting plates that lie below the earth's surface. Endless conjecturing and surmising as to who pulled the trigger, who operated the remote control devices to detonate the bomb or the mine, who flung the grenade. Whether the weapon was a T 56 or AK 47. Suspects are rounded up. But these are the decoys. The innocents. Confessions are extracted, whispered through bloodied, pulped mouths and bruised tongues to the High Priest, the torturer. Whom does it all help? Talk, talk, talk. What's the point?

I'm given orders to silence a voice. I don't want its echoes ringing in my ears. I want to dwell in a vast and endless space where a landscape will have no impediments. Cascading waterfalls, rivers rushing headlong in spate, a sky rent apart by tissues of lightening, the dull boom of thunder—all this would lead to a disturbance of the mind. My world is uniformly grey, silent with its absence of human voices. My bullets reach swiftly. There are no agonizing cries, no death throes. No echoes. Nothing haunts me. No voices whisper endlessly in my ear. Silence is my only companion. Before a blank wall I see only the image of a single man, blindfolded, hands tied behind his back, standing, face to that wall. I hold the weapon of execution in my hand. I pull the trigger. The machine gun splutters. The body is pitted, pricked out with an indecipherable message. They are the braille marks of the new fictions. People are still so slow to comprehend their meaning. Each indentation fills with crimson, the white page of the shirt suffused with blood. I walk away. The blood does not splatter on me to sully my clothes. The image recurs. The single man. The blank wall. Blindfolds. Hands behind the back. Knotted ropes. We never face each other. Neither of us knows the other's identity.

Tonight, it's this man, Nilame, who is my target. We know, my men and I, that he has no bodyguards. He is very confident, perhaps overconfident, of his own strength. He knows he has an enemy but he has underestimated the power of hate and the ruthlessness that goes with ambition. It will all be over shortly after midnight. Every move has been plotted and planned to the minutest detail. Perfect timing is vital. I must not waste time in searching through the maze of rooms in the old *walauwa*. I'll deploy my men so that whoever discovers him first will summon me without delay. One utterance.

'Nilame.'

I'm used to being there, always, at the correct time. The act can take place on the road, at the entrance of a man's house, on the political platform, at his desk in his workplace. Nothing is haphazard. I'm no explorer discovering the unknown. My mind is the map. The landmarks are clearly drawn in red ink. I am as meticulous as a scholar or scribe. Knowledge of a man's personal habits is integral to the task. Where and at what time precisely he breakfasts, the exact hour when he will step out of his house to enter the car that will take him for his assignation with high-ranking policy-making diplomats and ambassadors. Then again I must have the order of the speakers on the political platform. I don't listen to anything they say. My mind is blanked out. I prepare myself. Concentrate. Take regular breaths. Screen off the crowds who are hysterical with the euphoria generated by the speeches, and by the provocative and aggressive body language of the election candidates whose voices blast through the grating loudspeakers with all their shrieking distortions. Against the banners, the flags, the blank-faced bodyguards, the spotless white sheet covering the table with the jug of water and tumblers, the man stands up. He begins:

'My *mithrayo*, my friends, you have suffered deprivation for so many years. I promise you your freedom. And I promise you jobs, yes, employment, your right. We shall remove all abuses that have hindered you. We shall have religious toleration. We shall end this war, end the terrorist problem, have negotiations, dialogue, debate. Look into the grievances of these misguided youths . . .'

As the crowds surge forward to cheer, he is mown down with a barrage of bullets. Or the grenades are flung onto the platform. There's mad confusion. Stampede. Then there's the quick getaway. There are plenty of decoys too. Where is the assassin? He's never to be found. Where is he? Does he exist? Has he found refuge in a safe house? I permit myself a wry grimace that could pass for a smile. It's always 'the other'. Some poor fellow pulled out of a cell, one of those supposed terrorists with an ID planted on him, and finished off, bullets pumped randomly into his body. Just another victim to add to the growing numbers. Can no longer protest his innocence. The dead man lying in some squalid cul-de-sac beside on overflowing municipal garbage bin. Every bit of his clothing, his looks, his past, his career, minutely reported by the investigators. And photographs to give credibility. The enemy is so easy to identify in the confusion that exists in the current political scenario. We're living in a country rent apart by forces of violence, ethnicity, subversive elements, violations of every right under the sun. There's this huge power struggle going on behind the scenes so that it's never clear who the real enemy is. It is a society where the assuming of masks is easy. Not monstrous *vesmuhuna*, but bland, smoothly hypocritical masks. That man who is most vile, most corrupt, looks like a sage or an innocent householder. It's so easy to hoodwink the masses before whom a few crumbs are scattered. The huge drug cartels, the arms dealers, those who bag the biggest tenders, manipulate the small men. The powerful remain inviolable for a long, long time. Their corruption can even be interpreted as virtue. They'll be quoted to eternity for the good they have done mankind.

I am one man who never wears a mask. I don't have to. I'm perfectly safe with the one face I bear. It is distinctive only in it's ordinariness. The eyes have no definite colour. Sometimes they are like chips, splinters, of grey, blue-black stone hacked off a granite quarry. I have no one feature that stands out to distinguish me from the man on the street. Not a face that stands out in a crowd. But the sense of power I carry with me is felt by those who stare into the muzzle of my gun. It's like a hot, suffocating wave of air that overwhelms and inundates them. No one has yet been able to pin anything on me. It's because they never see me. Never hear me. It can't be one of ours surely who was the brutal slayer, they say. The victims are the saviours of our land. Those who engage in such acts of terrorism, they think, are from that other distant part of the island, that

Peninsula where the militants, the guerrillas, wage their unending conflict to divide the Motherland. Those men have know-how. Or else it's that Subversive Group, the 'misguided youth' so easily identified.

But those killers are different. Not like us, me. They come on their scooters and motorcycles, faces covered by their helmets, ride right upto the threshold and fire their revolvers. Nobody makes the slightest attempt to arrest them. They ride away swiftly, traffic is at a standstill, people gape, too shocked to move, the body of the fallen hero lies where it is being slowly inundated and saturated with his own blood. They may even be present when the body lies in its bier, passing by the resplendent corpse with the crowds of mourners, the hoi-poloi who stream into those elite drawing rooms where they would never have had entrance before. They tread with dusty feet on the plush red carpet brought from the undertakers, breathing in the heady fragrance of wreaths with their tightly packed clusters of orchids, gladioli, hydrangeas, lilies, carnations and chrysanthemums, smoke rising from the coconut oil-soaked wicks in the great brass ornamental lamps. Men, women, children, from all walks of life, people used to standing patiently for hours in bus queues, bow their heads in respect before death, weeping at the sight of the dead hero, fearful of *apaya*, hell, and of the supernatural world. Consumed too by an enormous sense of curiosity and even a feeling of secret pleasure that they, with the cracked soles of their feet and gnarled, knotty hands, are still alive with all their poverty and deprivation. The wreaths, opulent and ostentatious, pile up before their admiring eyes. A garden of death. The politicians enter the hall, give a swift inclination of the head and condole with the bereaved members of the family who are worn out with genuine grief and exhausted by the public show they have to engage in before the blaze of TV lights and the flashing cameras of the media reporters. The pallbearers lift the coffin, the sleek black hearse is ready to drive away in the motorcade. At the cemetery, crowds surge forward, breaking through man-made barriers, women faint from exhaustion, heat, emotion. The coffin is placed on the pyre and with a swiftly burning brand the ornate paper structure is set alight. A heavy grey blanket of ash is all that remains of flesh, blood, bones, cloth.

The dead hero becomes a cult figure. Sensational stories begin to surface in the villages. In some remote hamlet the parents of a small child say that their son is a reincarnation of the dead hero. Crowds visit the humble dwelling where he lives, the diminutive figure wearing clothes similar in design to those of the great man, the walls of the hut plastered with huge pictures of the dead handsome hero's smiling face. Where does it all end? The fake, the fraud? Is imposture a means of gaining fame, of lifting you from obscurity? Who's searching for honesty these days anyway? To be in the limelight, even briefly, to be the focus of attention of the media, to have the whole country conjecturing on the idea of their hero being reborn, of being a cult figure—that's enough for the moment. Everybody's trying to cash in on someone else's fame or image of popularity and power. Probably I have my followers too, though I'm not aware of them. Plenty of imitations. I'm the real thing—this they know, those who deploy me or use me. I use them too. I sometimes amuse myself by thinking, 'What if I stand on the banks of a *wewa* taking aim at wild doves or *batagoyas* or teal?' No, I don't want to kill those innocent birds. Wouldn't give me any pleasure. I don't kill for pleasure anyway. I just want to excel in my job. Like many others. Only you don't have to know my name. Everybody has aliases. So do I. My real name is tucked away in some niche in my brain. That's only for me, to remind myself of who I am. My parents gave me that name. It belonged to a great guru, a swami. That name could have taken me along a different path, had I wanted it. At the end of all this, who knows, I may be the leader of a great new cult that carries a message. And the watchword? 'Destroy before you are destroyed.'

I already have my acolytes. No one knows from where we emerge. We have our safe houses, in respectable residential areas. Alsatian dogs. Gates opening only through remote control. High walls. Bodyguards and security men. The gates are always kept locked. We wait for the next call. There are always the go-betweens through whom we first negotiate. We are then informed of who the architect of the master plan is. And of the price. The risks we take are our own. No betrayal. Cover-ups if we are discovered but we never are. We have too many high-ranking officials and politicians on our side.

Time is always limited, that's one thing we must be prepared for. Planning has to be done within forty-eight hours or even twenty-four. I have no time to lose, from the moment I open my eyes at 4.30 a.m.—no dawdling about in bed—to the hour when I close them (the hour is not always certain).

I function in a very special way. First, my breathing meditation. I keep the body still, without motion, the mind alert and keenly observant. 'Just as the tortoise shelters its limbs under its shell, so should the meditator guard his five sense organs and overcome the sex impulse with mindfulness.' So I have been taught in my lessons from the *theras*. I am always mindful of my breathing. This has served me well in my tasks. I am aware (*sati*), attentive and observant (*anupassana*). I breath in and breathe out rhythmically (*anapanasati*). Without my early morning meditation I am not prepared to face the day. As for those who work for me, I do not ask them questions about their private lives but each one of them has been carefully screened before recruitment. I cannot afford to make any error of judgement in my choice of men. They have to be part of a very elite force. They're well paid, well fed, clothed in the best of uniforms. Uniforms always instil fear, and respect for authority. A top designer has created them for us and they have passed through the hands of the best cutters and tailors. There's a very ancient Saville Row master tailor among them. We have both presence and personality. We're not attired in motley garb. We do not hack and kill. We do not mutilate or merely wound. Our killing is clean. We're not clumsy. Plenty of target practice. We don't take pot shots at trees. We have the real, live quarry.

While on the job there's to be no drinking, no smoking. After everything is over my men can relax, to a certain extent. There must be no excessive indulgence, no talking too much.

Strict vigilance is exercised by those who oversee the younger ones, especially those who are fired by political ideologies, who want to change the world, alter the status quo, carry on the struggle against neo-colonialism. They have got to concentrate on the job at hand. That's where you can't go wrong. As for political beliefs, I don't possess any. We don't betray, we don't change sides. We give our word and it is trusted. Not through any sense of morality but because that's the only way we can build up our select clientele and establish our credibility. There are those hit-men who'll carry out any slaying for a mere one thousand rupees or less and the fanatics who do it for nothing. We count our price in the region of billions and the account is safe in Swiss banks. Those in power are able to lay their hands on immense quantities of gold, of dollars, of sterling. They will let nothing come in the way of holding onto that power. And in the present political climate all kinds of personal vendettas, killings, massacres, abductions are thriving. It's easy to blame everything on the Proscribed Party or those terrorists, as they are called, from the North.

As we drive along, the faces of my companions are impassive. No one speaks a word. I demand strict silence, concentration on the mission before us. We have got to get this job over and done with. Tonight. No postponement. No failure. We cannot fail. We are prepared and armed to the teeth. The man, Nilame, isn't. Strange how men like himself are often caught unawares. Sometimes there are intimations, rumours, but they feel so confident in themselves that they disregard these warnings. The face of that young journalist flashes across my mind. No chance of escape. They came at dead of night. Surrounded the house. Blocked off every exit. Wrenched him from his mother's arms. Took him away. Tortured him. Murdered him. His body found the next day, quite by chance, by a fisherman, as it drifted in the ocean. Didn't that young man know he was in danger? Didn't he receive any prior warnings? Didn't he guess he was being followed? A senseless killing. Our executions are swift. We don't interrogate. We don't torture.

I know where the turn-off is. I guide the driver.

Dark paddy fields lie on either side of the road. The little boutiques by the wayside are shut for the night, their plank doors closed tight. Men are stretched out, sprawled in sleep on the cemented ledges. Drowned in sleep. Covered against night chills with a light cloth flung over their bare-chested bodies. A lorry carrying vegetables, coconuts and bunches of half-ripe plantains wrapped in sacking and straw is parked on the roadside. The driver and cleaner sleeping under it, feeling the warmth of the tarred road from the day's heat. A night *kade* is still open, neon lights blazing away. Hopper batter is being tilted in the pan. White, crisp-edged hoppers are piled up on a single plate. Rows of Fanta, Sprite, Pepsi, line the shelves. Bright orange, green, red, brilliant shining colours. We now take the road which leads into the interior. We pass tea and coconut estates, earth walled huts. We reach our destination.

It's the family property, a coconut estate of a hundred acres. Several family members have built their houses on this land. None of them will dare come out. No one does, these days. No one wants to risk life. These are dangerous times. The knock on the door at midnight heralds the unknown threat. Abduction. Disappearance. Death. The leader of the revolutionary movement for that locality lives closeby. Although 'our man' belongs to the ruling political party, they are both on good terms. So the killing won't be pinned on him. Death will come from his own people, those whom he has served for years, so faithfully too.

I look at my watch, a Rolex Gold. It's 11.30 p.m. By twelve midnight everything should be over. We drive into the heart of the estate. Switch off the engines. Night sounds clog our ears. The chirping of cicadas. Cries of birds disturbed. The screech of bats ravaging the wild guava and mango thickets. The rasping of the wind-shaken fronds of the coconut palms. The doors and windows of the houses remain shut. Shrouded in silence. They play safe. No one will raise any alarm. Even if they do, who will come to their rescue? People prefer to shut their doors by seven o'clock or even earlier, as soon as dusk begins to fall. The 'other' group is active, the one that is working to destabilize the establishment. Posters are pasted everywhere. There are strikes that cripple the country. Transport is affected. Also water, electricity. Shops and market places are ordered to close overnight. Tea factories are burned. Arrests. Reprisals. Tyre burnings. All these happenings are the order of the day. Mass graves in certain areas. I know a thing or two about these mass graves. Their exact location. One day they'll be excavated but can skulls, earthfilled skulls, talk? Tongues shredded into perpetual silence, bones like frail twigs encrusted with earth. Skeletal remains branching out in the dark underground, groping like roots searching for light. The fungi of mouldy scraps of cloth lying buried deep within crevices in the soil. Clumps of hair. Seed-hard teeth. Jawbones. One day the remains of the missing will be unearthed. But by then it will be too late. Will those who are guilty of these deaths of ordinary people, of bhikkus, of school children, many of them the offspring of peasants, of those young men and women called 'misguided youth', insurgents, and other anti-establishment terms—will they ever be held to account for their crimes? They know they'll escape. How strong is the evidence against them? They'll appeal against their charges. State that they were given sanctions to kill. I had a younger brother. I don't want to think of him. Who knows where he is or even whether he's alive. My power and influence meant nothing to him. He revolted against the 'corruption' it entailed.

Criminal. The corrupt. The immoral or the amoral elements. All criminals are not found behind bars. Killers roam free. Because they are in power they have the licence to kill, torture, abduct. Everything's changed overnight. Even the funeral rites. If you're known to be the enemy by 'the other side' and you're killed then you are not allowed burial in a coffin. You are 'the enemy', corrupt, a thug, the informer, pro-establishment. Oh, there are a thousand reasons why you can be considered the enemy. No mourners are allowed. No white flags or funeral orations. Everyone must know that your killing was justified. So the body will be carried in a certain way, the way a trussed pig would be, and flung into the grave. For this man, Nilame, it will be different. There'll be a big funeral. Orations. Eulogies. The *pansakula* ceremonies. Processions of mourners following the hearse with wreaths and banners. Weeping of a distraught family. Politicians in white garb will visit the house and solemnly bow their heads before the bier. The police will be at the scene of the funeral. The evidence will be recorded and documented minutely but they'll never find us. We're the men who do not wear masks but we can melt away and become invisible too.

We step out of the Pajeros. Nothing, no one impedes us. The surrounding houses are shrouded in silence and darkness. But we know which one he lives in. The big house. The *walauwa*. The family house. I've never seen the man before in all my life. That's not important. His political career has been unimpeachable. A seasoned veteran campaigner, loyal and faithful to his own Party, the very Party which now wants him out of the way. He belongs to the village. Has worked tirelessly for his electorate all these years, never changed sides. Selfless man, they say. Never acquired wealth for himself. An old, well-established family. Why get rid of him? Aren't men such as these valuable to the 'side'? I'm told that the reason is that there's a new man who has joined the Party, wants to oust him and contest this seat. He's just returned from abroad, one of the western countries, is enormously wealthy and wants to be the political candidate for this area. Nilame won't give in. Refuses. The man from the States has been lavish with gifts. Expensive gifts to all the important people. Mercedes Benz cars as birthday presents. Millions of rupees spent on election campaigning. There's someone behind the scenes manipulating the whole affair. Well, the only way out is to just get rid of the big rock that impedes the oncomer's path. It's my job to do it. I'm confident in myself and my men. We're well equipped. Have the necessary firearms. Machine guns. T 56s. We don't use swords and other such primitive methods of disposal. No *galkattas* either. I pride myself on my efficiency, my lack of political scruples, my unemotional attitude towards my job. My men are well disciplined and tightlipped. They won't give away secrets although they do not bite on cyanide capsules like 'the others'.

We don't knock on doors. We beat on the wood with the butt end of our weaponry. Naturally we find the front door looked and barred but there are other, easier entrances to walk through. My men get in first and open up the front door for me. That's how I always walk in. No leader ever enters through any other way. I establish my authority in this manner.

Here we know that no resistance will be offered. Nor will the occupants come forward to greet us and extend the traditional welcome. The *walauwa* is about two hundred years old with wide verandahs. Ten whitewashed pillars support the jak wood beams of the tiled roof. There are barred inner-windows. A brass spittoon stands beside a shabby rattan armchair. The front door opens for me. Inside the spacious hall with an ornate ebony couch and a few straight backed chairs, *sesath* with glittering prisms of mica lean against the walls. Family portraits in their heavy frames are lined up with their stiff, formal gazes. Silent and dead as the past.

My men walk into the rooms, searching. The curtains swish aside. Empty.

'Look under the *viyan andha*, the four poster bed.'

A young man in white shirt and sarong, ashen-faced, is cowering in fear beneath it. They drag him out.

'Where is Nilame?' they ask.

He's a young servant boy. He's speechless, his tongue stilled by terror. His body is trembling, his expression livid. They push him aside and walk into the next room. There are so many of them in the *walauwa*, half of them empty. An old couple, relations of Nilame, an uncle and aunt of his, this much I know, sit on the edge of a bed, side by side. Resigned to whatever has to happen.

'Spare Nilame. Take us,' they both beseech.

Naturally, this offer is spurned. Who wants this kind of noble self-sacrifice.

He has to be here. Couldn't have escaped. The house is surrounded.

'Nilame? Nilame?'

Shadowy forms are reflected in the old tarnished mirror of the dressing table.

I walk along a corridor and find myself before an open door. His study. He's there, standing at his desk, back turned to me, intent on what he is doing, going through files and papers. Bookcases are crammed with hardcover books. There's a glass-framed portrait of the President on the wall. Silver trophy cups won at College. An old, green, baize-lined writing desk with innumerable pigeon-holes. He gets no time even to turn around and face me. We never see each other's faces.

I fire three shots. He falls where he stood. I shoot again. Several times. I have to make sure. There was a large rock on the road. A boulder of considerable weight and size. It had to be cleared out of the way.

My men come running to the door when they hear the shots. So do the servant boy, uncle and aunt.

'No, don't go near him. Leave him where he is.' I order. My mission has been accomplished. Back to that empty room which is my life. The only place where I feel safe. Just myself and my weapons. I trust no one. I have had no one's love. My men are loyal because they fear me and value what they could gain. Their passion for killing dictates their actions.

We leave the doors wide open. Everything remains in darkness. We climb into our Pajeros. Prepare for the return journey. The neighbouring houses show no signs of life. Afraid to come out. All of them. We hear the wails begin in the *walauwa*. Tremulous sounds of aged people who now have no reason to live.

The job is done. Twelve thirty. Perfect timing. The arena is free for the other man to contest the elections. I'll report back to the bosses as soon as I get back. the telephone will ring in that house in the city. The Boss will be waiting to take up the phone.

'Boss,' I'll say, 'everything's fine. The coast is clear.'

'You'll find the amount agreed on in your bank account tomorrow. I'll telegraph it along to the Swiss account.'

Boss will sleep easy tonight. So will I.

The speeches begin. The great orations. The promises to build a brave new world free of the shackles of colonialism and multinational exploitation. Create a society which will not have discrimination against the underdog. End unemployment. Subsidize essential food items. Enhance scholarship allowances for university students. Investigate allegations of bribery, corruption and human rights violations. End the war in the North. Bring the misguided youth back into the democratic process.

The banners and flags are strung up once more. The new colourful portraits are blazoned everywhere. The loudspeakers blast out the polemic. Security precautions are taken and yet the grenades are flung. The fifth speaker and his bodyguards are blown to bits. Nilame's opponent. Probably the other faction was responsible. Those loyal to the old campaigner. The new man hadn't a chance. I removed the rock. Just ahead of him was the mine.

Big funeral for him too. Processions. Wreaths. Orations. The pyre was one big conflagration. The leaflets and the posters with his picture, his name and his Party's are blown into the gutters, trampled underfoot, scraped off the walls and hoardings to give place to the new candidate. He would still have been alive if he had remained in the States.

Well, there's bigger fish in the sea now. We have got to set our plans for the next big job. I have a feeling I know who the next man will be and the next and, finally, the biggest fish of all in this endless, polluted ocean. I'll be there, directing operations, behind the scenes, right in the heart of it, and in broad daylight with the coloured banners, the coloured flags, the cleared highway. I can predict it. My timing is perfect. Only this time I'll be at a safe distance, watching. He'll be blown to extinction, and others with him. This time the entire funeral will be dramatically presented on a colossal stage. But first, the streets will be swiftly cleared. The blood washed away together with the pieces of flesh. People will tread those streets, place their dusty feet on that very spot. They'll remember nothing. The monuments, the statues, three times larger than life portraits will tower over the common highways and somewhere in a remote hamlet the stories of rebirth will emerge. As for me, I'm waiting for the next job. I'm a professional. That's my only skill.

From Distant Ophir

It was time to think seriously of a bridegroom for Sulochana. Her mother was a widow and she was eager to see her daughter settled as soon as possible. Meena, Sulo's mother, was assailed with a barrage of questions:

'Meena, what's happening about your daughter Sulo? How old is she? Isn't she getting on in years? Not settled yet? Soon she'll be past the marriageable age. It is time you found a suitable proposal for her or she'll be on the shelf. All the younger ones are getting married, no? Education is one thing . . . . It is very good that she has her degree and all that, but young men are not looking only for education today. They want a wife who will be at home, looking after her family. Not that education is not important, especially if she can help supplement the income ...

and if she goes abroad, she too can work and they can have a good life. Better find a good matchmaker who can arrange all these things—dowry question, family connections, all the details . . .'

Meena, already anxious, would panic when confronted with these questions. Love affairs, romantic attachments, the ideal partner whom Sulo had envisaged all along—the dream mate, tall, dark, handsome, educated, wealthy, with liberal ideas— had been too much of a mirage. So far nothing had happened. Youthful bloom would not last forever. As time went on the prospect seemed to be gloomier. They would have to resort to a widower, a divorcee, or an elderly bachelor who needed a mate-companion in some far away country where he lived in exile. Sulo was approaching thirty. Yes, it was time to think seriously about a husband. A stable partner for a life-time relationship with a steady job and professional qualifications—a lawyer, doctor, computer engineer, accountant. The partner would most probably be living abroad. A political refugee or one who had gone for higher studies which spread over an almost indefinite period, or one who had decided that the good life was to be found only by the waters of Babylon.

For Meena, the responsibility of having an unmarried daughter on her hands was growing progressively weightier. Her somewhat frail shoulders would not bear it much longer. The young woman herself, Meena's daughter, had survived very well on her own all these years and had developed a tough resilience which had stood her in good stead through childhood, adolescence and now to a slowly maturing womanhood. She was quite conscious of her charm, confident that the ultimate choice, when it came to acquiescing, would be hers. She could not imagine that any suitor would find her irresistible. Fairy tales like the Princess and the Swineherd were not for the likes of her.

Meena, too, now felt that she was growing older and needed to be looked after and assured of a place someday in her daughter's home. That someday would have to be soon.

'I am not keeping so well,' she would complain softly, 'the upcountry climate doesn't suit me. It is so cold and misty there and I have phlegm trouble also. And how long can we stay in a boarding house sharing a room? We must also have our freedom. Sulo too must make up her mind, no? She is getting on and then it will be difficult to find a husband. I have put away money for her. My jewellery also is here for her. See, she has a nice gold chain. All that she needs. Dowry, also, I can give. And she has her education. Only we must find a good man. See, will you, already she has refused so many proposals. Look, let me show you the letter that Mrs Selvaratnam sent me about her son. He is a lawyer with a house in Barnes Place. Only child, so no in-law problems. And Mrs Selvaratnam is longing for a daughter! Sulo will be in Colombo and she can get a good job at the International School for twelve, fifteen thousand a month.' Sulo would keep silent. Then she would burst out: 'How to marry him, Aunty? He is going bald. All his hair in front is getting thinner. How to go out with him? I'll be embarrassed. He is tall, sharp-featured and all, but no hair, no?'

Meena put the letter back in her purse. It had been a pleading, propitiatory letter extolling the virtues of the son, of the family, and showing eagerness to have Sulo as a daughter-in-law. There were families which had built up respectability and standing in society—sons educated and professionally qualified, mature men in their late twenties or early thirties, house and property in Colombo 7, wanting to settle down with a wife of the mother's choice. Virtue and chastity were essentials in the game. Young women with these rare qualities were diligently sought out.

'Once she is settled then I can also rest,' Meena sighed. Meena was still attractive. She had blossomed in widowhood. She had always looked after herself carefully, nourishing herself with milk and eggs, her skin smooth and soft with rich emollient creams. She was soft and plump and gleaming like the burnished pearl that nestled in the blue velveteen folds of her jewel box. For the moment she showed no signs of ageing or of any great decrepitude. She was a carefully preserved woman in her fifties but still looked youthful in her elegant sarees with their pastel shades, her traditional jewellery, her *soignée* air and softly parting lips which revealed pearly teeth when she smiled. Her husband had been rather a loadstone in his lifetime—talented in his own right, with a gift for writing on a variety of subjects in a somewhat journalistic style of prose, he was also a skilled pathologist. His little addictions grew as he mingled with friends and acquaintances. Ultimately his world and his life crumbled and he became the victim of the political upheaval in the country, forced to join the dreary convoy of refugees back to the Eastern Province from where he and his wife originally came, and then through boredom, through human weakness, through loss and despair, as if impelled by the deepest death wish, forgetful of his wife and child, drank himself to death—the death which was his only escape.

Meena was now free to develop on her own, to acquire wealth through her own strategies of lending money on interest, money and gold being two useful commodities in that society. She also profited from her husband's pension which was now wholly hers to put away safely to accrue interest. She had the respect of the community without the embarrassment of a husband who 'indulged' himself, who was never strong enough to release himself from the guilt of his bondage, drink—that powerful, all-consuming passion—draining him of his manhood. Meena had a delicate, rather helpless air that appealed to those who felt protective about her. She also saw herself as the mother figure in young families, young families with young children who felt a certain emotional security in her presence. She, too, was a teacher, a teacher of English. That was a greatly respected profession, to be valued in a small provincial society where parents wanted their children to improve their English, conversational style, manners and cultivate social skills. And now if Sulo made a favourable marriage her mother's gentle sighs would cease. She would be proud to say, 'You know, Sulo is now so comfortably off—her husband lives abroad and draws a big salary. She will have nothing to worry about now. Her husband looks after her very well. He does everything for her. He even cooks for her. She has an easy time. I'll be flying there one of these days for the confinement. She wants me to come. How can she, poor thing, do everything by herself . . . .' Yes, she was waiting to utter those words. Soon, soon, the event must take place, that negotiatory settlement called marriage. To settle down. To be settled. To find someone to settle down with. As if the effervescence of youth must subside, grow quiescent, and bubbling youth must dispose of its iridescent bubbles and shining froth into some murky, opaque substance in which the mirror-reflection of the face drowns and vanishes.

Sulo, too, had a responsibility towards her mother. It was unacceptable in that society to have a spinster daughter. What would all the friends and relations say? So valuable a commodity as a well-brought up daughter was certainly an asset. Meena had every intention of living with her daughter to the very end. She was tired of living in a boarding house. She had sold her land in the Eastern Province, and with the political turmoil in those regions, could not dream of returning there. How long could two women share one bedroom? Share one life? Meena needed the stability of her daughter's marriage. In a culture such as theirs, marriage was coercively justifiable; love and romance secondary.

Right from the beginning, with the onset of nubile womanhood after the coming of age ceremonies, marriage was the desired end. That day when she had attained age, dressed in her mother's saree of vermilion silk and gold lace, with her mother's jewellery adorning her, Sulo knew that whatever happened in her life, marriage would be her destined end. All the friendly neighbours had risen to the occasion, giving the family a helping hand on the auspicious day, preparing rich food and the traditional sweetmeats. The father had found all this so exhausting that after some potent refreshment he had spread a mat on the floor and fallen asleep. The womenfolk, powerful, dominant and pityingly lenient about the lapses of men, had held sway. Sulo had looked so pretty in all that finery, so elated with herself at being acknowledged a woman. Yet, bad times had come and the same jewellery that she had worn on that occasion had, together with her mother's *thali*, to be hidden under a mattress for safekeeping during those violent times of the ethnic disturbances and Sulo had had to lock herself up for safety in the bathroom where she had knelt and prayed to Our Lady—she being a Roman Catholic—while the mobs rampaged upstairs in the landlady's apartment and then came downstairs to break up all the furniture in the annexe. They had left behind the debris of shattered glass, furniture awry and broken, books thrown everywhere. Sulo's parents were not home that day. They had gone on a sympathy visit to the home of friends to commiserate with the parents whose son had been beaten up in the bus. Sulo had been unscathed. No one opened the bathroom door. The jewellery too was safe. No one had thought of looking under the mattress. All that jewellery had been carefully preserved and added to. There was a golden chain of several sovereigns, bracelets, *attiyal*. Sulo's grandmother's jewellery, too, which had been apportioned out between both daughters, would be inherited by her.

To be single, in the eyes of Sulo's mother, was not to be envied, especially when all the other young cousins were getting married and going abroad. They appeared to have made favourable matches with doctors, accountants, lawyers. There had even been love affairs which had won parental approval. In this instance dowry posed no problem—love marriages did not require dowries. Sulo was attractive but there had been no wild and passionate love affair to transform her life. The choice would have to be made by the matchmakers. It was time to arrange something for her. A proposal. Nearing thirty meant that the choices would narrow. Sulo was no longer a teenager and the twenties were rushing into the thirties. She had educated herself, obtained a degree and was now following another academic course in the University. Mr Saldin, a member of one of the charismatic churches that Sulo had occasionally attended, whose own daughters had disappointed him by not going in for higher studies, had, together with his wife, exhorted Sulo to find a husband. 'Education will hinder you rather than help,' they said. 'Most men do not want women to be more educated than themselves. Better learn how to run a house, cook and look after children.'

'Must be jealous, no, Aunty?' Sulo would comment.' Their own daughters didn't study, that's why they are saying like that.' She was quietly ambitious and wanted to excel in her studies. Compensations. She wanted to do her Masters, her Ph.D. To reach the top professionally one day. Her dreams of the romantic hero were diminishing. She began to see the practical aspects of settling down. She was proud of the fact that she was a graduate teacher. She felt above the class of trained English teachers. 'I am the only English graduate in the area,' she would say with a sense of pride. 'I am now in the National School. I teach A Level English.' This was indeed prestigious. She had attended week-end classes in order to get her degree, qualifying stage by stage. She had to travel miles and miles by train, by bus, by van, on long and tedious journeys, spending the greater part of her salary on tuition fees. She had also to pay her boarding fees. In spite of it, she was always well dressed, well groomed, took care of her skin, of her hair. After her bath she would emerge, her skin golden with the tinge of *kasturi manjal*, wearing the clothes with their darts and crosscuts, the two-piece suits sewn for her by a little provincial seamstress or brought by an aunt from a thrift shop abroad, ready to sally forth to her classes in English Literature or Philosophy or Greek and Roman Civilization.

Sulo considered herself to be attractive. Her skin

was fair. She was conscious that this was in her favour. She worried about the slightest blemish and would go to Millicent's Beauty Salon. Millicent had many qualifications in hair care and beauty therapy from the U.K. and would give you a nice facial and shampoo with all the imported beauty products. There was always a lot of lively conversation in the salon and generous advice as Millicent steamed, painted on a face mask, removed minute blackheads, tweezed eyebrows into shape, creamed and patted your skin and then showed you your image in the mirror with a pleasant compliment. 'Just like Joan Collins' was her favourite comment.

Sulo had a romantic bent of mind. She waited for the chance encounter, the magic alchemy of recognition. She was convinced that the right person was there, just at hand, for the taking. She bore the image of the romantic hero in her mind, handsome, liberal, who could socialize easily, ready to unleash a grand passion and sweep her off her feet. He did not necessarily have to belong to her community. She desired some one with good looks, an easy charm, a daring and adventurous bent of mind with whom she could float on the wings of both illusion and reality. Sulo had not had a very happy childhood. Her father's death had left her with a sense of great loss and deprivation. She did not speak of her grief. That father of hers had somehow betrayed her by his own excess, by squandering his life. All her close friends had protective fathers. She had no one to lean on, be proud of, depend on. She lacked the security and love her friends basked in. She had missed all this—her life had this gap and sometimes she would be provoked to burst out with: 'But you have a father. How lucky you are! He does everything for you. I have no one. I have to do everything for myself.' It sometimes sounded almost like a grievance. A grievance against those friends who cared for her the most: they had what she could never have. Nothing or no one could make up for the father she had lost. She had loved him, admired him. Perhaps pitied him. He was weak. His fatal flaw, his addiction, prevented him from giving this only child of his what she needed most. His own inadequacies had driven him on to pursue a selfish path. His despair had led to his destruction. The destruction lay not only in his death wish but also in his rejection of a wife, a daughter. They, too, were too weak to throw the rope across the chasm. Too weak to stretch out a hand and draw him out of the putrid water in which he choked and struggled. Who, then, was there to fill the gap? The man whom she chose would have to be everything to her.

On her weekend journey she encountered young men who were swiftly attracted by her smiling, pretty face with its slightly-pouting lips which parted ever so slightly to reveal delightfully idiosyncratic front teeth—it added to her charm, this slight touch of imperfection. It could not be considered a flaw, rather those two little front teeth which appeared like milk teeth made her look childlike and innocent. The young men were charmed by her. The hope of a new relationship would begin but somehow nothing seemed to last. A few letters, a few promised meetings and then the ephemeral bubbles would burst and end in nothing except the faint iridescence of memory.

Sulo loved nothing more than to enjoy life, to watch videos of romantic Indian films, to go on holidays anywhere, to even live in the houses of strangers, to go visiting places where she would observe in minute detail the lives of individual families—the ageing daughters for whom it was difficult to find husbands (and they were not half as attractive as Sulo who had both colour and academic qualifications), or the pretty daughter, the only daughter, of another family who had not realized either her own or her parents ambitions and had settled down to an amorphic, vegetable existence. There were some who had neglected their family duties and responsibilities and had hastily married before their sisters. There were all the others, too, who had found husbands abroad. And there were bored husbands jaded with their wives who gave her the glad eye.

Everybody, it seemed, wanted to marry someone settled abroad. Abroad was Elysium. Abroad was El Dorado. Abroad had become another country which could be anywhere on the map. Anyone who went there lived not in Germany, Canada, England, but 'in Abroad'. It was a country, exotic, mysterious, flowing with milk and honey, much sought after. 'In Abroad' was where the money was. Comfort. A higher standard of living. Clothes from abroad, even a strange accent acquired from abroad marked you out as someone special. You were wealthier, more prosperous, more professionally qualified and educated if you lived and earned abroad. No loneliness, no locked doors, no cold winter or feeling alien, no racism. To be 'in Abroad' was to live in Xanadu.

Sulo's cousin, Neela, had married a doctor, a widower. She was a trained English teacher herself, but one of a large family of girls. The proposal had been accepted, the marriage had taken place and Neela was now comfortably living 'in Abroad'. The only child by the doctor's earlier marriage was wisely in the hands of the earlier in-laws. Neela was now happily settled. Her mother, a seamstress, with all those daughters on her hands, was relieved that her daughter would now be very well off in England. Of course, news would trickle across. There was no supportive family system there and so when her first baby arrived, the mother had to fly to England for the confinement.

At home the confinement would have been a very special happening—the traditional ceremonies, in spite of the fact that they were Roman Catholics, would have to be observed. Gifts of gold for the baby, special food for the mother, herbal baths— where could all this be done 'in Abroad'? The body to be laved with the boiled concoction of medicinal herbs in an English bathroom with the porcelain bathtub and tiled floors? The boiling of the herbs on an electric cooker would have been impossible. All that had to be dispensed with. When the second baby arrived, Neela flew back home on a holiday. Now they had the money to search for a maid. 'A thousand pounds a month they will pay,' Sulo and her mother had said, 'but it is difficult to find one.'

'What about a convent girl? An orphan, perhaps?' advised some of their friends.

'A thousand pounds a month? For a maid? How to believe. So much for a maid you think they will pay?'

'I don't know, but they said they will,' said Sulo.

Strange, but no one seemed willing to go to England. Yet, they clamoured to go to the Middle East in search of jobs where they faced much harder realities. Neela, however, was to be envied. She had found a wealthy, professionally qualified husband. Staying here, at home, living on a teacher's salary, married to someone whose salary would not be much higher, in a small annexe or in some remote, out-of-the-way place, with no car, no holidays abroad, was much less to be desired. Romance, compatibility, exciting relationships, were out. It was the fashion to be married and living abroad. Yet Neela was always trying to persuade her mother to come and live with her, to help cook, look after the babies and provide companionship. The mother preferred her life in the country of her birth.

Sulo felt left out in the cold. She would come and say, 'I'm going abroad in August. I'm going to Canada to be married.' Those were the first intimations of the winds that blew in from foreign lands laden with promise—'The Quinquereme of Nineveh' which would bring her all the exotic gifts she so desired.

> *Quinquereme of Nineveh from distant Ophir*
> *Rowing home to haven in sunny Palestine,*
> *With a cargo of ivory,*
> *And apes and peacocks,*
> *Sandalwood, cedarwood, and sweet white wine.*

Winds of hope. Winds of fertility. Where would Sulo reap that alien corn? In what distant field? Her mother grew more anxious every day. When could she proudly announce that they, too, had made a good match for Sulo? If love and romance had not played their destined role in her life, the professional matchmakers must. Business was thriving in the city of Colombo at the moment. Rosie Aunty's business was flourishing. Herself elderly, her children all comfortably settled and living abroad, she found that matchmaking was indeed an exciting and lucrative pastime. It gave her a respectable standing in society. It also gave her an insight into much else as she got to know all the personal details of other people's lives to be dossiered in her mind. Each life had its fictions, its plot, its characters, but the main theme was the marriage of young couples who entered into the contract which several parties had to arrange. Family secrets, skeletons in the cupboard, desirable and undesirable features were all laid bare. There were all the young men who wanted wives from their own country, ethnic group, religion. So the go-betweens were necessary. There were, of course, the advertisements which appeared in the marriage columns, but some of those proposals were questionable, especially where they said that wealth, religion, caste, age, etc., were immaterial. It made even desperate parents suspicious—'There must be a snag somewhere,' they would think.

So, they would all go to Rosie Aunty.

Rosie Aunty's professionalism was appreciated in a changed and changing society. Her motives could not be purely altruistic, especially since her services were much in demand. Marriages were made no longer in heaven—they were made by negotiators. Rosie arranged for the exchange of photographs and meetings concerning the hypothetical partners with parents, friends and relatives living in Sri Lanka. The photograph was all important—the groomed plumage exhibited for the mating dance. The young woman would be attired in her best saree, her hair coiffeured, subtle make-up enhancing her looks. Not casual clothes like pants, jeans or skirt and blouse. The traditional look was important. The illusion that nothing had changed the chastity, virginity of the well brought up young woman must remain. These marriages would not end in divorce or separation; there would indeed be gratitude for the new experience, or so they thought. Colour photographs were very popular. In the course of time they would graduate to videos; perhaps cassette recordings of voices. The photographs of the young men from abroad were always against the background of affluence—large cars (Japanese in make), tables laden with food, smartly cut suits, winter overcoats, scarves, well-furnished apartments, lounging in outdoor cafés or at parties, always engaged in eating, drinking in convivial gatherings. There were other scenes too—sons hugging or being hugged by mothers, sisters, showing how family-oriented they were. And in reality they were. A prospective mother-in-law living abroad hankered for a dutiful daughter-in-law from the home country who would bow her head and be subservient to her will. The burden and responsibility of cooking, too, could be passed on to her. A quiet girl, a modest girl, who did not flaunt her looks would be suitable. She could sit by the old lady and massage her feet. The old lady would keep an eye on the young wife. Marriage was a serious pursuit. It was also a transaction. Sometimes the young man would come on a holiday. There was more than one proposal to be looked into. If the first one failed, there were a host of others. The young man would leave for the country he came from with either a bride or with the promise that she would follow later, after she had got her visa. Every young woman was ready with her passport.

There was one special proposal for Sulo. The young man had studied in a Roman Catholic seminary but had not yet found his vocation. He was seen in the photograph kneeling in the holy city of Jerusalem, at the altar of one of the churches. His sister, a Roman Catholic nun, had brought the proposal. 'I want him to have a happy life,' she sighed. The mother-in-law to be looked formidable. The man had rejected other proposals because the girls had either lived abroad too long or looked too westernized with western clothes and too much make-up. Whether Sulo would be considered suitable was the question asked by the nun, Sister Felicitas.

Sulo's mother also consulted Rosie Aunty. A meeting was arranged. Sulo was led like a sacrificial lamb to the altar. They met, parents, relatives, matchmaker, the proposed bridegroom, Sulo, Meena. The bridegroom to be had come from the Middle East. He was a computer engineer with a salary of forty thousand rupees a month. He liked Sulo. So did all the others. Then he took her to a quiet corner for a private conversation. He stood beside her, compared their heights. He was short, wore heels to look taller.

'Are you worried that I am short?' he asked Sulo anxiously, and then continued: 'The woman I marry must not wear even a drop of make-up. No tilak even on her forehead. She must dress simply and be well covered. I belong to a religious sect which lays down such rules. We do not socialize much either. No parties or elaborate functions . . . . I would like to marry you without delay and take you with me. Are you prepared?'

'I want some time to decide,' Sulo said. Her mother was happy. So were the boy's parents and relatives.

'Marry him. He's a good match. You'll be well off too. Think of your mother,' said Rosie Aunty.

'Sulo, marry him,' the mother pleaded.

'How to marry him, Amma? He is short. Same height as myself. Also I can't enjoy life with all these rules of his religion, no? No parties even. Can't dress up nicely also. Not even *pottu* on the forehead to match my saree, and praying, praying all the time.

'Please, Sulo, please. He's a good boy. He will be a kind husband,' cried her mother, continuing to plead. Sulo cried the whole night through. Protested. Refused. The young man continued the search and ultimately was to find someone who was less selective. Sulo had had her way but her mother and all the others were greatly disappointed. She had found favour in their eyes, in the young man's eyes, but she was adamant. Here Sulo asserted her rights as a young woman who had her own ideas of what her life partner should be like. This man was short and conscious of being short; that she would have to wear flat heels all her life was something irksome to Sulo. Not even the promise that he would bring her back home once in every two years. She was not prepared for the simple life he offered, she who loved pretty clothes, a social life, visiting people. Shut away from everyone, how could she indulge her avid curiosity for life—curiosity in a pleasant way, of course. She knew a great deal about many people, many families: how much older than the husband the wife is, how they occupy separate bedrooms, how the wife is critical of the husband and says that he is a frivolous man. She observed that all the cutlery must be laid out on the table even if it is only dhal and bread for the meal, how daughters are rebellious with dominating mothers, and so much else. Little intimate details that titillated her fancies about the intricacies of lives—a vicarious interest but one which showed her the pitfalls of an unsuitable marriage.

Rosie Aunty never gave up. More exchanges of photographs. More letters from anxious and despairing mothers who wanted wives for their sons who looked as if they were going to be confirmed bachelors or who might end up living with a foreign woman. Sulo's mother was happy when she heard of the proposals—and she was confident that no one could resist her daughter, that untarnished, pure commodity who had still not had a passionate affair of the heart. A desirable object for a young man to bed and procreate with, carrying on the traditions he had embraced in the country of his birth.

For a change, Rosie Aunty brought a proposal from a lawyer who lived in Colombo. He had a car, a good income. Sulo could get a teaching post in an international school and enhance their income. He owned a house in the posh, elite part of the city— Colombo 7. The house was in the same area as that of a former Prime Minister of the country. There were no sisters in the family. There was an understanding mother-in-law. The in-laws would live separately. They would live in Sri Lanka and Sulo's mother would also have a home. The young man was tall, good-looking, but he had one flaw. He was balding prematurely.

'How can I marry a man who is bald!' Sulo wailed. 'How can I be seen in society when I go out with him? How embarrassing to be married to a man whose hair is all thinning in front.'

'See, will you, this girl! Can't satisfy her, no? What a good match, and a house in Colombo 7 too. Rosmead Place. And no mother-in-law problems also.'

Sulo was adamant. 'He is bald, no? How to marry him aunty. Shame, no? I'll be embarrassed.'

And then another proposal. This time Rosie Aunty was out. It was a retired teacher who was going to arrange everything. She too had daughters, marriageable ones, but they had faith that at the right time the Lord would provide husbands.

Mrs Sriskandaraja was careful. There were preliminaries. 'Is she a good girl? No affairs? Not a flirt or anything? She's not giddy, is she?'

'No, Mrs Sriskandaraja,' Sulo's friends stood up

for her staunchly, 'she's never had an affair. She is not a flirt. She is a good, steady type of girl. You can go ahead.'

Mrs Sriskandaraja went ahead. Sulo and her mother were invited to lunch to meet the parents of the prospective groom. He himself had been in the U.K. since 1983. An accountant. Very good job. Earning well. Had just one more examination to pass. Went to the U.K. during the civil disturbances which interrupted his studies. He was in his late twenties, a good age. He had his own flat there. There were a few fears though. Surely the young man must have had affairs in England. A free society, lonely life, how could he resist? But all in all, a good match. Christian. Caste-wise, too, everything was in order. Just a few other matters to be discussed, like how much are you prepared to give as dowry, in the way of property, money, jewellery . . .

'I said I can give three lakhs, plenty of jewellery also—there's mine as well as what my mother left me and what I made for Sulo,' said Meena.

Sulo and her mother came all the way from upcountry for the weekend in Kandy. It was all very secretive. Where these things were concerned, there was so much jealousy, character assassination, things said behind the back . . . one had to be very careful, very circumspect. On the day of the meeting with the parents, Sulo and Meena had come in a three-wheeler. Sulo wore a simple blue saree of nylex. A lunch had been planned. After it was all over, two very exhausted humans had dropped in at their friend, Menaka's place. Menaka had known Sulo from the time she was a little girl of seven years. Both mother and daughter collapsed gratefully into two easy chairs and fanned themselves with rolled-up newspapers.

'The ordeal is over at last, what a relief. Now we can talk freely,' Meena said.

'What a grand lunch we had, Menaka Aunty,' said Sulo.

'Yes, yes,' continued her mother, 'so many things Mrs Sriskandaraja had prepared—there was chicken curry, fried rice, cutlets, salad, vegetables and two desserts. What a lot of money they must have spent. We must really be grateful to them all.'

'Aunty, the father was a nice man, but oh the lady . . . very dominating. Husband was silent most of the time.'

'Yes, yes, the mother talked and talked,' said Meena, 'all about her family, about how great they were—their high connections, professors here, judges there, mathematicians, priests, bishops, all brilliant intellectuals—and have you read this book, and have you read that book, and I have read all these books, and what do you think of Nehru's letters from prison to his daughter?'

'She said she was a teacher, Menaka Aunty. No wonder she talked so much. Her son must be perfect according to her.'

'Oh dear,' Meena kept on saying, 'I can relax now. I was scared that she would ask me whether I had read all those big books. I think she wanted to show off how clever and well read she is.'

'But Aunty, the father seemed a nice man. A bit scared of the wife, I think. He kept looking at me all the time. He couldn't get a word in . . . before they left, Aunty, he gave me a wink and said, "We'll be seeing you soon."'

Some time elapsed before Menaka met Sulo and her mother again. 'So what happened to the proposal, Meena?' she asked.

'Didn't Sulo tell you? The whole thing fell

through. The young man wrote and said he wasn't prepared to accept the proposal. And what a lovely photograph we had sent. Sulo in her graduate gown. Mrs Sriskandaraja said she didn't look natural in it, like a painted doll, and as for that fellow—what a disappointment. He was certainly not in his twenties. Must be in his late thirties. Not at all good-looking also—balding, thick-lensed spectacles.'

'Teeth also projecting, Aunty,' Sulo said. 'Short also.'

'And funny thing,' said Meena, 'the photograph they sent was strange. Sister is embracing the brother. Why should the sister hug him like that?'

'What to do now? Rosie Aunty is getting angry with me. She is saying that she won't do anything more for this girl. See, will you, Menaka, others are dying to marry, no? Rosie Aunty is saying, 'After this you all find a husband for Sulo. All the good matches I am bringing and she is refusing all.''

But no one really gave up. Menaka met them again, mother and daughter. Proposals were still coming in. Meena pulled out a letter from her handbag.

'See this, will you, the mother has written such a nice letter. Son is in Canada. We knew him when he was a little boy—look at the photograph also.'

Sulo gave a shrug. 'Aunty, look at his ears. Millie Aunty is saying they are flapping in the wind. Also she says he has adenoids. What is adenoids, Aunty? Does it change the voice—will it sound different? What shall I do? Nasal tones you say, Aunty? Shall I write and ask for a cassette with his voice? If I don't like it I can refuse, no?'

'No, no,' Meena went on, 'he's tall, handsome, fair also. Nice, good boy. We know the family. They can't remember but they played together as children.'

'But what to do about the voice, Aunty. They say he has adenoids. Then how to marry?'

Meena was silent, but there was a quiet gleam in her eye. This time Sulo would not have so easy a victory. The next time Menaka met them she asked, 'So did you get the cassette with his voice?'

'No, Aunty, I telephoned him. The voice sounds all right . . . but now there's another proposal. Doctor from West Indies. That, of course, sounds better . . . '

The Golden Apples of the Hesperides

Domingos would say such crazy things. Just to
attract attention and appear outrageous. He was the
only person who filled any space in Marcia's new
life with so much sound, so much laughter; in that
life which was yet to discover voices of familiarity
and friendship. From that first silence which was
empty and cavernous, sounds, echoes, began to
reverberate. Domingos and Marcia were both in a
new country. They had first to ask for directions to
know which turning to take. There was kindness
enough in this country where people already knew
their way. 'Come with me, lass, I will show you how
to get there,' any stranger would say and lead Marcia
through the landscape of late summer, through
George's Square where the pigeons pecked at crumbs
and those humans, whose names she would never

know, sat eating crisps out of paper bags.

At the beginning of the journey it was only Domingos. His voice would boom and echo. He would laugh with so much gusto, yet there was a certain air of melancholy about him. His laughter was actually for himself. A reassurance, a sign that he was still alive in this grey and drizzly climate. It was now almost the end of the journey. Marcia shared a small, compact apartment in the University village with two Scottish girls, an English girl, a Malaysian and a Chinese, all students in the University. Domingos, after his many journeys, had at last come to live next door to Marcia and they were once more where they had begun from, yet each one changed, different. The world came in to meet them. Life had become easier after their manifold experiences.

On a Sunday evening, as Marcia and Domingos readied themselves for a walk, there was a knock on the door. There were consecutive knocks on other doors too. The African students—the men dressed up in their Sunday best, coat and tie; the women in chic two-piece suits, hatted, stockinged, wearing high-heeled shoes, Bibles in their gloved hands—knocked on the closed, locked doors of each apartment, bringing with them the message of salvation, the Good News. Marcia stood in the doorway and watched their reception as the Scottish and English students, their legs stretched out on the tables, showed indifference.

'We are non-believers,' they said in unison. The same knocks on those doors in another continent had yielded different results more than a century ago. The African students good-naturedly accepted the rebuff and soon, engaged in friendly, unbiblical, untheological conversation, went off on a long walk with the non-believers.

Yet, the Christians were very alive in this city—the churches always full, with fervent sermons resounding from impressive pulpits, harmonious singing from the choir. Some of the churches, vaulted and embellished with rococo carving, resembled opera houses. But some of the Victorian-looking churches were closed—churches with heavy, red brick walls with exquisite stained glass windows: the deep wine-red, the cerulean blue, emerald green, gold and sunset orange set within the brick-like pages from a mediaeval Psalter. The University had acquired some of these churches and the doors were heavily padlocked.

How cold, thought Marcia, those unheated churches must have been in winter, the Congregation warmed, perhaps, only by the brilliance of colour that was shed from the glowing stained glass windows and by their own lusty singing filling their bodies with blood heat.

Beyond the churches was the Necropolis, the City of the Dead, with its tombs and mausoleums, a whole city of convoluted towers and domed structures inhabited by ghosts. Spirits that always hovered in the air, speaking through the wind. Strange, those experiences of death, and the emptiness of cold rooms that had once been inhabited.

Once, Marcia had walked into a house, an uninhabited house open to sightseers. A woman, whose name she had forgotten, had once lived there. The table was laid for tea as if visitors were expected—Scottish tea with shimmering preserves of strawberry or plum, tea cakes, and a warm pot of tea brewing with sugar and cream. She went from room to room as if following some compulsively beckoning shadow, observing the arrangements, so ordered, so perfectly in place, observing everything that had belonged to that past life, from the blue glass bottle of milk of magnesia in the tiled bathroom with its old-fashioned porcelain bath, to the suitcases piled on the top of the wardrobe which must have been carried on journeys to unknown destinations, to the pile of books for bedside reading. A young woman had hovered around like a disturbed gnat among the preserves and then followed Marcia as she entered each room, creating her voyeuristic fictions. A lonely bed, she observed, the bed of a woman who had never married, never even had lovers, the linen so smooth and unruffled. But her spirit must still dwell here, thought Marcia, and, as if to confound and perplex her own musings, a faint strand of hair, perhaps imagined, lay on the white pillowcase.

Marcia stood before a photograph in which this unknown woman was seated at a city banquet and the lens of her imagination focussed on those satiny shoulders with their thin taffeta straps, on that careful coiffeur of marcelled hair, on a face that gazed at hers and established a never-to-be-broken, never-to-be-forgotten bond.

Marcia walked out to the road and gazed out at still unexplored vistas of a still unexplored city, feeling the wind ruffle her hair and plucking wild Scottish flowers. A nun came along, young, with a beautiful, virtuous face, and they talked.

'Where is Woodland Church?' Marcia asked.

'Let me take you over the bridge,' the nun said to her, 'I'll show you the way.'

But it was growing late and Marcia thanked her and said goodbye, for they would never meet again. The convent the nun went back to, that safe haven, would never be for her.

So she returned to Domingos, her first friend, as he unrolled the reels of his life and his fictions. He had lived with an American woman for fifteen years, a student he had met in the American university he was studying in. She had left him. There were no children.

'Domingos, you must have a child. You are only forty years old.'

'No, no, I am too old. I have my sister's children.'

Domingos loved his food. Food and laughter. Sadness, too, sometimes—melancholy and depression. The walls of Duncan's Hotel were sometimes shaken by the echoes of his laughter. Sitting among the staid Scotsmen and their wives in the lounge, among retired Empire builders, businessmen and lonely transients, Marcia and he listened to stories. There was the man who told them of his alcoholic brother who died of exposure on a street after being out all night. Or the hall porter told them of his plans to get married. (That was in the month of September. By December he was divorced.) Or Margaret, the cook, would bring in her daughter-in-law, a dark-haired Celtic-looking girl, to talk to Marcia because she was lonely, but the young woman spoke Glaswegian which sounded like Gaelic to her and they both spoke to each other in seemingly different tongues. And the Fat Boy would bring in trays of biscuits and tea.

Domingos would come in, plump himself down among the petrified Scotsmen and middle-aged Scotswomen in sensible stockinged brogues and tweeds with their twin sets of Pitlochry knits, then guffaw and laugh with an untrammelled ebullience as his florid face grew redder and redder. He almost made them leap out of their seats with his laughter. Laughter which had both joy and defiance in it. He wanted to make his presence felt. Anonymity, wherever he lived, would never be for him.

Quite suddenly, quite dramatically, he would stand in the lounge of the flat in Birbeck Square and declare: 'My mother is a castrating woman. She castrated me.'

'Castrated you? Are you impotent, then?'

'Ha! Carmencas would laugh if she heard that,' he would say.

Yet, his conversations about his family, his mother, his sister, her children, and his girl friend Carmencas, revealed how much he was attached to them. He saved his stipend to make long phone calls to them in Colombia, calls which cost hundreds of pounds. He bought gifts for them. His thoughts were always with them.

Marcia had first set eyes on Domingos in the foyer of Duncan's Hotel in Glasgow on a cold, drizzly day. He was leaning over the counter, all wrapped up in oilskin garments to protect himself from the weather. He looked like so many characters put into one—a brigandish-looking macho type with dark moustaches, eyes like tiny beacons setting off sparks on a distant hill. He looked a Hemingway character, or even Conradian—a lighthouse keeper, a revolutionary. He could even have been a plain and simple Scotsman. For one moment, since he looked at her with such welcome warmth and unmitigated curiosity, she, being Asian, different, thought he might be the proprietor of Duncan's Hotel. Duncan's Hotel—the home for transient students close to Glasgow Central Station. A caravanserai. The first home of the British Council scholars on their Commonwealth scholarships, all newly arrived in Scotland to study in Scottish universities. Hollow-sounding, disembodied voices announcing arrivals and departures against a background of pleasant music filled the lonely passengers disembarking from the long train

143

journey with a sense of euphoria.

Marcia had been seen off at Euston by a young English university student who did part-time work for the British Council. She had requested and been grateful for his presence. They had taken a cab from the Regency Hotel in London for which she had paid with crisp, new English pound notes. She had wanted to dispel the feeling of loneliness by being seen off in her carriage. She bought his platform ticket, quite grandly let him keep the change and slipped into his hands a slab of Toblerone chocolate. So she had not had such a lonely send-off from London and felt his friendly presence, a sense of comfort and security.

On the train she had been befriended by a Scotswoman who spoke of missionaries who lived and worked in India and now lived in retirement in Glasgow, and Marcia felt, yes, perhaps this would be yet another point of contact with the colonial history of her country. It was all this, then, that had culminated in this journey.

On the way to Scotland she had felt as she had on a previous journey to this country in her youth. Remembered scenes, recollections of prints from the illustrated books of her past with Scottish country scenes: sheepfolds and sheep dogs, bales of straw like shredded wheat packed in cardboard boxes of cereal, riders in hunting gear on horseback, on a foxhunt in the countryside, coppices and woods flashed past her bemused gaze.

And now, mounting the steps from pavement to hotel, she was already being enveloped in an easy sense of familiarity, with the Hall Porter already telling her about his life, his long relationship with a woman of means and of his approaching marriage that year.

And then the stranger at the counter spoke: 'I am

Domingos. From Colombia. I will be working on my thesis at the university. You too are a student, right? We can have high tea together this evening.'

They soon became friends. They shared a table for meals served by young Scottish girls wearing bright red tartan skirts, their golden brown hair in clustered curls, with a high colour on their fresh-skinned cheekbones. They carried pots of tea and the lavish portions of food which Margaret the cook turned out in her kitchen—pans of thick pea soup, Scottish pies, chips and baked beans with ice cream for dessert.

Domingos loved food. He was welcome to eat most of Marcia's at Duncan's Hotel. After the enormous meals served at Willowby Hall, at the University of Nottingham, she had lost her appetite completely. The meals there had been gargantuan, exquisitely prepared, cooked by the Nottingham women. Tables groaned with platters of roast beef and chicken, new potatoes, salads with exotic fruit and vegetables, fruit flans. Here, too, food was plentiful. Breakfast was piles of toast and butter, good, nourishing oatmeal porridge, cereals, fruit juice, pots of tea. High tea was again hot soups, and raised pies with crisp pastry filled with meat and potatoes. Marcia toyed with her food while Domingos buttered piles of toast and ate her share of ice cream too.

They spoke about their families. Back home Domingos lived with Carmencas. Marcia began to feel her presence. She emerged strong and dominating from his description. She began to feel the presence of other human beings too, people with their own strong identities. The hotel had its own mystery occupants like the elderly lady who lived upstairs all by herself. It was home to her. Her sister, with whom she had shared her room, had just died, and she felt that living there, in the same room, in the same hotel, she could commune with her spirit. Almost all her meals were taken up to her by the sympathetic young waitresses. Marcia remembered the beautiful and dignified widow of one of the Scottish lords living in a hotel room in Glasgow many years ago. Her husband had been Loch Leil, the head of his clan. He was dead, and she could no longer live in the great echoing rooms of her Scottish castle and so found refuge in that hotel with the spacious rooms and rococo-style ceilings, where she was to live out the rest of her days.

Marcia felt nostalgic, recalled encounters from the past. Loch Leil's widow must now be long since dead. She had opened a door into the past and vanished, leaving behind a recurring memory connecting the then with the now. The Scottish landscape of the highlands with the castles rising grey and towering on the banks of lochs, ruined castles with battlements, spires and crumbling walls that rose from wooded acres. Macbeth. Battlements. Hundreds of acres of forest where deer still bounded. Crags. Fields of heather. And the castle of Culquhound, one of its wings jutting out over the azure waters of the North Sea. She had visited that castle once. It had been so strange, walking from room to room with the silver-backed mirrors and the hairbrushes of unseen occupants lying on the dressing table. Yet another room had its walls covered with swords. Returning from that journey she had written these lines:

Death is not a decoration
Swords slash walls not flesh
Polished blood burns metal
The blade blunts not on

Bone but brick
Time has no hands
To hold these weapons
So they are put away
Are soon forgotten
But death will stay
And we surmise that ghosts
Do battle.

But life was moving on—people going away or remaining with you. There was loneliness here, muted voices, soft, subdued, except on Friday nights when the silence of the grey streets was shattered by noise, loud voices, laughter, screams from the pubs and the tinkling of broken glass on the pavements. Disembodied voices. Footsteps clicking on the hard flagstones. Journeys. Destination. Marcia's journeys. Beginnings. Loneliness too.

When Marcia moved from Duncan's hotel, Domingos came with her to the new Hall of Residence which had once been a big hotel in the thirties on Sauchiehall Street. They sat together in the large, bare room which had yet to be filled with her life, her thoughts, her presence. It was to be yet another room to be locked from within. One room in a passage with many other rooms where, before faces became familiar, only the sound of footsteps was heard. Sometimes, walking along the corridor to the room where the students heated water, or where the cleaning ladies sat down casually to drink tea or smoke cigarettes, she could see other lives in other rooms. An immigrant family inhabited an apartment in one of the old, grey, stone buildings, their lives open, naked and exposed to the view of any onlooker. The one room they lived in served many purposes. It was full of enormous, shining pots and pans with food simmering and boiling on the cooker. The women waved to Marcia and made friendly gestures of invitation when they recognized her as being, like themselves, Asian. The sink was perpetually piled with crockery and cooking utensils. One day Marcia saw a young man acrobatically washing his feet in it, first one, then the other, with great meticulousness. It was all quite natural, people and their lives and their needs to be catered to within that space in one small room, just as Marcia's own life would gradually be. People would come and go, sit, talk, read her books, drink lambrusco, eat Scottish oatcakes or haggis or fish and chips.

But Domingos could not fit his own life into one of these rooms among hundreds of other students. The size and girth of his personality could never be contained within these walls. He came to see her at Halloween, the time when the young students went crazy, whooping and racing madly through corridors with painted faces. 'Let's go and see the fireworks and the carnival near the River Clyde,' he said.

They walked, it seemed for miles and miles, through street after street until they came to the river. Fireworks spluttered in the air. The lights sparkled. They stood on the outskirts of the carnival and gazed at the brilliance like two happy children. On the fringe, outside the gaiety and fun, watching. Spectators. They had only to step in to be part of it, and yet they held themselves back, like strangers who were unsure whether that happiness was for themselves as well. But Domingos and Marcia were adults, afraid to be children. They gazed to their fill, feeling the Glaswegian accents swing past their ears—voices, high, excited, of children holding their parents' hands or held tight in their arms.

'Let us return,' said Domingos. 'Shall we go back?'

Marcia's feet were swollen with all that walking. He was so tall, walked so rapidly with his great strides that she had to take running steps to keep up with him.

'Domingos, walk slowly,' she cried out. To Marcia, walking was also gazing around, feeling the kaleidoscopic whirl of colours and bodies around her—the tall, solid stone-and-brick George's Square with its brilliant tulips, the dray-horses trotting along as they dragged their carts through the heart of the city. She picked up conversations with people who, even in that brief moment, shed their strangeness and accepted her as one of them.

Marcia began to see less of 'Domingos as she began her own exploration of the mazes within herself, peopled with newcomers into her own life. She glimpsed him in a Greek food shop, at a film, and once he came to her room to talk. He was, he said, lonely, waiting to go home.

She felt that she had failed him as a friend. By this time she was making a life of her own and she only needed to know that his comfortable presence was there for her, whenever she needed him. But she could not forget how he had once stood at the threshold of her room at Duncan's Hotel. She had been lying in bed, her books piled up beside her, listening to the voices from Glasgow Central, snatches of music and the hollow boom of echoes. At the knock on the door, she had opened it cautiously, to see Domingos. He had come to inquire whether she was settling in, to show her the way to the University library, to ask her about her permanent accommodation.

To him she had offered apples, those golden apples of the Hesperides. The wish humans have for those apples of illusion, those apples of eternal life which grow on the Hesperian trees of their private worlds, their private Edens. Apples too soon consumed, too soon to disappear. But this was the most tangible gesture of friendship that Marcia could make. It was an acceptance, as Domingos stretched out his hand to take the apples, of an eternal friendship. He did not venture beyond that door, but they were now no longer strangers to each other.

'Come, let us go to Stirling Castle,' Domingos once said. 'Bring all your friends. All I want is to listen, to watch you talking. I'll be there in the background. I will not disturb you. Let us go. I'll come with you to church. Then we can go for long walks.'

Yet, Marcia did not pay enough heed to him. The pursuit of her own happiness made her selfish. And then the year was drawing to a close. It was again a time for departure, for moving on, for beginning to accumulate memories.

Sometimes Domingos would say: 'I am neurotic. I am sick. I am depressed.' They sometimes drew together in their sense of homesickness. She still needed him. Had they forgotten that they were all transients here? They could not stay here forever. Yet, why did they imagine that they must feel at home in this country to which they did not belong? What had they left behind? Their entire lives, their closest, most intimate relationships, their families. Yet, here the bright crimson and red apples enticed with their strange, exotic flavour; they ached to reach that garden, to pluck, to taste, to acquire, possess. And having eaten of those apples, life would never be the same again.

If ever Marcia felt too lonely, she would go to Domingos' Research Room, the one he shared with Hayford, a Nigerian scholar who would sometimes have people over to pray in his room.

'I knew you were coming,' Domingos would say. 'Share lunch with me.'

In his paper parcel there would be two kippers, fresh mushrooms and oranges. They would sit and eat as if they were re-enacting the parable of the loaves and the fish.

Marcia enjoyed Domingos' admiration for her which was unreserved. 'You are a warm woman,' he would say, 'very charming. You are a poet.'

She read her poems to him, like little secret messages with their magical connotations. Who else was there to listen to this personal language of hers, to explore the metaphors of the new life in this country? He would listen, listen to everything she told him, comfort her if she complained of imagined hurts and slights. Then he would complain too. This was a world which appeared like a mirage. They were travellers in the same desert, thirsting for food, water, rest. Waiting for that nightingale to sing in a grey city, but only pigeons rustled their wings in flight from the eaves of ancient spires and towers.

Marcia was not the only lonely one here. The natives themselves were lonely. But she seldom saw a lonely immigrant in the streets. The Indians walked about in close-knit groups, speaking their own language. The women dressed in bright-coloured satin salwar-kameezes of emerald green or magenta or Prussian blue embroidered with golden and silver silken threads; their hair in long braids, adorned with bows and shining slides; and wearing danglers in their ears. If you walked into an Indian saree shop, the women would be found sitting at the counter with lengths of shimmery cloth in vivid rainbow hues studded with sequins, minute pearls and fine chainstitch embroidery, as if they were in a silk shop in their own country. The shop was a social outlet for them.

Marcia saw them pouring out of one of those terrace houses in Woodlands which they had converted into a temple and where they carried out their rituals, pooja and *darshan*. Or she would see them carrying banners in protest marches, asking for equal rights, jobs, better housing in this alien society.

In the grocery shop, the Indian proprietor told Marcia: 'You come here. I will give you good prices.' He was lonely too, and wanted to talk about his country, his home. He wanted to go back one day. His wife was not so friendly to Marcia whom she saw as just another Asian. She was more polite to the Glaswegians whom she went out of her way to be nice to. But one day Marcia found that the shop had changed hands. Two Scottish women had now taken over and from them she bought her apples and oranges and nuts. The melancholy, homesick Indian had vanished into those anonymous streets, who knows where?

Loneliness followed her everywhere. It was in the Savoy Centre, with all its warmth, music, food, people shopping and eating, that Marcia became aware of the lonely old people, sitting patiently, quietly on the benches, walking sticks leaning against their knees, just watching the crowds and savouring the aroma of life; or the forgotten soldiers in George's Square, on Poppy Day, remembering, wanting to be remembered with all those faded ribbons and medals pinned on their breasts, and people passing by without noticing, wanting to forget the wars of the past.

Domingos was always there when Marcia felt lonely. A shoulder to weep on. Yet, there was an element of selfishness in her. She never thought how lonely he could be, how lost, how much he missed Carmencas, or his family. He spoke so much of Carmencas.

'I wish I could meet her,' Marcia would say.

'But you won't be able to talk to her. She speaks only Spanish.'

Carmencas, he told her, was a nurse in the University where he was teaching. She spent only the weekends with him. 'I could not live with a woman for a whole week at a time. I am too neurotic.'

'Why don't you marry her?'

'There is no divorce in my country. She was married before and has a son. I, too, was married for several years to an American woman. We met as students at the university in the States. We had no children. She left me after fifteen years.'

'Why did Carmencas leave her husband?'

'He was cruel to her. He used to beat her up. He now has another woman. Carmencas spoils her son. She has to do everything for him, yet sometimes he even hits her.'

'What do you do on weekends?'

'We sleep till late on Sundays. Have breakfast in bed.'

'What do you feel about the political situation in your country?'

'Carmencas is very politically committed. Once she had to serve a prison term because she had nursed a political prisoner. I lost ten kilos at that time but she was strong, very brave. She told me, "Don't worry, it's just like being in another hotel, only less comfortable." Even now she prepares food every weekend and takes it to the prisoners.'

And so their conversations would go on, each tentatively exploring the other's life. For Marcia, in this country where they moved among strangers, they needed friendship. Both of them had to learn when to be silent too. And to accept silence, not as a sign of hostility but because privacy and silence were part of one's life. Even at the big refectory tables students would bow their heads over their trays of food, each in his or her own little private world. Sometimes a nod, a smile, a reaching out, and then in the privacy of your room, over coffee, those endless sagas would begin—stories of home, families, different countries, loves, hates, turmoil and confusion. The loneliness of the would-be suicide would be unfolded. The whispering in the heating system would drive someone crazy, keep him awake, listening to hidden, torturing voices.

And so it was important to have friends. Marcia would sit for hours, listening, while they ate oat cakes and fish and chips with coffee and lambrusco. Outside, on Sauchiehall Street, the Saturday night voices would smash through the night after the pub crawls, and the world would lie in smithereens, bleeding on those grey pavements. She often started up from sleep, terrified at the screams and violent abuse that would sweep through the night, expecting someone to be hurt or even killed, but the next morning, when she opened the window, the streets were clear, empty. Well-coated figures were going to the churches in Woodland Terrace and a Sunday silence gripped everything.

When Marcia moved to Birbeck Court, she invited friends to supper. Over food, which she cooked in the little apartment, the loneliness was often dispersed. Over a large stir-fry of chicken, cauliflower, mushroom, carrot and spring onions and sauces, together with rice and a dhal or curry with fruit afterwards, her Filipino and Chinese friends, Ken, the English boy, and Domingos ate, talked, drank.

Domingos needled Ken, so much so that he cried out in exasperation, 'I can't help it if I'm white.'

Domingos was extravagant when it came to food. He had to give up sharing a flat with one of his countrymen who lived on a lesser stipend. Domingos spent lavishly. He got an extra five hundred pounds every month from his University in Tunja. At first his compatriot and he shared the food bills but one day his friend said, 'Let's eat separately. You spend too much on food.' Domingos was sensitive. He was hurt. He moved out, found another bed-sitter, but he was unhappy with his landlord. 'The apartment is filthy,' he complained, 'the dog messes up everywhere and my landlord is so surly, never talks to me or greets me.'

Once, he nearly took a plane back home. At the University he was quick to take offence at any imagined slight. At the water tap someone pushed past him . . . someone said, 'What are you doing with those files on the professor's desk?' when Domingos was searching for information to corroborate facts for his thesis having obtained the professor's permission to do so, and now he felt he was being suspected of crime. He was touchy, took umbrage, lapsed into black moods of depression when he felt he was alien, not accepted, an outsider; when he missed Carmencas; when he missed his family.

Krishna, Marcia's friend who was an Indian professor doing Commonwealth studies, was sensitive too—followed on the streets, called names like Paki, lived like an avatar in a seaman's hostel where he learned colourful cusswords, where the young men went on the rampage and bashed in the telly or pretended to shoot at the screen, rat-a-tat-tat, or even destroyed all communication with that greater world by ripping apart the telephone wires. Krishna lived and suffered there so that he could manage carefully on his stipend. None of them knew that Krishna was writing his thesis on Commonwealth poets, where he explored a different tongue. They left him alone most of the time. They sailed on different oceans, reached different harbours, yet each man here was his own Odysseus.

Domingos now became a part of her life, part of Glasgow, a city which now had become home to her. Yet, she had to share him with others too, for soon strangers, other strangers, had become friends; but in all those friendships, sometimes so brief, sometimes stretched into eternity, there was the latent sadness of parting. Each would go away, back to his, back to her own country—but there was so much safety in the knowledge that they were there when they were needed.

They shopped at Spaar, the supermarket that catered to the University Village, filled with haggis, black puddings and fruit puddings. One day Marcia felt herself being clasped from behind, someone's strong hands covered her eyes while she was choosing her vegetables and fruit. She struggled to release herself, turned round and found herself looking into Domingos' eyes, sparkling with fun and excitement. Marcia felt shy. In front of all those customers and salesgirls! It did not matter to Domingos. You did not have to feel self-conscious with him.

'I am shopping today so that you can have lunch with me,' he told Marcia.

He took great pains to prepare that lunch. Almost everything was out of tins except for the salad. In the apartment at Birbeck Court, the food was set out in bowls and dishes. It tasted like champagne and caviar.

At Birbeck Court, everyone who shared the apartment with Marcia wanted to be Domingos' friend. The Scottish girl. The Algerian girl. The Moroccan girl, too, thought him very handsome, very attractive. They admired his macho looks—he was so manly, so tall . . . his ruddy complexion, his thick, closely-growing dark hair and dark moustaches . . . . He went to Paris for a short holiday and Marcia found herself missing his voice that called out every day as he passed by her flat. He sent her a gay froth of a picture postcard, something light and frivolous to enliven her days of deep and serious reading. When he returned, he told her he had lived in the apartment of another Colombian friend of his, a brilliant Russologist. As a young *émigré*, he had become the protégé of a woman twenty-seven years older than himself whom he had married. She was now in her seventies, a frail invalid. She did not mind any more if her husband had lovers. She accepted it. She lived with its reality. It did not destroy her. She was wise. Her husband still looked after her. She needed his attention and he was grateful to her. She had made him, the once young *émigré*, what he now was.

Domingos was faithful to Carmencas with whom he had lived for eight years. In Paris, where he went for a week's holiday, he admired the beautiful women. 'The most beautiful in the world,' he said, as if he were moving through the galleries of the Louvre in his quest for the ideal, for that which surpassed the ordinarily beautiful. There he met a woman. 'She was not beautiful,' he told Marcia, 'but I found her fascinating, interesting. We talked all night.' Yes, he was faithful to Carmencas.

Domingos would never accept an act of kindness without some token of its recognition—a pineapple, a box of chocolates or an evening at the pub where they would sit talking while Domingos drank a frothing glass of ale and popped red glace cherries into Marcia's avocat.

Sometimes they would sit in the sunny courtyard. Winter was over and the lean cat stretched itself out, stalking something in the hedges. Yes, winter was over, the ice had melted, the snow had thawed. The crocuses were pushing out of the earth where they had been imprisoned for so long. A woman beckoned Marcia from one of the windows. The pale sunlight fell across her white shoulders as she leaned over the ledge. She was in the room of one of the African students. Marcia went up to her and she started talking. They asked each other questions and the woman began reading aloud from the open pages of her life. She unfolded sentences from the first page, then the second—a life that would, like all their lives, be important only to herself and to the casual lovers she had in those momentary and transient encounters. But she was to remain forever in Marcia's mind, a painting of a woman within a window frame, in a white slip, the sunlight falling like wings of light on the silk of her skin.

'Why are you so open,' Domingos chided Marcia when she returned to the stone bench, 'you talk to everyone.'

When Marcia had first come to the university village, she had smiled at a stranger, someone who she thought was a post-graduate student, someone who appeared to come from nearer home. He crossed over to speak to her. He wasn't a student. He was from Pakistan but had settled down in Glasgow and was the owner of a restaurant. He became very friendly, but within that friendliness there was too easy a familiarity.

'Can I come up to your room?' he asked.

'No, I have work,' Marcia replied.

'When can I come to see you?' he persisted. 'Tomorrow? When, when?'

What did he think of her? Another Asian, someone with whom he could share his feelings of homesickness? He kept returning. Marcia retreated into silence. She hid from him.

Late one night, he came to the door of her apartment and rang the bell. He kept his finger pressed on it. The building was silent, everyone asleep. Marcia peeped from behind the curtain of her room with beating heart. He would not go away. Her heart thumped. She was filled with trepidation. Marcia felt he would wake up the whole apartment but there was only the silence of its sleeping occupants. He did not move for ages and ages. At last he turned to go. He walked away but kept looking back over his shoulder as if the windows, the doors would open for him to be invited in.

He returned one morning.

'Tell him I'm not here. Gone to London,' she entreated her flatmates with great cowardice.

Joyce, Brenda, Lam, all peered out of the window and said, 'The lady from Sri Lanka has gone away.'

'Gone where?'

'Gone away.'

That was the last Marcia was to see of him.

'You talk too much. You talk to everybody,' Domingos had warned her.

Yet, wanting, needing human contact, Marcia could not stop smiling completely, like Browning's Last Duchess.

And then, there were the phone calls from a mysterious stranger, phone call after phone call. The man kept changing his name. He called himself Ravi.

Then Shankar. 'I must meet you. I came to the Hall but you were out. I am lonely.'

'Why don't you make friends? Go out with some of the Scottish girls.'

'No, I cannot. I am afraid. You and I are Asians. I want to be your friend. I want to send you a book.'

The book arrived but it was a journal with suggestive pictures. A sales book which advertised all kinds of paraphernalia for people who needed to be titillated. A glossy catalogue. Inflated, almost life-size human figures. Was this the only overture to friendship that a lonely human being could offer? Was there no other language? Marcia felt sick. This was not the kind of friendship she had envisaged. Ahmed, another of her friends, admonished her, 'It is you who encourage these people.'

Marcia was filled with sadness. Sadness for this man who thought that she would be prepared, away from the confines of her own society, to taste a new freedom. It was not what she had wanted at all. She shredded page after page of the glossy catalogue into the waste paper basket. The tokens of an undiscovered relationship.

The phone calls, however, persisted. The next time he called, Domingos was by her side. She had summoned him for strength and told the mysterious stranger so. 'My friend wants to speak to you.' They were never to meet or speak to each other again.

Domingos was packing his gifts to take home. Marcia was invited to see them. They went up to his room and he pulled out a suitcase from under his bed to show her all the toys and presents he had saved his precious pounds for. Presents for his nieces, nephews, mother, sister, Carmencas. There was a barking toy dog and a tartan skirt of one of the Scottish clans, the Black Watch, for Carmencas.

The day before he left, Marcia planned a farewell evening for him. They were to have supper together and spend the rest of the evening in the pub. Their last meeting. But it was not to be. Everybody invited themselves for supper. Marcia felt resentful. Joyce, who alternated between frigid silence and occasional friendliness, wanted to be invited too and even offered her own supper of grilled chicken as a contribution. Marcia could not understand her. She would sit every evening, having her high tea of hot, baked potato and grilled chicken alone, absorbed in the act. The table was often not cleared. Her dishes stacked, unwashed, in the sink. She was a pretty-looking girl, slim with curling, brown hair; her eyes were like water-washed pebbles at the edge of a loch. She was difficult to live with. For one thing, she never volunteered to take the black bag with all the food leavings down to the courtyard, even if the flies buzzed round it. Either Lam, Catherine or Marcia would do it. Joyce felt pressurized if anyone offered her food, even an apple. Lam and Marcia, with their different cultures, felt it was alien to eat alone. Sheila, the English girl, often shared their food. But Joyce felt that all of them could afford to feed themselves so there was no need for sharing.

Everyone shared Marcia's TV. Not just the TV but her friends as well. When her friends came, Joyce, who seldom had anyone but a single girl friend visiting her, would want to speak to Domingos. She was attracted to him, to his macho good looks. Yes, everybody was crazy about Domingos—the Algerian French girl with the blond hair; Joyce, the Scottish girl; and the Moroccan girl. Lam's sister, Shirley, from Hong Kong, was different. She was truly delightful. Generous and hospitable. On Marcia's first lonely evening in the University Village, she had walked over to Shirley's flat where she had at once set about cooking a meal for Marcia—rice, soup, stir-fry with pork chops and mushrooms. She was lively, open-hearted and amused everyone by going about proclaiming that she was the only virgin in Glasgow.

Marcia had to prepare supper for everyone on the day of Domingos' farewell—chicken, stir-fry, rice, salad, with wine and fruit. After supper—and Joyce was so pleased and happy that she offered to do the washing-up—Marcia felt a sense of loneliness and emptiness and went back to her room, switched on her cassette and began to write letters home. Snatches of Scottish dialects came to her ears—voices, music. She fell into one of her reveries.

Walking on the grey Glasgow pavements one morning, she had been interviewed by Scottish television. One of those on-the-street interviews.

'What are your impressions of Scotland? Of living in another country?'

'We have to understand a different culture. Live with it. Others too . . . it's important that they understand ours. We are not alien. There's a kinship . . .'

Marcia felt a sense of restlessness. Others had taken over her evening. She resented it. They couldn't relinquish Domingos. They wanted to go with him to the pub. They came to the door and called Marcia.

She became stubborn. 'You go down without me,' she said.

'You must come,' Domingos pleaded, 'this is my last evening. Don't spoil it.'

Marcia had to be persuaded. In the pub, she gave Domingos her farewell gift. A poem.

'Read it aloud even if we don't understand it,' Joyce said with slight tones of irony.

Marcia read it. Around her, people were drinking

foaming mugs of beer, whisky on the rocks, cognac. In her memory the red cherries floated on the golden froth of her glass of avocat. They would sit and talk for hours, the two of them, feeling a sense of closeness among the others, each absorbed in their own concerns. Outside the glass windows, the pigeons flew about. Marcia would drop crumbs for them. Domingos would go away. She would not come to the pub again. She, too, must prepare to pack her bags, her memories, store up images, pictures of the routes, the maps, the journeys she has taken. Back to her own familiar country.

Marcia presented the poem to Domingos. There was silence as he read it. He looked up at Marcia. 'Let me propose a toast.' He lifted his glass of wine. 'To the warmest, most charming and talented woman,' he said.

It was getting late. They walked across the grass to the flat. Everybody kissed Domingos goodbye. Joyce hugged him, clung to him. 'Come up for coffee,' she said.

In the apartment, coffee was brewed. Marcia switched on the TV. It was a late night documentary. She did not want it to end. She felt content, not alone, with Domingos' presence in the little lounge. He was part of all she had lived with—the table where they had sat and eaten, the chairs, the refrigerator, the electric cooker, the cupboards and shelves with the crockery and cutlery, Marcia's dishcloth with its patterns of flowers and fruits. It was here that Domingos would come, eat stir-fry and rice, drink wine, peel fruit, bring his own offerings of a pineapple, a bottle of lambrusco.

The last programme was over. Marcia went down the stairway with Domingos. They said their final goodbye. She had managed to salvage that little bit of time alone with him to re-establish their connection, their friendship.

He went back to his room, to his box of Christmas gifts, his mattress on the floor. It was too late to say and do the things that Marcia regretted she had left unsaid and undone. When Domingos had needed her, she had been selfish, callous. He had had to visit the University doctor for advice for his depression, taken tablets to ward it off. She remembered how he had shared his meal with her in the research room he shared with Hayford, the Nigerian Methodist whose friends would come for prayer and comfort. It sometimes grated on Domingos' nerves, the sound of fervent prayer as they knelt together, while he was writing his treatise on the Latin American debt. Each man had to share his comfort the way he could. Domingos had opened his parcel of food and had spread it out before Marcia. Fresh, unwashed mushrooms, his Scottish herrings, his fruit. She would never forget that shared repast.

Domingos had angered some of Marcia's friends, teased them, embarrassed them by his openness. He would stare unabashedly at Katherine and say, 'You are so beautiful; one of the most beautiful women I have seen . . . .' This was something that Ken and Jonathan felt was just not proper. Domingos could justify himself. 'In my country,' he would say, 'a woman, any woman, can come up to you on the street as you're walking and talk to you in friendship.'

Domingos wanted friendship. He was seldom alone, unlike Marcia who would go off on her own to the Cinema Royal to watch films like *Kiss of the Spider Woman* or *The Tempest*. He would be with one of his Colombian friends on Sauchiehall Street, at the Greek food shop or at the cinema. Never with a woman. Marcia was his only woman friend, but she had never told him how much she had valued him. It was he who had come with her to an empty room at Baird Hall to settle her in when she was a stranger. He was always there. A shoulder to weep on. It was he who had first stood at her threshold, offering her friendship while she had offered him the golden apples of the Hesperides. They had exchanged gifts. He had always protected her. He had advised her. He stood by her shoulder when nuisance calls came to her. 'Give me the phone,' he said, 'I'll tell him off. He won't dare ever again.' That had ended those phone calls with offers of a different kind of friendship. 'You want to smile and talk with everyone,' he would say, 'I have to drag you away.' Yet, that was the very quality he liked about Marcia. They never misunderstood or hurt each other.

Marcia tossed all night in bed. She woke early. 'I have to make it up to Domingos,' she thought. He was going away even before his time was up, to his country. He couldn't take the loneliness any more. Marcia put on her overcoat and wrapped a scarf round her neck against the early cold of a Scottish morning. She ran down the stairway in haste to tell him all the things she should have told him. Even go with him to the airport as a good friend would.

She rang the bell of his apartment. The Chinese student whom he had become friends with looked out of the window. 'Domingos has already left for the airport. He went early.'

Birbeck Court seemed cold and empty, bare without Domingos. The stone seat where they had sat, catching the warmth of the sun, stood like a monument to remind her of his presence.

He had left, generously as ever, room for someone else.

All is Burning

> Bhikkus, all is burning. And what is the all that is
> burning? Bhikkus, the eye is burning, visible forms
> are burning, visual consciousness is burning, visual
> impression is burning . . . . Burning with what?
> Burning with the fire of lust, with the fire of hate,
> with the fire of delusion; I say it is burning with
> birth, ageing and death, with sorrows, with
> lamentations, with pains, with griefs, with despairs.
> —The Buddha's Fire Sermon

SHE BLEW OUT the flame of the bottle lamp, leaving
the room in darkness. She took a towel off the line
and wrapped it about her shoulders. Seela, her
daughter, a young woman in her twenties, sat at the
table with her head in her hands.

Night sounds filtered in through the clay walls of the hut. Not just the sounds of insects rasping against the leaves or of wakened birds, but also a vast sighing that rippled through the thick blue-black shadows that lay like welts on the earth.

Seela lifted her head wearily. The weight of melancholy, of despair pressed each image onto her consciousness. She had aged. Felt older than her mother. In the cavern of her being images of dead fish, silver bellies upturned, floated in an inky pool.

'Mother,' she whispered. 'Mother, shall we go in search of Sena? He may still be alive if he has not been taken away. I'll come with you. You can't go alone. They may still be there, who knows. We can guide each other. It's still not light, we have to search for the path. It may be an unfamiliar one.'

Alice was already at the door. She spoke under her breath. 'No, you wait. Don't open the door to anyone. Remain in darkness. Don't light the lamp.'

'Mother.'

'Yes?'

'Don't go alone.' Seela rose wearily and dragged her feet to the door.

'No. It is my mission. A journey by myself will be safer. I'll come back here. Don't move. Wait and keep that door barred. Just don't open to any knock.'

Alice stepped out, treading softly, warily on her bare feet. It would be easier that way. No sound of any footfall. She closed the door behind her very quietly. She peered into the darkness with yet its hint of light. Her nerves felt on edge. Her instincts alert, she must let herself be guided, by odours— unusual odours of gunshot, of blood, borne by the slight, chill tremors of wind. There would be that human odour too, of fear, that rank smell of bodies through whose pores fear had breathed.

The sky began to lighten very faintly. Pale innocent streaks of colour appeared before the darker, reddened contusions that bruised the clouds. She walked along in a half-blind, almost groping way, feeling the roughness of tussocks of grass and dislodged stones that trembled beneath her feet.

She still felt her flesh raw, hurt by the events of the night. That sense of peace which came with late evening and the dusk which settled over the river, the trees, the road and their little hamlet had been deceptive. The bathers had returned from the river, they did not linger very long these days. The water, silver shot with ripples of gold, soon turned dark and opaque, vanishing into the dense clumps of trees. The woodsmoke curled up from the huts, spiralling into the sky, a pale wreathing grey.

She had been busy preparing the evening meal. The pot of rice was still on the fire, the fish and vegetables simmering in their pots. Seela, her daughter, was talking to Sena, the young man whom she was going to marry. Alice wanted this marriage for Seela. Her own man had deserted her when she was pregnant, leaving her to bring up the child alone. She had been a servant in so many houses, cooking, minding children, washing piles of linen, dressing her child in the clothes outgrown by other peoples' children—her mistress's daughter's clothes and those of her friends' children. No more of that for Seela. She had been a bright, intelligent child, had gone to school, passed examinations. She had a future before her. All that was through the efforts, undoubtedly, that Alice had made.

But it had come to their hamlet too—the

bhishanaya, the trouble. Yes, it had reached them. There were rumours. The young men in the village, were they too involved in all those happenings? The country was on fire. Everything was on fire. All was burning, burning. Yes, the fires were burning. Fires that burnt down the huts. These and hundreds of other villages burning. The self burning. The unconscious, the visual impressions, burning. The fire of lust and hate, the fire of delusion. The Buddha's Fire Sermon that the villagers heard in the temple— the monk repeated it on the last poya day when they went to hear him, to find some relief for their suffering minds.

'Burning,' he said, 'with birth, ageing and death, with sorrows, with lamentations, with pains, with griefs, with despairs.'

And what do we do? Alice thought to herself. Become dispassionate, detached? To reach that liberation must I first go out among the dead and their ruined houses? I cannot forget the sound of the vehicles on the road . . .

They had stopped at the entrance to the village. The darkness had moved like an open door to admit them. And they had entered. The villagers heard the sounds of their boots. The knocking at the doors. The commands.

'Open up.'

There was nothing else to do.

Screams. Dying away. Growing fainter. Fainter. She had to go. But not at once. Wait for sometime. Till they heard the sound of the vehicles moving off. Then she would go out, in search of Sena, for Seela's sake. She thought of herself. An ordinary woman. Very ordinary. Even the name Alice did not matter to anyone. She knew that she had to do it. Even if there were a vestige of life left she would confront those last moments. And she would have to do it alone.

Seela too had been strong during those last moments. 'Mother, our generation, my generation, we know the consequences. We are not afraid.'

Now Alice was walking along pathways. They had to lead to the deathspot. Through the grove of trees—wild guava, hard-shelled green belly fruit and straggling palms. A cluster of thambili nestled among some of the thicker fronds, a very pale orange. Her throat felt parched, as if death were already clutching at it. Dry tongued, her belly cavernous and hollow. Out of the trees, out of the grove, she emerged like a sleepwalker into a space where the grass had been trampled and crushed.

Now it was over. The sound of gunshot still echoed in her ears. Yama had visited every house in the village where there were males. They had all been taken away. She had to summon all her strength for this mission. The vision of Yama, the god of death, filled her mind.

I am an ordinary woman, she told herself. I have been a servant in other people's homes for the greater part of my life. Always subservient, obeying orders. Eating after everyone else had eaten. Sleeping on my mat in a corner of a room, seeing that other people were comfortable. And now, now that I had hopes for a different kind of life, now when I thought things would change—but no, things *have* changed, though not for the better. Yet I have to do this for my daughter, look at the faces of the dead and dying. No, Seela couldn't do it. I'll do it for her. I am her mother. Who else has she had all her life? Myself and her grandmother. Two women. There has never been a man to give me strength. I have done things that I never believed possible for a woman to do.

No, it will never end for me. My strength grows with each crisis. I've been well trained through the years. There's no one else I can turn to. I'll do it by myself. I can't help it if my mind keeps going back to all the events of the night. I'll relive this experience for ever.

The knocking on all those doors resounded in her ears. She had opened the door. What else could she have done? They wanted Sena. As they did all the males in the village. Behind them she saw that vision—Yama. Yama, the god of death. He too was with them. On whose side was he? He was a constant guest on both fronts these days.

They pointed the guns at Sena. No, he couldn't escape. Nor could all the others. Weeping, shrieking echoed through the night, the night that Alice had thought would be so peaceful. She smelt burning rice. The brands crackled and the fire raced, shedding sparks as it blew up.

Yama, Yama. Was it only she who saw him? Eye for an eye, tooth for a tooth, the men kept saying as they pointed the gun at Sena, prodded him with the butt.

'Don't try to resist,' said one of them. 'And don't say you are innocent. You want to be martyrs. Then where are the victims? Someone has to be the victim. Who put up all those posters with their violent messages? Who carried off the weapons after the attacks on police stations and the army camps? To use for what purpose? To use against whom? The men of this village—we have proof. The last attack . . . there were deaths. Now get on, move on . . . . The fires are spreading all over the country. Come on, hurry up.'

Her daughter had fallen at the feet of the men. She had pleaded and wept.

'Don't take him away. Don't. Don't.' It had all fallen on deaf ears.

There had been so much shouting outside their walls. Commands. Tramp of boots. Sounds of running feet. They had heard the guns. The volley of shots. Went on ceaselessly. Would they ever stop firing?

It seemed a lifetime ago. Alice now smelt the odour of death. Rank. Foetid. Like rotting vegetation. They lay there, clumps of them, their bodies spreadeagled on the earth. Men. Bodies. A mirror of light flickered across her gaze with their distortions, black specks, rust coloured streaks—chiaroscuric images that almost stoned her eyeballs.

She knew she had to go among them. How else would she find Sena? He had to be there. He had to, unless . . . but could he have had a chance of escaping, in the dark? No, there must have been flashlights. The darkness violated by those coruscating beams. At least if she could find him . . . . She was a woman who needed certainty. The certainty of truth. It had to be one way or the other. She had never deceived Seela. Nor had she deceived herself. At this moment she did not want the comfort of any human being. This would be her final test, her trial. And Sena, if he still had some life in him, even if he was barely breathing, perhaps he could gasp out a word, perhaps she could even drag him out of this welter of bodies.

She looked at them, almost dispassionately. They were finished. There was nothing more left for them. Their women would have to fend for themselves now. The women were strong enough. And they had their children. They couldn't give up at this stage.

She wiped her face with the edge of her towel. The towel was damp with morning dew. Her face chill and sharp like the edge of a keen blade.

Death walk. That's what this is, she thought. I'll have to turn them over. I have to see the faces. How else can I recognize them? How can I recognize Sena? Men who had belonged to other women. I would never have touched them at any other time.

Her bare feet slid cautiously through the huddle of bodies. They felt so soft. Even the sinewy ones.

She bent over, turned up face after face. All she recognized were the empty faces of men. Men who were all akin, all brothers, husbands, fathers. All gone. To leave life in so unfinished, so haphazard a manner.

She stumbled, almost fell against one of the bodies. I'll have to be careful, she thought. I mustn't jostle them even in death. Perhaps, some of them still have that last breath . . . the soul that's reluctant to leave the body. No funeral orations for any of them. Individual burials are no longer practicable. It is within our minds that we carry those reminders of what each man was to each woman. Till each one is claimed, if ever they are claimed, they are anonymous. It's happening elsewhere too, perhaps at this very moment . . . . Soon there'll be no birds left in the village. Startled by gunshot, they'll fly away to another village. Who's going to start life here all over again . . .

Her movements now became mechanical. But she wove her way through, a searcher who could never give up the search.

Where would the pyres be lit? And where the secret graves? They would be silently carried away, secretly buried. Their names would be mentioned only in whispers. So this was the journey that Yama took daily? Difficult. But she had the strength.

She flicked at a fly with a towel. They were already there, the bluebottles. The smell of death, it

173

was choking her. She felt suffocated but could not
stop. She would go on till she found him.

Could this be Sena . . .? She peered into a face,
called his name softly: 'Sena, Sena, Sena.' It could be
Sena—a young body, but the face all smeared with
blood. If she wiped the blood off she might recognize
him. She wiped his face gently with the end of her
towel and gazed into the face.

No, this was not him. Resembled him . . .

She stroked his head, caressingly. A woman's
gesture. Her towel was sodden. Her clothes felt damp.

He is still warm, she told herself. My towel is
soaked with blood. My clothes too . . . damp, stained.
She felt dead, her limbs numbed. She stumbled
against yet another body.

There must be so many . . . so many of them . .
. . Forgive me, she whispered softly . . . . Respect for
the dead, incantations, prayers . . . I can't forget it.
Forgive me, son, brother, father, husband, forgive
me for touching your sleeping body with my foot, it
is not that I mean to insult you . . .

No, not this one either. Where was he? And such
a silence in the village. Where was everybody?
Asleep? Awake? Afraid to come out? All the women,
the children? Such a silence in the village.

Her head was full of images, strange thoughts .
. . . All the blood must seep into the earth, as if the
gods must be propitiated, as if we have had a long
drought. What new plants will grow here? Or will it
remain a desert, haunted by ghosts and spirits?
Shouldn't we leave it this way, to remember them? I
must go down to the river, wash my clothes, bathe,
watch the water change colour—like my dreams, the
dreams that will visit me night after night.

When can I ever complete this journey? Yama
told me—somewhere—that this is my first journey

into the darkness of the underworld . . . . What's that sound . . . a groan? Not all are dead then.

She knelt down. Her back ached with so much bending. She felt the man's breath touch the palm of her hand like a slight vapour, a cobweb of mist that faintly wreathed round her fingers.

'I won't leave you alone. I'll stay by you,' she said, sitting beside him, wiping his face with the corner of her towel, pushing away the tangled strands of hair from his forehead. She supported his head in her arms.

'Mother,' he uttered faintly. His life was ebbing away.

'Mother,' he repeated. 'Thirsty.'

'Wait, I'll bring you a sip of water. I'll go back to my hut. Wait. Don't move.'

No, there wasn't time to go back, to fetch water, to give him that drink. Life-giving water? No. It would soon be over. She felt the spasms of his chest, the painful heaving of that wounded breast. She held him until he was still. Her hands were stained with blood. She wiped them slowly but the blood felt sticky, oozing into her skin, her flesh.

That was the end. All she could give him was the hope of that sip of water. And he had called her Mother. That was enough. She was a comfort to him and that was more than all the others had on all the battlefields where they gasped out their lives.

Already, so many bodies and she hadn't found Sena yet.

What could a village do without all its men? We'll have to take their place now, we women, she thought. I'll go back to my daughter. Perhaps there's still hope. They may have taken him away for questioning. Seela will have to continue living, like all the other women. It won't be the end for us, not while we still have breath.

She rose wearily. She wanted to retch but her mouth was dry, her throat parched.

Two hundred and fifty of them. All the men in the village. Gone. Swept away in that great flood of death. But the women would bear more sons. Life had to, would go on.

The Sand Serpents

THE TAXI TAKES me back from the airport all the way to Mahawa through a familiar landscape. As we pass through Kurunegala the road grows straighter with paddy fields and coconut groves stretching on either side. Sometimes scattered herds of cattle cross the road and the taxi slows down to let them pass. The sun is hot; the heat grows but not like in Doha. There, in a few seconds my clothes would be soaked through and through with perspiration, especially because the kitchen and the hall did not have airconditioning and that was where I spent most of my time working. I had only two sets of clothes which Bossa madam had given me for the whole six months that I was there. I would wear one set of garments which would soon be wringing wet. Then I would change them, wash and dry them and get into fresh clothes. This went on, it seemed interminably. And the heat was so unbearable. The house was like an oven during the day, but the nights were chill. In the desert the deadly poisonous snakes would be under the sand and you could tread on them. At night, when it was cold, they lay concealed.

My heart begins to grow lighter as the taxi speeds along. My companion is returning home from Saudi and we will share the expenses. She is returning to Kurunegala but she is kind enough to come all the way with me to see me home safely. She has brought many things with her—gifts for the family, things for the home. I have been able to save only a little money because I did not stay there long enough. I bought a saree for my mother which cost seven hundred and fifty rials. It was very expensive. I came to Colombo and bought a gift for *loku mahathmaya*, a pair of trousers and a shirt. If I had waited longer I too could have brought back many things. Perhaps I shall go back one day, so that I can earn more money.

I have missed this countryside—the freedom and openness which I always had, before I went to Doha—the wide fields which are being harvested in some areas, the silvery channels of water, the *wewas* with the nelum flowers blooming. The men are sitting on the *pila*. Their work is done; they have sown the fields and are waiting for the paddy to grow. The paddy *bissas* with their thatched roof covers must be full of grain and the pomegranates must be ripening on the trees in the village gardens. Pumpkins lie piled up by the roadside, enormous golden yellow pumpkins. I never ate vegetables in Doha. It was always mutton and rice. Bossa madam would cook the food herself. She would cut up the meat and boil it with rice and spices—coriander, cinnamon and lots of cardamom. I have not tasted chillies on my tongue for six months. I longed for the taste of fish from the Mahawewa—tilapi and loola cooked with red hot chillies and coconut milk.

Coconuts are plentiful in *loku mahathmaya's* estate and everyday I would scrape coconut lavishly—as much as I wanted for curries and *sambols*. Big bunches of plantains hang in the *kades*, kolikuttu and ambul. Divul and pomegranates fill the *vatties* woven out of dried *pan kola*. I think of the guavas and mangoes in the garden. During the season the trees are laden with honey-sweet fruit pillaged by parrots. At Doha there were plenty of apples and grapes but the people I lived with were *loba*, stingy. The rest of the family would buy crates of fruit and send up a share for Bossa Sir and madam and the children but they never gave me any. They would eat and drink before me but they never shared with me. I was, after all, a lesser being to them, a slave. I was there to do the work. There were five children in the family and Bossa madam was a teacher. The children were good except for the eldest girl, Menoor. It was because of Menoor that I could not stay. She made life unbearable for me.

Soon, soon I will be in Mahawa. I can see from this distance the towering pinnacle of the rock temple of Yapahuwa. The eagles and sparrow hawks wheel about the summit. Below the rock, covered with trees, are caves with figures carved in stone. Life never changes here at this temple. The chairs with their embroidered covers are ranged against the walls of the wide verandah, brass spittoons beside them. A teapoy stands in the middle with a vase of flowers. The monks who dwell in the *avasa* go about their business calmly as if the outside world hardly exists for them.

I will pick jasmines and araliya to take for *mal pooja* to the temple for my safe return. On Poya days the villagers all gather at the temple precincts to listen to *bana*, the sermons preached by the High Priest. I was like a prisoner in the house at Doha. Even Friday, which was meant to be an off-day there, was never granted to me. So I never had a chance of going out and meeting the other maids from my country. My loneliness grew greater and greater. There was no one to speak my language with, no one with whom to share my thoughts and feelings of homesickness. True, they looked after me, they protected me, but how long could I live locked up in their house where they did not want me to even open a window? They would shut the window immediately I opened it. I would weep from loneliness.

The greatest happiness that those people had was to go to the desert. They were free there, to drive out and sit under the date palms in an oasis, take off their heavy, constricting burqas, cook food out of doors. But I never liked the desert. I did not feel the same happiness that they felt. It was just white sand with little dunes, small trees, beginning to sprout, planted on small mounds. Since there was no path, no road, the car would jolt badly on the sand and I would feel sick. But, if I stayed back in the house to be alone, Menoor would also remain. She took a perverse delight in torturing me. As soon as the parents left she would take the little baby and twirl it round and round fiercely until the baby cried. Then she would complain to her mother that it was I who was responsible.

I loved that baby. I wanted to carry and look after it, pet it, but Menoor was jealous. She did not want anyone to show affection to me. She was disturbed in her mind. Very disturbed. Even in school they found it difficult to control her and would telephone home. No maid would stay because of her. The last maid had stayed for only two months.

She found different ways of tormenting me. One day she put water in the plate of rice Bossa madam served for me and I had to go hungry. Her mother beat her but she would never change. If Menoor was watching TV and I came in to join them, she would immediately switch it off. I used to sleep on the ground, and if she wanted to open or close the window near where I lay, she trampled my body as she walked towards it. I was not human to her. I did not have feelings. My pain of mind or heart meant nothing to her, or the fact that I was far from home, among strangers who belonged to a different culture, who spoke a different language. I could not even lie down on my mattress in peace at the end of a day's work—all the bed clothes would be missing; or she would put ink on my pillowcase or dirty the sheets. She did not want me to rest even at night. She herself would not sleep for a long time. She would stay up, put on all the lights, sometimes until two o'clock in the morning, and disturb me. But no one cared.

No one could control her. She was restless, very mature for her age. All those young girls are very mature even at an early age. They marry young once they have attained age, and bear children. They are largely built and very attractive. Even with children they go to school. Menoor loved to take photographs of the Indians who used to come to wash the cars in the family home. It was an extended family that lived there, and there were twelve cars in the house. The young women were heavily veiled but when they wanted to attract the attention of the expatriate workers they would lift their veils and stick their tongues out at them. They were restless, perhaps because they married too young—their burqas were like prisons in which they dwelt, hidden away behind the coverings.

The men were afraid of the women, were dominated by them because they were afraid they would lose them. It is a very expensive business getting married there because the men have to pay a big bride price for their wives. But Bossa Sir's mother had gone mad because her husband had taken a second wife. She had dropped one of the babies— Bossa Sir's sister, who as a result was mad too. But this sister was kind to me, and would come upstairs and sit and talk to me. The men were very good in the family. They would never even look at my face. It was Menoor who caused me all the unhappiness. Other maids came back with lots of gifts from their mistresses. Bossa madam promised to give me many things at the end of two years. Before I left she gave me two dress materials after taking me to the shops. It was a very rare thing for them to buy my return ticket before the two years had elapsed, but I persuaded them and pleaded with them. They knew they could do nothing to keep me back.

It was not because the work was hard. They had machines for everything. But it was so lonely. Shut in, not allowed to mix with the other Sri Lankan maids. They told lies—that it was I who didn't want to meet them. If any of the maids came there, I was sent upstairs. My letters were not given to me when they arrived. I knew this by the post marks on them. Sometimes in my loneliness I would stand at a window and listen to the voices of the workers speaking in Sinhala as they passed by on the road. One day a maid came to help at the wedding preparations of the younger son. She was from Galle. I was not allowed to talk to her for long. She retaliated by scolding her mistress under her breath: 'Bitch! Bitch!' I was sent upstairs and my food, too, was sent up to me. Didn't they realize that I would have stayed back if I had been less lonely? Were they afraid that I would learn too much from the more experienced maids, make demands?

I went to Doha because I hoped I could make a lot of money. I was given three thousand rupees a month. I could have saved much more if only I could have stayed. I needed the money to help my parents. In my village in Kolabissa the house is small. It has two rooms. I wanted to cement the floors and replace the tiles that had blown off in a great gale. I am the only one to help my family. My younger sister has to go for classes, for English and singing. All this needs money. I will spend for the English classes but I do not like her to go for *sangeethaya*. I myself never went to school, but when I came to work for *loku mahathmaya* he insisted that I should learn akuru, the Sinhala alphabet. I can read and write now. I can speak English too. This helped me when I was in Doha.

Oh, how afraid I was at the beginning! We first went to Bahrain. We were given sardines and *parippu* and bread to eat by the agency that employed us. The maids were waiting to be sent to their various destinations. Bossa Sir and Bossa madam were the only couple to come and choose their maids. Out of the twenty of us I was chosen. When Bossa madam held my hand I was afraid. She was big and tall; she was completely covered in a black burqa. She laughed when she saw me recoiling from her and moved aside the veil that covered her face. It was a pleasant face. They went back to Doha and when my visa was ready, I too flew there. But I had to remain for three days at the airport until they came to fetch me. I felt so alone and abandoned. I wanted to return home immediately but a young Sri Lankan Muslim boy who was working at the airport consoled me. '*Akka*,' he said, 'you must face the suffering now and not turn back.' He brought me bread and tea. At night I was afraid to sleep alone. The policemen would open the door and look in. My clothes grew loose on me, my saree sagged at the waistband.

At last Bossa Sir came. He gave me a salute and smiled. He said, 'Bossa madam gone on business, come with me.' Bossa madam was a teacher. When I went to their house I was given tea and asked to sleep. The reason, I discovered later, for the delay was because in the house of my master and mistress the telephone was kept off the hook all day because they were at work, so none of the calls reached them.

The house was large, with many halls and rooms but with very little furniture. There were carpets everywhere. When I reached the house I was still scared, wary, but they were kind to me. But they were also often thoughtless about my comfort. Once I had no tea to drink for three days. I kept reminding Bossa madam that there was no milk and tea in the house. No one paid attention to me. One morning I was washing the clothes when I felt dizzy and faint. I came out of the bathroom and sat on the floor with my head in my hands. Then they quickly sent for tea. Bossa madam said: 'Ah, you feel faint because you did not have tea. Tea is bad for you. You will die soon.'

But what was life worth if I could not have even a cup of tea? What else was there for me, what pleasure could I have there even with money, living with strangers who did not care, really care, about me? What about the others who stayed on, and who remained behind? Some of them went mad, or committed suicide or even murdered their mistresses. When they returned they found that their men had taken other women. They, too, because of loneliness, became friendly with other men who were equally lonely.

Abba came back soon although there was nothing to complain of in the house she lived in. There was very little work but she was bored. She felt that the house was like a *hira kuduwa*, a prison. The house was large but walled in. You could not see beyond those walls. In that house crates of apples were brought in regularly. The children used to play with them, rolling them across the floor like bright red balls.

Abba's sister has come and gone back now for many years. She hopes to open a pharmacy with the money she has earned. She has learnt the Arabi language too and can speak it fluently. But the separation is bitter and the loneliness great when wives and mothers leave their husbands and children and the men leave their families. The climate is difficult, the food is strange. Many get sick because of the unbearable heat during the day when they have to work out of doors, and the chill at night.

Gamini's young wife left him and their baby and went to Saudi. Gamini had no future in Mahawa after he had married out of his caste. His parents would not accept him. First the couple stayed at *loku mahathmaya's* estate as caretakers but then the wife got a chance to go and so she left. Then Abdeen, who was also the watchman at the estate at one time, went to the Middle East. His wife had been there for some time and she was earning well. Now they have returned and bought property and a house that had belonged to *loku mahathmaya*. They are prospering.

Abdeen was saved by the old master in 1971, during the insurgency, when he was arrested by the police. He was innocent but he was then about to be shot. He owes his life to the old master. Now the old master is dead too. The man whom *loku Mahathmaya* wanted me to marry changed once he found that Abdeen's sister Farina was rich and could send him money and gifts from Saudi.

I am getting on in years and I do not know what prospects of marriage I will have in the future. The men prefer money nowadays. But some of the women have grown more selfish; they have come back and built spacious houses. They do not want to marry and share their wealth with the men.

There is the other side too. Ratnayake's wife has gone for the second time to the Middle East but she is very sick. Just before she left she was in hospital with asthma, being given saline. She is as thin as a katussa, one of those garden lizards. Hardly any flesh on her. All bones. Her mistress does not allow her to cook the food or come near the children. One day there was a big fight between the two of them; the mistress beat her and she, too, beat the mistress. She ran away but was caught by the police. She was considered the wrongdoer and was put into prison. Now they are trying to get her back but they have had no news. Sompala's wife came back three months pregnant. The husband did not want someone else's child, so she had an abortion that went wrong—it was performed by a quack. When she was taken to hospital it was too late and she died.

There are many more changes now in Mahawa. The old houses are now abandoned—the huts with

the mud walls and thatched roofs with their windows
barred with jungle sticks. The new houses have
plastered walls of pink and green with tiled roofs.
There are no longer fences of jungle wood but parapet
walls with gates. The houses are full of cassettes and
transistors. It was very different in the past. Nona,
loku mahathmaya's sister, remembers many things—
the big, flat round *kurakkan* rotis that the people of
the Wanni Hathpattuwa ate and the jungles full of
bear, deer, leopard. The thalagoyas, the giant lizards,
used to crawl into the garden at night and the jungle
cocks would crow in the garden, she would tell me.
The wild fox, the nariyas, used to scare her at night.
The jungle was close to the property but it has now
been cleared and the animals have had to go far into
what's left of the jungle. The last time Nona came,
she knew that things had to change in her brother's
life. Brother and sister had stood watching the
coconuts being plucked, talking about how *loku
mahathmaya* too could not live here much longer. The
loneliness was too much for him. He was growing
old. There were many changes taking place and the
estate was too much for him to manage. Not like
Arthur *mahathmaya* who still has his coconut
plantation in Chilaw. He will never give it up. He
prefers to be alone there rather than live with his
wife in a foreign country, however rich he could get
there. *Loku mahathmaya* has already given away most
of his possessions to his children and soon the house
and property will be in the hands of strangers. I will
then have to find a new place to go to, but it will
never be like this. Here I was treated as a person, an
individual, a human being. And even when I go, he
will see that I do not go empty handed.

The taxi stops at the gate. I open it for the car to
go up. *Loku mahathmaya* is lying back on the long

chaise lounge, reading a book. 'Ah, Nanda, you have returned,' he says, smiling.

I enter the house and sit on a chair. A luxurious feeling assails me. I have never felt such a flood of happiness in my whole being. It is an indescribable sense of peace, *santhosaya*.

For six months I had no chair to sit on, only the floor, and when I was tired and weary I had only the wall to lean back against. When I sit on this chair I feel I will never want to return to that country again.

This, alone, is enough for me.

The Innocents of the World

The Arrival

JASMINE HAD RUNG up from Colombo. 'We are coming to Kandy on Saturday. A friend of mine, a very rich businessman from Hong Kong, wants to see your antiques. He admired the chiffonier in my house and I told him you had one exactly like that which you might want to dispose of. I had told him the price tentatively but, of course, we shall leave room for bargaining. They don't have this kind of furniture there. Now don't prepare any food for us. I shall bring a picnic lunch. There will be about nine of us in the picnic party.'

Camille waited for the sounds of her friend's

arrival with a sense of eagerness, almost elation. Jasmine was the comet that streaked through her life bearing with her so much presagement of the future.

Jasmine arrived. She came up the steps with her eyes and face full of that joyous light which she always bore when she saw Camille and Raj. Where did all that happiness and ebullience come from? She had at various intervals been separated from her father whom she had greatly loved and had had to spend most of her time with her mother and half sisters. But she had also lived part of her life with her father's relations who were extremely wealthy. After her father's death she had inherited everything, being his only child. Every year in his memory she gave a *dana* for a hundred people, cooking the food herself.

'I feed the crows too,' she often said. 'I give *dana* to the birds to appease Saturn.'

Her first marriage had been disastrous. She had married young and gone to London. She was now married to an Anglo-Indian whose forebears had once belonged to the great Dewan families in Colonial India. His first wife, an Englishwoman, had been killed in a car crash. They had both come together out of their personal tragedies.

Jasmine stood on the threshold with her arms outstretched and flung them about Camille. 'My darling, how are you and Raj and the girls? How are my innocents? Have you got your family house back, your ancestral property? When are you going to live in the family house?'

Three Chinese came quietly behind her. One of them was a small man with shaggy dark hair falling over his forehead. The light struck his spectacles sharply. One could not see the expression in his eyes. He wore a loose, baggy shirt. He was the boss.

The other two Chinese were very shy, diffident, muted, completely effaced. Very slender with white, ivory skins, very low-keyed, unexcited.

Kendrick, Jasmine's husband, came up slowly, puffing his pipe; the children followed, a girl and a boy—the son towering head and shoulders above his father. Kendrick was never effusive in his affections but was greatly concerned about Camille, Raj and their family. His bland, smooth face and placid brown eyes did nothing to betray his feelings. The turmoil of living, of violent emotion, was not reflected in his expression. His humane instincts surfaced when it came to his family and friends. The aliens were the intruders and the trespassers. If one of the girls was too thin, he would say: 'I say, Camille, are you feeding Savithri well? Is she taking her milk and eggs? Stand straight, my dear. Look, straighten up at the waist. My, how you've grown.' And then he would query impatiently, 'Now for God's sake, Camille, what are you doing about that house of yours?'

'I'm helpless,' she would reply, 'the tenants will not leave. I'm tired of fighting. I've had to pay off the mortgage. I have to keep the other pieces of land from being sold out of the family. I've sold my jewellery. I had to sell the furniture to pay off the bank loans. I'm going to sit back and live as if I'd never possessed it!'

'Now come, come. For the children's sake you've got to do something.'

Kendrick and Jasmine were always so concerned, not only about their own children but also about those of Camille and Raj. Their own children went to the best private schools which had been set up by the English missionaries. These schools were for the creme-de-la-creme of society. They were expensive.

They imparted the best of English education. The girl had her ballet lessons and swimming. The boy had his tennis, cricket, rugger and body-building.

Kendrick knew the value of land, the inherited acres of coconut at Duwa. The estate flourished; the vegetables they grew, the prawns they caught in the lagoon, everything brought in money, but hard work went along with it. Jasmine even catered to the tourists who drove in for a day in the country, cooking food on the hearth with firewood collected from the estate, arranging the table with frangipani and hibiscus to give it an exotic setting. The lagoon yielded so much fresh fish and prawns and Jasmine delighted in creating these country banquets. The enormous koduwa fish was cooked in an earthenware pot and brought simmering hot to the table; it was flavoured with country herbs. The tender young coconuts were scooped out and filled with fresh fruit. She remembered every detail which contributed to the comfort of her guests. Coming in thirsty after a hot drive they were offered a choice of beer or fresh *kurumba* or *thambili*. She was enchanted by her role of hostess. They were both hard-working and had learnt the necessary skills to survive.

And here was Jasmine now, bubbling over. It was always she who hugged them all with crazy abandon, laughed until she cried with her crazy wit, pulling out boxes of surprises from the car, basket after basket, carefully and thoughtfully packed with goodies, as she called them—vegetables from the estate, woven bags of *pan kola*, *kalu dodol*, delicate embroideries, enormously rich chocolate cakes set on mirrored stands which reflected the extravagant sugared roses and layers of cream.

They all trooped into the house to drink coffee and lime juice. First Melwyn stepped forward. He was the Chinese who seemed to possess all the authority. He sat quietly on one of the chairs; the rest followed suit unobtrusively. He looked carefully away from the chiffonier which dominated the room, its golden, polished wood glowing. The gleaming top was arranged with porcelain ginger jars, Dutch plates and cut-glass decanters.

Jasmine pointed at the chiffonier.

'Yes, I saw it,' Melwyn said, without even glancing at the chiffonier. Or perhaps his shrewd glance had already appraised it at once and valued it. No; rather he had appraised not so much the priceless bits of furniture as the owners themselves. They were marketable and he had priced them in his mind. He felt their lack of money. He had summed them up, found that their possessions were indeed beyond price but that they themselves did not have what he had—an overwhelming abundance of money.

To him barter appeared easy. There was a powerful lack here, in this household, of what gave Melwyn the necessary bargaining power over other humans. After all, he was in this country for a purpose. He did not need to be philanthropic. He had come not to fulfil their needs but his own. He looked around: the sagging cane and the torn-up upholstery with the cotton stuffing coming out; everything was badly in need of being refurbished. He could not see anything beyond that fact. He had already set his price on everything, and that price was not high. But looking at their faces he felt a twinge of doubt; perhaps it would not be all that easy to buy them over with the contents of his fat leather wallet. He felt its weight in his trouser pocket; it gave him a sense of security and power over them all. But they appeared to be so nonchalant about their possessions. They belonged here as he did not. Their roots were far more deeply embedded in this soil than his would ever be anywhere.

A fragile blue and white teapot stood on the carved Dutch sideboard. 'Can you read the Chinese characters on this teapot?' Camille asked Melwyn.

They all crowded round it. The Chinese grew excited; they huddled together, peering at it. It was of delicate white porcelain as thin and transparent as an egg shell, with blue bamboo leaves and chinese characters, perhaps a line of poetry, perhaps the name of the artist, painted on it.

'Yes, yes, that is Chinese but it is difficult. We cannot read it.'

It was their language but they could no longer understand it. They had lost the key to that identity. Relinquished it, together with the names—their own names that had been changed in the missionary school. The delicate brush strokes of the Chinese characters defied their understanding. The teapot reminded them of a lost identity whose recollections remained as faint and ghostly as the aroma of the jasmine-scented tea which it had once held.

Melwyn walked everywhere, looking, touching, assessing. He suddenly came to a standstill and stood thoughtfully by the satin wood and ebony centre table supported on the wide-branched antlers of a slain stag. It must have been a magnificent stag; both wood and antlers had come from a long-ago-ravished forest.

'I like this,' he said.

'Melwyn likes your table,' Jasmine announced happily. At last he had shown approbation. They were all so pleased at this significant remark. He would surely want to buy this piece.

'You will sell?' Melwyn asked, looking at Camille.

She felt that what had attracted him most deeply, even more than the golden grain of the satin wood, were the immense and impressive antlers. But certainly he would never see himself as the vanquished stag. Rather, he saw himself as the hunter who had vanquished the stag. This table would be his trophy.

'I don't want to part with this,' said Camille. 'It belonged to my father; he had it made many years ago when he was in one of those distant, remote outstations in Batticaloa, living alone, with his family far away from him. He would take his gun and go hunting into the jungle and come back covered with tick bites from a wilderness of thickets. He would layer the walls of his dwelling with glistening snake skins, and hang weaver birds' nests and antlers with the date and the place of the shoot inscribed on the wooden mounts. They were the trophies of his expeditions.'

Perhaps he had shot that stag; she did not know. She could not remember. All he had told her was that he had designed the table himself. The octagonal satin wood with its carved ebony edge like black lace belonged to that youthful period of his early married life. It had always been part of their home. Carefully arranged with various objects that were meant for decoration and ornamentation—a little brass bowl with a Hindu deity, a cherry blossom tree, a miniature marble bird bath, things that were brought back from the aunts' Continental tours in the great Cunard liners . . . things that mingled strangely with the assortment of brass bowls, trays, vases.

Yes, a strange, haphazard assortment. Later on, the family Bible also found a place, and a pen stand of some golden, varnished Australian wood. Above

the table was the big portrait of Camille's dead
brother, Arthur. There were too many associations
with that table to ever part with it.

They had grown up with these things around
them, accepted them naturally. Camille's parents had
lived with these objects for years, built up their
home, created that home for their children and then,
piece by piece, given over everything. All these pieces
of furniture handed down from generation to
generation were part of an inheritance which emerged
out of an European colonial ancestry. Yet within that
heritage there was an identity to be explored which
entailed investigating how these many racial strands
mingled in their veins. Within the context of that
imperial ideology lay several clues. They had
involuntarily become part of the political and
historical mission which had resulted in colonialism.
They had to live with these inescapable facts but not
condone them. Perhaps they were clinging to what
they would inevitably have to give up, what would
eventually be a requiem for the past. They would
not sell it so cheaply. Rather they would keep it till
the very end, the bitter end, until a different kind of
migration took place. For displacement was to be
expected. Where would these wanderers find new
territory for their habitations? Where, in what strange
new clime would their cumbersome possessions fit
in? The wood would surely warp.

Relinquish, relinquish. Not cling . . .

Now, suddenly, all these things had a different
value. These artifacts had a greater price than the
lives of their possessors. They could be bought,
taken away; they could enhance other lives that had
lost their identities and took their colour briefly
from a cosmopolitan social milieu. These outsiders,
these aliens, could pillage with their money, create a

new history for themselves out of those ravaged lives. The invasions were subtle. Melwyn had the power of money which these two schoolteachers, Raj and Camille, did not have. Indeed, could never have.

Melwyn padded about the house, walking with a panther litheness. He moved swiftly onto the verandah, lifting the cloth spread on the old oval-shaped teak table stained with ink and water marks. Thick lenses concealed the colour of his eyes. His smooth face betrayed nothing. He eventually looked at the chiffonier, opening out the drawers which were filled with books and papers, peered into every bowl and jar on the shelves, opening doors on spaces crammed with cut glass decanters and cruet sets swathed in cobwebs.

Camille and Raj stood at a distance, mere onlookers in their own home as this man, this stranger, this transient rummaged in every nook and cranny of their lives. They felt exposed, ravished. So much so that they disassociated themselves from each object, however delicately wrought, however precious.

'How much is this? Your last price?' Melwyn kept asking.

He went to another room with its carved settee and chairs. 'These chairs I like. These two. But not the settee.'

The settee and chairs had come from Martha Barry. Martha was one of a large family, her father an old British engine driver in the Ceylon Government Railway. They had once been next-door neighbours. Dottie, her sister, had been married briefly; her husband had left her and she slept alone in an enormous old four-poster bed. The chairs were again part of old houses. They had belonged to friends and settled in comfortably with all their memories.

It seemed to Camille as if she was swathed in strong cobwebs of the past which would not release her. The furniture piled round her stood for the past, in fact had taken the place of all those who had gone away, leaving her to fend for herself without resources. A wasp buzzing about her head kept building its clay castles on the leg of one of the tables. Potter wasps, her mother had called them. Potter wasps. How hard, how firm and unbreakable those dwellings were and the larvae safe and protected inside with their store of food.

The table was piled with books and an old porcelain basin. Everything was covered with dust. In Camille's old home this quaint table, European styled with its stretchers that could hold out trays or draw them back, sliding in and outwards, was filled with brass trays and blue glass Chinese vases. There was a tray with a hunter engraved on it. On either side of him were a tiger and a deer—the hunter was between the two. There was no escape anywhere, not in that jungle. Not for the deer that he was hunting, not for himself who was the hunter. Only the stronger predator would escape. The others had to face annihilation.

All these things belonged to a life where the objects were not valued merely because they were possessions. They were used, shabby, part of a life which, with all its conflicts, had stayed secure. Camille's father had brought them newly minted coins and poured them out onto their palms. The money bought nothing but was merely an extension of his love, inarticulate and undemonstrative, for his children. He would take the big iron signal lamp and slide the coloured panes into yellow, red, green, to delight them. Signals which meant a matter of life and death on those train journeys through endless tunnels. The lights had been put out and now there was no one to warn her of the impending danger from earthslips and landslides or even sabotage on the tracks. She had to find her own way. That lamp had been lost long ago.

What was she trying to sell and for what reason? Money could not replace any of these memories that would vanish with each object. In the cellaret cupboards of the Victorian sideboard there had been glass stoppered jars of lime pickle so ancient that the liquid had jelled, the limes preserved like flies in amber. The bottles of golden whisky, the deep red claret and bees honey impregnated the seasoned jak wood and left its aroma for years. The Dutch chest had been filled with childrens' clothes and Christmas decorations. Her father, her uncles, their friends had lain on the arm chairs and kept their glass tumblers of whisky in the hollowed-out niches in the wooden arms which could be slipped out. They stretched their legs and drowsed. Somnolence lay on their eyelids like butterflies drugged with nectar. But they were all ghosts now. Did she imagine that her safety lay in anything as tenuous and evanescent as memory? The cobwebs must be reft away, the dust wiped off. The wind must blow through the window, clean and fresh; new voices brought in new values which were signposts that things could not remain as they were any longer.

'You must see Jasmine's house,' said Melwyn.

'Yes, I can imagine what it is like,' said Camille, reminded of polished floors, immaculate furnishings, handmade crochet bedspreads and table cloths, handlooms of brilliant colours, choice antiques that had belonged to her father.

'My daughter,' Jasmine's father would say with his arm possessively around her. He was immensely proud of her talent and beauty, her wit and intelligence and she loved him in return. She had rented out the family home, her father's home, to foreigners. She gave a lively description of the state it had been in when she got it back:

'Of course there are advantages in renting out the house to expatriates. They pay good rents—thirty thousand rupees a month. I was able to live in a pretty good flat paying a rent of a much lesser amount. But can you imagine, my darlings, the state it was in when I got it back? The cupboards were painted orange and black, black and green and the doors were cut and slashed. Well, in twenty nine days everything was in place. Why do you think they would want to slash my doors? Well, everything was restored to what it had been before.'

That was Jasmine all over again, her nimble fingers, her mind and imagination wildly creative and yet so ordered. She preserved what was worthwhile, extending its life a little longer. She had taken the old rocking chair from Camille that was well over a hundred years old and had come from her old teacher. The children had rocked on it until it had broken. Everyone said it could not be repaired and it was cast aside. In Jasmine's home it would not be desecrated once it had been completely done up. Re-rattaned with all the broken joints mended. Jasmine had loved it.

'Take it,' Camille had said generously. The only way she could repay Jasmine's kindness, her largesse, was by giving her something that Camille herself had valued.

The rocking chair had a history behind it. Both Camille and Jasmine used history to dramatize their lives, create exotic backdrops. They needed to have something to talk about beyond the conformity that marriage and family responsibility had bestowed on them. Potter wasps, both of them. Camille felt strongly about the fact that marriage was the merging of her identity with that of another. It was important to assert and define the culture that came out of her family history. History did not belong to the archives alone. The artefacts which surrounded you in your home had meaning because they were part of life, a personalized life, one which belonged to what seemed almost a secret enclave.

Her children would have the continuance of a heritage and an inheritance, if such values did have importance in this world of theirs where the young preferred anarchy as a way out of their own confusions. Camille felt, however, that she should offer her children the choice of either accepting or rejecting this inheritance. Their identity had become a dual one—the children of parents who each came from widely diverse cultures. The names of Camille's forebears were engraved on the memorial tablets that filled the Dutch Church in Galle. Yet who would ever go in search of those ghosts, retrace those sea-routes on tattered maps that disintegrated in your hands? She, Camille, had made her own choice. She had had no map to guide her, no astrolabe, no mariner's compass for her own voyage through this life. Yet, with the same sense of adventure, of daring, as her distant forebears she had plunged to this marriage with Raj. For her this marriage had provided an entrance into an entirely new culture which would take her on altogether different routes. She would map out her own passage with each newly discovered route, face the hazards of the oceans.

While Raj spoke of the mystical experiences and

the supernatural happenings of his life in a village in the north, his own children grew up detached from their father's family whose narrow hierarchy could not contain them. They were sustained by their own independence. They surveyed with detachment the values that their dual inheritance had bestowed on them. It gave them the greater sense of compassion through their own rejection. They were largely ignored by their father's family but they missed nothing from being left out. Those others in their closed niches remained the poorer. Their wealthy aunt who was a socialite kept them completely out of her life. The rooms of her mansion were closed to them not because there was not sufficient space for them but because their presence would cause disturbance and upheaval in the hierarchical order of her way of life.

Her house was full of period pieces too. Indo-Portuguese sofas, Victorian couches, marble-topped tables, pier tables, chandeliers and English carpets. The maintainers of tradition sat comfortably on their well-padded chairs and sipped their sherry and courvoisier. They, too, were hybrids, although they did not know it. Caught between the confusion of two cultures, the westernized way of life which was part of their social circle, and the other—caste and wealth-consciousness and a deep religious-mindedness. This was not a way of life that Raj's children could accept. Like Jasmine, they drew their strength from the fact that they had a choice of identity. Where Melwyn was concerned identity did not matter at all. He could be as gregarious or as anonymous as he desired.

But what of those who worked for Melwyn in his factory? He himself wore the sweatshirts churned out by them. The girls sat day after day, cutting and sewing, going back to their boarding houses where even their sleeping areas were chalked out, where they could not even move their limbs naturally, leaving the village to earn enough money to send back to their families. Their survival depended on people like Melwyn who assumed new personalities and new identities to enable them to have an easy passage through different worlds. They were a new race of people who, with their expense accounts, could purchase pleasure, could buy over bodies and souls. Melwyn could not read his own language, those exquisite characters on the porcelain teapot, but he had the language that would help him get through all worlds, and the name that would give him the anonymity he desired.

The Picnic

The grass was wet after the rain. The fat mynahs were all over the place, feeding on the earth teeming with insects and grubs. The birds with their sleek, waxy feathers stalked through the lush green blades. Everything looked fresh, the grass springing green and thick, the leaves shining, their blue green surfaces shaking off droplets of moisture. Bushy-tailed squirrels ran along the branches. All the summer houses in the Botanical Gardens were crowded with people. The party of picnickers, some of them in the car, others in the blue truck, drove round and round the gardens, coming back to the same point from which they had started. The flowers flashed past, blots of brilliant colour. It was cool after the rain. They peered again into the summer houses. The white dome—sparkling, sugar-crusted— was occupied. So was the other by the rickety old suspension bridge.

'I used to love to run on that bridge when I was a child,' said Jasmine. 'Look, I remember that's where a woman was trying to commit suicide,' she said, pointing towards the bend in the river. At that point the river swirled and frothed. 'She was struggling in the water with her children. I was only a child. We had driven up to Kandy for a picnic. We saved her and her children. My uncles jumped into the river and brought them out. Poor woman. She had been cruelly treated by her husband. Beaten, burned with fire brands. She had no hope. We took her home and she lived with us for years. She never went back to the husband. The children, too, grew up with us. It all comes back to me now when I see the river flow at that point.'

Camille, too, remembered the story of the young poet who had died here on a picnic many years ago. The party of schoolgirls had been brought here by their teachers—they had gone down to the river to wet their feet when Sunethra had started hopping from rock to rock. No one knew whether she had actually slipped on the treacherous rocks and was drawn into the quicksands. 'The river is calling me,' she had cried out. That was all the onlookers had heard. Three times she had surfaced but there was no one to save her. It had been an ill-fated picnic. And a mystery. No one knew whether she had slipped into the water or whether she had wanted to commit suicide.

'What shall we do?' cried Jasmine. The party reached the avenue of palms and stopped. Tall, straight, stately; towering over the rest of the trees.

'Let us go and sit in the shade,' said Camille. 'We'll sit on the grass under one of those wide-branched trees.'

Canopies of shade, spreading branches, a roof of

leaves thick as closely laid tiles. Twisted, snake-like roots spread out on which ants scurried up and down in dual trails. The grass from afar appeared to be as smooth as on a well-mown lawn but when they went closer the ground was uneven with gravelly patches, knobbly humped roots, sharp wet blades of grass. They got out of the car and stretched their limbs. The blue truck stopped ahead. They all got out—Melwyn and the other Chinese, Kendrick and the children.

Kendrick stood puffing his pipe, very straight, very proper, very British. 'I say, Camille,' he said in his habitually serious tone, 'why don't you and Raj go to Nigeria? I hear they're paying teachers as much as doctors and engineers. It's a lot of money, you know, thirty, forty thousand rupees a month.'

Kendrick did not need to go out of this country. The coconut estate yielded enough profit to give them a comfortable lifestyle.

'Yes, perhaps,' Camille said, 'we should think seriously about it. Unlike you—there's no point in your going away.'

'Yes, my dear, it all fell into our laps, you know.'

They walked up to the shady trees; the girls, young teenagers, walked in a manner of stately reserve, apart from their own ebullient and extrovert elders. The young ones were careful with their emotions; almost constrained. They held back their enthusiasm and watched with an expression akin to hauteur. They were cool, aloof; they felt that Jasmine and Camille displayed an almost childish lack of reserve. The young were a critical generation, embarrassed by loud laughter spilling unreservedly from eyes and lips, although they enjoyed Jasmine's sharp satire, her uninhibited laughter, her ironical comments.

'Mummy,' Jasmine's daughter had said once in sulky petulant tones, 'my teacher is not like that at all. You just say things because you want to be funny and make everybody laugh.'

'Oh but dear, she is like that too,' Jasmine had answered with crimson face, laughter seeping through every pore. One wondered whether she could ever cry. Or ever had cried.

Beneath the trees Jasmine started to unpack the baskets of food for the picnic lunch. On the grass she laid a starched pink damask table cloth and arranged the matching pink damask serviettes beside each flower-patterned plate. She took out the large flowered flasks filled with fruit drinks, the cutlery and crockery and the food. There were four round pizzas topped with minced beef, tomato, cheese and dotted with green peas; there were vegetable pizzas, salami and egg sandwiches, lasagne, meat balls, a fish pie in a pyrex dish; plastic containers of stuffed buns, boxes of chocolate cake. Jasmine's picnic. She had worked hard to give everybody pleasure. Plates were piled with food. While they ate the tourists drove past them swiftly, skirting the blazing flowers; all these strangers hardly looking at the stately avenue of palms or noticing the brilliant bird-studded grasses. Their eyes were attracted to the group under the trees, a little private group of humans. A little island in a vast ocean of trees and grass and foliage and marooned humans. It was the briefest curiosity which helped them peer into lives of strangers and create fictions out of them. They did not need to hear what was being said. Those people could be left behind. There was no sense of responsibility towards them. One naked look in which one strips people and says: 'We are all alike, all base and beautiful and so vulnerable, but I have no time to discover you.' So they drove swiftly past and went out of those lives; intimacy would be too self-revelatory.

Melwyn, too, would go away. Unlike Jasmine and Kendrick there was no obligation, no ties of friendship. He had rejected these ties wherever he went by implying that only money had power and that this power could be wielded over people: 'You are poor, you need money. I want these beautiful things of yours but I do not value their memories. They can belong to me, they can be taken over, and then these things will be mine. They will be given a new veneer, a new polish and the imprints of your fingers on their dust can be wiped off completely. After that you can be forgotten. I see the frayed collar of your shirt and the tear in the armpit and I know I cannot afford to pity you. Nor do you ask me for pity. We will both survive in our own ways, even if it means I have lost my identity. Even if my names have been taken away and I can no longer read my own language. That is why we are in your country. You yield to us so easily, because of certain needs. We can exploit them. You let us set up our factories here and pay wages to the girls who work in them. I know they can hardly keep body and soul together, but without even that wage they would starve . . .'

After lunch Camille, Jasmine, Kendrick and the girls wandered away, leaving Melwyn, Carey and Ivan—the other Chinese—with Raj. They walked slowly across the grass. Snatches of disjointed conversation drifted across the air.

'Look, this tree was planted by the Czar of Russia. I didn't know that he had been in Ceylon.'

'The Czar of Russia? It was he who was assassinated. Yes, he's the one who was assassinated.'

'Yes, soon after the Revolution broke out. Look,

the Prince of Wales planted this.'

'And this, I'm sure, was planted by that, what's-his-name, the one who was assassinated in Bangladesh.'

They peered at the name. 'Yes, that's right. The plant is dying too. Strange, isn't it?'

The name boards stood in front of each tree, some were upright, the others crooked. In some the writing was almost effaced. Latin botanical names now as exotic and forgotten as some of the plants. They were like menu cards from a long ago banquet, the ghosts of revellers still clinging to them. The tree, the plant brought from far away, rooted in alien soil, flourished or decayed. The mynahs pecked idly among the grass blades. The Czar of Russia and the Prime Minister of Bangladesh were both dead. Forgotten events in history. Only the trees remained, put forth their leaves or shed them seasonally, bore fruit and flowers and grew with time into time.

'Do you know Kendrick wept when he heard the commentaries on the Queen's visit? He wept with emotion when he heard 'Rule Britannia'—or was it 'God Save the Queen'—played by the band,' said Jasmine.

'Kendrick, were you so overcome?' asked Camille.

A pleased smile stretched his lips and his cheeks with their firm taut skin flushed with colour.

In the orchid house they moved through the green lights, listening to the sound of trickling water. People came and went, clicking their cameras. An elusive fragrance emanated from the waxy blooms. They felt they were wandering in a cool, dark jungle. Some of the flowers looked tigerish with their dark stripes. Camille felt herself enclosed within a wall of flowers and leaves, lost in an ancient temple which stood forgotten in ruins within this proliferating forest—the grey roots stained with green; flower clusters springing out yellow, purple, orange and mauve; the dark shades of leaves.

She joined the others and walked across to the green house with its tropical foliage. Water slipped over the mossy stones, gurgling and falling into shallow pools. The great monsterras, the gigantic ferns, the velvety purple-green leaves with their thick veins grooved in crimson into the fleshy surface seemed somehow menacing; a gigantic spider's web of green in which Camille felt herself moving tentatively, knowing that she could not escape. Her insect life felt drawn along those threads to the centre, the strands shaking and trembling yet holding her strongly, not letting her go.

Suddenly Melwyn appeared, his footfall soft, passing like a pale fish through moss and water and leaves; yet a fish that had its own armoury of spiky fins and tail, the survivor in this hazardous ocean. He peered at each plant, hardly making a stir. He would be safe in any jungle, move without disturbing the masses of foliage, scenting danger and adroitly avoiding it, without stepping on the coiled serpent. He could avoid temptation.

Melwyn wanted to visit one of the greatest, the most famous painters of the country. He lived across the river Mahaweli. Melwyn loved paintings and had stood gazing at an old water colour, a still life with flowers and fruit which Camille had once painted, with a certain wistfulness in his manner. Why that air of wistfulness? He had turned round and said: 'He offered me a temple painting for sixty thousand rupees. I offered him thirty thousand.' These were skillful copies of paintings from the ancient temples in the island, done on paper in water colour.

Jataka stories with their glimpses of the world of bodhisattvas, kings, queens and ordinary humans. Their dwelling places, the patterns on their cloths. A God world and a human world.

'Did you get your painting?' Camille asked.

'No, I lost it. He sold it to someone else.'

Outside the orchid house Melwyn had stood talking to Ranee, a relative of Jasmine's, who had also come along for the picnic. Melwyn and his friends knew her well as she often provided catering services for parties and banquets organized by expatriates.

'Melwyn,' she drawled, 'I thought you said you wanted to see the paintings.'

Camille watched Melwyn's face. It did not change its expression. Bland. Imperturbable. Not to be shaken.

'No, not today. I don't see them today. If we go without an appointment, we disturb the artist. We must first inform and then go. Not proper.'

'No, it's quite all right. We can go with this lady. She knows the artist well. The others can stay in the car. I have only to mention my father's name.'

Ranee's father belonged to one of the foremost families by virtue of wealth, birth and political connections in this country.

'No, I don't go. I haven't brought money. No cheque book. We go another time.'

He walked away and looked at the gold fish in the pool. They swam, glittering in the sun as they surfaced and then disappeared beneath the leaves of the lotus flowers.

Curious, Kendrick, Jasmine and the rest of the group came up to them.

'What have you been talking about?' Kendrick asked Raj and Melwyn.

Raj smiled. 'He wants me to come and teach

English to Carey, to stay with them. There is a vacant room. I can eat Chinese food if I wish. He wants Carey to be groomed to run a restaurant in Colombo.'

'What else did he say?'

'He touched my collar and said, "A teacher's shirt. I send you shirts from my factory."'

The Return

It was no use standing in this primeval garden and looking at birds, paddy fields, the river, the mountains, the massed foliage under which flashed the dark water. Along the earth banks the garandiyas slid along, disappearing into the clumps of sword-like plants.

It was no use. They, Camille and Raj, had nothing; no share in the power they felt pressing its weight upon them. The aura of power. They had no money. People like Melwyn and others less kind would always assess, evaluate, measure and find that they did not matter in this world. Their talents, their skills were worth nothing because they could not go out into the human jungle and fight for their survival. People like themselves, whom Jasmine called the innocents of the world, would perish in the onslaught, buried under the volcanic flow that erupted, of money, money, money. They would be buried under it. The innocents of the world. All that they valued was nothing: their fine old furniture, the books, the gentleness, the desire not to hurt or wound, not to kill or take by force what belonged to others, not even to wield power over others. All this was despised. Those in power were the kings of the gameboards. And people like Camille and Raj were the pawns so deliberately set in their squares; the ivory or wooden pawns that bled as they fell, suddenly transmuted into flesh in pools of blood, while the brooding silence of the victor gave way to a grimace of delight over the discomfiture of the vanquished.

Camille thought of an acquaintance, Ananda, who reeled from shock on his return from abroad. He mumbled incoherently about the books with gold bindings, the marble-topped tables, the carriages with their horses, the land gifted by his philanthropic parents to build a convent. He had come back to find a stranger wedged firmly on his land and refusing to budge. He fell ill, went mad, spent two months in hospital. With all his philanthropic ideas he still wanted his land. But he was helpless. He would never get it. He wanted his wife, who was a doctor, to give free medicine to the poor. Don Quixote tilting against windmills.

'I leave it all to God,' Ananda had finally said. God willed it then that Ananda should relinquish all claims to his land.

'Live life from minute to minute', Kondanné Thero, the monk, had said. 'Avoid greed, hatred and delusion. It is karma. Your karma.' Kondanné Thero had changed from a man of the world who had spent years of his life in London to a Buddhist priest, having joined a Forest Order in Thailand. It had not taken him long to change. From thence he had returned to his island home. Raj had met him years later at a bus stand. They had both been friends in their youth. Now he wore the yellow robe of a monk and would not touch money even to buy a bus ticket. Yet his vision was to set up a meditation centre and, later, an ashram in the Knuckles Range on an abandoned tea estate. Lakhs of rupees would need to flow in from every part of the globe for this.

He would go on his missions, taking with him his message of freeing the mind, the spirit through meditation. The donations he received would help in the realization of his dream.

And that antique dealer who visited the home of Camille and Raj for good buys. He had once thrust out with a crude gesture his wallet bulging with banknotes and started haggling for possession of the old wooden Dutch writing desk. 'My wife says I am too softhearted,' he had said, pitying himself, 'I get taken in too easily.'

Yet, with an expert and not too gentle hand he shook the two Indo-Portuguese chairs until Camille felt the bones of ancient spectres rattling in their graves. He thrust back the bulging wallet into his pocket. It swelled out obscenely. And he went away. He had gone away empty-handed.

'See, I have brought all this money to pay,' he would say. But he bartered over the dead wood as if he was bartering for the ownership of their souls which he wanted to purchase as cheaply as possible.

They must go away, she and Raj, far away and be forgotten, yet they held back. There was always someone, something that kept them back, even more than the people. It was this landscape with its light and dark, its rocks and hills, the fields, the water, birds, wild flowers, the calm of nature that kept the storms at bay. The black ebony gleamed, polished with beeswax. The old painting throbbed with life, light shone through fine green glass, books, papers, clothes lay exposed. They didn't bother about the shabbiness. These things were priceless but no one could take them away because the money was much less in value to the happiness of living with these things, savouring their history and building wasp houses of memory on their wooden surfaces.

'Let them be,' Camille thought to herself.

'I will write to you,' Melwyn said.

Camille knew that they would never see him again. Nor would he ever write to them.

He had promised that he would go back and make up his mind whether he wanted to buy the chiffonier. He had come to their country, opened his factories where the young girls sat day after day, hour after hour at the machines which churned out expendable garments to be shipped to other faraway countries. He would soon be forgotten like all the other Melwyns of the world who filled their homes in new lands with whatever bric-a-brac they could lay their hands on.

Melwyn looked up at the tall shabbily dressed figure of Raj with pity and contempt and superiority. He admired him and despised him at the same time. Looking at the mended, frayed shirt of the schoolteacher he said: 'Yes, I will send you shirts from my factory. You come, you live in the dormitory and you teach my friends English. We will feed you and look after you. After that I open a big restaurant with Chinese food. Then my waiters talk good English. You teach them.' But Melwyn had lost even his real name. The missionary teachers could not pronounce it, so they changed it. He couldn't read his own language. He was like his friends, depersonalized.

'I say, Camille, do you know Nero's Palace?' boomed Kendrick. 'At the casino they serve you any kind of drink you fancy—champagne, cognac, courvoisier, anything; you should see the chips flying . . .'

Before they left Kendrick came up to Camille who was standing on the drive leading up to the house. She waited suspended against the late evening light to lift her hand in a gesture of farewell. Waiting for the act of waving them off and turning her face once more to the fields and the river. He stood before her, pipe clenched between his teeth, and hissed, spitting out the words: 'Sharpers, I say, these fellows are absolute sharpers.'

The words were uttered softly yet fiercely. No one else heard them. 'I'll never give anything to anyone free. Not a thing,' he continued.

Camille looked at him wordlessly. She waited patiently to turn her face away from words and from people. The water was darkening in the river. The cranes were flying homeward.

They all got into their cars and drove away. One of the uneaten pizzas which was now cold and hard was balanced precariously on the retaining wall which was giving way—a wide crack slashed across it. The earth bulged out through it, sprouting ferns. Jasmine had left the remains of the picnic feast behind. Lifting the pizza down they bore it back to the house. The green peas stuck in it seemed to stare balefully at them like small vicious eyes. Camille picked out one and bit it. It was hard, cold, unappetizing. She kept taking them out and then stuffed them back again, arranging them in a careful pattern like the disks on a gameboard. It was all that remained of the pizza and she suddenly felt that it was a leaden weight in her hands.

She looked once more at the familiar landscape before her. As the dusk thickened and the water slipped slowly through the shadows that gathered depth, the river followed its serpentine course and vanished into the distance of hidden perspectives. She knew that their faces were already receding into the darkness. They would be forgotten with time, one by one, elusive as faces in dreams that lie floating on a river of sleep, borne away by a strong current that drifts into that distant world of dark. Wakening from that dream, the sleeper throws a stone into a vague reflection that shimmers on those flowing waters. It shatters, dispersed in fragments so that there can never again be a connection between remembrance and recognition.

Prayers to Kali

I<small>T WAS MY</small> birthday. I went to the temple to make an *arichenai*. The Brahmin priest was from my village in Jaffna and we were talking about the new Vishnu statue that had been enshrined in the temple. It was a statue of the god sleeping on the coiled serpent in the Anandasayanam pose. There had been a nadhesweram *kacheri* in the temple for three nights and one of the virtuoso nadhesweram players had come with the other musicians all the way from Jaffna to play his instrument.

How different this *kovil*, this temple, in Katukelle was from that of my village, Navaly, in the north. Katukelle had once been a thorny wilderness just outside the township of Kandy, a fearful place which was dangerous after dark, without even streetlighting. Now, the teeming streets of Kandy lay outside its gates. In the inner courtyard the beggars sat and waited for alms. In the *mandapam* marriage rituals were performed.

In my village the Chintahamani Pillaiyar Temple was close to my home. The veedhi of the temple was on part of our land. My father had been the patron of the festivals and rituals in his lifetime. His sons were expected to follow suit. Last year my mother had written and asked me to be present at the *Kodiyetham* but I had not been able to go.

It was years since I had been to the village. Only part of the great house remained. In the past some of the heirs had carried away the great limestone blocks from the structure, brick by brick. I myself had no share in the family house. After my marriage my mother had written away her share in her ancestral house in Jaffna to my brother's name. The rest of the land had been divided up among my brothers and sisters. I had given up my share in the Colombo house as well. The whole house and property was given to my sister at the time of her marriage. I had made no protest. The curse of the family would have been on me for spoiling her chances of marriage. I had no longer any part in the life of my family.

In the past we had been close, like the ring of thetpai grass which had bound our fingers to that of the Brahmin priest in the sacred rituals. But with time the ring of grass had been worn away. There was nothing left to bind us any longer, even one to another.

As a child I had ranged my father's property freely. As I remember it, the palmyrah grove was dense and dark. It was a desolate uninhabited land. The mango trees budded and burst forth into blossom, fruited and fell unpicked, among the withering vembu flowers that carpeted the ground. But, having once left that land, the journey back seemed too long, too complicated and difficult to make. What could I have done with my life if I had stayed back there? We had all uprooted ourselves and gone to Colombo. Life had changed in the village. There were no paddy fields left from which a harvest could be gathered. They too had been sold at the time of my younger sister's marriage. So many people had to make so many sacrifices which even entailed taking away another's rightful share; each act of sacrifice led to the further alienation of the family. In the end everything would be in the hands of strangers.

Here, in Kandy, I walked among strangers. There was no one to call me by those familiar names of Rasa or Nainar. I stood alone at the altars of the gods, making my pilgrimage. And as I touched each part of the gods, I touched my heart, my eyes too, so that my body would become the abode of those spirits.

As I washed my feet at the tap I thought of the *kerny*, the watertap in my village, adjoining the temple. It was here that the deities were given their ritual baths at the culmination of the annual temple festivals. The rituals were long drawn out and milk, coconut water, sandalwood paste and *kumkumum* together with the juices of fresh fruit like lime were applied on the idols of the gods and goddesses before they were bathed in *theerny*. The nadhesweram, the conch and the cries of 'Haro, Hara!' heralded the event.

I rubbed one foot upon the other under the flowing water tap, washed my hands and walked up to the niches where Ganesh, Skanda, Amman and Kali looked out. The Brahmin priests were performing the poojas. My friend, the Brahmin priest from my village, Navaly, came up to me with the tray containing the split coconut halves, ripe plantain, tulsi leaves, flowers. He entered the sanctum and intoned the Sanskrit slokas. The inner room glittered with light. I glimpsed the bright gold which shone inside on the faces of Parvathi and Shiva, their bodies arrayed in brilliant silks and jewels. I prayed for the blessings of the gods for my family.

I wished I had come for the concert which was held when the Vishnu statue had been brought. My grandfather had held similar concerts in his home. In those days the artistes were given gifts of golden sovereigns for their virtuosity. All I had now was the portrait of my grandparents hanging on the walls of my home. Earrings glittered in my grandfather's ears and jewelled rings encircled his fingers. My grandmother looked out of the portrait with her heavy, inscrutable face, her *attiyals*, *padakkams*, necklaces, *mukukuththi*, bracelets, earrings. Where was all this wealth now? The jewellery had come down from generation to generation and adorned my mother and my sisters in their turn. After the deaths of my grandparents, acre by acre, house by house, the greater part of the property had been sold by my mother's guardian. Of the houses that were left, neither of them was any longer my home. There was nowhere to go back to. Now that my father was no longer alive there was nothing to take me back. I had stood on the seashore and, looking towards the land, thrown his ashes into the sea, then walked back swiftly towards the land . . .

I stood praying to Ganesh.

Our family guru had always told me that I must study; for the others in the family he had pointed a different path. We had grown apart with the years. I was never, after my marriage, ever asked to be part of the festivals. I was alienated from them by my marriage and they were alienated from me by their possessions. Like the gods and goddesses, they hardly ever stepped out of their chariots, those elaborate *chapparams* which bore them through the world. I sometimes thought they had forgotten—my mother that she had a son, the others that they had a brother.

After I had finished the *arichenai* and stood talking to the Brahmin priest, I became aware of a woman dressed completely in white who was having a long dialogue with the gods. She stood as if in a trance, rapt, before the statue of Kali with folded hands. She was a stoutish woman, middle-aged, with black hair greying slightly that was oiled and combed smoothly back and knotted into a neat *konde* at the nape of her neck. She went from god to god, burning camphor in the halved coconut which she held carefully in her hands. She was talking and talking, speaking out her troubles aloud. She didn't seem to care who heard her. I watched her. There are many like her who come to the temple not only to pray and ask for blessings but also to curse those who have hurt or harmed them. 'Destroy, destroy,' they would keep saying, 'destroy even my own flesh and blood' . . . 'protect me from their evil ways . . . .' They pray and curse together. They seek vengeance, a destructive vengeance on their own sons, daughters, in-laws. They have no resources of love or natural affection whereby they can protect themselves. Yogaswamy, our family guru, would always say: 'If you are truthful and straightforward no evil can touch you.'

The *thirtham* still tasted sweet on my tongue. The crushed tulsi leaves in the coconut half that I held were fragrant, so was the ripe plantain, its yellow skin already blackening. I rubbed holy ash on my forehead and pressed *kumkumum* and sandalwood on it. The last time my wife and children had come to the temple—how long ago it now seemed—it was during the Ther festival. It had been a very special day when a family well known to us had been the patrons. They sat round the cushioned cradle in which lay the god, rocking it to and fro, lulling him to sleep with softly sung *thevarams*. The god was tired after his journey of several nights in the outside world in which so much good and so much evil both existed. In my village, too, we had the same ceremony—the Pillaiyar god was taken round in the chariot and on the final night, weary after his long journey, he would be lulled to sleep before he went back into the temple sanctum.

The woman continued to pray. She was oblivious to all that was going on around her. Families came in, or single individuals. They prayed, they offered poojas; the priest chanted the Sanskrit slokas. The sharp sounds of the coconuts being cracked interrupted my thoughts. The fragrance of burning camphor, the smoke of incense drifted, clouding the air. People came and went but the woman remained before the Kali statue. People went round from statue to statue as if on a pilgrimage.

As I was preparing to go home she came up to where I was standing. She looked at me as if she wanted to say something.

'Why do you come to this *kovil*?' I asked her. 'To which gods do you pray?' I asked her this question because I knew she was a Sinhalese woman, a Buddhist.

'*Mahathmaya*, I come here because the gods here are powerful. I pray to Skanda, I pray to Kali. They will help me to overcome my problems and protect me from my enemies. Kali will also help me destroy those who harm me.' She began to talk about herself and her family. 'I need the help of the gods. What can I do by myself? I am surrounded by evil forces, I live in fear. There are people, my very own people, who are waiting to take everything that belongs to me. Yes, my own children, my sons, my sons-in-law, my grandchildren.'

Her voice began to grow more heated. Faint beads of perspiration appeared on her upper lip. Her eyes had an anxious, worried expression. 'My daughters have gone away to the Middle East to earn money, leaving their children behind for me to look after. I am the slave. I have to serve everybody. I have to do all the work. I do the marketing, I cook and look after my grandchildren. My children expect me to do everything for them because I am their mother and they, in turn, do nothing for me. They don't respect me or obey me. My sons do not support me. All of them are living off me.'

The coconut cracked, parted into two perfect halves in the hands of the Brahmin priest. Milky white kernel appeared. After the pooja the flesh of the coconut would be fragrant with fruit, flowers, leaves and streaked with crimson *kumkumum*.

'*Mahathmaya*,' the woman continued, talking to me as if no one else existed, talking as if this were an interlude before she returned to her dialogue with Kali. 'My daughters have gone away to earn money, but this money has ruined our family life. They use this money to make a slave of me. If they hadn't gone to earn all this money, my daughters would have carried on with their duties and responsibilities here. I have brought up eight children of my own, did anyone help me? Did I leave them in anyone's care? I nursed them, I fed them, I cared for them . .

This money has destroyed my grandchildren. They ride on their new bicycles, they are always in new clothes, they have wrist watches, they listen only to cassette music. They don't study, they loaf about everywhere. Do they ever listen to my advice? My grandson is seventeen years old. Only once did he do his examination. Now he wanders around, wearing his imported clothes and new wrist watch. He doesn't go to the temple with me on Poya day. They are all useless.'

The woman stopped for a moment to wipe the tears that trickled from her eyes. She wiped them with the *pota* of her white, starched saree. 'My son-in-law doesn't care about the children. He is a vegetable *velenda* in the market. The children spend money lavishly. My eldest grandson has stopped going to school. The mother sends all the money for them to live a life of ease while I have to work for them. I have to buy and carry baskets of vegetables from the market, grind the chillies, cook, and wash the clothes alone. There is no one to help me. I have a house of my own. It is worth two and a half lakhs. My sons want that too. They are waiting to chase me away, to grab that house. They have forgotten that I am their mother.'

The gold chain round her neck quivered slightly. She adjusted her saree carefully on her shoulder. A faint, proud smile appeared on her lips. '*Mahathmaya*, I could tell *sastraya* too. I had my own shrine room. Everybody respected me; people came to my house to hear *sastraya*. I had a big statue to which I prayed and made poojas every day. I could foretell the future.'

Her voice grew faint, her face lost its brief brightness as she continued: 'Do you know what my sons did? They smashed my statue into pieces. They crushed and ground every piece under their feet into dust . . . they tore down the pictures of all the deities on the walls of my shrine room. They laughed and laughed at me and mocked me. "Look at us," they said, "we have done all these evil things and yet we prosper. What has happened to us? Nothing. We eat meat, we drink arrack, we smashed all your statues into bits, we have a good time, we enjoy ourselves. We do all these evil things and yet we prosper. Look at you, you mad woman, visiting all the *devales*, praying, offering poojas, and see how unhappy you are."

'My children want only what they can get from me; my money, my house, my land. I'm the slave in the house. No, I won't give my house to anybody. I will hold on to it. After all, it's in my possession—my children can look after themselves. No, no, I won't give my house so easily to anyone. I am holding on to the *oppuwa*. Are they waiting for me to die? Well, till I die everything will be mine. If I sell the house now they will take everything from me and throw me out on to the road. This is the only thing I have . . . this too they want to take from me. The deeds are with me, they won't get them.'

I could not understand how a mother could feel this way towards her offspring, nor how children could feel as her's did towards their own mother. All natural feelings seemed to have been eroded; how could they all exist together under one roof in this atmosphere of hatred, suspicion, distrust?

'Look at my younger son,' she continued in her distraught way, 'he was going to marry a young girl. But what happened? He ended up living with her mother. She is an old woman. I am just a year or two older than her and she is living with my young son. And what does she do with her daughter? Gives her in marriage to the younger uncle, the mother's own brother. And my son, I am sure he is charmed—he has a stomach ailment. He cannot eat. He has all this pain. This woman is to blame. He doesn't do anything for me—he only comes and worries me for money time and time again. One day I had to make a complaint to the police—yes, about my own son.'

Had the memory of the milk she had nourished her sons with turned so easily to gall? How had they all turned against her, I wondered. I thought of my own mother. In the past she had made *arichenai* and *abishekam* for me to propitiate the gods. Had she forgotten me now as had my own brothers and sisters? Would the gods help my family to turn their faces in my direction as they once had? When I stood before Kali I too asked for protection from the forces of evil which surrounded me—but these forces of evil emanated not from my own people but from strangers who acted as if they must expend whatever evil they possessed within themselves on me . . .

The woman went on talking. Didn't she know who I was? Had she been wearied by the silence of the gods whom she spoke to so that she had had to turn to a human being once again, this time a complete stranger?

'*Mahathmaya*, every day I take *kiribath* to the temple. I give *dana*. I pray to Kali. Yes, Kali will hear my prayers . . . . Let me tell you how my prayers were answered. One day I had gone to bring my grandson from school. He was thirsty. I wanted to take him to the Brahmin hotel to drink water but he wanted his own way. He let go of my hand and darted across the road and was knocked down by a bicycle. He broke his ankle. That was his punishment for his disobedience. Oh Kali, oh Skanda, protect me.'

She continued in a tone of despair. 'The family is

broken up. My daughters have left their children. As mothers they do not carry out their duties towards their children. They are tempted by the money. In the past where did we have all these cassettes, transistors, TVs? Where did my sons ride bicycles when they were children; where did they wear imported clothes? They wore blue shorts and white cotton shirts to school. On Poya days we went to the temple. We picked flowers from my garden, araliya, jasmine, and offered them in pooja. Sometimes we went to see a picture and the whole family went together. If we left home it was only to go on a pilgrimage to Sri Pada or Kataragama or Anuradhapura. Why don't my grandchildren fall at my feet and worship me as they should? Why don't my sons obey me, respect me? Have they forgotten all the hardships I endured to bring them up? Today also, I took *kiribath* to the *devale.'*

The woman turned her eyes towards the Kali image and prayed. Kali held in one hand a sword, in the other a severed human head dripping with blood. A necklace of skulls hung round her neck. The expression on the face of the image was one of ferocity. The woman seemed to be praying for vengeance—not against unknown enemies but her own children.

People were coming and going, worshipping, lighting camphor, doing poojas. The gods watched from their niches, the lights blazed in the sanctums. The bronze and stone images, the gleaming silver and gold statues seemed to emanate a certain power. The lights flickered around the *navagraha*. The smell of burning coconut oil reached my nostrils. I loved its strong smell. I too prayed to Kali to protect me from all evil just as the soldiers in the past had done, before they went forth to battle. Kali was not evil.

Kali was strong. She was the goddess of war.

I had to step out into the crowded, teeming streets. I too had my own conflicts . . . . I prostrated myself at the entrance to the temple before I departed. I had now to think of my own problems. With a certain reluctance I left my own area of peace and calm. I hoped that the planets would be favourable for the coming year. I went out from the darkness and coolness of the temple into the blazing sunlight. The woman remained behind but before I left she came up to me and said, '*Mahathmaya*, I have spent all my money—please give me some money to go home.'

I pulled out some change and put it into her hands. '*Amme*, continue praying. Perhaps the gods will hear your prayers some day . . .'

As I walked out I saw her once more, in her hands the coconut with its camphor, standing before the image of Kali, as if her pilgrimage had only just begun.

Fragments from a Journey

Dewa STANDS ON the balcony of 'Hotell Arun' and looks out to the road before her. The starting point of their journey. A huge container passes along State Bank Road, 'FLAMMABLE MOTOR SPRIT' painted on its sides. Sprit, spirit, what did it matter anyway? The message was clear. It reached me as all messages would on this journey. I would nearly have to reread them, then all would be clear. Language would take on new, richer meanings.

All three of them, Sri, Dewa and their daughter, Anna, had wanted this journey. Each had come in search of different things. Sri had taken a vow for his daughter some years back when she had been very ill and this vow he looked forward to fulfilling by making a pilgrimage to the great Meenakshi Amman Temple in Madurai. Sri was also looking for a place where he could finally find peace. Before his marriage he had had many uncertainties. To resolve his doubts he had wanted to go away to Kataragama for a period of quiet and meditation. He had gone there on so many pilgrimages since childhood and had been inspired by the swamis and holy men who had relinquished the world and lived there, spending their time in meditation. The very thought of marriage had been daunting. To him it meant the end of a carefree student life, the taking on of new responsibilities—being a householder, bringing up a family.

'If you go away you will never make the decision to marry,' Dewa had told him. 'Remain here and grapple with your conflicts. Don't run away from them.'

Dewa was a woman who had the courage to change. For her, marrying into a different culture, a different community, held no fears. Her ideas were eclectic. Sri was different. He was, in a sense, timid, unprepared for the commitment that marriage entailed. He had lived, up to that time, in the sheltered environment of a tradition-bound Hindu enclave. His people had not mingled freely outside the enclave. And he was reluctant to face the enormous changes that were inevitable if he married outside his community.

Finally, though, he paid heed to Dewa's suggestion. He did not make that pilgrimage to Kataragama and married Dewa against all opposition. Years of married life had given him the strength to live as a good husband and father. Now, many years later, he was making this journey to one of the most ancient temples in India, and he thought of it as a long deferred pilgrimage. Only this time his thoughts were not about staying on but returning here after fulfilling his responsibilities as a householder. Here perhaps he could spend his last days in peaceful meditation. But there was time enough for that yet. The presence of Dewa and Anna drew him back to the world. He would return once more with them to the island, to Sri Lanka, from where the journey had begun.

Anna, his daughter, was in between two journeys. She had returned from the States where she had been away for one year studying in a College in the sea port town off Maine. She had returned home but found that her sojourn had been incomplete. She could not settle easily into the life she had come back to and was going back. But before she re-embarked on that journey she had this most profound wish to go to India, as if she felt that she might move too far away from a world that she might never return to. But here, in this country, she needed a guide—her father. Both she and her mother needed him. They had to travel great distances, thousands and thousands of miles from city to city, from temple to temple, and Sri could speak, often, the language of the people; he could translate and interpret for them and make their passage easier. And when they wanted to be silent they could be silent, each with his or her own thoughts, retreating into their private chambers, their inner sanctums.

Dewa herself had returned from the West where she had been living alone away from her family, self sufficient and fending for herself. To return home was important. But once she returned her confusions grew and she felt her strength ebbing away; a traveller at the crossroads, not knowing which route to take. For her the rank undergrowth of tangled roots and matted creepers grew overwhelmingly close about her and her skin felt bruised, grazed by red-tipped thorns that clutched at her. Her skin had grown too sensitive in the West. It had changed colour. Her voice had grown muted. Even the colour of her clothes had changed. In the West she had worn sombre blacks, beiges, browns. The food she ate was bland but it had nourished her. In her own country she had to taste once more the flavours she had lost, she had to see and touch the colours and textures of leaf and plant and flower that would have blinded her with their brilliance in those cold, grey streets. Her daughter had wanted her to come to India and Dewa too had felt that she had to go to that country where she had been so many times, that it would help make the hard and difficult passage of her return easier. She longed to go on this new journey to touch, to taste, to feel. She wanted her senses to come alive. It would not matter here if she were among strangers. She would be a transient, a pilgrim, a traveller.

Here, then, at this point, in a hotel room on State Bank Road, in a family room with three comfortable beds, blank walls, an attached bath, a washbasin in the alcove and a little balcony with potted roses and bougainvillea, the journey begins. The room is impersonal, vaguely western in its decor. The hotel itself is neutral except for the strange spelling— Hotell Arun. From its windows can be seen the plush Five Star Hotel Rajaliya. At night both hotels are ablaze with coloured lights.

When Dewa steps out on to State Bank Road she sees into the lives of families in their thatched and woven dwellings. They have the minimum of furnishings and furniture. Cool, smooth-floored, with rolled up mats and cooking vessels, the alponas drawn at the entrance. Bared open to the onlookers gaze, there is nothing to hide. No one would want to take their simple belongings. A mat to sleep on. Vessels for water, for cooking. These people are no refugees. This is home for them. It is they, the three of them, wandering along these streets, who are refugees but they cannot pitch their tents here. They are passersby. The sacred cows stand in the wasteland on the outskirts of the township, feeding on the refuse that is thrown there. The flies buzz and rise in clouds. All life is sacred here and nothing interferes with it. The cows wander freely about the streets and the black swarms of flies savour the sweet cane syrup, the fruit and the sweetmeats as freely as humans do—the people on the streets of Tiruchy or Dewa or Anna or Sri.

Dewa walks into the bathroom for the rituals of cleansing. The day must begin like this. She wakes early, the call to prayer from the muezzin and the Hindu *thevarams* from the temple fill the whole city with waves of sound. There is no contradiction, no argument between gods and prophets, only reminders of man's sinfulness and his need for both hope and penance. In the heart of the town, at Main Guard Gate, there is an impressive church, but the sound of its bells does not reach as far as their hotel room.

A room becomes home for them. It is here that they renew themselves for the next strenuous exploration. At Madurai it is difficult to find accommodation. College House is where they want to be, the buildings set within a green quadrangle, but there is no room. Another hotel nearby is recommended to them. The proprietor is very polite, asks them to first go up the lift and inspect the room to see whether it is to their satisfaction. The lift does not work. They go up the stairs. Their decision is made, all they want is to stretch out, rest. The fan stirs the sluggish air above them. The room has just been vacated, the linen not yet changed. Sri lifts the telephone and begins to make what will be the first in a series of calls to the manager.

'Please change the linen. Send someone please.'

'Yes sir, now he will come.'

Little boys in shorts, barefooted, who look as if they have just been lifted off the streets, run about the corridors. Sri rings again.

'No one has come to change the linen.'

'Yes sir, now it will be done. We are waiting for the laundry to come.'

Dewa has seen where the laundry is ironed. Men spread out the clothes on the padded surfaces of their wooden carts in the streets and wield their irons. Streets which teem with life. Open stalls heaped with bags of grain, of jaggery moulded into coconut shapes. Streets with open drains in which black pigs wallow like huge bandicoots. Crowds gather beside a tree where a miracle has taken place. Milk exudes from its trunk. People have decked it with offerings of flower garlands and saffron cloth while the Brahmin priests chant Sanskrit slokas and offer poojas to the tree. Dewa thinks of the temple sculptures, of the goddesses that wind their limbs around the trees, cling to the fruit- and flower-filled branches. Anywhere on the street can be found temples, shrines, gods. Here you can pray, do penance, engage in barter and trade. There is no one to interrupt your private pilgrimage. But you must have a room where you can close the door, finger your thoughts like prayer beads as you recollect, meditate.

The room boys are scuttling all over the place, little boys who fetch and carry, going up and down in lifts with flasks and water jugs and bedding, but there is no one to actually do what you really need to get done. The room is hot and close. An extra bed is needed. Here, in this country, a little space can be shared by many. A double room can be easily converted into a family room. It does not matter how many members belong to that family. Space is an extension of the mind, so that you can fill it with the dimensions of your thoughts or with as many manifestations of your being, of your self as you wish. You can generate sakti, the female principle, and become Parvati, or Uma, Bhairavi, Ambika, Sati, Gauri, Kali or Durga and Kailasa will accommodate you and all your offspring. There is space here for all these manifestations. But Sri, Dewa and Anna need that extra bed. There is no difficulty, people accept that you have needs; Dewa has learned that much so far on this journey.

A room has four walls; you can do as you please within them. The room belongs to you while you are here and there are no inroads on your most sacred privacy. It is the inner sanctum of the temple, while the crowds mill around the courtyard and jostle you in the great halls.

'Yes, yes,' the manager says, 'we can provide extra bed. You pay a little more. Sixty-five rupees for double. Fifteen rupees more for bed.'

'Where is the bed?' Dewa asks. 'Where are you going to put it?'

'We will bring now.'

After a long wait a bed is brought. It is a soiled, stained mattress with soiled, stained pillows. The linen is soiled too. Other pilgrims, other transients have left the impress of their memories, as if their reluctant psyches still remain.

'Who can sleep on this?' Dewa demands.

'This is a bed.'

'Please take it away.'

More telephone calls.

235

Repetition becomes wearying. Finally another mattress is brought with some pillows. They accept it. There is no use protesting. Going along the outer passage Dewa sees a small room where the dirty mattress has been flung down. These are not mattresses for guests. They are for any room boy who can snatch a moment of sleep here. A tired boy sleeps as if it is the most comfortable place in the whole world.

The view changes at night. Dewa peers through the narrow apertures of the hotel windows. She can't have enough of these glimpses into the unknown life that lies beneath her. In the West everything had been closed in, shut in. There was always privacy—locked doors, subdued voices. People there walked with closed faces. Here, everything is open, naked, exposed. Life seethes everywhere. From one corner she looks down on the kitchens of an eating house. A bare-bodied man brushes his teeth at the water tank on top of the flat roof. Another man dips clanging buckets into it to carry water down to the kitchen. There is much hustling and bustling going on down there. Barebodied men, barefooted, their veshtis tucked up, are fetching water, chopping, cutting, peeling, cooking, washing. They move quickly and lithely through the confined space of the small wood-partitioned room. Basins and pails, enormous cooking utensils fill up with all kinds of meats. Mutton for kofthas, chicken for tandoori. One man squats down on his haunches and with a long sharp knife peels and chops some long tubers, manioc yams perhaps. Smoke rises into the air as the food cooks on great wood fires. The men, talking volubly, carrying utensils from one room to another, work throughout the night. The kitchen floor is wet, they are barefooted, but it doesn't mean anything to them.

To and fro, to and fro they move from kitchen to outer rooms lifting cauldrons of cooked food. In another building an old man massages oil into the arm of a young man, smoothly and deftly kneading the aching flesh. The shelves of his little room are covered with bottles of different oils which he pours into the cusp of his palm. Rhythmically, with long swipes, he patiently rubs the oil in. Other rooms reveal clotheslines strung across and rolled up bedding. From the open passage that fronts the rooms Dewa looks down on rows of bathrooms. They are only for men, who spend hours brushing teeth and performing their ablutions, water splashing on their bodies as they pour bucket after bucket on themselves. This is part of their ritual, pouring water over head and body, something she always missed in Europe.

They travel by night to Bangalore. They leave Hotell Arun at 8.30 p.m. and drive along straight roads with carefully planted avenues of shady tamarind trees. They pass through townships and villages on the way, villages that come alive as soon as the bus blasts its trumpet horn. Huddled figures wrapped in shawls disengage themselves from the shadows. The lights are bright in the little eating houses. The kaapi maker busies himself, the tumblers and *lotas* are arranged before him. The milk is boiling hot. The sugar dissolves instantly in the hot milk and kaapi. On a heated aluminium sheet food is sizzling, rotis are flipped over repeatedly to bake evenly; a passenger from the bus stands beside it, getting the onions sliced fine while condiments and spices from various bottles are sprinkled on the mixture. Everything is fried in one corner of the baking sheet. In another corner meat is being stirred about with a metal spoon, all this is then piled onto a plate and the roti cut up to be eaten with the fried onions and meat at one of the tables inside.

Calls of nature are answered in little alleyways. From a huddle of huts covered figures drift out. 'Don't come this way,' an old woman wrapped in a shawl calls out, 'the wind blows the odour in the direction of our houses . . . go elsewhere.' People vanish into the shadows and are almost left behind till a blast of the horn brings them rushing back to clamber in. The bus sets off. A young man's parcel of rice spills out. He is imperturbable, sits with a blank face, staring ahead as if the rice does not belong to him. The squishy mess lies at his feet. Not a single passenger grumbles or complains. The young man is clad in western attire—blue jeans and T-shirt—his hair is oiled and brushed, his moustache neatly trimmed. He detaches himself from the packet of rice that his mother must have packed for him. The conductor says, 'Will you keep your mother's house in this condition?' The young man pretends not to hear. He is embarrassed. Later on, very carefully, he cleans up the mess and throws it out. Very little fuss is made. A man's pride and self respect are preserved.

They arrive in Bangalore in the early hours of the morning after the long night-journey from Tiruchirappalli, four hundred and fifty kilometres away. They have spent eight hours in the bus. Alighting at dawn when all is veiled in a mist, they see ghost figures under the feeble glow of street lamps through the chill haze, Amrita Sher Gil figures standing like wraiths covered with blankets and shawls. Where do they go now? This is a journey without carefully planned routes. But they must know where it is that they have arrived before they set out to discover the reality of treading on this soil which seems already to be losing its firmness, slipping away from under their feet so that the steps they take towards they know not where are tentative and uncertain. They trust to luck, confident that lodging houses and hotels will open their doors to them automatically. They walk across the bus station through a silent street and up the steps of the first lodging house they see. They enter through the open door. People are sprawled on the ground or are untidily asleep on scattered divans.

'Can we have a room?' Sri asks. 'Single, double, family?'

'No vacant rooms. All full.'

They drag their bodies down the steps. A figure disengages itself from the shadows on one of the steps where it sleeps huddled up.

'I take you to hotel. You want? Come.'

'Where?' they ask.

'Come, I take you. Here.'

They follow his young slight figure wrapped up in a blanket. He lopes along through the street, takes them to a brightly lit building. 'SALEEM'S TRAVEL AGENCY.' They are ushered in, greeted, welcomed, offered seats. Tumblers of hot chai are brought in from one of the hotels outside. They long to sleep, to find a room where they can close the doors and fling themselves down on some mattress. But it is not easy, not with Saleem. He has inexhaustible energy. He flashes a smile of great charm at them.

'Sister, please sit, you can have double room. No family room. We can put extra bed. You pay fifteen rupees extra for bed.'

'Can we go at once?'

'Sister, now please sit. At six o'clock only you have room. Till then sister, sit, please sit. You can also take our tours. Bangalore, Mysore, Ooty.'

They sit with other weary travellers like themselves. There is a big placard on the wall before them advertising the tour: 'TOUR TO MYSORE, SEATS SOLD OUT, SPECIAL SEATS RS 100/-'.

Dewa decides to take all the tours, preferring the easy way out. The bill is written out and presented at once. Saleem is happy. They take one step nearer the room. The room is no longer maya, illusion. They feel they are already in it, each sleeping like Vishnu on the serpent Ananta.

'Don't be a fool,' Anna hisses under her breath to her mother. 'They are going to play you out.'

'We have changed our minds. We will not take the tours. Perhaps one, to Brindavan,' Dewa says weakly, placatingly. Faces fall, enthusiasm wanes. Mr Saleem had appeared to be so friendly and co-operative at the beginning. Flashing his gem-studded ring and brilliant white smile at them, he had promised to communicate in whatever language they wished. 'Urdu, Gujarati, Kannada, Tamil, English. Sister, I know all languages. I am an international,' he had said. Now he grows silent. He appears not to see them. They are ignored. Others who have promised to take Saleem's tours fly off in their trishaws to hotel rooms. Sri, Dewa and Anna are left behind. The trishaw drivers are huddled at the door waiting for their hires. Clad in tattered cardigans against the cold. Rubbing their hands, stamping their feet. The guide has vanished into the shadows. Mr Saleem is disappointed, very disappointed in them. They know intuitively that they will not get a room. No tour, no room.

Saleem decides to give these reprobates yet another chance. He inclines his head towards Sri. 'Sir, can I have a word with you? You are taking tour with us?'

'No,' Dewa answers for her husband. 'We prefer to make our own explorations. All we want is a room.'

Saleem remains silent and unsmiling. They decide to leave Mr Saleem's little haven. They climb into a trishaw. The thin young guide who suddenly appears is pushed aside by a burly individual, one of Mr Saleem's guides, who prepares to get in.

'No, no,' they protest. 'We want him, we want our first guide, the young one.' The guide is scolded in Kannada but he manages to get in, strengthened by their insistence.

'Let's try Saleem's hotel anyway,' Dewa says.

Sri is led up the stairs. Of course there is no room. The telephone call has not reached. No tours, no rooms.

'I will take you to another hotel,' their guide says. 'There is Voyshella Hotel.'

'Where?'

'We go there now. Come.'

They begin to drive crazily through unknown streets. They are lost. They know it. But Bangalore is beautiful in this early light. Wide streets flash by. Rows of shady trees spread their branches protectively over the straight clean roads. They glimpse houses set in spacious gardens. They pass by several hotels. The trishaw driver does not stop. 'Voyshella,' he insists. 'Other hotels, common bathroom.'

'Voyshella expensive?' they ask.

'About hundred fifty rupees per day,' he answers.

'Too expensive for us. Take us to that hotel, that tourist hotel. That's good enough for us.'

The trishaw driver is now angry but he stops and they get off at 'Hotel Tourist'.

'Pay me double fare,' he says.

'Why?' they ask.

'Before six in morning you pay double. Night fare double.'

'But we left after six. Rooms are vacated only after six.'

There is a loud argument. The young guide is guilty and silent. He does nothing to protect them.

'You are to blame for all this,' Dewa says, turning on him. They are all pent up. The trishaw driver is belligerent.

'All right, then you take me to police.'

The other occupants of the hotel come out into the corridor and look on.

'I took them long way,' the trishaw driver says.

'What, Saleem's Tours is at the next corner. Very close,' says one gentleman.

'Look,' said Dewa, 'we are tired. You don't even want to give us a room. The receptionist says that there are no vacant rooms. We are being cheated all the way. We are your guests in Bangalore. Everything was fine in Tamilnadu. We expect hospitality. After all, your country and ours, aren't we neighbours? All right, pay him at least part of what he wants— they're poor aren't they? And we are green horns, easy to take for a ride.'

The trishaw driver takes his money and disappears. They turn to the young guide. Sri pays him extra. He is so young. He has been sleeping in the cold. No room for him. It is his karma. He is so much like one of those tender dawn-wrapped Sher Gil figures.

'Why did you take us to Saleem's?' Dewa asks him sadly.

The heavy key is handed to them at last. There are vacant rooms. Several. Safe at last. The first thing they have are hot baths. It is all there, and also predictable—the big brass tub, the hot water, the brass *chembu*. They feel cleansed once more. The hotel is old-fashioned and conservative. The beds are narrow four posters with rock hard pillows. They are thankful for this room which appears to cater only to Hindus. The walls of the corridors are full of photographs of the founder of the hotel and on one wall of the room hangs a framed set of rules and regulations. There are indeed lots of vacant rooms but the receptionist had been so wary of taking in strangers and 'foreigners' like themselves. And their entrance had been so dramatic, unannounced, with no booking.

The hotel is full of interesting people. Mostly men. They are all very friendly and very lonely. They want to talk. There is a famous film director from Kerala. A film photographer. A police officer who speaks openly of corruption in politics, of the Indira Gandhi assassination, of the death of Sanjay Gandhi, of the Sikh problem, of his family and of the Sri Lanka-India cricket match that is going on. He has a long moustache and is a tall handsome man. An old army batman looks after him and brings him trays of food. There are lots of students about. Everybody is talking cricket. Sri makes friends with everyone but Dewa must not be overfamiliar. Ladies are expected to observe a certain decorum. They do not talk freely to gentlemen in this society. Everybody seems to be walking perpetually along the open corridors, calling out cricket scores and listening to the commentaries on the transistors they hold to their ears.

Anna falls ill—high fever, headache. They search desperately for a doctor. He gives her antibiotics. He is very happy that Anna is his first patient for the New Year. His premises have only two rooms but it is called a Nursing Home. The nurse talks only in

Kannada. The doctor keeps describing his own experiences of by-pass surgery. Anna comes back to the hotel and sleeps most of the time, is fed oranges, grapes. Dewa misses a step on a broken cement staircase as she hurries down to catch the tourist bus to Mysore at six o'clock in the morning and sprains her ankle. She has felt disorientated, disturbed by Anna's illness and woke up at midnight to start getting ready. It was with relief that she had gone back to sleep. Punctuality has become ingrained in her after her years in England.

Dewa is the first passenger in the bus. The bus drives round and round the city collecting other passengers. Blazered students from an Indian College fill the back seats. A small boy is with his parents. By the end of the journey he becomes very difficult and calls his mother a 'bloody basket.' A pleasant nun from Aurangabad sits next to her. It is difficult to imagine that there are convents in a Muslim stronghold like that city—but one does exist. Though the nun is herself from Bombay. She is the only child of elderly parents. When she decided that her vocation was to be a Roman Catholic nun, they had accepted her decision without demur. As soon as the bus takes the road to Bangalore the videos begin. What one sees is the impossible, the fantastic; maya, illusion, is part of the accepted reality in this country. What you see, you believe actually happens: incredible battles, warfare that wipes out whole armies, conflicts from confused ideologies, and love, ideal and romantic, with lovers who sing to each other with the bravura of operatic singers. The heroines are impossibly noble, ever ready for death and sacrifice. And in defeat there is total destruction. Yet another video is switched on when the first one is over—a villain is portrayed, the tyrant of the village who has the power of life and death over people, tortures his enemies, wrests children from parents for obstructing his passage through the streets of the township in his chariot. The heroine is tortured. She slides down a chute into a room where she is imprisoned. Enormous crabs creep out from every corner as she lies helpless; they crowd round her, scuttle over her body. She shrieks in fear and pain but does not die. She is rescued by the hero in the nick of time and the villain finds himself there in her place. He is not rescued. The students adore it. The rest of the passengers are spellbound. Clapping, cheers, greet these heroic feats. Some passengers wipe tears from their eyes.

They stop to visit the gumbaz of Tipu Sultan, Fatima Begum, Hyder Ali. Sightseers of history, of time, viewing all that is left, monuments and ruins.

'How was Tipu Sultan killed?' Dewa asks the guide. He mentions two names, one of them is that of Captain Harry.

'This place Tipu Sultan body found,' he continues. He points to a grassy spot with a brick wall that is in ruins.

Am I to view history only as a tourist—no, it cannot be, Dewa can't help thinking to herself. Anyone who has had some involvement in that whole colonial experience can only see himself or herself as having been there, part of it all, having held the sword in one's hands or the flint lock, seen those cannon fired that razed a civilization to the ground. For this one tomb, for this one deathspot in a desolation of weeds, there are thousands and thousands of nameless graves and a thousand Captain Harrys. Looking at the others, Dewa sees even the Indians with her as tourists within their own country with its vast distances and diverse languages.

Everything changes on these journeys—food, clothes, religion, dialects, the very air that is breathed, the fruit and flavours. Ambrosia is here to taste but you must not wait too long—the thin-skinned plantains spoil, the grapes ferment, turn sour and the flies buzz over their early decay. The freshly-skinned papaw reveals its succulent and thirst-quenching golden flesh, the sapodillas are honey sweet. Here with all their fruit—the apples with their *kumkumum* streaks, the juice-filled oranges—you too can partake of the *theertham*, the offerings to the gods.

Going into Mysore is going back into history. Everywhere in the city colonialism has left its impression on the administrative buildings, on the churches, on the bungalows. They have impressive facades yet they are touched with a certain melancholy, the green mould and fungus of time, the peeling plaster and the sense that these are monuments of an age that one would not even wish to remember. Yet, side by side with the race course, the golf club and the boating club are the ancient fortresses, tombs, temples and shrines. One culture is juxtaposed with another. Even on the road to Thanjavur the graffiti on the walls had read: 'Hindi Never English for Ever'. And everywhere, processions of bicycle riders carrying flags with slogans on them and lorry loads of youthful political supporters of the Congress party filled the road.

Bangalore and Mysore are towns full of ghosts, full of monuments. They still bear that aura of a vanished colonialism. Amongst the sandalwood trees, the crisp cool air, the glittering temples and the great stone sculptures of Nandi, the spires of churches and Christian colleges reveal a different kind of reality. Here, colonial rule ceased to be alien, took root in brick and language.

The guide goes on and on in the bus, speaking his part. 'Now we come to place named Mysore. You stop fifteen minutes. No delay please.' He rattles off a number of facts. The students first take notes. Then they get bored. They prefer the video. They refuse to pay him the extra rupees for additional information which he offers to give.

'Two rupees more you give me for telling about hydraulic feats in Brindavan Gardens.' There is an altercation here. 'Why should we pay him extra? Already we have paid him at the beginning of the journey,' the lecturer from the Indian college says. He is a fair-complexioned, placid-looking man who appears to be immensely popular with his students.

'We could not understand a word also of what he was saying.'

The guide gets very angry when the students raise their voices. He turns upon them and berates them. 'You are students. Pin drop silence.' The students pay him no regard. He continues giving his instructions unperturbed. 'You must be punctual for homeward journey. If you not come in time, we leave you behind. No buses back to Bangalore also that time. Town also many miles away.'

Dewa is in dreadful pain after her fall but how can she miss walking through Brindavan Gardens. It is a world of water, green grass lawns and flowers, and Indian families taking in the air. There are no solitary Indians here. Dewa keeps company with the plain, down to earth Indian nun from Aurangabad. They share biscuits and sweets. She doles out money to a younger nun who escapes on her own most of the time. 'She loves gardening,' she says as the young nun is seen far away, lost in a pavilion on a grassy knoll surrounded by flowers. Dewa's nun friend has an upset stomach. She eats only buttered bread for lunch in the restaurant to which the guide takes them. Dewa talks to her about Aurangabad as she and the others eat naan and biryani.

'We have a shortage of water,' the nun says.

Dewa has memories of Aurangabad, of shehnai music trickling through the night-silence and gypsies singing round their fires. Then too, a young guide, as young as themselves, had taken them to the Ellora caves to walk among the sculpted deities of Kailasa. He had been a graduate of history. Dewa and Sri had stayed in an old hotel. It had a courtyard with a lotus covered pool and four poster beds. There had been a young couple there who sat beside the fountained pool for hours. They were newly married. They must be middle-aged now, thinks Dewa, far away like myself from the music of the shehnai and the gods of Kailasa.

Busloads disgorge their families in the Brindavan Gardens. The ladies are attired in rich silk sarees with gold lace and *butis* of gold and silver scattered over diaphanous folds. They wear necklaces and earrings of gold and their wrists are covered with bangles. Dewa feels strange, an outsider in her cotton Sambalpur saree. She has not taken enough pains to be lost in a crowd, to be as grand as the others are, attired in silks and jewellery. She has even forgotten the vermilion *pottu* and the *sindhur*. For the first time, she feels foreign, strange and conspicuous without these ritual ornamentations.

The ladies drift like stalked flowers among the arching jets that criss cross and dazzle in the late afternoon light gently changing to softer evening shades. Poor children with garlands in their hands run up to elegantly dressed ladies with sweet-smelling jasmines. This is a country of flowers.

The fountains flash like shooting stars. Water

glides and spills over steps or lies calm in lotus covered pools. As it grows darker the coloured lights begin to flicker through the jetting sprays, green, violet, crimson, gold. A stream of people surges over the bridge. The coloured lights touch their faces so that they appear to be mirages that lie beyond the green grass lawns. Dewa watches from afar and sits talking to one of the party who has been on a scholarship to Germany. Watching the people eating at the stalls from the piles of food, he is reminded of the canteen at his workplace in Aurangabad. The young men, he says, order different dishes, everything that is on the menu, then grumble about the food and leave the dishes virtually untouched, wasting all the food.

'Why?' Dewa asks.

'They don't have to pay for it. It is all subsidized. These young men take the attitude that it is their right.' The food stalls here are piled with vadai, samosas, pakoras, kadalai, murukku, idli, and the people stand around drinking tea and kaapi and fruit juice. The nun and Dewa drink fresh grape juice and eat kadalai.

It is time to go back to Bangalore. The students ignore the guide's warning and wait until they have had their fill of the coloured lights of Brindavan. Dewa and the nun settle down to wait patiently until every student has returned.

On the bus journey back, the videos appear on the screen again to keep the students quiet.

Dewa is the last passenger to get off the bus when they reach Bangalore. It is late. There are no women in the street at this hour. She hurries back to the hotel as quickly as possible. It is only the Indian male who is out this late. The streets are silent.

In Madurai a Brahmin with a *poonool* across his

shoulders leads them through the crowds at the Meenakshi Amman Temple. Crowds of devotees within the inner buildings wait in long queues to offer poojas in the sanctum. Bands of pilgrims walk together, wearing black veshtis with orange shawls on their shoulders, their torsos lithe and wiry. They are followers of Ayanar and they go from temple to temple, walking with a peculiar swagger of their hips. Wild black hair tumbles about their foreheads, prayer beads click round their necks. They walk barefooted, treading the pathways of their pilgrimage.

It is sweltering inside the great temple. Sri carries the pooja offerings in his hands—the coconut halves, sacred herbs, bananas, flowers, packets of *kumkumum*, incense, camphor and holy ash. These are bought for eight rupees at the entrance to the temple or at the place where tickets are bought to keep sandals and shoes safe. The soft pilgrim-trodden stone feels almost buttery underfoot like the ghee that flows from the brimming oil lamps. The press of bodies around them is suffocating. Dewa wants to feel with her whole being that the experience affects her spiritually but she can feel nothing. All she can feel is this sense of admiration for the perfection of the sculpture and architecture that surrounds her; she draws breath at those sculpted forms of gods, the idealized human figures that some anonymous artists have so perfectly realized. Their faces she has seen around her on the streets; the ordinary men and women whom she walks with have the faces of deities. She feels closer to them than to the gods and goddesses. The world is her heaven; here, she prays, makes vows, does penance.

The Brahmin with the *poonool* leads Sri and Anna away from her into the inner sanctum. The devotees are full of *bhakthi* and one man is so overcome that he edges himself into the shadows and prays and prays, refusing to move until the priest hits him and chases him away.

One must find God, then, in other places, quieter places, where there are fewer people, Dewa thinks to herself. In that case, perhaps all temples with their inner sanctums exist only within oneself. But many need to be with others when they pray so that *bhakthi* flows from one to another, a giant ocean that engulfs them.

Dewa is separated, momentarily, from her family. She stands among the heavy pitted outer stone pillars and looks down on the *kerney* empty of water. Groups of people are being led by their guides, Indians from all parts of the country and a scattering of foreigners. The experience of the West seems so far away. Here she feels at home, an accepted part of the crowds, the colour of her skin does not single her out as an alien. She feels, looking around her, that she can be anything here, part of a pillar, or an ancient sculpture from the past, or even a flower already wilting that lies within the coconut half that is smeared with holy ash and incense. She feels a pang of sadness, a loneliness as she remembers her past in that other country with its seasons of spring, summer, autumn and winter, and calls out silently the names of friends whom she has left behind as if she would wish the gods to keep them in their memory, perhaps even to protect them.

She is summoned by Sri to another part of the temple as if the centuries old gods are impatient to meet her. Here within this pillared hall the poojas go on and on as if the deities are under some compulsion to give ear to the Sanskrit slokas that are being intoned by the priest. The camphor splutters and a cloud of incense rises as they touch the heat and light from the *aalathi* to their eyes and pray with folded hands and bowed heads to the flames that spring up and burn so steadily. The gods are safe here within their sanctums and for Sri and Dewa and Anna too there is a feeling of safety. There is worrying news from the south, across the waters, of bombs going off in streets and railway stations. But for now, for this moment in time, they establish a connection with the ancient glittering gods within the safety of this sanctum, gods decked in silks and jewels and garlands. Day in and day out the Brahmin priests carry out the poojas, their entire lives lived according to rituals—the plants they see are those that lie within the coconut halves, the *kumkumum*, red as blood, spilled on the white fleshy kernel. They do not walk on the streets of Madurai as the people do, among the dead rats with bloodied mouths that are flung on the pavements. Sri, Dewa, Anna along with all the others, have to walk along these streets, prepared to risk any kind of pollution because it is part of human life. Yet the priests are there to lead the penitents along the paths to salvation on this brief pilgrimage.

Sri, Dewa and Anna propitiate the *navagrahas* and light the *aalathi*, watching the flame that bursts out of an oil-soaked wick like a glittering flower— the air shimmers with its light and then it burns out to a blackness. Butterballs exquisitely shaped like pearls spilling out of oyster shells, float on the surface of water vessels. Each pearl is flung onto the body of Durga. Durga, the ten armed goddess, each arm with a weapon. In one hand she holds the lance which pierces the heart of the conquered demon, the demon who has changed form often—first a buffalo, then an elephant and finally the giant with a thousand arms. Her right foot rests on a lion and her left is placed on the demon's neck. They continue to hurl one butterball after another onto the body of Durga. The butterballs swirl past her, hurled through what appears to be a cosmic space, to disappear into annihilating darkness. Some of these white pearls splatter on Durga to bloom incandescently—a strange prehistoric moss that clings like mould to the stone. Dewa stands before Shiva. She feels the force of motion in the tandava dance. It is an act of cosmic creation. Shiva both destroys and creates, and from this act emerges the absolute. The air seems to quiver with a rush of movement as he raises his foot and sets in motion the cosmic functions of creation, the symbol of divine activity, the source of all movement in the universe.

It is an endless pilgrimage that seems to be taking place in the streets of Madurai, from one temple to another. The streets are alive with people moving, eating, cooking food. At an outdoor stall huge vessels are filled with different kinds of rice— tamarind-flavoured, plain white rice and saffron rice. People sit on benches at long trestle tables and eat off banana leaves relishing their hot food with sambara, curd, chutneys and ghee. Men sit before pans of sizzling oil in which fritters are frying; bananas in batter, crisp and golden brown, lie spread out before them. The metal ladles turn over the fritters in the frying oil. The crowds surge through the narrow streets and with them Sri, Dewa and Anna are drawn compulsively along with no destination in mind. A wooden cart is filled with pyramids of fried fish, a woman in a blue cotton saree with glittering *mukukutthi* stands behind it. Her little daughter assists her in selling the fish. She holds up a fried fish and dangles it like a mobile before their eyes. Customers carry parcels wrapped in leaves from her stall.

They go into a Muslim restaurant and eat hot samosas with fruit drinks and kaapi. Little saucers of lightly roasted cumins are placed on the table to aid digestion.

You cultivate, Dewa thinks to herself, a taste for what is unusual, savour it as if it is something you must add to the experiences of your palate, tasting just a little more of the great cauldron of flavours that emerge from this continent, changing constantly, teasing the senses, making you take pleasure in what, in a different life, might even repel you, so that you feel that even in this tinge of bitterness that lays its aftermath on your tongue, there is more, there must be more delight than in the predictability of sweetness.

They search for more food, sit down and eat hot dosai, crisp and light, plain or masala—filled with onions and potato—with chutney from some white seed finely ground, and sambara. They ask for coffee. Two stainless steel *lotas* are brought in so that the hot milk and kaapi can be poured from one utensil to another to reach that perfect mixture of hotness and sweetness. They enjoy the food, say it is excellent. This is conveyed to the proprietor of the restaurant. He comes and sits at their table.

'I am not so satisfied with the dosai today. It can be better,' he says.

'No, no, we find it very good,' Sri remarks.

The waiter wants to talk.

'I am from your country. My father was a milk vendor there. I know Pettah, Kayaman's Gate. Maybe I will come back, one day.'

There is a certain feeling of regret, of homesickness that these exiles seem to bear. Many come up to them and say, 'We were once there in your country. We remember. Come and see us. Have a meal with us.' It is as if they too want to join them on that return journey to an island they had once lived in. A country better known, more familiar than the place they now live in. Yet it is within the ambience of this very strangeness that new discoveries and explorations must be made. Perhaps that once easily acquired familiarity has grown so stale that there are no more subtle gradations between what is sweet, or sour, or bitter. Taste and flavour are what they have always been so that the taste buds find nothing new. Here, in this country, biting into an apple is not like biting into a fruit. It is like biting into, tasting the flavour of, breathing in the fragrances of flowers—jasmines and roses from the garlands which are piled up in baskets used to deck the hair and adorn the gods.

Sri, Dewa and Anna will go away, back to their home, back to their island, the starting point of each new journey. What they have brought with them, to share with these exiles, is the knowledge that looking back on the familiar past carries with it the regret of nostalgia. But for the exile familiarity is to be reclaimed through the chance encounter. It is here then that he or she must remain until this strangeness too grows with the passage of time into familiarity. The paradoxes will always remain, and therein the poignancy of thought and feeling caught up in that conflict.

There is this last glimpse into life, ordinary everyday life on the street of Madurai before they go back to their hotel—a little girl sits crosslegged inside a room on the street, writing in her exercise book as the father sits at the threshold of their house and sells towels to the passersby.

People drift in and out of their lives. Are they to be remembered, these people who become part of the sights and smells that accompany them in this reincarnatory journey through the continents of their individual selves. Addresses are taken down, with promises to write, but in what ways can transience give any kind of permanency through encounters so brief that they leave only fleeting impressions of faces, bodies, voices?

They had met Mr Thandampani, an official from the State Bank of India, at the Tiruchi airport when they had first arrived in India. Dewa had begun it all because she had started discussing philosophic concepts with him while changing currency. It was something she would never have done on that other journey at Heathrow or Gatwick. Everything had been cut and dried there with only a polite interchange between herself and the official who stamped her visa giving her entrance into another of her reincarnatory journeys. When she was coming back home, another official had asked her, 'Will you return?' 'Only if I am invited back,' she had said. There was time only for such cryptic utterances there, unlike in this little room where she could start her journey by attempting to explain to someone, who she hoped would understand why she had come here, her need to explore the myths and legends that she felt existed as pointers and landmarks in her journey of discovery. The others with her had their own explorations. There was Anna's longing for discovery of this mythological continent where part of her life would always remain. She would think back on that childhood illness where in fever and delirium she had felt that she would never see again and Sri who had suffered so much for her had made this vow to Ambal. For Sri this was a pilgrimage.

Thandampani came into their lives needing sympathy. This official, this bureaucrat, felt he needed to explain his mystic name to them, to make them feel he was some kind of avatar of the gods himself. But he wanted an audience too. He would visit them in their hotel room, sit himself comfortably on one of the easy chairs and begin. 'I am a misfit,' he once complained. 'I cannot talk to anyone as I talk to you. My ideas are socialist. I do not follow the rituals of religion which my wife believes in. But I have faith.'

They invited him to share their meal of idli with chutney and sambara. He ate sparingly, an idli or two. 'These are not fresh,' he said disparagingly. 'You must come to my home for a meal. My wife makes idli daily for me.' But how could they have kept these promises which they made so earnestly on the spur of the moment? Moving from place to place on their pilgrimage they had to spend their brief time in thought and meditation rather than in conversation with too many gurus. They had to avoid confusions, reach the source of their search directly themselves. Yet Thandampani enjoyed his conversations with them. He could talk freely because no one would disagree with him or interrupt the words that flowed from the full cornucopia of his thoughts, a melange of everything from politics to Hindu mythology. Moreover he knew much more than them about what was around him.

There were places which they would never arrive at, places concealed to them which were not part of their pilgrimage.

'There are refugee camps here. They are crowded. There is nothing for these refugees to do here.'

He also told them about his beginnings.

'I was a B.A. in chemistry and studied in a Catholic College. We had discipline there . . . . I remember the time I was working in a bank in a village. Everybody brought gifts to the manager. He was invited to big feasts. He was very important in that district. He had a car. I lived a simple life . . . my wife complains that I do not take her to temple often enough. She likes to wear nice sarees when she goes.'

When Sri, Dewa and Anna left Tiruchi temporarily to go to Bangalore, Thandampani had missed them greatly. Now, as soon as they return he visits them on the last evening of their stay here. He is upset that his new friends cannot have supper with him and taste his wife's idli. 'If the others cannot then you come,' he tells Dewa who he thinks is truly liberal and broadminded.

'You come, you are an enlightened lady who has been abroad and has been influenced by the West.' He wants them all, he wants Dewa especially to meet his wife who, he says, is fair with a wheatish complexion. They are too tired to go. Anna is recovering from her bout of fever in Bangalore. There is much packing to do and a comfortable bed, a hot bath, hot kaapi are what they look forward to most. 'You are a villain,' Thandampani tells Anna accusingly. 'Because of you, your mother cannot visit my home.' Anna is too weary, still recuperating and does not want to go anywhere even to eat fresh steaming idlis made by Thandampani's wife. And Dewa, however broadminded and liberal in the west, will never, here, embark on a journey with Thandampani alone.

'Next time,' Dewa says placatingly. 'I will return.' Thandampani settles back happily to drink hot kaapi. He turns patronizingly to the room boy who is very friendly with them and who obviously resents Thandampani lording it over him. He knows that this man on another occasions would not deign to look at him.

'Thambi, how much you are earning?' he asks. Thambi does not answer.

The conversation continues. It is on the topic of his wife.

'I took my wife to the temple. There was a big crowd that day. She was not pleased with me because I did not manage to get a good place for her right in front where the poojas were taking place. I will take her to the temple but that is all I will do. I cannot push through the crowds. She had not got a good view of the inner sanctum and the gods for the blessing. But what could I have done, crushed on all sides by the milling crowd of devotees? That is not the way to worship. How can you pray with so much sound, so many bodies jostling you?'

Dewa never meets his wife whom he is educating with his liberal ideas. He takes her on his Bajaj scooter to open university classes. He is proud of her fair skin which appears to be an important consideration for marriage. He is ambitious. In his hands he holds the blueprints for the house he is going to build with a bank loan. He is fascinated by the materials and sarees that Dewa has bought to take back. He has never seen, never heard of their richness—the real, the traditional Kutch work, the ikkat-dyed sambalpurs, the kalamkari khadi and the bandhani, all very inexpensive, very unique. He sees a batik cotton, implies that Indian ladies of the elite social strata will not wear this.

'You can say what social class a lady belongs to by the sarees she wears. That saree perhaps she will wear to the kitchen.'

Dewa is not offended by his remark. And Thandampani is fascinated by all he sees, touches, feels; he looks carefully at colour and design. He tells them about the legends and myths associated with his name, Thandampani . . .

They have packed their bags which overflow with what they have found precious enough to take back. Dewa carefully puts away the sweets she has bought for her second daughter who could not come on this pilgrimage. They are very special, bought from a little shop in a street in Tiruchi. The glass showcase in that shop was full of swan popli, Mysore pak, barfi and the most succulent muscat. In the inner room an old man clad in pure white veshti had sat before a wood fire, stirring with a huge ladle the sugar, milk and ghee for fresh sweets. The old man's son went quietly into the room and measured out very carefully the colours and essences to be added to the mixture. The old man did not cease stirring even for a moment—he handled the ladle like an oar. Neither Sri nor Dewa nor Anna were allowed anywhere near. The whole act of making sweetmeats appeared to be as holy as the ritual of preparing the food of the gods, the nectar and ambrosia, the *pancha amritham.* The sweets were carefully packed for them. Dewa saw a fly savouring the milk barfi in the glass case. Feeding on the same rich ghee, milk and sugar as humans. And she had felt then how close the sharing of those pleasures could be. Each morsel of barfi that crumbled with sweetness on the tongue was no longer something kept apart for selfish beings like themselves alone. But to the fly both sweetness and decay were as one. She had seen flies swarm over the urinals in the bus-stations. Those roofless, half-walled buildings of the urinals, with their cemented floors, flies buzzing furiously over rivers of urine frothing and swirling about or lying in stagnant pools and puddles about your feet. You step gingerly through that flood. Dewa remembered the lady who had sat on her haunches before her in the urinal at one of the bus stations. She had seemed one of those delicately bred women, sleek oiled hair and gold earnings. She had been munching murukku and eating grapes in the bus. She had been very silent on that long journey, not exchanged a word, yet, within the urinal they shared a strange intimacy. There was no sense of violating the other's innate sense of modesty in this act of nature. And the flies around them there were perhaps the same flies that had buzzed over the baskets of crisp sugar-coated murukku, fresh grapes and oranges in the bus. The flies followed you everywhere. They had also hovered around the silk and organza clad ladies who had stood in a queue at the waterless toilets in Brindavan Gardens. The flies are no respecters of persons, Dewa thought as she stood at the shop, watching them buzz over the sweets. They alight on the jewel at the throat, gold at the wrist, feeding off ripe or rotting fruit, flowers and flesh, sweetness and ordure. Their endless ragas celebrate life, announce death. While they were sampling the muscat at the shop, a very charming old gentleman had become friendly with them. (It is their foreignness that attracts, in Tamilnadu they were taken for North Indians.) The old man had a very young son. While the father talked in his careful and meticulous English, the little boy tried to drag the father away by the hand, refused all fruit drinks, muscat, barfi, swan popli, everything. All that he wanted was to flee from them while his father persisted in being friendly . . .

Dewa puts the sweets away in the bag and zips it up. She closes her eyes. Thinks. Of Thanjavur. In the great Cholan temple the goddess Amman was being given an abishekam. Anointed with oil that was cool and rich and fragrant. The stone appeared to breathe through its pores as the statue was bathed with turmeric and coconut water, sandalwood, *kumkumum,* fruit juices. The body of the goddess glistened with oils. The act of cleansing and purification was symbolic. It was the purification of the stained and fatigued human flesh. The sacred light from Agni's fires warmed the cold flesh, brought it to life and the Sanskrit slokas were the prayers that beseeched the goddess to heal the cripple boy who stood before her . . . . The *abishekam* wiped away, cleansed whatever each man considered his individual sin, crime, guilt. Threaded garlands wrapped round her body and a silk cloth of red with gold zari was draped on Amman's body.

Sri had felt so much at peace in Thanjavur. 'This is where I want to return and allow my soul to have repose,' he had said.

A party of French tourists with their guide had passed through, going from shrine to shrine. A woman had stopped for a moment and raised her hands to Dewa in a gesture of namaskaram. She had smiled and passed as another of those fellow beings who were part of this new journey which had really emerged out of millennia of travelling from one life to another. That flash of recognition had told each of them that they had met before.

Dewa, Sri, Anna. They have encountered so many stages on this journey. Each stranger has been destined to meet them, to share the journey, to act as another pointer, one more landmark to the familiarity of that which is so ancient in their past and yet so immediate in their present. Some of them had stood at the entrance to their rooms and begun stories of their lives. The sources of rivers which journey through landscapes of time to destinations Dewa will never know of. Perumal, Skandakumar, Mani and so many others. Sometimes they needed to leave words like those indigo tattoos on the mind: 'Skandakumar my name. My parents dead. No mother, father. I am sixteen years. I cannot read. I never went to school. My brother works in another hotel. When you finish I will eat.'

A Fistful of Wind

CROWDS MILL ON the pavements. They brush past you, knock into you, jolt you, poke their umbrellas into your eyes, prod you in the ribs; your hair gets caught in their umbrellas. They walk in family groups, the grandmother carrying the baby in her arms, the mother following behind, the husband leading the elder child by the hand. They are bodies, just bodies, brushing past impersonally. Sometimes faces, the eyes directed only at what they want to see. Among them mingle the foreigners in their kurtas and swinging skirts importuned by the sellers of coloured seed chains and spice packets. The woman who sells betel on the pavement outside the Baptist Church has had a new baby this year. The child plays beside her, unaffected by the street full of people.

Eyes survey you coolly from the seat of a car.

Sitting there, leaning against the leather seats, those people can watch you as they drive past, and in that split second see the lives of strangers, open and revealed before them. Beggars stand beside the windows of the cars for alms. The back seats are usually stacked with boxes and bags. The parking girls in their yellow uniforms and black belts stand beside the vehicles with their notebooks and pencils. In a corner of the street an old man, hunched after years of bending over bits of leather, sits with his legs drawn up, painstakingly putting white stitches on a pair of old leather shoes. It is old leather, but good. How absorbed the old man is, his white head, his white beard and the white stitches creating their own pattern on the grey pavement, the sunlight slanting on the man's worn-out clothes. How precise each stitch is, how neatly placed on the leather. People no longer throw away their old shoes but have them mended, re-soled, or stitched together.

I forget to stop and ask him to mend my shoes. The soles are thin, worn out, the stitches have come undone near the toes. I have worn them for a long time, so long that I feel my feet are part of the road, as I walk and walk.

The shop windows filled with sarees, lengths of dress material, imported goods—crystalware, cut-glass, stainless steel and electrical goods—tantalize window-shoppers. They can only afford to stand and gaze longingly at the things displayed, overcome by a powerful urge to possess at least a few of them. But what can they do if their pockets are empty— only grab at fistfuls of wind. Outside one of the big shops stands a larger-than-life Santa Claus. The cloth that covers his body is thick, red and warm. He is shod in strong, heavy leather boots. Is it real leather?

I don't stop long enough to see. The giant Santa Claus holds a brown paper parcel in his hands. I turn to my daughter.

'Shall I take the gift?'

'What do you expect to find inside? What if its empty?' she says with an ingenue's cynicism.

'Let's go into the shop and look around.'

'What do you want to buy?' she asks. 'I don't like these big shops. There's no point in going in unless you have lots of money.'

'Oh, we can look around. At least we will know what we can do without.'

At the saree counter stands a former student of mine with his wife and relations. The salesman is pulling out the sarees which are in vogue—expensive chiffon Manipuris, sheer diaphanous things with heavy gold borders. Saree after saree is flung open on the counter. Behind the salesman are stacks of more sarees. I go past my student. He is shy with his new young bride beside him and without the slightest knowledge of what will please her. All he has is the money to purchase whatever she wants. Heavy gold earrings glitter in her ears, bracelets slip up and down the length of her forearms as she lifts the sarees and holds them against her, feeling their textures.

Kandy is a small town. I often meet my students around. The majority of them are much wealthier than me, drive about in their big cars and wear expensive clothes, imported shoes.

'Teacher, how are you? Are you still in College?'

Sometimes they look up gratefully and say, impelled by some compulsive need to appear grateful: 'Teacher, I am grateful to you. I am what I am because of you'.

I too had spoken like this to my old teachers, but

in a different context. I meant that they had helped me to learn. But my students mean something different. I have helped them to become successful. This is of much greater importance to them. I have never thought of success in this way. They grow up and go to their tea plantations, high administrative posts in the Government, jobs in hotels, their rice mills or their gem businesses and I remain behind, sometimes even having to ask them to help me sort out some of my problems.

'Are you still there, teacher?'

'Yes, I'm still there.'

'Is College still the same?'

How can anything remain the same. The faces in those class photographs have altered so much.

'I'm glad that you're doing well.'

I am really proud of them. Proud when I read of them, hear of them doing well in high places. Why didn't I ever get out before the walls began to press me in and the empty pitch grew dark with a solitary shadowy figure walking across it . . . . The old tress are being cut down, the ancient tamarind tree, the flowering trees have all disappeared. Why didn't I leave earlier?

Roots, roots, too firmly embedded in the soil have kept me back. But now the shallow earth is eroding around these roots. A lot of debris is piling up around them. The branches are being lopped off, a rough stone rears itself against the gnarled and spreading roots. Soon the old tree will be cut down before it topples over, the roots wrenched from the shallow earth. New young saplings will be planted but it will be a long time before they fruit or provide staunch nesting places among their branches for birds; the drifting winds will twist their branches and slender trunks—they are not seasoned hardwood of the true forest tree. The wilderness too is receding. The wild things that sheltered there are scattering: the jackals have had to swim across the river into another wilderness, the reptiles stay on a while longer and creep into the niches of stone parapets which they share with the great brown lizard; the bear stumbles towards another cave, the leopard falters at the drying waterhole and turns away, the deer and sambar slip away, shadows flit behind the trees, the ruby eyes of crocodiles shine in the dark. Everywhere in the ruined landscape stand the charred stumps of trees and the great silvery white *thumbasas*, anthills that have grown out of the earth—the whitening bones, the bleached bones and fleshless skulls shimmering in the sunlight, the grass springing out of creviced ribs.

I lean against an electric cooker in the shop— smooth, white and shiny. I feel a warmth engendered by so many bodies crowded in the shop. How comfortable the kitchen was in my old home: the hearth with its wood fires, the simmering pots placed on them, the firewood, coconut husks and coconut shells which fed the flames piled up in the *porane*, coconut shell spoons suspended from the spoon rack—one for the rice pot, the other for the milk, others for meat, fish and vegetables. The splutter of frying oil; the ground condiments in little mounds on saucers . . . an old *amme* would do most of the cooking in the dark kitchen with smoke-blackened walls, cooking until she couldn't eat fire any longer. She did everything for us—even ironed our clothes with the *polkattu* iron or comforted us with stories when we were sad or tired, sitting by the side of the bed, massaging our feet with her small strong hands and beginning her story in slow, measured tones: 'Once upon a time, in a certain country, lived a

Gamarala and a Gamamahage . . .' she would go on until we drifted into sleep.

The salesman catches my eye. 'Yes, madame?'

My eyes take in everything that is placed on the shelves with one expert glance. I know the prices of everything, and I assess every commodity against the price of our daily bread.

'A cake of soap, please.'

He slips it into a little bag; the soap fits in perfectly. Then I do my rounds: electrical appliances for every purpose under the sun—for broiling, baking, steaming, frying; canned foods, plastic flowers, readymade garments, rolls of cloth, sarees, Christmas cards, shoes . . . . I can't afford a single thing other than a cake of soap. Twenty-five years of teaching, and my whole salary will buy just one saree, a pair of shoes and a little food, perhaps enough for a week. Not even a house of my own. Twenty-five years of teaching . . . I can't buy books—I can only read from libraries.

I run into another old student of mine.

'Teacher, how are you . . . I have just returned from the Middle East. We are building a house at Navayalatenne. I am opening a motor spares shop. I have brought five lakhs back . . . . No, I don't think I shall go back again.'

'If you have made your money then there's no point . . . can you get a job for my husband?'

He is silent for a moment.

'Aren't there jobs . . .?' I ask.

'Not for men of his calibre.'

'Oh, not teaching . . any job . . . clerical?'

'Ah, clerical, yes, that's possible, but through an agency . . . and the work's hard; there are many hours of boredom, there's nothing to do . . .'

'Oh, he can spend his time at the typewriter . . .'

I don't recognize some of them.

'Teacher, this is my wife. I was away for five years . . . .' Was it so long ago that we had sat at a table in the library reading *Pride and Prejudice* and hearing the sound of the cricket ball against the bat, or the sound of feet scurrying up and down stairs, running along corridors, or even the swish of the cane as the master of discipline punished a student for the slightest misdemeanour. The sound of the whip-like rattan falling on flesh is repugnant to me and has always caused me pain. Nothing can be more humiliating to watch.

Roots . . . the roots are appearing, bare, humped, gnarled, out of the shallow sand . . . . Roots.

We go out of the shop. Anton comes running after me. He stands in his dirty brown shirt and trousers, unshaven, gaunt, barefooted.

'Please bring me a shirt . . . Sir promised me a shirt. I'm hungry, find me some work, I'll do anything. Please, please give me two rupees, I'm hungry, hungry, hungry . . .'

I dig into my purse and pull out some money. The loose change has spilled out of the broken purse. One day a pickpocket had put his hand right into my bag in a crowded bus. I had what was left of my salary in it. I hurriedly peeped into the bag; the purse was intact. I gave him a hard, cool stare and he calmly withdrew his hand. An expensive watch flashed on his wrist, his sarong was a finely chequered silk. What a precarious existence. I would have had to starve if that money went. Yet, I always feel sorry for pickpockets when they are caught: the terrible humiliation, the hot chase, the bloodied heads. Pity . . . . No one pities teachers. I have seen them sitting in little tea rooms and eating one bun each and drinking cups of tea; and buying cut-pieces, not whole sarees but cut-pieces. No one can see where the deception begins and where it ends. And why are they cut, these identical pieces? Shariff says that they are smuggled, or that people have to pay less duty on cut-pieces. They are much cheaper than whole sarees—one third the price and no one knows the difference.

Out on the pavement I suddenly miss the old man who used to sell his kitul pani, kitul piti, kitul jaggery, papaws, vanilla beans, aanamalu plantains. Where is he? There is no longer any room for him here. A brand new Santa Claus stands in his place. At the next shop there is a fresh pine-scented Christmas tree covered with bulbs, baubles and streamers. Where is the second-hand bookseller and the man who would sit scrubbing spurious gold in his basin of frothy water. It is difficult to walk on the narrow pavements . . . I really must get my shoes mended. I can't walk as swiftly as I used to either. There are many cobblers in the little alleys, at streetcorners and under the billboards of films, men who sit for hours mending shoes, stitching pieces of leather, sitting there with their scraps of leather, re-stitching, re-soling, re-stitching. My father always had his shoes made by old Peterson, the cobbler. He never bought shoes in shops. His shoes were made of good strong leather or elkhide. Every Christmas old Peterson would come with a new pair of shoes for my father which he had made after carefully measuring his feet. He would be given his Christmas drink and a gift for his family—so many mouths to feed had Peterson, yet how cheerful he was.

'Sir, I have brought your shoes.'

'Have you done a good job, Peterson?'

'Yes sir, look at the sole. It will never give way, see how strong the stitches are . . . all handstitched,

271

sir. Fine leather, sir. Fit on, sir, fit on . . . good fit, sir, it fits your foot well . . .'

'A little tight at the toes, Peterson, pinches a bit.'

'No sir, it will stretch. Look at the fine polish I have given it.'

'Hmmmm. Not bad . . . now what do I owe you, Peterson?'

'Sir, only fifteen rupees—price of leather gone up, sir.'

My husband has only one pair of shoes. How much longer can he walk in them before they disintegrate?

'Oh, I'll get them repaired. They'll do,' he keeps saying.

He has had them re-sewn at least three times over.

When we were children, every Christmas we would be taken to buy new shoes. Shoes lay strewn all over the place, cardboard boxes with tissue paper wrappings . . . feet gently eased into them: suede, patent leather, wedgies, brogues, court shoes. Nobody wore slippers then. Now the only shoes I buy are those that can help me walk over all kinds of terrain— rough, uneven, broken, muddy, with potholes and slush—always walking towards what I had been taught is 'A vocation': one which can no longer help me keep body and soul together. With time, the shoes are impelling me in another direction: the earth heaped up, piled on the sides, the dull clang of the spade knocking against the sod. How many graves, not yet my own, have I stood at, peering in, the thudding, hurrying sound of the coffin falling, falling . . . but this time I will not be able to walk away, my broken shoes will lie gathering dust in some corner where I will have kicked them off among the papers and books strewn about.

At the bar a few people stand sipping drinks. The man with the basin of hot kadalai and boiled manioc is no longer there. The bar looks new— polished counters, clean floors; in the past the strong smell of liquor would assail your nostrils and you would quickly hurry past, averting your eyes. If you glanced inside all eyes swivelled round and transfixed you with that brave red glare. What a lot of foreigners now stand here, without a trace of self-consciousness, enjoying their drinks, some of them absorbed in conversation, some drinking silently, others laughing loudly and guffawing—it isn't a tavern anymore. It is a pub full of the many foreigners working on the different development projects in the environs of Kandy.

The faces of the old buildings are changing. The aapana salawas and the Siripura Hotels are now three-storyed buildings with carpeted entrances, potted plants, polished stairways. The old carved screens which retained the privacy of those who ate and drank at the little tables, the steaming, hissing tea urns, the glass cases with their piles of stringhoppers, hoppers, cakes and buns have all disappeared. Everything looks more sleek, more expensive, filled with imported sweets, chocolates, biscuits. You need to have lots of money to walk into one of these shops. I had stood outside one of them once, gazing at the new building with its bamboo scaffolding. My lawyer, who stood beside me, had said: 'You know, the man who put up that building had to pay three lakhs of rupees to get the last occupant out. That's what they are doing these days.' He gave me an oblique glance as he spoke. 'You may have to pay your tenant at least ten lakhs before she agrees to go.'

Ten lakhs! But I can hardly afford to feed my

family on what I earn and she has immense wealth herself, land, estates . . . . From where can I get even a lakh? My husband has only one pair of trousers, one pair of shoes that has been re-sewn three times at least. After twenty-five years of working what have I got? I can't even afford the basic necessities of life.

'From where can I get ten lakhs?' I had asked the lawyer.

It is better to be silent; you avoid having to utter hot words, recriminations; but silence is a blunt weapon, others are armed against you with sharper, more lethal ones. Yet greed is sometimes the spade with which you dig your own grave, greed for a piece of earth, greed for four walls, greed for the lush possessions of others.

I spot an acquaintance who has returned from Nigeria. I don't stop to talk, and she too appears not to see me. Wealth has imposed barriers so easily. Everybody finds it difficult to understand why I have stayed back. In the past I had no cause to complain. But now I am being edged slowly, slowly, towards the precipice of rejection; I am dispensable.

'What are you doing here. . . why don't you go abroad?'

Has it come to the final answer so soon?

'We have to find work for you on the time table.'

'Teacher, Teacher, Teacher . . .' each echo retains the timbre of remembered voices. Twenty-five years ago I had not thought I would reach the end of the line so soon. The old masters, the old servants had stayed, stayed on, becoming part of the walls of the classroom until they died; and then the funeral was held in the College hall and the altar servers with their candles, led by the Bishop and priests, came in a procession chanting softly, and the boys filed round the coffin and the mourning family stood weeping on one side. Twenty-five years of service celebrated with a special assembly, a special dinner, a special photograph and an empty bank balance. No, I will not let myself enjoy the farce, I will not allow them the chance to forget; I will take a quiet walk outside, never to return.

'Teacher . . . .' Mad Suriyapillai who has been a student in College walks about the pavement in dirty clothes.

'Teacher . . .'

'Yes?'

'Teacher, I am spoiling the name of the College. Everyone is telling me that I'm letting down the College.'

Why don't I have the courage to tell him: 'Go in peace . . . you're free.' Instead I say, because the whole world is watching: 'Yes, Suriyapillai, you must think of the name of the College. You must not let down your school, your teachers . . . wear clean clothes, I'll bring you a shirt. Go back to your parents . . .'

'Yes, teacher, I must change.'

But he won't; he will suddenly disappear off the streets, no one will know where. Both of us to our anonymous graves. Someone, somewhere, has let him down. One does not question guilt on a pavement in a crowded street. We cannot even speak the truth because the eyes of the world are upon us.

Why am I still here?

You must go away, you must go away, my friends tell me. You are wasting your time here.

My answers had come out pat in the past: I don't want to be a second rate citizen anywhere; I don't want to be in a country that is politically unstable; What I earn is enough for me. I have peace of mind here; my father is old and alone, my brother and sister are out of the country—who will care for him if I go too?

But there was something else that was keeping me back—roots, the deep roots that stretched and snaked their way through the corridors and classrooms, through the acres beside the river. Behind the classrooms there is a wilderness that I love to gaze on. Tall old jak and breadfruit trees. Swarms of hornets had once clung to some of those inaccessible branches. Undisturbed they had clung and made their dark, thick honey in the great brown honeycombs, the close mesh of their cells thick with swarms. The roots of those great trees were buried deep in thick grass among the wild cannas and the disused, abandoned wells, their water gold-green and glittery with sun and scum . . . . But then suddenly the swarms had disappeared, no one knows where; though the wilderness was left undisturbed, the reptiles coiling within the maze of tall *thumbasas*.

No, I couldn't remain in that milieu any longer. The trees of the flamboyant are bare of flowers, the wind blows, the rain falls, the leaves grow dark and dense. In the Clock Tower there are piles of old registers, birth certificates, group photographs, messages from Popes, addresses to principals, old record books with instructions for disciplinary action, all gathering dust in a corner. Crumbling fossils. I must get out before it is too late.

In one of the shops, my friend, who is the proprietress, comes up to me. 'I have just what you like. Aren't you going to buy something today? My sarees cost a little more because I go specially to Colombo to choose them. Have you found anything you like?'

'Yes, there's something . . . this red and black. It's beautiful. But if I buy it what will we eat for the rest of the month?' I turn away. 'I'll look for something on the pavement, in one of those little shops.'

My daughter and I walk past the grocery shops with their sacks of rice, chillies, onions, past the hotels, the booksellers, the antique shops. We rush shoulder to shoulder along the pedestrian crossing and onto the pavement jungle. There is a babble of voices, all calling their wares. The pavement shops overflow with yards and yards of Japanese polyesters, Swiss voiles, ponjees, shirtings, trouser lengths. People walk and talk and stop to buy. The pavements are too narrow to hold the crowds.

The pavement hawkers stand behind their makeshift counters lined with dazzling mirrors through which flash a coloured whirl of limbs bathed in sunlight—the whole town, its glittering snake of humanity uncoiling itself through the streets, restless, seeking, walking, walking, lifting, touching, feeling, stretching, holding against the body, feeling the textures. The shimmery soft folds of cloth to cover their bodies with. Yes, they all seem to be women. 'Does the colour suit me? Will this fit me?' They . choose the skimpiest measurements to sew a dress or skirt or a pair of trousers. They don't leave much room for growing. The skirts are short and uneven, the sarees joined together out of cut-pieces. Cheap rubber slippers lie on the pavement.

They stand in little groups, the young girls, hardly ever alone. They all look the same, even the colour of their skin, the shapes of their bodies and faces, in their standard attire. How lost their youthful insouciance is in the shoddy clothes they wear. As fashions change, so change their uniforms: they all want to share the same identity—the printed T-shirts from Taiwan, the corduroy skirts, the permanent-pleated synthetics, their hair caught back in pony tails, their faces powdered white with talcum, the heavy shoes with thick rubber soles, the coloured hair slides; and the older women, the young married women, the clerks and the teachers, the middleclass housewives, counting their money in their little plastic purses and handbags or untying their knotted handkerchiefs to take out the crumpled notes. The neglected hands criss-crossed with dark lines, the marks of knife cuts, the worn-out finger nails—the result of cooking, chopping firewood, scrubbing pots and pans, cutting vegetables with rough-handled knives. Occasionally the prosperous new returnees from the Middle East pass by—gold bangles, earrings, high-heeled shoes, perfume, that special aura, that gloss of new wealth glittering in the bright clothes and handbags; the children in their brand new imported clothes, shoes and socks.

I peer at a blue flowered print. 'I like that,' I say.

'What, that? It's not nice at all. Buy the ponjee, the white or cream. Now don't ask the price of things on the pavement; don't make a spectacle of yourself looking at all those cheap things,' my daughter murmurs disapprovingly.

On the other side of the road are all the eating houses. There is the Muslim Hotel which has stood there for years. People are walking in and out, sitting at marble-topped tables, eating and drinking. In the past it had always been biryani, or godamba or wattalappan or tandoori chicken. What is it now? I have not been inside for a long time now. There used to be trays of rich Turkey bread, boondi, jalebis too, and the little porcelain cups of rich syrupy wattalappan. I stand for a moment and watch. I remember coming here with my father. We would go upstairs to the long dining room with our friends, and commandeer a whole table to ourselves. It would be swiftly covered with spotless white tablecloth, the tumblers of water set on it and the steaming hot dishes of chicken curry and biryani, the long-grained rice soaked with ghee, placed in the centre. My father laughed and joked with the waiter and taking his red fez, placed it on his head.

My father was a big man; strong and always laughing. Couldn't be still, couldn't contain that vibrant energy he had, until he was very old. When I was a child, at Perahera time—the annual pageant where homage is paid to the sacred Tooth Relic of the Buddha and the streets are filled night after night with dancers, drummers, caparisoned elephants in their trappings of silver, gold, velvet and brocade, bearers carrying torches of burning copra, whip crackers, Kandyan chieftains in their traditional regalia—he would carry me on his shoulders, high above the crowd of heads. Every year I waited with bated breath until the casket, the *karanduwa* in which the sacred Tooth was kept, borne on the great tusker of Dalada Maligawa, appeared. Each year I counted the number of elephants that appeared in the procession as if it was the most important thing in the world and I could exclaim, 'This year there were a hundred and fifty elephants! Many more than the last time . . . .' Their tinkling bells, their sad, wise eyes, my having to pass under their bellies during the day perahera to give me strength, my father feeding them sugarcane sticks . . . . Memory after memory remains . . .

'Come, come, don't dawdle; where are you looking,' my daughter says.

We stand before a row of pavement shops which sold sarees. My friend had told me that you could buy cut-pieces cheap here. I recognize Shariff who wants me to use my influence or power or whatever he calls it, as a teacher, to help get his young son into the big school where I teach.

'Shariff, did you succeed?'

'No teacher, I failed. They didn't take my son. What to do, teacher, I was away on business in Budulla.' His hands make a gesture of hopelessness. 'I was too late.'

'What will you do now?'

'Send him to another school, anywhere . . . Katugastota, Siyambalagastenne, Mavilmada . . .' his voice peters off sadly.

Shariff stands islanded among his bundles of cut-pieces, short and stocky in his white shirt and sarong, his dark moustache looking strange, incongruous on his bland, cherubic face, although behind that smooth exterior he is a shrewd, very shrewd businessman.

Bundles and bundles of cut-pieces, Four-by-Fours, American georgettes that really come from Japan, and Korean silks lie tumbled about at his feet. He can't take a step backwards or forwards. He can only turn his body from side to side, stoop, pick up something and throw it at you. The bundles of cut-pieces, knotted together, look very tempting. Some of the designs and colours pleasing to the eye. You have only to sew a fine seam and join the cut-pieces together. My friend says that the seam will not be noticed. It will be hidden among the pleats.

Shariff is most obliging. He does not mind how many pieces you wrest out of the pile and fling aside. As you grasp and pull, he too tugs at the piece of cloth or takes another cut-piece and thrusts it under your nose.

'I show you something nice,' he says.

'No, no, I'll choose,' I insist.

It becomes a delightful game. We clutch at hundreds of cut-pieces, rip them out of their bundles and hurl them at each other.

'This, what about this? You like this? This colour, this design? It will suit your complexion.'

The shop is crowding up.

'You come Friday. I get another bundle then. More cut-pieces. American georgette.'

Beside me stand two village women, dressed in printed butter nylon. They too can't make up their minds.

'*Akke*, isn't this nice for me?'

'Yes, this border is good. The colour will suit you. What about this? No, this is better.'

They are standing at the narrow entrance, blocking it. The salesman standing close to them is grumbling. 'Almost two hours you have spent choosing and choosing and still you have not chosen.'

Does he mean me? Whom is he talking to? I turn round startled. The man's face changes. It is rather a rough sort of face with stubbly cheeks, sharp, narrow black eyes, a long thin nose, thin lips curling at the corners. He stands outlined against a background of flimsy, rainbow-coloured sarees. They are not all cut-pieces.

I look at Shariff. 'I am sorry I have taken so long,' I say apologetically.

The salesman is discomfited. He begins to murmur incoherently. He slurs his words and stumbles over them in embarrassment. 'No, no, no, not you, nothing, all right, not you.' Shariff breaks in smoothly, 'Madame, not you—that—' he lifts his eyebrows in the direction of the two women. 'Poor people, let them choose, let them take their time.' He has immense patience and tact, but then, that is the only way in which his business will progress.

I am still gazing rather anxiously at the salesman. I hadn't noticed him before. It is Shariff who dominates Ali Baba's cave. I had first thought the man to be the husband of one of the village women. His aggressive expression now begins to melt somewhat. A tentative, completely false smile masks his face.

'Madame,' Shariff says, 'Madame don't get offended. He didn't mean you.'

Each of us tries to mollify the other. I try to put Shariff at ease and he tries to placate me. But I still feel uneasy with the man who, I have now discovered, is a salesman. The two women are completely oblivious to what is happening. One of them turns aside and taking out a large white handkerchief which has been tucked into her sarong at the waist, begins to mop her perspiring face. As the perspiration trickles down her cheeks, I too begin to feel hot and uncomfortable in the shop.

'*Akke*, what about this?' Their heads together, they are still choosing.

'Here, take,' Shariff thrusts a folded saree into my hands. It is viridian, with brilliant green flowers. 'For presents, very good. Only sixty rupees'.

More and more people are entering the shop. I feel I will be pitched forward into the pile of soft, shimmering silks. My daughter is pressed into a corner against the bundles of silk. Her knees seem to be buckling under her. The parcels in her hands are slipping. Her face is red.

'If you are buying, buy something and come quickly, or else give me my bus fare and I'll go home. Look, all the parcels are falling. Don't blame me if I lose any of them.'

Books, umbrellas, foamtread slippers are being juggled by us. I stand still for a moment, stop being so frenetic. Flimsy pieces of cloth cling to my hands. I look at the cut-pieces again. Would these be suitable for wearing to church on Christmas Day? I think again of my childhood, those Christmases. My mother would take us shopping weeks before the great day with her handbag full of the money my father gave her for all our clothes and shoes. We would sit comfortably on chairs with the foot mirrors before us while the salesman opened box after box, each with its rustling tissue paper.

I feel my head reeling. I would go mad inside this place, day after day, if I were Shariff, shut out from the sun, light, air, all my possessions being touched and tugged at as if they cost nothing. And even the people who wear them—what value do their own lives have? Aren't we all nothing too?

The babble of voices eddies about my ears. Shariff's voice suddenly rises shrilly. 'Be careful of your bags, your purses, your umbrellas,' he shrieks. I have let my bag slip out of my hands in all the commotion and it lies at my feet.

'Be careful,' he pleads, looking at me, 'be careful of your bag.'

My bag. Does he know how much my purse contains? Its contents are meagre. It could just as well belong to any of the poor people who stand around me. Only I don't tuck my purse into my blouse like some of them, or, like the old village women, tie the money into a knot at the edge of my saree *pota*. If I take out the paper notes they might just drift away, vanish like scraps of soiled paper on the pavement. Does my whole life, my whole career amount to just this minuscule amount? Do I have to sweat year after year to buy just two cut-pieces of cloth and join them together to lend an air of respectability to my occupation? What if I leave my bag behind? I have discarded many things that do not matter any more. Shoes that have to be repaired,

for instance. I never collect them from the cobbler's.
I suppose I have walked long enough in them. They
have served their purpose.

Cut-pieces . . . . And second-hand clothes . . .
the shops by the station are full of second hand
clothes—soiled, faded, frayed. Who buys them? There
are people who do. I am fascinated by the thought of
the bodies, the lives they must have once wrapped.
I sometimes stop and look hard to see if I can find
all those garments that have been stolen from me
through the years. I have often been betrayed by
those whom I have shown kindness to. This does not
make me bitter; I have accepted it. They were poorer
than myself.

I remember the wild-looking man with his light
grey eyes on fire, a flame of madness flickering in
them, who sits in one of the shops near the station,
sewing away at his machine, converting old silk
sarees with their dull gold thread into pants, skirts,
salwar kameezes. Among the sarees heaped on the
floor and hanging on a rope stretched across the
front entrance I had once spotted a faded turquoise-
blue Kashmir silk with block printed designs—
stylized figures of women, peacocks, flowers. It was
genuine silk, the kind, one has heard, that will pass
through a ring.

'Where did you get that Kashmir saree from?' I
had asked. The saree was quite obviously old, tatty.

'I went to Kashmir. I brought it from Kashmir.'

'It's not new,' I said.

'Yes, new.' His face shone with a crazy light, all
on fire.

The old silks swung like curtains before his face.
The shop looked ghostly, the machine went on
whirring. He kept hoping that I would be taken in
by his deception which was so innocently transparent.

'Tell me the truth. It's old silk. I like old things.'
'New,' he insisted.

Most probably all those clothes had been brought there for sale by the *parana coat karayas*, men who go from house to house collecting suits of tweed and wool and silk sarees disintegrating with age, taken out of almirahs where they must have lain for years, with camphor moth balls or dried fragrant savendara roots in their folds. Once a friend of mine had given away her husband's wedding suit in exchange for some new plasticware. 'At any rate, it was out of fashion and didn't fit him any more,' she had excused herself.

All of us need to discard a great number of things we have accumulated through the years. It doesn't matter where they all go, bits of our lives go with them too, lessening the burden we have to carry.

'Haven't you chosen yet?' my daughter asks, bringing me back to the present. I can feel the impatience welling up inside her. 'I'm tired,' she says. She looks elegant in her imported jeans and T-shirt, her hair sleek in a carefully combed pony tail.

'Wipe your face. You're perspiring.'

I embarrass her sometimes, wearing the wrong colours, staring at the wares of pavement hawkers. The young have a certain decorum which their elders lack. They want fewer possessions, they have fewer memories, their lives are relatively uncluttered. There is still time for them to give their discards to the *parana coat karayas*. How many of the young sons and daughters are earning more than their parents! One young person had said: 'My first salary amounted to more than my mother's who had been teaching for twenty years.'

I have chosen nothing yet. I can't. What am I

doing here anyway? Shariff throws another saree over my head and says: 'Sixty rupees but no colour guarantee.' The saree is a virulent magenta. Loud enough for his audience to hear, he keeps on talking: 'These people are strangers. If I don't tell them the truth they will blame me and never come back again.'

'Come in, come in, come in,' the man at the entrance invites all and sundry.

Shariff suddenly calls out again, 'You purses, your handbags, your umbrellas. Be careful.'

I can't move out. My elbows seem to have been pinned back.

Shariff stands islanded, stretching out bundle after bundle of cut-pieces. I can't bring myself to buy the cut-pieces that drift out of my hands and fall on the pile before me. I can't subscribe to the transparent cheat, the camouflaged poverty. And how patient poor, sad Shariff is. All the money he earns from his cut-pieces will be spent on his son to get him a good education in one of the best schools in Kandy and here is one of the teachers from that same school turning over in the craziest fashion cut-piece after cut-piece. What does it matter? Who cares anyway? The cut-pieces help hundreds of people to wear an air of respectability.

'Here, take . . . .' Shariff's attention has shifted. A head, like an intrusive bird, suddenly thrusts itself over my shoulder. Shariff stands unmoved by the din and confusion around him. People push us, jostle us, casually dropping in to finger the silks. However, there is a sense of his being protected, however flimsy the barrier, by his own sarees.

'Don't you feel crazy inside here, Shariff? Don't you feel you're going mad inside this shop?'

'What to do, teacher, this is my life. Teacher,

please try to get my son into the College. I will give anything they ask for the building fund. Tell them I promise five thousand, ten thousand, anything they ask.' Shariff lives in hope to see his son get the kind of education that will make him a gentleman, so he won't have to sell cut-pieces in a pavement shop. Cricket, rugger, prize givings, sports meets—he envisages all this for the boy whom he wants to see in one of the leading schools in Kandy.

'No, I cannot,' I think. 'I'll wear something old to church on Christmas morning.' I recoil at something I have never done, never can do. My whole being cringes and withdraws from the choice.

Do we then all belong together? The masses of humanity on the street, the crippled boy crawling with matchstick thin legs on the pavement, the beggar women with their babies being lulled and fed in the street. Is it only these few flimsy pieces of silk that mark the difference or do we think in and speak a different language?

Suddenly I begin to laugh hysterically. I don't know why. There is nothing to laugh at.

'Stop,' my daughter says, 'everybody is looking.' She has given up and is sinking into the pile of drifting sarees that has been pulled apart. I am laughing at myself, the ludicrous figure I cut, and as I laugh an image of the whole suffering mass of humanity rises before me. Mirrored in its distortion is my own face, with its grimace, its laughing, tear-filled eyes. It is myself I am laughing at. Bleak humour. Black comedy.

I can't contain myself. My laughter is out of place, as if I am laughing beside a newly-dug grave. The faces around me seem to come together in a manic jumble of incongruous expressions. My daughter wears a worried, serious look on her face.

'Why are you laughing? I don't see anything funny to laugh at.'

But there is, there is. We are all so serious about things that do not merit any seriousness. It is the revelation of utter futility that makes me laugh. To negate myself and all my values makes life, existence, survival, bearable.

I hear voices echoing in my mind . . . . 'Please tell me, teacher, please have the courage to tell me that you are a failure. You are a fool. You haven't learnt a thing in twenty-five years. You can barely survive. It won't take you long to starve to death. You can hardly fend for your family. You're looking for the cheapest clothes . . . cut-pieces, cut prices. You're nearing the grave without having learnt a thing unless now, at this point, you confront your exploiters. Your subversion of all those sham noble ideas will at least rip that veil off your eyes . . . revelation . . . the stark truth . . . teacher . . .'

My laughter is really a shriek of pain, the death throes of the desperate. As I dissolve in helpless and hysterical laughter the world around me splinters, disintegrates. In the street reflected in the shattered mirrors of light I see dismembered limbs, shreds of flesh trampled upon by those who flee to avoid disaster. When I look up and wipe my eyes the world lies before me bathed once more in sunshine. Voices grow recognizable again. Limbs are whole again and flesh and blood take on the semblance of reality.

We walk quietly to the bus stand.

'Look,' my daughter says, 'a Christmas tree.'

Beside the garbage heap with its wads of cut hair, mounds of pineapple skins, scraps of food and paper, stands a Christmas tree. It is an old, withered jam fruit tree, a street tree, dying, doomed to be cut down soon. On its puny branches hang an abundance of empty tins, scraps of coloured paper and cloth, fluttering like pennants; an old tyre slung on one of the branches. Also a few crumpled flowers, old shoes.

'The beggars' Christmas tree,' I murmur.

'Ah, we can share those gifts,' my daughter says, not without a trace of irony.

'Look, *nonamahathaya*, our tree, our *nattal*,' the vagrant children call out, the children who clack their arms against their shallow chests, the hollow caves, through which echo the dull boom of ghostly voices. *Nonamahathaya* . . . not *amma*, not mother. Where are their own mothers? I too am a woman, a married woman with children, but I do not belong to them. When they address me in their poignant tones they already know I belong to others—to a husband, to children of my own . . . . Their ribs protrude like some ancient bone instrument, a vestigious harp on which their tender fingers play to leave livid bruises on the thin skin. These are the children whose lives last as long as the shadows of the bo tree leaves that fall on the street, effaced when darkness falls. Hadn't these very children once invited my husband to partake of their food—scraps of pastry from a restaurant which had been thrown on the garbage heap? They had built a small fire and set a zinc sheet on three rough stones to bake the pastries. 'Come and eat,' they had invited.

Beneath a tree sits a thin young beggar woman with a newly born infant in her arms. We bend down to give her our gifts.

'Gold, frankincense and myrrh for the Hope of the World,' my daughter utters as we count out the coins.

Bali

HOLDING MUNGO'S HANDS, the two sisters, small girls
in their smocked chintz dresses, socks and shoes,
walk to the village. Mungo's own children are looked
after by her mother. Her husband is dead. They live
in an earth-walled hut that seems to emerge out of
the hill. It is very dark and cool inside her hut, like
a cave. The floor is of smooth cowdung. The interior
of the house is so dark. You feel as if you are a
lizard clinging to the inside of a clay pot. The roof of
the hut is thatched with new straw. It is dry and the
strands rustle in the heat. Menike, Mungo's younger
daughter, comes out of the hut blinking at the strong
rays of the sun. Her eyes are red and sore, the lashes
matted with pus. She is half blind with an eye
disease. The sun spins like a silver disc through the
screen of green plantain fronds and dark dhel leaves.

The village is close to the house of the two children; but they are small, to them distances seem long, the path rugged and stony. The snakes are coiled in the undergrowth or lying hidden inside their *thumbasas*. The green snakes, the *ahatullas* twine among the creepers. 'Eye-peckers', their mother calls them. 'Be careful when you go out into the garden, the green snakes will peck out your eyes . . . .' Janine sees them on the granadilla vine like fine green tangled stems, pliant and supple, their heads watchful and raised.

The children's house is one of the railway bungalows on the hill. The roof is tiled, with glass skylights set in it through which light filters into the bedroom. There are no ceilings. The glass globed lamps hang from the rafters. The night lamp is brought into the bedroom at six o'clock in the evening. It is placed in a niche where it burns, flickering in the dark. Shadows dance against the whitewashed walls with their borders of black tar to keep away the termites. The rooms are full of furniture, the settees with cretonne-covered cushions, the centre table covered with brass ornaments and blue Chinese glass vases. There are heavy gilt-framed paintings on the walls, of Scottish landscapes, glens, forests, waterfalls. A leopard-skin backed with red felt lies on the floor, its jaws open in a grimacing snarl, its hard yellow-fanged teeth sharp against the exploring palm as the children thrust their hands inside its mouth.

Green tats hang in the verandah—rolled up and tied. They are pulled down to keep the sun out. Stepping out into the verandah, the children walk under the arbour of thumbergia into an enchanted world with thornless roses and hollyhocks, crimson dahlias, white mugerines, the Holy Ghost orchid, scorpion orchids; the world in which they played exploring every nook and cranny with Mungo.

The children walk along the path, a narrow earth path. They cling to those hard flat-palmed hands encircled by silver bracelets with a curious design engraved on them. They must have been put on Mungo's wrists when she attained age or got married. Attaining age unlocked, through the puberty rites, the gates of womanhood. After the period of seclusion, when it was taboo for her to be with the rest of the family, she lived isolated and apart in a separate room of the hut, fed with special foods and then she had the ritual bath, the cleansing—pots of water poured over her head, her body laved with culled herbs. The pot was broken at her feet, she was dressed in new clothes, in her ears and on her wrists was put not gold but silver. She was ready for marriage.

Mungo is a simple village woman. But she is their guardian and protector. She looks after all their needs, tells them folk tales, lulls them to sleep chanting her stories as she sits beside them on long hot afternoons while they lie with their heads in her lap . . .

'The fox wanted to eat the milk rice, the labu kiribhath, and so he waited and watched while the gourd, the *labugediya,* swelled and swelled and grew rich and round and the *rakshasa*, who was waiting to catch and eat the children, tempted the children with kewun, which he had placed on a tree, kewuns that were full of honey . . .'

The children hold on to her, cling to her, completely trusting her because to her this is a familiar pathway, the safe ledge along which she alone can take them.

The women of the village are bathing at the well.

The water is dark green. Dragonflies skim its surface. The children, as they move along the narrow footpath among the dark green-leafed ala kola, the bushes of red pinna flowers and the brazen sunflowers, feel their bodies slide through a lattice of light and shade. Their flesh takes on a transparency, compounded of silvery elements, and becomes insubstantial. The densely massed earth bank is crowded with attana flowers—the Devil's Trumpets, as their mother calls these white-throated flowers. Through the flowers the children think they can glimpse that secret world where the snakes are coiled, asleep.

Mungo looks after the two children, but it is the younger one who is most attached to her. She sleeps with her head on Mungo's lap, her body spreadeagled on the stretched-out legs. Mungo rocks her gently to and fro to put her to sleep while she croons to her like one of those birds that move in the long grasses that sway in the wind. Or they play together in the garden for hours and hours, sitting under the shade of the red-blossomed mara tree, the flowers sweeping down silently to fall at their feet. The split sapu pods lying about them are filled with their bitter-sweet orange-red seeds like bright parrot beaks, seeds which the father feeds the selalihinis with—the caged selalihinis, light black and yellow, that have learned to talk with human voices.

In the night the bali drums and chanting are heard from the village. The ceremony is being held tonight for Mungo's daughter. The rites and rituals are carried out to propitiate both the deities of the planets and the demons. There is dancing, drumming, chanting of verses. Offerings of betel and flowers are made. Mungo's daughter, Menike, lies, covered with a white cloth, on a *padura* beside the bali figure. She holds one end of a cord in one hand while the other is held by the exorcist. As the drumming and the incantations rise to a crescendo, Mungo's brother, the *kattadiya* who officiates as priest of the demon ceremonies, whirls in a trance and leaps into the air as he swallows the flame from a burning torch. He spews out a column of fire which bellows out into the night in furious swirling eddies, scattering sparks . . .

As they continue to walk, the pathway narrows, hedged in by cobra-hooded leaves which sway from side to side. At last they reach the village of the exorcists. It is the aftermath of the bali ceremony. They step into the compound where the great effigy of the *yakka*, moulded out of clay, lies on the ground, as if felled by some cataclysmic supernatural force. To Janine the demon is gigantic, mythic, tall as the arecanut palm. The huge protuberant black eyes seem to devour the sunlight. From what ancient memory have these faces emerged? From what time and age, until the form, shape and aspect assumed the terror and fear of man's imaginings . . .? For the *yakkas*, the demons, were here long before man had set up his habitations by rivers and streams and waterfalls and forests. These spirits dwell in darkness and desolation, you encounter them in graveyards and in lonely places. They bring sickness upon you and insanity. The *yakkas* have no relation to human faces around you. The lolling tongues, the tusked teeth, the bulging eyes—they are the reflection of the dreadful, awe-inspiring fear and terror within man's mind.

Measured against the length of her shadow, to Janine the bali images appear to be colossal. They are the cause of all maladies that assail man and release lies in their propitiation and exorcism; for the pent-up trammelled feelings to be freed from the prison of your self.

To exorcise the demons of sickness and evil within, writhing in you as you lie wrapped up in a white cloth, stretched out on a mat, with your blind dark stare, your mind twining with snakes, the *kattadiya* chants his incantations and you are rid of your burning fever and delirium. Red, yellow, blue, white and black colours from the barks of trees, from seeds crushed to yield juices, have been used to paint the folds of the cloth and the flesh of the body. The black bulging eyes leap out of the white protuberant orbs, fearful and hypnotic, opaque with matt darkness.

Flowers, yellow, white and red, marigolds, araliya, hibiscus, lie scattered, fallen from the *pideni tatuvas* woven out of leaves containing the offerings to the demons. Janine stoops to pick up the bright flowers strewn about.

'Do not touch *bebi*, do not touch,' Mungo gently cautions. 'Never pick up the flowers that fall after the *thovil*. The demon that has caused the illness has been cast out. All the evil powers that had affected my daughter, all the *vas* that has been exorcised, lies in those offerings.'

'What will happen to me?' Janine asks Mungo, her hand half stretched out to pick the flowers.

'You will become afflicted with sickness. You will get sores on your hands. Then there must be a bali for you too. So let them lie where they are.'

The flowers are left then to wither in the sun and to lose their brightness.

Every afternoon Janine calls Mungo out into the garden at the hour when the lizards are asleep. Her mother too is indoors, the green bamboo tats pulled down, sleeping on the French bed. Morning, afternoon, evening, time is measured by light and dark. It is night when the leaves of the thumbergia bower grow dark, almost black, and the honeypeckers have had their fill of nectar. The green snakes twine like slim fingers in the hair of the grenadilla creeper. The night owl hoots from the anodha tree. But in the hot afternoon light under the shade of the mara tree Mungo and Janine play for hours with the red flowers dropping down gently, soundlessly, like red rain upon them. The petals are caught in snares of light and shadow cast by the intertwined branches.

Janine picks up the flowers, the meat and food of her fantasies, and crushes and pounds them on stones. The juices run out. The flower meat cooks in the sun and is served out on leaves for her invisible guests. She mixes the new earth with rain water and bakes cakes in the sun, embellished with petals of wild flowers and ferns. She puts them away on shelves, awaiting the advent of her brother and sister from boarding school in Kandy. She imagines that the wild flowers will never fade; that the earth will always bear the freshness of sun and rain. Mungo teaches her to pick up the tender kurumbetti, peel off the outer layers, stick ekels taken from dried coconut fronds into them and make toys, fold dried jak leaves, skewer them with twigs and set them soaring in the air. They twist leaves and fix them onto thin fine sticks. Then, holding them aloft, Janine runs all over the garden. Bambaras which spin with the currents of air. The air sings with their whirring as they turn and turn in the wind.

In the trees the red ants weave their leaf nests lined with a soft fleece of cobwebby fluff; the grenadilla slowly ripens on the hedge; the thornless roses grafted by Janine's father bud and bloom. The cream roses are streaked with a flush of pink, the petals bear the faintest blush, the stalks smooth, free of *visa*, the poisonous, vicious red-tipped thorn. The shiny black millipedes scuttle on feathery legs and snails hide in the cool mossy shade safeguarding the glistening moisture of their flesh that soon dries in the heat. The bees fly in and out of their blue-painted hives, their buzz presaging a threatening sting when they are smoked out and the thick honeycombs taken out. Janine has felt the sting, the red swelling with the white needle embedded in it. Her father had carefully removed it and Mungo had rubbed it over gently with white *chunam* that was cool against the soreness.

Among the flowers and trees scurry squirrels and millipedes; bees and wasps buzz around; birds carry wisps of straw for nesting, butterflies rest on the thornless roses and caterpillars eat slowly into the leaf. Who can think beyond the here and now in this garden, the preserve of innocence where you can smell the earth and air, the plants and the ripe fruit, the mangoes, guava, jak and passion fruit. The golden orioles, yellow as the segments of ripe jak, flash on the branches. Mungo has so much patience sitting by the child hour after hour in this timelessness of childhood in which Janine never seems to grow up.

Mungo and Janine pick up small pebbles, place them on the back of their hands, toss them into the air, then catch them in their palms . . .'*Athuru, mithuru, dambadiva thuru*', they chant . . .'*athuru mithuru, athuru mithuru . . . .*' Or Janine tucks herself into the hammock of Mungo's lap, into the striped cambaya cloth, and intones the incantation that she has learnt: '*Kaputu kaa, kaa, goraka dain, dain, Ussi kaputa!*' and she springs up and waves her arms wildly to shoo away the crows that fly away, flapping their wings, crying raucously, to perch elsewhere, their purple black beaks tearing apart the carrion flesh of dead bats and maggoty flying foxes.

Rather than be separated from Mungo even for a moment, Janine would prefer that the whole world go up in flames. Fire. At the bali ritual it had sprung from the burning torches to surge skywards, the darkness slit by streaks of crimson like the blood-red winking eyes of the black cock bird slaughtered in the rituals that exorcise the demons that dwell all around you, your mind crawling with white-bellied snakes with black markings like the speckles on the trunk of the coconut palm. Dark brown snakes, black ones, snakes wreathing the head of the demon . . .

Mungo carries the night lamp in her hand shielding the flame, carries it into the bedroom, and it casts shadows on the whitewashed walls. Janine wants to hold her back, to take her by the arm and hold back night and dark, to still the sound of the bali drums, to lead her out into the garden and play games with her. But she cannot hold back time. Janine follows her, chases her round and round the house, overtakes her and grasps her by the hand; the lamp falls from Mungo's hands and Mungo falls too. The fragile glass chimney splinters and the flame flies up, takes its last breath and is still.

So tonight there will be no night lamp. The room will be wrapped in darkness. Janine cannot run and hide from what she has done. She is punished for hurting Mungo. But no one can understand why she has done it—this whole game of keeping time at bay, of holding Mungo hostage, of wanting to possess Mungo for herself, to keep her imprisoned in the shadow of her childhood forever.

She sleeps in the dark. The moon wrapped in flames from the torches that reach the sky becomes blood red. Then, burnt to a cinder, it goes black and falls in ashes at dawn. She lies in bed thinking of the bali ceremony. Far bigger and greater than the golden snakes that emerge out of the red anthills were the serpents that had writhed and twisted round that demon head crowned with wide blue-black hoods. Those serpents had eyes that saw into the night through the flames to where those demons, the *yakkas* dwelt—Maha Sohon Yaksaya, Riri Yakka, Kalu Kumara Yakka, the Gara Yakku and Ratha Yakku. The *peretayas*, spirits of the departed, lurked in graveyards and desolate places. All power and fear lay within the great effigy of the *yakka*, with its towering figure, its huge loins.

This *yakka* must be propitiated with offerings and rituals—offerings of flowers and fruit, the slicing of hundreds of limes, the slashing of the neck of the sacrificial cock bird. The *kattadiya* dances through her dreams, leaping into the darkness torched with flames. Yet, before she sleeps Janine kneels every night at her mother's feet and says her prayers. Mother sits on the four poster bed and the two girls kneel on either side of her. 'Gentle Jesus meek and mild . . .' they repeat after her. They wear cotton nightdresses that billow out, fresh white cotton sun-dried and ironed out by Mungo. They lay their heads on their pillows but sleep does not come easily. The sounds of the bali drums start up from the village of exorcists. The anodha tree in the garden comes alive with the stories that Mungo has related from her own childhood store of folklore. There are *rakshasas* in the trees, hiding there to catch you and carry you away. You must be careful not to be tempted by the kewun tree, where the kewun, soft and dripping with honey, hang like ripe fruit. If you eat of that tree you will be charmed. You will have to follow the *rakshasi* and be killed, eaten up, your bones cracked and split for the marrow. If you drop your fingernails or the hair from your head, you will be charmed. The charm will have to be dug out by the exorcist or you will get ill or go insane. There is poison and evil in speech and in sight and in thoughts. Evil in the mind of others—*kata vaha as vaha. vas dos;* the evil may be uttered or thought. You can languish away. The plants will shrivel and die. The black clay pot in the paddy field is painted with white *chunam*, a grotesque grimacing face, to scare away the birds and keep away the evil eye from blighting the harvest. The faces of the people round Janine are gentle but can they protect her from the demons that they themselves will never see?

As Janine grows up, her mother feels her weight grow heavy on her lap as she flings herself onto her. 'Child, you're too heavy,' she exclaims and shakes her off impatiently. She is a small-boned woman with ivory white skin through which the blue veins show. Almost always stockinged, gartered, corsetted, her flesh and spirit held at bay. She is a soft, gentle-mannered woman who listens to reason, unlike Janine's father who is volatile and impulsive. She allows her children a great deal of freedom. She does not impinge on Janine's world of fantasy, lets her sleep till late on a school morning so that Janine often goes off absent-mindedly, leaving her books and pencils at home, rushing to catch the train still half asleep. The train flies past on the tracks, cinders blowing into her eyes.

Janine's companion is Milroy who goes to the same school. He is a quiet boy but one day he turns cruel and punches her black and blue, cuffing her on the ears as she cowers helplessly, unable to fend him off. She is enraged at her own helplessness . . . . One day, sitting on the rocks of an abandoned tea estate with Milroy and Menike, Mungo's daughter who is a servant in Milroy's family, looking down on the railway tracks, Janine has a sudden impulse to hurt. She wants to hear the hollow boom that echoes from the cave of the human body, like the echoes of voices that strike the hills of Belungala. She gives a short sharp blow on Menike's back . . . . And she is punished for something she cannot explain. This feeling of aggression, all dammed up within her. She cringes with guilt as she is called a wicked, cruel girl. 'You have been naughty,' Mrs Jones says, 'it was cruel of you.' Janine cringes and bends over the food that had lost all its savour. She does not understand her own aggression. She knows that she has done something wrong. Isolation is her punishment.

Janine also quarrels with her sister Elsa when they play together on the verandah. All her precious dolls which the aunts have brought from England are being petted and cosseted by her sister, so she holds Elsa by her hair and starts knocking her head hard against the wall, until she howls and Mother comes running out to stop her. There are no words to express the blind rage within Janine.

A telegram arrives, informing Janine's family of her grandfather's death and they travel by train to Colombo with Mother. Father does not want any of them near him. He feels grief but he does not want their comfort. He has lost a young son too and the earth is still too fresh in the newly-dug grave. Janine watches him step forward from among his brothers and sisters and place a wreath upon the mound of piled-up earth. What is death? She does not even know that it is like sleep. She has never seen the body of someone who has died. Only the shape of the coffin, like a flower-covered boat moving slowly on a dark ocean.

She remembers Jock Young, the Scottish scoutmaster, who had come with his scout troop to which her brother belonged, to their home in Kadugannawa. They had gone up the hill where Janine used to wander alone, the preserves which she knew so well. She liked his gentleness, his lean wiry body, his fine featured face. She had watched him hold up his binoculars to gaze at the vistas before him—Dawson's Tower, the hills of Belungala, the small township with its railway station, turn table, siding shed and scattered bungalows. It was a small world and he tried to look beyond it. What did he see? A world that could not contain him? He had gone away to fight in the Second World War and no one knows in which battle he had died or even where he was buried.

And Jem Smith, the foreman platelayer who brought them toys at Christmas time, had also gone back to England where he had died in the Blitz. This was the beginning of her awareness of grief and sorrow, loss and bereavement. Some months later she had stood and watched from afar as her father carried the dead Belle, the Airedale which he loved, in a gunny sack to be buried under the chow-chow creepers; and Timmy, the long-eared black Cocker spaniel had to be put to sleep, with her beautiful black velvet-furred litter, because she had been bitten by a rabid dog . . . . And she thinks of how the tails of new-born puppies are cut. They are a special breed that her father rears and the little stumps are bound in iodine stained bandages. But when she falls down and bruises her knees, she makes a salve of wild herbs to staunch her blood, the wild hulanthala crushed between her fingers, the green juice mingling with the redness.

She wanders up the hill alone among the scented

tea bushes with wild flowers and wild strawberries. She has no fear of being alone; the snakes coiled in the deep undergrowth of ferns and leaves. It is the season of her growing.

The wild strawberries taste both tart and sweet on her tongue. She allows the leeches to cling onto her flesh and bloat with blood, glowing like incandescent bulbs and then she lets them fall off after they have had their fill; wounds here do not leave deep scars.

So many years afterwards, the child who is herself now a mother with big children goes in search of Mungo. Janine's journey begins out of danger, the loss of hope and the loss of faith in all human nature after she had had to flee from her home and live behind barriers in a camp for refugees. After she came out of the dark tunnel she did not know which route to take. She felt alien and homeless. She longed to find Mungo again, that pure soul whose only desire was to protect and care for the two children in her charge. The days when Mungo could hold them back from touching evil have long passed. Out in this world those words of warning have not helped. Janine has known all human fears and sorrows; tears have burnt her cheeks; all the bloom has vanished, leaving them pale and wan. Yet she has returned as if to reassure herself that there had once been a past innocence, not that it can ever be recaptured; to be reminded that it had once been there in the world she had inhabited. She goes out on to those wide and crowded streets, into those proliferating gardens where no one had been present to hold her back from picking those brilliant blood red flowers of evil.

She climbs up the steps which seem too narrow

to hold her feet. She reaches the verandah of her old home; strangers live in the house, sprawling on easy chairs. The green tats have vanished, the thumbergia bower with its golden honeypeckers is no longer here. Here, on this verandah, she begins to remember. She had come back from Mrs Swan's to silence and emptiness. She had been sent there to spend the day. Where was her sister Elsa? Mungo had come out of the room, held Janine tenderly by the hands and told her: '*Bebi*, your sister has been taken to hospital, she has had an accident. When she was running along the verandah while she was playing she fell into the drain and fractured her wrist. Your mother has taken her to the hospital in Kandy, but do not be afraid, tonight I will sleep beside your bed. There is nothing for you to be afraid of now, is there? Tomorrow we will all go and see *loku bebi* in the hospital.'

When she went to see her sister in hospital she found that Elsa had already made friends with a little boy who was a patient there. She now had a new playmate while Janine went back to an empty, lonely house. The loneliness continued when her brother and sister returned to their boarding school in Kandy. The rains came, families were flooded out of their bungalows and the beautiful Sylvia Craighlaw came with her children to stay temporarily with them. Janine would watch her admiringly, her dark slanting eyes, ivory skin and dark wavy hair. She had a secret inward look about her as if her inner life and thoughts were walled in. Her husband was a blue-eyed, red-cheeked man, an official in the railway and Sylvia's life appeared to be devoid of the romance she longed for. Some years later she was to leave her husband and children, flout all the conventions of the time, divorce her staid husband

and marry a small, dashing Captain in the British Army. Her secret, she would tell the other ladies, was that in order to win a man a woman must always be a good listener. But Janine knew that it was Sylvia's supple body, ivory skin and dark secret gaze which really drew men to her.

Janine remembers watching her young cousin Lorna walking with her lover under the thunbergia bower. They stood under its green shade, with the honeypeckers dipping into the nectar that welled in the cerise throats of the flowers, with their arms entwined about each other. Lorna had brilliant blue eyes and Titian red hair, she was as beautiful as a Renaissance painting. Bert's looks were dark and saturnine; they were both so young and vulnerable, on the threshold of life, and they had come to announce their betrothal to their aunt and uncle. But they would not be like this forever. Time would pass, they would cross the seas and Bert would grow to be an invalid and die, leaving Lorna alone and bereaved.

Baby Uncle visited them and laughed and joked as if he had never known sorrow in his life. He was the only son of a Sinhalese family, rich, with many acres of land. Yet he never married and never had children, and no one remembered him when his laughter was finally stilled and he died.

Janine is reminded also of her father's grief and sorrow after Budgie's death. 'Janine,' her mother had once told her, 'your father was so disappointed when you were born. After Budgie's death he had wanted another son.' Was that why when she was very small her father had once wanted her to be dressed up in a pair of blue shorts and a white shirt. He had asked her to come to where he was with his friends, near the engine turntable in the railway yard. The children used often to go on the big steam engine as it was turned slowly round on its steel rails.

'This is my son,' he had told his friends. Janine had blushed and felt very shy. How many disguises do adults always want children to put on? Are they not too old to play these games? Or are they so serious about them that fantasy may be transformed into reality?

Janine feels she must find strength in the fact that innocence had once existed not only in those closest to her but also in herself. Mungo had sought to protect her from all the manifestations of evil. Those pretty flowers of orange and gold, of white and red, that lay strewn and scattered from the *pideni*, still bearing their freshness—Janine had wanted to pick them up, but they had been touched by evil. The moon had been wrapped in the flames that swirled above the head of the exorcist, the burning brands scattering their sparks. The sky was red and the great bali demon, Riri Yakka, had loomed out of the dark, towering over her life.

She will never find Mungo again. She finally knows that that safety would never have endured. The protected garden had belonged only to childhood. The stones and pebbles they played with in their ritualistic games have grown into sharp, jagged rocks to be hurled with great murderous force, to kill and maim. The blood from the slaughtered cock bird is now the blood from the virgin who is raped in the forest where the flying foxes screech as they maraud the fruit.

There is guilt and sorrow now in the lives of those around her. Janine had known it all along. She sees it once more as clearly as she had once done when she had stooped to pick up those flowers, red hibiscus, yellow marigolds spilled from the *pideni*, lying on the red earth after the bali drums were stilled and the flames quenched from the exorcist's torch. And once more in the *kamatha* the cobra with its outspread hood has crept out.

She stands suspended, for a moment, before she takes the next step, nearer, nearer, towards that inevitable confrontation with violence, with death, with destruction.

A Husband Like Shiva

Man desires an apsara in bed and the woman, a husband like Shiva.

THE YEARS HAD passed. The garden had diminished. The leaves had not been swept and lay scattered where the wind had blown them. The araliya flowers lay strewn about beneath the trees, the smell of their wilting petals overwhelmingly sickly-sweet. The bird bath was empty of water. Radha felt a sense of oppression within the rooms of the locked house with its massed and heavy antique furniture which belonged to an epochal and alien civilization. The Victorian style furniture in the drawing room draped with its dust covers gave it an untenanted look. Years and years of living in the same house. How many years? Over fifty perhaps. Growing older each day and trying desperately to hold on to the joyousness of her youth.

Her veena, where was it? She hadn't touched it for years. She tried singing a verse where the goddess describes Lord Shiva, the Destroyer and Creator:

> *Protection, promised in hand uplifted*
> *His arms adorned with hooded serpents*
> *A tiger skin his garment,*
> *The crescent moon in his hair,*
> *His feet beautiful as the petal of the red lotus,*
> *And anklets sounding music as He dances*
> *His face alight with divinest compassion,*
> *A third eye on his forehead.*

Her voice had lost its musical quality. She had neglected to use that gift. Where was her veena? Nowhere to be seen. It must be in the storeroom, abandoned, dust-covered, in some corner. The house was silent. Her husband, Maharaj, was quietly dozing on the armchair. He had given her everything that a woman desired—expensive clothes, jewellery, cars, houses and estates. Whenever she wanted she could go on holidays abroad. He had not been like his father who had had mistresses, had even fathered children by them. Her own three sons were now grown up and living abroad. The house was filled with the sighs of emptiness.

She walked along the corridor, going past the kitchen where her maid Saro was cooking mutton porial for lunch. They ate well. Crabs, prawns, chicken, mutton. On Fridays Radha fasted and went to the temple. She stopped at the door of the backroom, opened the door and peered in. The veena was there, covered with an old silk saree among the cabin trunks, leather suitcases, odds and ends of furniture and piled up mattresses. She bent over it, lifted it up and carried it to her bedroom. She took an old piece of linen from a torn bedsheet in one of the cupboards and gently began to wipe the dust off the surface; the golden brown wood was dull beneath its patina of accumulated dust, a gossamer of cobwebs was puckered up between the strings, stifling those hidden, ghostly notes. Her fingers tried to pluck the strings. The veena had not been tuned for years. She sounded only discords. The delicate paintings on the surface had lost their lustre. Dust motes shimmered in a beam of light that came in through the lace curtains of the open window. Fanciful images uncoiled in the piercing shaft of light.

At her birth itself tradition had decreed the course Radha's life would take. She had, when she was young, done all that was expected of her. Her marriage had been part of a heritage into which she had been born. It had been a comfortable alliance. Her husband, Maharaj, would always be there, until his death. But which one of them would go first? She loved life. She would not relinquish it so easily. She had gathered wisdom through the years. She would never squander those gifts of wealth and comfort. Not like that woman Saradha who had had everything, who belonged to the same stratum in the social hierarchy and had sacrificed it all. And for what? Leaving her husband, a distinguished lawyer in the city—Saradha herself the daughter of a judge of the Supreme Court—to run away with a foreign lover to a tragic tryst in the romantic landscape of Venice, her El-Dorado. But she had failed, failed and returned with her half Italian daughter to beg on the streets of Colombo, displaced and homeless . . . . Radha shuddered. She had never allowed herself to

310

be swept away, carried away by the lovers who had importuned her. No, never. Her feet in their gold sandals had never felt the dust of the road. But she had lost—what had she lost together with her youth and beauty? Why had she allowed the strings of her veena to snap, to gather dust, the cobwebs to wreathe its wooden frame? Her life was now crowded with social engagements. She no longer had time to play the veena and sing *kirthanams*. Her singing voice would not bring enchantment any more. It had vanished with her being scarcely aware of the passage of time after her marriage.

When Radha was young, she was always made to feel special. Everything was in her favour. Her reputation was impeccable, her chastity and moral purity assured. She would do nothing to mar the status of her family in the social circles they moved in. Her mother, Mrs Shivalingam, was a woman greatly revered and respected in her generation. It was always the dignified personage of Mrs Shivalingam who was at the forefront of all the marriage rituals even while bathing the bride with milk and honey. It was what women of their privileged social standing had to submit to—subject themselves to a kind of subtle sleuthing, a prying to detect flaws and imperfections in the most intimate parts of the female body. What if there were scars, signs of former misdemeanours? To submit to this ritual was the tradition of these high-caste Vellala families. Submission was ingrained in the woman from the time of her birth, carried on to these prenuptial rites. Virginity was a special requirement or she, the woman, would be spurned. The milk and honey that was poured on the as yet unviolated body, the virgin body, made her feel she was a goddess, part of that mythology of fertility, being prepared for procreation. When Radha had come of age, she was fed special food—eggs, sesame oil, the flour of different grains stirred into a thick porridge, and fruits—to make the womb strong for bringing forth many children. Radha had seen the goddesses bathed by devotees in the temples of Thanjavur and Madurai and Nallur, with milk and honey, with *theertham* and *kumkumum*. The bride to be who stepped shivering and naked for the ceremony had to submit to the scrutiny of those experienced eyes of women who had acquired knowledge of the men they had slept with for years, whose most intimate habits they had grown used to with acceptance and submission. The woman's awareness of her own sexuality was not of any importance. The Kamasutra was generally read by the men. A woman's compliance with those unwritten strictures on chastity and virginity were the guidelines to a happy and successful marriage. Sometimes things did not always work out as expected. During one bride bathing ritual, Radha's mother had detected an early pregnancy in the young woman. What secret terrors of being discovered the young woman must have had, and yet she had escaped. Mrs Shivalingam had kept it a secret. The bride was swathed in her vermilion *koorai* saree and led to the *manaverai*, her eyes cast down demurely, to await the bridegroom. The fires in the sacred *yaham* continued to burn steadily.

Radha herself was now ready for marriage. Opposite the house where all these women, Radha and her cousins, were living, was a huge mansion with tall iron gates on either side of the high walls. The young women were in a state of suspended living. They had nothing else to look forward to but marriage. They were all waiting for the elders to bring proposals from well-known families, eligible suitors with unsmirched lineage who wanted family name, caste and virginity to be assured. The young women would gaze at the two storeyed mansion with the ornate wrought-iron gates locked against all intruders and indulge in fanciful couplings with the two eligible young sons of the family, sons who would ride the white horses in the wedding procession wearing the white and gold silk of their caste and lineage, their cockatoo-crested turbans fanning out erect and crisp; senses overcome by the heady fragrance of *attar* of roses sprinkled from silver flagons and jasmine garlands streaming on the *manaverai* and swinging massed and heavy on the braided oil-sleeked hair of the bride . . . the vermilion silk in its heavy folds, smooth yet stiff and unyielding until it is draped around the woman's body, imprisoning her still further in its swathes and wrappings; feet flashing with anklets and toe-rings of silver, hands beringed, throat, wrists, ears, nostril laden with family heirlooms, henna patterning the palms and soles of feet with an orange-red tracery of intricate designs. The ordinary flesh disguised by the elaborate trappings of marriage.

And so they waited, waited and waited, each of them, for a husband like Shiva.

Sivam's story

Sivam, the bank clerk, sat in the small dark backroom in the house of his rich relatives, poring over the letters given to him by the go-between. Love letters. Letters from a young woman who professed her admiration of him. He, a humble clerical servant. He read avidly, the blue note paper still bearing a faint hint of fragrance from the flowers in her hair. 'What does she promise?' Love. Fidelity.

'I am prepared to marry you. I see you pass by the house everyday. I know what your feelings are towards me. I reciprocate them too. I know that my parents, my relatives will be dead against our plans, yet I am prepared to face all opposition. Nothing should deter us . . . .'

Recklessness of phrase. Could all this be true?

'I can then hope.' Sivam folded the letter, put it carefully away in a drawer of the cupboard which held his office clothes and his veshtis that he wore to the temple on Fridays.

'I can hope. I have compelled her to notice me. I am not the kind of suitor whom that family would ever consider for their daughter. Their aspirations are higher. They have such pride, they are so arrogant. It's just my status in life . . . too humble for them. Yet, what does she say in these letters? Isn't it attraction to me, as a lover . . . . I pass by the house everyday. She is dressed, ready, waiting for me. I have glimpsed her, once, twice . . . . Perfection. Who would not desire her? Her creamy complexion, wavy hair. That air of innocent playfulness.

'She wears flowers in her hair. Garlands of jasmines, half-opened buds . . . . I know what people are saying—there's this big proposal for her. A wealthy suitor. Drives me crazy to think that that's what they will ultimately go for. As for myself? Who will think of me as a suitable husband for their daughters? I come from a good family . . . from the North. We have our lands there, paddy, palmyrah groves, the family house in the village where we have lived for generations. But here, in the city, values are different. This backroom is all the space I have in the house of my relatives. They live their lives, I, mine. I suppose I must be thankful. I don't earn very much as a bank clerk and I send money home, to the North, for my aged parents, for my sisters' dowries. These young girls in the city . . . they are somehow different. Their parents had left the ancestral villages so long ago. They only go back for the temple festivals at Nallur, Sellachannadhi, Mavattipuram, or for holidays in their houses by the sea. The young women wait for marriage. They're all pent up, waiting for their bridegrooms. Nothing to do with their lives. Idling away their days. Locked up. No going out without chaperones, the old women with eagle eyes. But I know, I know what's going on in their minds.

'Renga tells me of their longings, their desires. He brings me their letters, takes them the gifts I send. The girls sit together, chat, eyeing the chocolates, the sweets I send them—laddus and ghee-rich Mysore pak. Oh yes, I've seen those ardent looks . . . . Those flowers in their hair, the crimson tilaks on their foreheads, those large bindis—they aren't for the gods only. They go to the temple every Friday, during Deepavali, Mahashivarathri and worship, pray, sing *thevarams*, make vows, pray, pray, pray, for husbands with the aspects of the gods . . . . In their fervour they imagine the gods stepping down from their pedestals and walking with them round the sacred *yaham* . . .

'All of them, all of them . . . . I could choose if I want . . . but it's only she, only she, really, Radha, whom I desire. The others mean nothing to me. They're all collecting silk sarees for their weddings. Jewellery. Dowries. They wear nothing but pure sovereign gold jewellery. Their *thalis* will be heavy with twenty gold sovereigns at least.

'These letters are proof that Radha is attracted to

me. Perhaps I can approach her parents? No. Useless. It's a vain hope and yet . . . . I've got news that things might not go too well with the marriage. I hear letters are going all over the city, to friends, to relatives and to the family from where the proposal was brought—the Vigneshwerans. Rumours of a secret love affair of Radha's. I know the consequences only too well. They will bring everything to a standstill. Everybody is gossiping here and yet the Vigneshwerans want Radha so much as a daughter-in-law. I know what the letters contain . . . . "Radha is having an affair with Sivam. She is carrying on with him in secret. She sends him love letters. Think carefully before you proceed any further. She is not a suitable match for your son."

'Yes, I know the people who are responsible for sending out these letters. I don't want to destroy her happiness. But what about my feelings? I desire more than anything else to sit beside her on the *manavarai*, to give her the vermilion silk *koorai*. I want so much to go round the sacred *yaham* with her. I want to clasp that *thali* round her neck.

'It's Renga's sisters who are concocting all these anonymous letters, casting aspersions on her reputation. There's not enough excitement in their lives. And there are distances too between Radha's family and the families of Sashi and Kokila, Renga's sisters . . .'

That was true. The two girls lived with their mother and unemployed brother Renga in another part of the city in a small house. One of their sisters, Shivarani, had married a lawyer and moved away. She had given birth to two daughters, Kamalini and Yogini, and died when the children were very young. The widower had re-married and had one daughter,

Ragini, who was Radha's cousin. The step-daughters lived in the same house together with their step-mother and step-sister but there was a great deal of conflict within the household. Ragini's mother sent her step-children away as often as possible to spend days with their grandmother and aunts in Kotahena.

The two girls, Kamalini and Yogini, felt left out and unwanted. They didn't get on well with the step-mother. The young aunts were unmarried and were envious of Radha and Ragini. They themselves lived in the Roman Catholic dominated part of the city, away from the big mansions and the solidly built houses of the prosperous Tamil families in Cinnamon Gardens. They felt, as a result, that they would not have the same chances of making a good marriage. They were not sought after. It had only been Shivarani who had managed to escape. Their minds began to plot and plan.

Everyone in the city, in their social circle, was buzzing with the news of the proposal for Radha from one of the Vigneshweran sons. Not for them such matches. They felt jealousy eating into them at the thought of the privileges she would enjoy. They themselves could never escape from their little middle-class house in Kotahena. Their brother was a dissolute young man, jobless, idle. He would visit his nieces, listen to their conversations, report on them to all and sundry. He was friendly with Sivam who confided in him his great attraction to Radha. All of these young girls stayed in the same house, especially since Radha's mother was often in the North in their family house in the village where the sons were being educated during the war years.

There was a great deal of innocence among the cousins. They walked about in the garden, sitting on a garden seat among the rose bushes, the sun warm on their skins, breathing in the coolness from the water sprinkled on the flowers and the potted palms. They had nothing to do with their time except to talk, laugh, play games, go shopping or visit the temple while they waited for their marriages to take place. Radha had her veena and singing lessons of course and her very sweet and melodious voice would fill the air with the ragas and *kirthanams*.

Days passed in dalliance. The piles of silk sarees in their tissue folds began to grow, stored carefully in their cardboard boxes in the wardrobe. Patu sarees. Kinkhab of Benares. Patola. Heavy with gold lace and gold embroidered flowers. Like Sita's, of whose elaborate trousseau Valmiki wrote, 'woollen stuffs, furs, precious stones, fine silk vestments of diverse colours, princely, ornamental and sumptuous carriage of every kind.' Wealth would be displayed through these rich clothes and through the jewels Radha would inherit from her mother—the *attiyal*, *mukukutthi*, bracelets and earrings. There would also be delicate nets, chiffons, georgettes embroidered in silk or silver thread or studded with sequins. After her marriage Radha would have to display herself in several changes of clothes on those visits to houses of relations or those occasions when she would have to entertain guests. The seamstresses usually visited the house and the sewing machines whirred as they sewed saree blouses and undergarments.

Until the day when she would be married, Radha was still free to sing and give performances at cultural shows. She was busy every day, practicing and rehearsing for special performances. Then the day arrived for her performance on Radio Ceylon. Her eldest brother and cousins were to accompany her in the family car. She never went out anywhere alone, unchaperoned. She had practiced the ragas she was to sing. She was prepared, her voice would be sweet and melodious as always. They entered the area where the Radio Ceylon building stood. As she turned the corner of the building, her brother carrying the veena, she saw him coming towards her. He was smiling, his face transformed by an air of expectation, sure of recognition and acceptance. She knew who he was. That man who passed by their house everyday, the bank clerk. She watched him, startled.

In his manner, in his bearing there was a sense of ease, complicity and familiarity as if they were old acquaintances. In his expression there was only pleasure at the dazzle of light on her perfect face. That face, which to him was like a jewel: gold, topaz, amber. His glance alighted on her face like a caress. He wanted her to greet him. He was confident that she would greet him. He did not fear rejection. She gasped at his sight, felt her heart beginning to thud. Her lips felt dry. A chill crept up her fingers, they were paralyzed.

'How can I play the veena! How can I sing the ragas!' she thought. 'My fingers are stiff. I can only strike discords if I touch those strings.'

A feeling of great terror engulfed her, as if she were alone in a jungle. She wanted to cower among the leaves, hide from the footpad that came towards her. The thick, fecund growth stifled her, the thorns snarled her smooth hair.

She screamed at him, 'What are you doing here?'

He stopped in his tracks. A look of stunned incomprehension arrested his smile. It was overtaken by despair.

'Go away! Go away! Not here, I don't want you here!' she cried. How could she escape him? That smile ensnared her with threat and fear. It was a sunny day but she felt only darkness and gloom encompass her. The gold chain was a thick liana round her throat. Tightening. The silk of her saree rasped against her skin.

He was almost upon her. She had intercepted him in time but she had felt the touch of that strong, bare, unknown hand violating her body, her life. She did not want it.

The faces about her, her friends' faces, her brother's, were disembodied, part of the tricks of light and shade in the jungle. Couldn't they save her? Their faces, shocked, spun, shining discs in the shattered light.

Her eldest brother spoke at last, addressing the man. 'How did you get here, past security? You have no right, no right to accost my sister like this. She must not be disturbed. She has come here for a performance that must go on the air and you appear suddenly to upset her. You know that you can be arrested. This is war time, you can be suspected of anything. I can have you taken in . . . you can be shot . . . . Look, you have nothing to do with my sister. She wants nothing to do with you. Leave her in peace . . . leave her alone . . .'

The man's face appeared to Sivam like a totem carving in a jungle. They were in a jungle. Now he was the hunted. He turned away, ran along the length of the wall, clambered over it and disappeared. A fugitive.

Radha felt her palms turn to ice. The ragas she had so carefully rehearsed would never emerge from the taut muscles of her throat.

'My voice! My hands! I'm in turmoil. This friendliness, this intimacy is not something I ever invited . . . no, I never meant . . . . It's a misunderstanding. A mistake. He's a threat to my happiness. I should have known. An obsession. This passion. It was not something to be taken seriously . . .'

Sivam had first believed everything that the letters had contained but now he began to think anew. He had been deceived. But by whom? And why? He had thought that she was prepared to love him. He did not want to think otherwise. At least his dreams lay within those letters. Her thoughts and desires had become part of his imagination.

He had passed by that garden, that house every day and he knew she was always there, he felt her presence. The garden was fresh with carefully tended flowers, the leaves and petals glistening with the glittery sheen of sprinkled water. Flowers that dazzled the sight and awakened the senses with their newly born fragrance. And the flowers the young women wore in their hair—overpowering in their sensual appeal. Women reposing in bowers heavy with the scent of jasmine, dallying with the hours of their youth. The chords of the veena reaching out of inner rooms and a voice singing songs that emerged out of Radha-Krishna legends. For him, there was the hope, the promise of all the delights that reposed like fragrant spices—the betel in a silver box, the cardamom and cloves, the slivers of creamy white areca, the white chunam that burned the tongue, the dizzying shreds of tobacco, the fresh green leaves. They would offer the leaf to him in invitation, he would carefully wrap within the leaf that amalgam of delights and close his eyes to dream while she sang the Krishna songs . . . .

And now they were threatening him. They threatened to interrogate him. Mortal fear. He tossed on his bed, the narrow bed in the small back room of his rich relative's house. Sleepless, night after night. Their voices dinned in his ears. Persistent. And his heart thudded in his chest. An irregular pendulum knocking at the hours that tortured him.

The brother had threatened him, 'There are severe penalties for what you have done. It is a grave matter. You have tried to ruin a young girl's chances of marriage. You have tried to ruin her reputation. You could have destroyed her life.'

'I believed that she was in love with me,' Sivam had stammered.

'What made you feel so sure, so confident?' Rajan, the brother had demanded.

'All the letters that she sent me . . . .' Sivam's rejoinder had been half-pleading, with a weak attempt at bravado. Yet there was innocence in his utterance.

'Letters?' Rajan had pursued relentlessly.

'Yes, letters.'

'What did they contain?'

'Expressions of her love for me.' No one could have expressed such naivete unless he was completely blinded by the illusion. So false in itself.

'But you know that it was wrong, very wrong of you to encourage a secret affair. Our people are of high social standing. This is not the way we do things in families like ours. Everything is arranged by the elders. In a formal manner. It is not for the young woman to chose her partner. Not in these circles.'

'But the letters were sent for me. My name was on them. They were signed by her.'

'But you have never even spoken to her.' Rajan's tones had been incredulous.

'It was not necessary to speak. We had seen each other, there was a go-between . . . a friend . . . he told me that she was attracted to me . . . that he would carry the letters for us.' Was this confession necessary? This interrogation?

'Did you really imagine that you had chances?

You don't belong to our social status . . . you could never have maintained her in the comfort she is used to or given her the life she expected . . . . What's your job anyway?'

The questions still hurtled against Sivam's brain. He felt the cold shock of realization grip him. These people considered him to be a nobody. Not of any worth or value because of his lack of wealth and power. He remembered some of his answers.

'I am a clerk in a bank.'

'And do you know whom they have brought a proposal from for my sister?' Rajan had said with a sense of pride.

'Yes,' Sivam spoke humbly. 'I have heard . . . everybody in Colombo is speaking of it . . . a favourable match . . .'

'You know of the prospective bridegroom and still you tried to spoil her chances. He's a much more powerful person than you. The family occupies a very high social status. They have wealth, property.

'Is that all?' Sivam had spoken with a certain irony. So that's what these people respected most then?

'Yes, the family has vast assets in the city. Coconut estates, houses up-country, temples, hereditary properties. And you think you would be given preference?'

'If she loved me she would make sacrifices.' It had been a dubiously confident yet pitiful assertion.

'What could you have given her?' What was Rajan assessing? Were they discussing the bargaining power of money or the couple's happiness?

'Everything. Myself. Would have devoted myself to her well-being, given her what young women desire most, a devoted husband. I wanted to be the father of our children . . . to adore her . . .'

'In such families as ours, we look for other things. There is no place for you there. There never will be. Give up all your hopes. Do you think there would ever be a welcome for you in our family circle? The doors will always be closed to you. To put it bluntly, you are a poor man. You have no wealth behind you. You have still to establish yourself.'

Sivam had turned and walked away. Out of Radha's life. Out of the lives of these people whom he would no longer disturb.

Yet the interrogation went on endlessly in his mind. He had to confront Renga. Ask him the truth. He met him, questioned him closely.

'Why, why, why? These letters, the letters with her name, surely she wrote them to me.'

'Don't blame me,' Renga said. 'My sisters decided that they would teach her a lesson. That family is too proud. Why all the best proposals for her? What about my own sisters? What chances do they have? They too are unmarried. Can you not sympathize with them? We are not rich, we live in a small house, my sisters do not have Radha's beauty, her talents . . . . They are such arrogant people. We wanted to teach her a lesson. And so did my nieces. She stays with them and their father, her uncle, the husband of my dead sister, is encouraging all the proposals only for her. What about his own daughters? And we thought in the end it would not really be wrong. What if it worked out? Isn't it just because you are a poor relation that they didn't pay any regard to you? There's nothing wrong with your looks . . . in fact you're much better looking than the proposed bridegroom. Only his wealth matters. We know all the inside stories . . . we could bring them into the open. She's not in love with him, it's just a social marriage, a continuance of their privileged heritage.'

'Then I have been deceived? And by you and the others . . . ?'

'We didn't know it would turn out so seriously. My sisters . . . they were jealous. They would never have the chances that Radha would have. There were no proposals for them . . . .'

He was stunned, bitter. There was nothing he could do. In time a marriage would be arranged for him, but not with such a beautiful woman as Radha. No, she was not for him, a bank clerk living as a poor relation in a back room . . . . A poor relation. In the village back home he would be someone, but not in the city. Never. He was a nobody here. He had been castigated severely for his presumptuousness. Radha would forever be beyond his reach. He would have to be content with his parents choice, a wife who would be suitable for a bank clerk. He would go back into the obscurity from which he had temporarily emerged but he would not forget, ever. He would watch and wait. He would be patient.

Yet when he would one day settle down to a predictable relationship and marry, bring forth children, he would look back on the days of his youth without regret. He had had his fill of that vision of beauty. And visions always elude. He would settle down to a different life. He would not forget her, Radha.

Tradition and Hierarchies

'Is there anything I regret after all these years of a well-arranged marriage, the wealth, status in society?' Radha asked herself. 'What is love, what is passion? I have never really known or understood, although I have sung time and time again of the passion of lovers for each other. The thorn has never pricked my heart to shed even a droplet of blood. But Saradha? That breaker of conventions . . . .'

It had needed a kind of reckless courage to break away from the rigid constraints of the Tamil hierarchy of that era, of the generation of Radha's mother. Women who knew men as husbands, fulfilling their ordained roles of obedience, chastity and the begetting of children. But Saradha had returned. Where was that ardent lover, the Italian ship's captain, Luigi Botticelli, with whom she had gone away leaving her home, her husband, her family? She had returned with her young daughter, Lucia, to beg on the streets of the city, to be shelterless, ostracized, spurned by the society she had once lorded over. Saradha, whose wardrobe had been filled with the richest Indian silks, brocades, organzas; her full-bosomed body swathed in turquoise, emerald, crimson, with elaborate jewels in her pierced nostrils, her ears, throat, wrists. A woman who had brought dowry with her, houses, land, money . . . she had returned perhaps to claim it all but it was lost to her forever. A woman so strong as herself, why had she not fought back to reclaim what was hers by right? There was no one to defend her. Women like Saradha were considered immoral. She was not seen as a woman who desired to free herself of the bondage of custom and rigid roles, but only as a loose woman. The long sea voyage had taken whatever money she had, and all her jewels. Everything spent.

Saradha's Story

Venice. That's where Luigi took her. That was where her youngest child was born. Where she herself was reborn, taking into her wide embrace more than the

326

Italian ship's captain. She had taken into her very being a whole alien culture and a civilization in her attempt to know herself as a woman. But to know it to its fullest she had to metamorphose into a different being, learn the cadences of a new language, change her tastes in food—here she drank much wine, Chianti, sweet muscats and lay with her lover in a room in one of those ancient Renaissance buildings, shutting out of her mind the past which had given her no role as an individual. She had been married like all the others after a formal proposal in which she had no say. She had brought her virginity with her, together with her dowry. Then she had escaped . . . . Luigi was her lover. She did not think of him as a husband. There had been no divorce. The passion that had been denied her flesh in that distant alliance that had wedded her to all the tradition and ritual of her inheritance was now realized to its fullest. Her body, her mind, her soul— all was now Venezia.

They lived in one of those buildings overlooking the Ponte Dei Sospiri with the gondolas passing beneath those high arched windows. She could cross those bridges on foot or sail in the gondolas—she knew every bridge, every canal, every church and palazzo through the long years she lived there. That entire panorama was hers to view. She, Luigi and the little girl, Lucia, would walk to the Facciata Chiesa S. Marco et Piccione where they would feed the pigeons. They would enter the great church of St. Marco with its enormous chandeliers and pillars and crosses. 'Will God forgive me? But then what is sin? What sin have I committed? Luigi kneels and prays at the altars in churches. Does he regret anything? His passion for me . . . has he any feelings of guilt at having taken me away from my husband and my children? There are priests at the confessionals who listen to him. As for myself, there is no turning back. I cannot have regrets. Tradition had shackled me, I had to break away. I had to know before I died what it meant to step out of my prison and into freedom . . .'

Venezia was home to her, the grand monuments, the palazzos, the piazzetas . . . but it had all come to an end. Luigi went away on a voyage from which he never returned. She had just enough money to pay for her return passage and that of Lucia. she came back but all doors were locked against her. The woman who had transgressed had to pay her retribution. There was no acceptance. No forgiveness. She could not even claim back what was rightfully hers. She had sacrificed that right and she had no resources with which to fight back and no money to go back to Venezia where she had had the freedom to cross the bridges over those innumerable canals—the canal Grande, the ponte di Rialto, to sit beside the palm in that sheltered enclosure of the Chiesa Della Salute, sipping wine out of a Venetian glass.

In the end Saradha was left with nothing but the memories which she would never relinquish but which drove her mad, demented, with a child who spat abuse at her. She was now spent, finished, yet with that wild light of a reckless and accomplished period of her life glittering like sharp daggers in those brilliant eyes. She had rebelled against a closed in society. Her present wretchedness she had to accept as a penitent would her karma. There was no forgiveness for her. She had to contend with a society which would ultimately destroy her. Saradha and Lucia carried whatever they possessed knotted up in bundles. They were both garbed in rags and tatters, the remains of their once fashionable modish gowns of silk and grosgrain with strands of Venetian beads round their throats and dangling from their ears. At night they slept in the corners of verandahs of the once grand houses where Saradha herself had been welcome in that almost forgotten, so distant, past.

Mother and daughter would live and die outside the pale of a tightly structured society with its invisible but unyielding facade. Lucia, the child of that misalliance, had a rare and unusual beauty—her skin like a peach ripening in a Mediterranean orchard. Her eyes, long, slanted and green, cat-like. Transplanted, vulnerable and unprotected on those strange streets that her mother had fled. The two of them displaced in the city, the daily path they trod, that of survival and endurance. Living on other people's charity. And Luigi? The man who had left Saradha or whom she had abandoned, dying somewhere, old and alone. All his voyages had perhaps ceased. The astrolabe would point to no new star. The compass in no new direction. Old age and death in some forgotten haven. Gerontion. His youth over, all passion spent. Perhaps he had steered his ship to the Happy Isles.

Mother and daughter had only each other to cling to. The girl trailed along behind her, unable to break away, unable to summon the strength to live on her own. She uttered harsh words that dashed like stones against the heart of the woman who had promised her refuge but could give her none. Saradha's mind shattered like those Venetian glass beads falling from their broken strands onto the hard pavements of the world. She was still tall and dignified. Her hair was cropped short. She no longer wore the traditional jewellery of rubies and brilliants.

All that had vanished. Days of her past glory and beauty remained only in those rare beads of amber, of lapis lazuli and the mottled glass that swung against her throat and breast.

No one was prepared to pity either mother or daughter, to rescue them from their wretchedness. Not even Saradha's own kith and kin. She would stand at the gateways, at the doorways of her people, begging for alms. And that was all they were prepared to give. They would not welcome her into their houses. There was fear too in their attitudes for she was still a strong and intimidating presence, one who reminded them of feelings and emotions that they would not, dared not, allow themselves to even envisage. So they let her go . . . they would not take responsibility for her. she would die and the daughter would survive. They would be forgotten.

Regrets

Radha remembered. She would not make such mistakes. For her, rebellion would have been calamitous. she could not have been a survivor like Saradha. Like Lucia. Her destiny was the acceptance of inherited roles, traditional roles, handed down from generation to generation. She would pay heed to her parents' wishes, to the wisdom of the family guru and the family choice of a bridegroom. That had been her life with all its predictability. There had been nothing to escape from. She had entered the fortress voluntarily, never to leave it. She had diversions, parties with laughter and trivial conversations. Cocktail parties, birthday parties, anniversary celebrations. These were the important landmarks in her life.

Fifty years ago, she had been a young bride

welcomed into the household of the Vigneshwerans. That man, the bank clerk, the gossip, the rumours, nothing had been able to mar the destined path she would take. She became an icon set in a niche of history. Women like Saradha served as grim warnings for those who transgressed the rules, those unwritten laws. she had taken her veena with her to the new household but soon her music was forgotten. Those whom she and Maharaj now entertained had no time for ragas and *kirthanams*. The veena was put away, forgotten, until this day when she had looked out on the garden with its wilting flowers, the unswept lawn, the empty birdbath. She remembered the hours she had spent in dalliance with her cousins in that garden of their youth, waiting for their husbands, waiting for marriage.

Under her breath she began to hum the bhairavi raga, *'Pasyati disi, disi'*—Radha in her arbour of flower creepers, weak with love, waiting for Govinda, for the fulfillment of that glorious consummation of which chastity and virginity were prerequisites. She had disappointed no one except perhaps her secret self long submerged and hidden away. She had waited for the realization of that love which she had yearned for all her life. All she had was the mundane view of the world. Others directed her sight to what lay before her. If only she could have lived out the myth and legends of the loves of the gods and goddesses she sang of. That was never to be. She prepared to put away her veena in the same hidden corner of a darkened room, never to bring it out again. She sang those lines softly to herself, lines which belonged to her youth: 'She mourns, Sovereign of the world, in her verdant bower. She looks eagerly to all sides in hope of the approach; then, gaining strength from the delight of the proposed meeting,

she advances a few steps, but falls to the ground.
Rising, she weaves bracelets of fresh flowers; dresses
herself like her beloved; and, looking at herself in
sport, exclaims, "Behold the vanquisher of Madhur!"'

She sang the final line before she laid the veena
down and covered it with an old silk saree—'It is
my beloved who approaches.' Turning back to resume
her life, she encountered only silence and emptiness.

'I Will Lift Up Mine Eyes'

I will lift up mine eyes to the mountains, from whence shall my help come

—Psalm 121

RUTH ALLEN, THE English missionary principal, sits within her arbour of bougainvillea, jam-fruit and flowering araliya, breakfasting at a table set out in her garden. Her lapis-lazuli blue eyes change colour in light, in shade. Sometimes a willow pattern plate-blue, or convolvulus violet-blue like the flowers that unfurl their fragile silk petals on the school hedge, or a pale, clear, cerulean blue. They gaze beyond her garden, an English missionary garden, into a distance where the peak of Hantane juts into the sky. Those eyes look at children, flowers, birds, mountains with the same steady, unflinching gaze. Eyes that hold light like mirrors, glittering with prisms that slant through the air. They change colour as shadows fall on the garden. They become amber, flecked with gold. These eyes have seen a myriad visions, visions that brought her to this earthly Paradise to form, to mould the lives of those who dwelt in it—those who had already been baptized at birth in the fonts of churches, but to whom the life of Christ was still an unknown mystery.

Ruth Allen is close to Nature in this primal garden where the balmy air lays the softest caress on a face, on a body that had once known only the English seasons. Ah, what had brought her here in the nineteen thirties from her English schools, from her English University, with her Bible, her hymn book, her books of poetry: Rupert Brooke and Wilfred Owen—for she was always reading, nostalgically, from those books every morning at school assembly. Often, she would bring guests, English soldiers, officers, who would speak to the rows of schoolgirls sitting on coir matting in the school hall. Or she would read from letters which came from prisoner-of-war camps . . .

> *Four ducks in a pond,*
> *A grass bank beyond,*
> *To remember for years*
> *To remember with tears . . .*

Time creeps like a ladybird over a leaf, gold, red, black, glittering, varnished by the light of the sun, its rays still pale, emerging out of the mist, but soon to become brassy with a strong white glare. A green caterpillar silently eats into a mulberry leaf. Her day is circumscribed by her duties, her responsibilities.

The garden is her private preserve before she embarks on the prayers, the hymns, the Bible lesson for the day and announcements at school assembly. Later, she teaches English, Latin, Maths. This is her quiet, private time when she sits alone at a table covered with spotless white napery; shining silver cutlery, her tea pot in its cozy, cup and saucer, milk jug, sugar bowl, toast, butter and marmalade. She scoops out a slice of papaw with a tiny silver spoon.

Christina is sent up from the school hostel by the matron with a message. She stands before Ruth Allen in her starched white uniform, straight hair combed over the ears and severely clipped back, filled with a sense of her own importance. The message is delivered as she stands before Ruth behind the barrier of the table with the English breakfast set on it. How golden and ripe the slice of papaw is. So like the beak of a glossy *selalihini* which feeds in the grass. They watch each other gravely, this child so solemn, so serious in intent, and this white, alien woman who has so much power within this little world bound by its tall, dark convolvulus hedge.

In the school hall, in the library, are paintings and photographs of missionary principals, Englishwomen, those intrepid ambassadors of Christ, dating from the latter part of the nineteenth century. Women. Women who had moved out of the restrictions of their Victorian whalebone, their high-necked gowns, their bustles and ankle-length skirts. With their solar hats they had ventured into a garden filled with pagan traps. There were souls to save. There was a new morality to impart. Their faces were strong. Beautiful faces, some of them Rossetti-ish in their beauty. It was sacrifice. Sacrifice. Sometimes burying their very young children, husbands too, far from home . . .

If I should die, think only this of me,
There is some corner of a foreign field
That is forever England . . .

Lines which Ruth Allen often reads out from the platform at school assembly.

Ruth eats little bits of the garden, a flower vanishes down her throat, a fruit, leaves, petals. Soon the garden will be denuded of its plants and the bare twig-like stalks will tremble awkwardly in the wind. She will settle her roots into the earth which will press itself against her pale, stalk-like body, the pale lily of her body, the necrotic stalk. Nothing will remain and the tumulus of her brick edifice will crumble with time . . .

All around her, orioles, magpies, mynahs feed off the ripe fruit on her trees. She is ambushed by their wild cries. Their appetites are enormous. They peck and peck, their beaks going deep into the very essence of the fruit. They probe into the lonely cave of her life and the seeds fall all day, float and scatter into faraway gardens.

But of the fruit of the tree which is in the midst
of paradise, God hath commanded us that we
should not eat; and that we should not touch it,
lest perhaps we die.

Her silk gowns are like the speckled sheaths that shimmer over the tender stalks, flecked, cobwebby, in silk, patterned in blue and crimson, veined with the shades of colour that merge and flow within coloured marbles. Christina's eyes gaze steadfastly into hers, into that blue ocean, unfathomable, that suddenly changes colour. Beyond her Christina sees a butterfly on a russet hedge, a bird upon a branch heavy with guavas. Babur, the Muslim tailor, sews her dresses. He lives in one of the little tenement houses on the main road beside a butcher shop with hunks of bloodied, fly-ridden beef suspended from black steel hooks, and scarred chopping board with flecks of white and blue sinew and blood, the sliced-off flesh exposing the bone with its streaked, whitish-red marrow. Next door is the barred goldsmith's shop. Babur's measuring tape is always spilling out of his pocket. Sometimes it is draped round his neck. His face is ruddy-cheeked and grizzled, smelling of sweat and tobacco. Raw carcases. Flies swarm.

Early in the morning—for Christina, too, lives on the main road—she hears the cattle go clip-clopping to the slaughter house. Behind the slaughter house, the deep gully flows with thick red blood. She hears too the throaty, early-morning voices of the men leading the lean cattle, their voices rasping and guttural, urging the animals on. Animals being readied for slaughter, half-starved, gaunt-ribbed, are seen feeding on piled-up straw through the wooden bars. Later on in the day, the road teems with vendors carrying their loads of fruit, vegetables, fish, clay pots. The bullock carts creak with their rasping wooden wheels, loaded with coconut husks and firewood. The old men from the villages come with fowls tucked under their arms and fresh eggs in baskets knotted in *pottaniyas* of old cloth or in red bandanas. The young seminarians walk two by two along the road, taken out for an airing.

Babur sits on his little verandah while his children tumble about and play in the city drain just outside his house, his Singer sewing machine whirring away, running up dresses for Ruth Allen out of lengths of silk sent out from England for her. Babur's wife is plump, fair, young, rosy-cheeked. She is almost always dandling a new baby in her arms. Babur spends his day sewing and sewing to feed them with juicy beef and sugared vermicelli. The dresses are completed and taken to Ruth Allen. Blue silk with faint marbling veins of colour. But Babur's life is hidden from them, especially the hostel boarders, behind the thick hedges.

In the little red brick Methodist chapel is set a small memorial plaque: 'In Memory of May Shipstone, the lost and forgotten child of one of the earlier missionaries. This is the chapel in which May's father had preached. Linda Uttley comes to Sunday School. Miss Bamford sits in the pew of the Methodist chapel in town wearing a jaunty crimson felt hat on her head. Ruth Allen and Elsie Shire never wear hats to church. Great, braided coils of hair are ringed round Ruth's ears. Elsie Shire wears her white hair shingled.

Christina delivers her message and watches the caterpillar on the leaf eating little bits of the garden. Miss Allen, as she scoops the papaw with the silver spoon, becomes the lost child in the woods, relives the tale of Hansel and Gretel, becomes a fawn, a fairy. They believe in fairies, these children, and spend hours making fairy gardens in the school hostel—little, magical, enchanted gardens with silver wands and toadstools and little wine cups and plates for those invisible, airy beings that visit on a moonlit night.

Christina's father has sent a star tortoise that lives among the flower beds; and the water diviner comes from England with her willow wand and walks over the lawn of the hostel garden. Secret springs are hidden here. The willow wand quivers as she walks over the grass.

Gravely, Christina takes leave of Ruth Allen who will complete her breakfast and come down the steps to the big hall for school assembly. It is a daily ritual. The girls file in through the doors which lead from the hall verandahs, demure in crisp, starched white uniforms of piqué and cotton from the Manchester and Lancashire mills. White socks neatly folded over the ankles. Canvas shoes pipe-clayed in white on drill days and country dance days— 'Hunston House' and 'Gathering Peascods'; school tie, badges, not a pin to be seen (or marks would be cut off); faces open and innocent, hair cropped, clipped and braided. Elsie Schoorman is not allowed to go up the platform to receive her prize on prize-giving day as she has had her hair permed for the occasion. On Prize Day Annie Reith, Elaine Fairweather, Elsie Schoorman, all the big girls wear ankle-length dresses, sweeping with frills up to their ankles. Christina and her sister wear ivory-white fugi silk with delicate smocking at the waist, pearl buttons and Peter Pan collars. Christina wins many prizes. She likes the Julia Bartholomeusz Memorial Prize for General Intelligence—S. Milne's *Winnie the Pooh*. Her dead aunt's prize for Courtesy she never wins: The Elsie Jansz Memorial Prize for courtesy given by the sisters. Elsie Grenier-Jansz had died very young. Auburn haired, blue-eyed Elsie Jansz.

The children sit on the rough coir mats that are spread out in rows on the floor. Dorothy Poulier lifts Christina's heavy black plaits and holds them in her hands, feeling their thickness and weight.

'Beautiful,' she murmurs, 'beautiful, thick hair.'

Dorothy's own hair is short, straight, without the slightest ripple or wave, but Christina admires her ivory complexion, her slanted eyes dark as sloes, her slightly purplish, plum coloured lips. Dorothy is from Singapore and has the exquisite fineness of a Chinese ivory carving.

The children stand in straight rows, sing hymns from the Methodist hymn book: 'All things Bright and Beautiful', 'To Thee I vow my Country', 'Guide me, O Thou Great Jehovah'; translations from Greek and German hymns of early churchmen and of John Wesley, Frances Jane Van Alstyne. Christina ponders deeply over the anonymous early Christian hymn writers: Anonymous c. fifth century *'Aeterne Rex Altissime'*; or the fifteenth century *'Gloriosi Salvatoris'*; or *'O amor quam exstatitus'*—fifteenth century; or the German *'Lobe den Herren der Machtigen Konig der Ehren'* of Joachim Neander (1650-80) translated by Catherine Winkworth (1829-78). Here, then, is the discovery of that early metaphor of praise and thanksgiving shaped by a Christian evangelism. They are the privileged ones, separated from the primitive heathens, from the pagans, born to inherit the kingdom of God. And into this kingdom the children are led gently, without threat of hellfire and brimstone, by the missionaries. After the hymns, the psalms, the prayers, as they sit on the rough coir mats listening to the announcements, the reading of long lists of mark-sheets, poems, extracts of letters from 'Home', from prisoner-of-war camps in Germany in the 1940s, pyramids of words build up before their eyes, too strong for them to break, and quietly, silently they lie entombed within those structures for all time.

On the wall behind Miss Allen is a large, life-size, impressive portrait of a former principal, Mrs Gordon. She had been Miss Mallet and, like the others, had married another missionary. She sits upright, severely straight in her dark graduate cloak, her white hair—a spume of silk—parted smoothly, her lips shaped in a faint smile over ever so slightly protruding teeth, her skin pink and pearly, unmottled by a tropical sun, her tapering fingers with their almond-shaped nails holding a pen over the white parchment of an as yet unwritten edict—something official, perhaps a prize-giving report or a letter to a missionary body in England. A portrait painted by the Estonian artist, Karl Kasman, husband of the music teacher in the school. Karl, who played with great passion Gypsy Czardas music on his violin and painted enormous canvases of mediaeval court scenes and of dry-zone vegetation with its grey-green cactii and gnarled, grey, tumbled trees in a sanctuary. He had painted with great truthfulness to reality the missionary portrait of Constance Gorden—Miss Mallet, strong, beautiful, austere, like a Renaissance painting of the apostles of Christ. On either side of her portrait there are paintings of 'The Fall' in the Garden of Eden. The flesh tones of the naked bodies are translucent, smooth, and gleam with mother-of-pearl tints. And there is the painting of the resurrected Jesus standing with a lantern before a locked door. The locked door? Of what? The human heart in its tangles of wild brambles, the brambles of darkened ignorance? The school crest is a brilliant blue, green, gold. 'A Deo Auxilium'—'Our Help Cometh from the Lord'—words against the blue, green and gold of a valley, mountains, sky, sun.

> I will lift up mine eyes
> Unto the mountains
> From Whence shall my help come;
> My help cometh from the Lord
> Who hath made heaven and earth.

Hantane towers over the valley. Over the school. It looms over the netball pitch, above the ancient tamarind trees, the convolvulus and hibiscus hedges.

Its defies the walls of the school; it brings the swirling mists, that envelop its peak, into the classrooms and fills the heart with terror when the flames rage upwards from the wild, burning mana grasses. But through their childhood, through adolescence, the girls are safe behind the hedges which screen out the voices and dust of the road. The chaos, the turbulence and turmoil of the cosmos lie outside this primal garden where sorrow, bereavement, loss of love, betrayal and death are everyday facts in ordinary lives. The horror of things glimpsed: the woman without a nose, the exhibitionists behind the hedges or in a park—weak and impotent men, the revulsion of seeing their sad exposures; the blind beggar, old, ragged, who sits on the roadside playing on the plangent strings of a violin made of a hollow coconut shell . . . . But all this is not enough to make them renounce the world—to abdicate, to reject, to escape from the world which tempts them with the apples of sin and guilt in Satanic whispers. They will go out to life, to death. Presagement is just the slightest intimation: 'Jesus Christ, *mein schonstes Licht . . .'*

My Saviour, Thou, Thy love to me
In shame, in want, in pain hast showed;
For me, on the accursed tree
Thou pourest forth Thy guiltless blood;
Thy wounds upon my heart impress
Nor aught shall the loved stamp efface.

Miss Aileen, the drill, art and music teacher, blows her whistle and the children leap up to catch the ball that swings beyond their sight and falls—oh, victory—with a plump sound into the net. Banda rings the bells under the jak tree. Pakiar sweeps up the fallen leaves. Miss Eva unrolls the map of the world and hangs it up on the blackboard, pointing at continents and islands they have never seen—desert, tundra, tropical, equatorial; tropical and coniferous forests. The pygmies creep through dark forests and the Eskimos draw their sledges with their huskies through the snow and ice. They sing 'Cherry Ripe' and 'The Lonely Ash Grove' and whirl round in the Maypole Dance. Babe Jonklaas teaches them ballet and they pirouette on their toes in imaginary tutus. There are no intruders here, but there are secret goings-on. Elizabeth is found kissing Lalani in a deserted classroom. The hostel matron peeps through the key hole and finds her little charges cavorting about on their beds, performing a Bacchic dance. The spinster clerk in the office has a favourite. Starved for love, she loves the almond-eyed, brown-haired Cynthia. 'Ah, my little white sugar ball; my sugar sweet one,' she says. And Cynthia receives very adult love letters from a lonely soldier. Indra brings her father's gynaecological volumes to the classroom and the children pore over the mysteries of life in the vividly illustrated pictures of birth and evolution. Soma brings books from home too—books which her father once read; lurid fictions which the children read without understanding any of the meanings.

Ruth Allen too reads verse after verse of poetry from the collections and anthologies she brings with her to assembly. She is easily moved and weeps as her voice intones lines from the war poets, reminding herself, so far from home, of life, death, mortality. Her voice breaks, quivers with a familiar grief as she reads aloud extracts from letters addressed to her from 'Home'. Letters from friends and family to an exile. Ah, yes, she is a valiant woman, bent on her mission to mould her charges in this Methodist missionary school. Ruth Allen reading poetry always reminds Christina of Suandhi, who had once been a student of the school. She would write poems, many poems. Did any of them bear presagement of her death? She had drowned in the river Mahaweli on a school picnic. She has become a legend here. Only a few of her poems remain.

Picnic at Hantane

Christina, Grace, Muriel, Nanda and Pearl, with their other classmates, decide on a picnic to Hantane with Miss Olga and Miss Elaine. They will take the road to that soaring peak, to Hantane, and look down from its summit on an all-encompassing view of the township where they live . . .

> *I will lift up mine eyes to the mountains . . .*
> *The Lord shall preserve thee from all evil;*
> *He shall preserve thy soul . . .*

The valley is left far behind. It is safe down there. The high convolvulus hedge shuts in the school from the busy road. They have seen, from the netball pitch, from the verandah of the school hall, from the classroom fronting the yard, Hantane rearing itself from the low roofs of Katukelle. The road, leading up to the dazzling white cube of the tea factory, is a silvery thread winding through the tea bushes. Hantane is a barrier, protecting yet threatening. The morning air is crisp, flecked with light; slender, wind-blown trees appear insubstantial in their pale transparency. Waterfalls turn into white froth. The grass is wet with dewfall. The valley is slow to wake. The doors and windows of the little Katukelle houses are still shuttered. The road climbing out of the valley takes its silence with it. It goes past the marketplace, rising above the hospital, the railway lines, the empty station and the shunting engines. The silence of lonely places overtakes them, trees growing closer together. The fern banks rise from the road, heavy with moisture. They listen to each other's words more intently. The whole landscape seems to be listening, carrying echoes to the lonely mountain. The wind intervenes with its syllables through the pale, gold-green light flittering among feathery-branched trees. The whole landscape is compounded of light. They hear water sounding from hidden streams and waterfalls which they are yet to encounter. They peer over the precipices which fall abruptly into the valley. They can place a finger on the spot where the school lies hidden among the red roofs peering out of the green.

The small group of figures struggle up the hillside. They have passed through rows of tea bushes and now the wild hillside slopes confront them. The mana grass clings to their limbs, their skirts, slashing them as they climb higher and higher to where the peak rears great outcrops of rocks impaling soft, cirrus clouds. They look down on the valley already distanced from them in a world of miniature perspectives. The Mahaweli, coiling through fields and densely wooded banks, is caught and held within a silver light. The mana with sharp knife-like edges, cuts the flesh as the children move, sunk upto their breasts, through this sea of swords. It sways and rasps against the skin. They feel its moisture at the roots, the earth damp at their feet.

In the dry season, fires are lit in the evenings to clear patches of mana. Their boisterous flares spread over the hills till darkness creeps over the purple ranges; red, orange, gold, they creep over the road, insidious flames coiling within themselves, ropes of fire fed by the animus of their own heat. They extend their peripheries of brightness until they burn out, leaving raw, black scars on the red soil.

The children are climbing higher and higher. They can almost touch a wind-blown bird. Its cry is shrill against their ears. The wind plucks a steely, discordant note out of the air to send it zooming and twanging across the space between ranges. Their lips feel cold. They arrive at waterfalls which have hitherto intimated their presence in echoes buried in rock. Water froths, ice cold, over ferny, slippery stone. Tea pluckers climb the sides of the hills rising steeply from the road.

Now they arrive at a point at which they begin the ascent to the summit. They feel trepidation. The slopes are craggy. There is no pathway. The earth is loose and crumbly. The sharp twigs of the bushes prick and clutch at the neat white uniforms, tugging at the ordered pleats. The air is cold and rasping, the mist, white and thick, billowing above the point of the summit. They walk along footpaths holding each other by the hand, but they are young and agile; they manage without stumbling. They steadily pursue the path which will lead them to the seemingly safe ledge.

They reach the point where a rock juts out, forming a seat. They sit in little groups on this ledge that seems balanced precariously over nothing but space. Beneath it lies the vertigo of blue emptiness and whirling wind. This is the summit. The lesser ranges lie below them, eddying above the green coronets of windblown trees and grass. The swift currents of air blow teasingly about their bodies. Above them are stronger layers of wind which seem to trap them. Below them, in the waves of wild grass, a secret current of wind travels. It is cold. A small rain cloud condenses over them. The air tastes like fresh spring water, chill against their lips, but leaves their throats dry, achingly parched. The skin feels taut and sore from the grazes of the mana grass. They feel the flutter within the green shadow: the movement of wild things secretly scanning them from coverts.

The children's songs and conversation do not remain within the space they create with their own bodies. The wind dissipates the sounds which are too frail to strike echoes against mountain walls. Their syllables are carried down precipices where they are lost in the murmur of streams, hidden rills and waterfalls. In the woods they become a different language, transmuted into cries that are primeval, hardly human. The voices eddy and waver in startled spurts which drown and the syllables of grass, murmuring, continue through time and space, endless, perpetual. The valley is left behind. It is safe here, now that they have reached the summit. They are all quite safe here for the moment on the rocky ledge.

> I will lift up mine eyes to the hills, from which cometh my help . . .

The promise of protection. The promise that has been assured them as they stand at school assembly and sing 'A Deo Auxilium'. Green valley, dark blue mountains, pale blue sky, golden sun. This is the heraldry of the school. Those missionaries derived their inspiration from this primeval world they had set their dwellings in.

Some of the children begin to wander off from the main group of teachers and children. They wade into a sea of green grass, pushing aside the sharp blades that hide their bodies one from the other.

There is no pathway here. Only silence. The further ranges seem to move away from them, leaving a greater space and emptiness to be explored. Coming towards them, carried by the sweeping mountain wind, a brutal stench of putrefaction assails their nostrils. Christina steps forward and parts a screen of tall mana grass. Eyes search, but she sees nothing. The others draw nearer. Their senses whirl with the onslaught of the stench and, feeling faint, they grasp the strong stalks of grass for support. Here, they seem to be groping for some kind of knowledge on a separate plane of reality—knowledge that has been withheld from them in that school in the valley below. Life. Sin. Guilt. Death. Salvation. Life after death. Resurrection. Not death, decay, putrefaction, stench. High above the township, where lies all vileness, hidden from the eyes, they are closer to the truth which is within reach but beyond their sight. In this rarefied atmosphere with its pure, clean air, that decay of mortality has penetrated. It follows them everywhere. Death of a stranger, an ordinary human for whom there will be no resurrection. The death of Christ—the cross, the tomb, the spices and perfumes for the lacerated body, the bright and shiny garments of the two men in the tomb where the body of the crucified Jesus had lain, the tomb soon empty but for the linen sheet in which His body had been wrapped . . . that death had been different.

And it happened, as they were greatly perplexed about this that behold, two men stood by them in shining garments. Full of fear the women bowed down to the ground as the men said to them: 'Why are you looking among the dead for one who is still alive? He is not here; he has been raised . . .'

This is a different kind of death, they know.

Human life has absented itself here. The mountains seem to reject the living breath within their territory. Eyes, tear-filled in the wind, look through a blurred pane at ranges of peaks, summits, trees, grass and cloud. If you step out of this perimeter the precipice drops steeply into the valley. The ledge on which they have rested is safe, but only temporarily. The children are enclosed in a world of tall grass which presses sharp, keen-edged blades against their faces and limbs, clouding their eyes with a hazy confusion of whirling images compounded of the closeness of flighting birds. Wings almost touch their cheeks. They feel the harsh touch of swaying columns of mana. They smell the tang of crushed grass underfoot. Their tongues are muted by terror. They feel that the confrontation with unknown mysteries is imminent. The strong odour of decay and disintegration beckons them to cross a frontier of sharp green stakes. Only serried rows of grass separate them from the revelation.

Their voices weave their motets in the wind. Tremulous whispers are bruited about this green, swaying wall. They have wandered too far from the others, too far from the safety of friends who had halted, resting on the rocky ledge.

'We're lost.' There is fear in their voices.

'Listen. Voices. Can you hear them?'

'No. I can hear nothing. They're not even searching for us.'

'There's no path back. How can we find our way? Listen.'

'Louder. Louder. Call out their names.'

Only the sound of wind and of water streaking the rock faces, dripping from secret sources high, high up in the mountains. The tough blades of mana grass rasping like stiff silk in the wind. Birds fly high above their heads, swoop down and are borne up again to glide in currents of air, drifting, devoid of conscious volition. Their voices emerge out of the silence.

'We made a path through the grass . . . it's trampled . . . the trail will guide us.'

'Look, my arms and legs are grazed . . . this mana grass cuts like knife blades.'

'We were safe with the others. Now we are alone. We shouldn't have wandered away from them.'

'When we go back shall we tell the others?'

'If we do, will they believe us?'

'Let's find out for ourselves, once and for all, what it is all about. Are you afraid? Wait. I must see. And you? Muriel? Grace? Nanda? Do you want to see? We're free. There's no one to forbid us. There are no rules, no one to make us obey them. Come with me.'

'It's . . . I know it's death. It's there, hidden for a long, long time in the grass. No one will discover. The grass will be set on fire and the body will char and be ash . . .'

'My father told me that the man who had disappeared from Hantane estate had never been found. A bloodied mana grass-cutting knife and bloodstained clothes had been discovered but no arrests were made. There wasn't enough evidence against the suspect. Perhaps the man who had killed was waiting for the fires to begin—you can see them like beacons on the mountains. But we have stumbled on what was meant never to be discovered—even if all of you go back, I must see for myself . . . don't worry, you'll find your way back. You'll be safe . . . I'm going on . . . .' Christina has made her decision.

Their eyes so liquid and unknowing hold fear.

The picnic was for pleasure, for laughter, for adventure of a different sort, not this confrontation with the slow disintegration of a body abandoned, unclaimed in a waste of grass, corrupting the earth, the air, with its vileness. But don't the birds of the air feed on its flesh? No, there are no vultures here, no birds to pick the white bones clean.

They can hear, very faintly, the sound of reed-like voices singing through the wind from a long distance away.

No one wants to go any further, to part the grass, to see death, the cold flesh which has lain for so long, shrouded in dews, swept by mist and rain until the fire from the mana grass consumes it. The high convolvulous hedge of their missionary school has protected them for so long and they feel that the earth is a safe world, that no mountain holds danger for them.

> He shall not suffer thy foot to be moved
> He that keepeth thee will not slumber
> He that keepeth Israel shall neither slumber nor sleep.

These are the words of the school psalm which they intone at Prayers. This is what they believe in. Sometimes Christina has seen the funeral processions pass by her home. The melancholy sounds of Chopin's 'Marche Funebre' played on the silver trumpets with the big drums beating out a sombre tattoo; sad looking men in starched white twill uniforms and pith helmets, bodies bent almost backwards with their weight. Their stiff arms lifting and falling, the upraised batons, the dull, monotonous thud, their measured tread on the hot, tarred road, the black hearse being slowly borne along, the coffin weighed down by the elaborate wreaths of flower.

The bereaved dressed in white with hair loosely tossed on shoulders, weeping, clinging to each other for comfort, follow in the old Ford and Austin cars, their grief for all to see. Mourners straggle behind with black armbands, talking in subdued voices. Death is concealed in an ornate, varnished coffin. Here, it is wantonly exposed.

> *I will lift up mine eyes to the mountains*
> *from whence shall my help come . . .*

But not for everybody, not for this lost soul. The violet blue morning glory cannot screen them or protect them forever from the outside world, within the fortress of the school. Here, then, is that moment of truth. The world has changed. All life, all pleasures of this world are subject to decay. 'Our voices will vanish,' Christina thinks to herself. 'Now we are young, but I am grown up, I am beginning to be aware of the bloom on my cheeks, the glow in my eyes as if fireflies have flickered and passed over them in the night. Everything will pass. The birds drop down in unknown coverts to perish, the wild flowers lose their lustre and are stripped of their frail transparent petals of gold and purple. The grasses burn. Our steps effaced. Our teachers grow old and die. Forgotten. We will have long since ceased to learn from them. The sky, the clouds take on the colour of flint, grow cold. The earth will be blackened and charred. All flesh will perish and go back to earth. How quickly life is transformed in death.'

The air is so still. The wind silent.

'I must see for myself what lies beyond this wall of grass,' says Christina. She is alone. The others have decided to return.

She separates the thick strands. They rasp against her skin. The valley flickers in her eyes, the serpentine river winds down below, coruscated silver. The mist has altered the perspectives of the further ranges and she steps into seeming safety, upon a ledge of vapour. She has a vision of her body plummeting down the precipice. Her step does not falter as she steps forward. But then she draws back. She closes the screen of mana grass. If she plunges from the ledge, stepping into vapour, there will be no foothold. But no, the act of dying is the ritual she must enact in her mind if she is to emerge out of her lonely discovery. The mountain must fall too, the summit of its strength collapse; its falling rock engulfing the valley, the garden, the school, the playground, burying beneath it those toy figures that no longer have any reality.

The others are safe, for the moment, where they sit, suspended in time on the rocky ledge. They will go back to the valley but the road will not return to the same conclusions. They will discover with the passage of time that the valley is as dangerously deceptive as the secluded mountain.

Two Women and an Apple

> 'Witness says that about 12.30 in the night she left the hotel. The man had given her an apple for her children.'
>
> —Evidence in trader's murder case

Voice One

I REMEMBER HIM because he gave me an apple for my children. It's not often they give me gifts. Hardly ever. Nor do I expect them to. It's only money that passes through our hands. Sometimes I carefully fold and put away the crumpled notes into my purse. The money is important. I have to think each day of where the next meal will come from. I am twenty-six years old. Getting older day by day. There's no other steady wage earner in my life. I could have gone to the Middle East to earn money but where could I find the thousands of rupees to pay the job agencies? This is easier for me. I can stay with the children too. As it is they are neglected. I have often to spend the whole night away from them. It's the eldest girl who has to look after the younger ones.

I keep going on from day to day. It's now a routine. I bathe at the well in my little garden, pouring bucket after bucket of water on my body. I sleek my hair with coconut oil and plait it or tie it in a pony tail with a scarlet band. Sometimes I leave my hair loose. It falls to my shoulders. It's easier to run a comb through it after I finish my business. I put cream on my face and powder my cheeks. I drape myself in one of those cheap sheer nylon sarees which I buy off the pavement hawkers. I have managed to save enough money for a pair of gold earrings and a fine gold chain. There are lots of coloured plastic bangles on my wrists. Naturally glass would shatter so easily. I give instructions to *loku duwa* to feed the children and put them to sleep and then take the bus from Kolonnawa to Colombo and then into the heart of the Pettah area. Kolonnawa is where my home is. I have a little house with a few coconut trees in the garden. That's all. There are no jobs for me here. No man to earn for me either. My parents are poor. My brothers and sisters are married and have their own problems and responsibilities, so I have to earn a living, somehow, to provide for my children.

I'm not the only one who walks these streets at night. There are other women too. It's a human jungle here, although the bright neon lights, the loud music from the cafés and hotels, the crowds jostling

355

each other on the pavements give the impression that it's a safe and recognizable world. It never is. Sometimes I fear that I may never see my children again. The men can turn violent. Many of the rougher ones carry a knife at the waist. They are used to brawling. They belong to the underworld of gangs and gang warfare. They live in danger too. Some of my clients are just lone men with money to spend. So, I do not know what the night will really hold for me. And with whom I will share a bed. I am now used to the beds in the hotel rooms. There is a familiarity about them. But there is never rest, never peace there. The shadows on the walls cast by our bodies are magnified, distorted beyond recognition. The shadows have a flatness, lack dimension—a sombre darkness over which the buzzing insects or the wingless ants crawl like maggots on festering flesh.

My bones ache. My flesh feels bruised but my senses are numb. I have a phial of *beheth thel* from the physician in Kolonnawa. I massage my body with this oil. The relief is only temporary. There are deeper wounds that need to be healed. All kinds of men come to the jungle waterhole to assuage their thirst . . . . Does the jungle ever suffer from drought? Does the earth grow parched? Still the animals come in unending herds. Deep, grooved fissures bite into the ridged and hardened mud. When it rains the mud is churned up and becomes a ploughed up field. Sometimes the animals lie down wearily at the rim of the waterhole and die of thirst. They give up the struggle and the carcass is soon hollowed out by the predators, leaving the concave arches of bone to form a canopy over the seething earth. That is their end . . .

But what about myself? The rain replenishes my

store of water. Sometimes a single nelum flower blooms upon its surface. Dragonflies skim over the tremulous ripples. A slant of light slashes the water mirror to reveal the struggling fish that the birds swoop down to feed on. Even when the sun has drunk up almost all the water and a muddy residue is left, until the rocks are bared like jutting crocodile sharp teeth, the animals reach out to quench their thirst.

What pleasure do I have now? It's a daily struggle to keep body and soul together. Soon my elder daughter will attain age and the puberty rites will have to be carried out. I must somehow put a bit of gold on her wrists. Earrings in her ears too. New clothes to be sewn with embroidery of gold thread and satin with ribbons. I shall see that she does not tread the same streets that I do. She must go to school, pass examinations, perhaps be a teacher someday. Only one feeling dominates my mind now—the children should not cry for food. I carry bags of bread, rice, vegetables, tea and sugar back home. Sometimes an apple. One apple that they will share. The handcarts are piled with apples. They come from another country, and look so fresh and tempting before the sun begins to crinkle their thin skins and make the flesh dry and tasteless.

When I reach home I stretch myself out on the *padura* with its smooth woven strands of reed and fall asleep. A restless sleep. A sleep disturbed by dreams. Grotesque faces, masks, the great *vesmuhuna*, grimace at me. The towering bodies of demons lean over me. Huge, protuberant eyes look deep into my very being. Raging fires engulf me and the screech of a slaughtered cock bird, long-drawn-out and shrill, echoes in my ears. My arms flail about me and my daughter shakes me by the shoulder and whispers anxiously, '*Amma, amma*, what is it? You are frightening the little ones . . . .' One of these days when I have the money to spare, I must invite a *kapurala* from the *devale*, the temple near my home. He will invoke the blessings of the gods and they will give me protection against any evil or sickness that afflicts me. He will carry out the *deviyage*, the ceremonies of propitiation. I will lose my fear, my terror. I will wear a protective charm in a silver *suraya* round my neck. Then perhaps the dreams will cease. I cannot think of giving up this job just yet. I have grown used to it too. I know I must be careful. I do not want to die and leave my children orphans. But they must not go hungry. Sometimes I am terrified. A great fear builds up in me. I feel I am being swallowed into this huge maw, stuck in the gullet of an unknown monster, struggling, still half alive, for breath. The men who come to me are all strangers. And will always remain strangers. I do not know how they will hurt me or abuse my mind and body.

I smoke cigarettes. I drink. Sometimes they want me to give them company when they drink. We eat the food which is brought up to the room by Suduputha, one of the hotel employees—string hoppers, fish or meat curry. But sometimes there is nothing. Nothing at all. And I feel myself bereft of everything, hungry, thirsty, weary, wandering though the dark streets with the ruins of buildings stark against the skyline. Roofs, walls, shattered windows, broken doors burned during the racial riots that took place eleven years ago look sinister and ghostly. I see the shapes, forms, faces of other women too, their faces, blue-dark with bruises and knife gashes half healed on their cheeks, and their expressions with that inward look as if they are locked in within dark rooms, rooms from which they can never escape. Their lips are caked and dry. Their skins withering like those apples in the city handcarts that wither and shrink.

I always go to the hotel with the men who invite me. The rooms can be rented out for so many hours. Sometimes for the whole night. The rooms are bare with the minimum of furniture. A bed. A chair. A teapoy. A calendar on the wall with the picture of a filmstar. Food is brought up from the hotel restaurant. Drinks too. My clients generally drink arrack and order Suduputha to run to one of the neighbouring bars to fetch a bottle for them.

It was the fifteenth of May. I remember the date clearly. I came to First Cross Street at about 7.30 p.m. That's the time I generally hope to get a client. I always stand at a particular spot where I know the neon light from the hotel will flash on me. I observed this man, alone, walking along the street. He saw me. Paused. Came up to me. I noticed his clothes. He wore a chocolate brown shirt and blue sarong. He had a small, pink *sirri-sirri* bag in his hand.

'Will you come with me?'

'Yes.'

'Where can we go?'

'I know the hotel just over there. We can get a room.'

He must have had money on his hands. He looked a trader from the Pettah. Doing business in spices or rice, coconuts or vegetables. No family in Colombo. Living alone in one of those ancient, thick-walled rooms with sagging plank floors and a rickety stairway above the shop with its sacks of rice and dhal, dried fish, dried chillies, onions and garlic. The sarong he wore was of good quality cotton. Imported, expensive. The shirt, polyester with white buttons,

could have been bought from one of the pavement
hawkers.

There were the usual hangers-on at the Siripura
Hotel, together with the proprietor and one of the
hotel employees. They recognized me. I knew them
well. The man . . . . I did not ask him his name—
names are inconsequential in this business—paid
money to Ratne, the owner of the hotel, and arranged
for the use of a room. Sene and *Podimahatthaya* stood
near by smoking cigarettes and talking. We went up
to the room, opened the door and walked towards
the bed. The walls closed in around me. It made no
difference. All rooms are the same to me. The walls
needed a coat of paint. The linen on the bed was no
longer fresh. I laughed mirthlessly to myself. White
cloths. Virginity. Age-old traditions. None of them
for me. 'Can I get some arrack?' the man asked.
'What I want is a bottle, not just a drink.'

'There is no bar in the hotel. You can ask
Suduputha who works here to fetch it for you. He
might be willing to run out and get it for you if you
give him a tip.'

The man went to the door and called out from
the landing.

'Here Suduputha, Sudu, come here a moment.'

Suduputha came up the stairs, stood at the door.
'*Mahatthaya*, what do you want?'

'A bottle of arrack. Can you get it?'

'I'll try. It's late. The bars may be closed.'

He pulled out a five hundred rupee note from
his wallet.

A ring, bright gold, flashed on his finger.

'Here, take this, go and try'.

I waited for it all to begin. To end. Then begin
again.

It is always like this. Then I must forget. Go

home. Think of the next day. Think of the next client. The next night. I walk blindly through the street, limping with weariness past the wine bars, the liquor shops, the arrack taverns, the men lighting their cigarettes from the twisted smoking rope, the basins of boiled kadalai steaming at the entrance. I have no appetite left. Only a great thirst. Nothing can assuage it. One day it will consume me, this thirst. I burn with its fire.

We talked desultorily before Sudu came. The man had placed the bag on the table. It contained three apples. My children liked apples.

'You have children?' he asked matter of factly.

'Yes.'

'Here, take an apple for them.'

My hand closed round its smoothness. An apple was something special. Expensive too. The cheapest was ten rupees.

He told me about himself.

'I am a *mudalali* in Maliban Street.'

He must have left his village a long time ago to come to the city. He had made his money here.

Was he looking out for a woman that night? Or was it a sudden whim which overtook him when he saw me?

Do I awaken lust, desire in men? I know their bodies so well now. I listen to romantic songs on cassettes. The garden with beautiful flowers. The hovering honey bees seeking nectar. Words that cloak the bare and necessary act of coition. Images flash on the TV screen of young girls decked in gold. Modest downcast gaze. Sweet-smelling soaps lather limbs that are already clean. My skin is still good. But withering gradually like the apples in the handcarts, growing crinkled in the sun.

I wondered whether the man would give me the

amount he had promised. Sometimes my clients don't. Since I am alone, I am afraid of coercing them. None of them ever remembers me or seeks me again. I am indifferent to whether they get pleasure out of me or not. We never have romantic background music to fill the senses. I sometimes feel more dead than alive. My emotions are never involved. What I do, I do impersonally.

Suduputha came back in a short while.

'*Mahatthaya*, the bars are all closed. No arrack anywhere,' he said

I needed a drink too. I would have liked some iced Fanta. The room was close. Hot. No fans in these rooms. Only a shut window. My reflection in the blurred mirror that hung on the wall stared back at me, surrounded by a nimbus of coloured light prisms. The ceiling bulb was dull and sticky with dead and crawling insects.

His chocolate brown shirt was draped on the back of the straight-backed chair. It was 12.30, past midnight. Four hours we lived in that room as man and wife. I couldn't stay longer. I had to stretch the remaining hours until morning with new clients. My saree that had been carelessly tossed on the floor was draped once more on my body. I flicked a wingless meroe ant crawling on it with my finger. It wouldn't last long, and soon the red ants would drag away its body.

We went down the stairs. A few stragglers were still eating hot hoppers with fish curry. The young man making the hoppers tapped an egg on the rim of the iron pan and tilted it into the soft hopper mixture. Sudu was running up and down with hot hoppers on a plastic plate and jugs of water. Fingers were wiped on squares of old newspaper.

This was my first client for the evening. I would

search for more of them and go home in the morning. Then my other life would begin. I had the apple in my bag. It would mean more to my children than the money. It was however the money that had more importance to me. I would remember this man for the apple. I was not likely to see him again. But how could I be so sure? Fate? Destiny? We are all travellers on the ocean of *samsara*. Perhaps I might meet him in another birth. The morning arrived. The city was coming awake. The sleepers huddled outside the Fort Railway Station were getting up, folding their clothes, preparing to move on. I was dragging my feet along the street looking forward to the journey home. A woman, a casual passerby, told me that a man had died near First Cross Street and the body was lying there. Why should she have told me this news? Did she think I would be curious about the body of a dead man? Why should I have been? I have no feelings towards anyone except my children. All bodies are the same to me. They are not gods whom I had worshipped before in any sanctum. I wouldn't place garlands round their necks. Or bend to wash the dust off their feet. I cannot name the fathers of my children. They had come. They had gone. Perhaps I have been widowed several times over. There is no man in my life for whom I will ever again cook a meal. I have no love for men. But they become providers even without being conscious of the fact. I ought to feel some gratitude towards them. They beat me up sometimes. Rage at me. Their abuse heaps up like garbage about me. I have learnt to live with that rage because to me it is only a passing storm. I know I can disarm them even if they pull out their daggers and threaten me simply by offering them my bag with the money in it. They have to leave me. They have to go on their way and sometimes are destroyed by the very violence they themselves generate. But I am tough too. My degradation gives me strength. I have nothing to lose. At twenty-six I know all things that are necessary for survival. An independent woman earning her own living and supporting three children. One day, if I live long enough—and I know the dangers attached to my profession—I will give my daughters in marriage respectably, and then earn my rest. Perhaps my son will earn enough to tell me, 'Mother, stay at home. You're weary. You've struggled for us long enough. I'll go out and get any job.' Yes, I must admit I'm worn out already. I am afraid of getting pregnant again. Then what will I do for a living? I never want to put my children up for adoption. Life is this long weary passage. I cannot see any light at the end of it. Treading these sordid streets night after night. The dust, the mud, slush, churned up by myriads of walking feet. Piles of rubbish heaped up everywhere. Scavenging dogs, lean, gaunt city cats. Piles of fruit, pineapples, mangoes. Apples sprinkled with water for freshness or polished with a piece of grimy rag. Oranges which look tempting and fresh on the surface but inside are black and spoilt. Grapes that grow sour and fermented.

I wanted to hurry back home but my curiousity got the better of me. Also this feeling that I was still alive. Who was this man anyway? A man whom I could have once encountered? I walked up to First Cross Street with the woman. She wanted to see the body again. The body of a man who no longer had any power over a woman. Would I feel pity for such a body? In this instance I recognized the man. He was still wearing the chocolate brown shirt and the blue sarong. Only now, they were soaked in blood. He had been stabbed all over his body. Softly under my breath I uttered the words, '*Sabbe Samkhara Anicca*' (All conditioned things are impermanent), '*Sabbe Samkhara Dukkha*' (All conditioned things are suffering), '*Sabbe Dhamma Anatta*' (All dhammas are without self).

Impermanence and sorrow are part of our lives. I wonder what happened to the rest of the apples he had and all his money. Why had he returned to this hotel? Did he come in search of me? Did he come with another woman? Yes, often men in this state of mind crave more and more of indescribable sensations. There is a hollow feeling, an unappeased hunger in the empty, cavernous mind and body, so they continue their search.

Who would bury this man? Who would mourn him? I had lain with him for a few hours. There had to be a bond between us. Yes, a feeling of *dukkha* overwhelmed me. I felt a pang but suffering was not something I could afford to indulge in. All life is suffering. 'Birth and old age, sickness, death, association with unpleasant persons and conditions, separation from beloved ones and pleasant conditions, not getting what one desires, grief, lamentation, distress, all such forms of physical and mental suffering . . .' all this is *dukkha*. This is what I heard as a child when *bana* was preached in the temple on Poya days. Then I would sometimes observe *sil* and meditate on the five or eight noble precepts of the Buddha. No, I could not feel entirely indifferent towards him. Part of his money would feed my children today.

I will go to the police and give evidence. I feel in a way that I am responsible for the whole train of events that took place. But it was our karma. We had to meet in this life. There were things we both had to atone for. We will be reborn. The currents of the ocean of *samsara* have dragged us on, beyond the shore. I have struggled out of its depths, even if temporarily. I will give *dana* for this man. Charity. So that his next birth will be less painful.

Voice Two

There is no other way to earn as profitably as I do. My husband Somi has no job. As long as I make money by offering my body, I can support my man and my children. For the last three years this is how I have earned my living. I don't look towards any future for myself. I am only concerned about what happens from day to day and what my children can look forward to. I want them to be educated, to go to school regularly. But how could I buy them their books, their pens and pencils, their clothes? Feed them? How? This was the easiest way for me. My man, Somi, is always around. He is there, waiting outside the hotel till I come out. He makes the arrangements with the clients. Sometimes he has to be careful. If the man looks too rough, a real thug, he puts him off. But then we cannot afford to be to choosy. The feel of their bodies, smells, odours, the roughness; their greed, violence, urgency, their weaknesses—these are all things I put up with, endure as long as I can take money back home with me, to my children. What can Somi do? How can I blame him if he cannot afford to find a steady job? He once had hopes that he could support his family. Provide for us, give us a home and keep me there to look after the children. He had studied, passed exams, tried hard to get steady employment.

When we look around us there are so many who appear to be prosperous. Building new houses, buying vehicles, travelling in Pajeros, Toyotas, BMWs,

beginning business enterprises. There are those who
have gone to the Middle East, to Kuwait, Oman,
Sharjah, Riyadh. You can tell by the way their wives
and children dress that they have money. The way
they shop at the super-markets, the gold that adorns
them. There is poverty too, all around us in this city.
The homeless with their meagre belongings camp
under wide shady trees, or huddle on pavements
and on steps leading to old, disused buildings. At
least I have a home to return to. I see those human
forms like carelessly strewn bundles, sleeping under
the stars at the Fort railway station, guarding their
little space jealously. Their territory. Where will they
end? Before the early morning trains set out, some of
the women and children limp to the station toilets
and perform their ablutions. They prepare for the
long, hard day ahead. When the monsoon rains fall
I do not know where they sleep.

Sometimes I feel my body is not a body. Just a
piece of used up earth, ploughed time and time
again. So many hands, through need, through greed
and desire, have reaped its harvest. Sometimes the
yield is been so sparse, the earth so drought ridden.
At others there is a rich harvest— a rare, plentiful
yield, an abundance of golden grain. And then, as if
a monstrous seed had been sown, dark and fungus
ridden, the husk becomes boll, the grain bitter. The
scarecrow set in the middle of the field grimaces. A
wry grin twists the black pot face. A hot wind
sweeps over the stalks and bends them, tangles their
roots. Over the grain the old women with their
bodies humped in toil scythe the stalks and sing
mournful dirges. A vast famine hits the land and
skeletal hands scrabble in the dust . . . . These are the
visions that often possess me. I must wear a *suraya*,
with its amulet, round my neck to protect me from

misfortune. I must save money for a *thovil*, the magical ceremony that will rid me of the demons of sickness that have taken over my mind and body.

Perhaps one day things will change for me, but as long as the children do not go hungry, as long as Somi does not desert me for another woman, I will carry on like this. Almost every day I take the bus from Panadura to the city the Pettah area with its shops, hotels, cafés, restaurant, bars and taverns, with its traders and ancient houses where once the rich and elite lived. Old houses with thick walls, wide-girthed pillars and verandahs enclosed in intricate trellis work. Tall steps leading up from the pavement. Inner doors, spacious rooms now dark and musty. Storehouses stacked with wooden crates and sacks of merchandise. Inner courtyards. The walls now stained, damp, with green fungus. The tiles on roofs awry. I am so used to these streets. The rich no longer live here. The *natames* lounge about after unloading the lorries with their huge curved hooks beside them. They use them to grasp the heavy loads and swing them over their backs already bent double with gunny sacks filled to bursting. It is so different in my secluded garden in Panadura where I have a small house. It has a tiled roof and walls whitewashed with *chunam*. There is an araliya tree and jasmine bush. My daughter loves to scatter fresh jasmines in a clay pot filled with water from the well. But it is no place to earn a living, so almost every day I take the bus with Somi into the city. I have a certain amount of freedom. I have a protector. Unlike some of the women who live in the very bowels of the earth, in subterranean chambers, caged up in barred cells. They are locked up, padlocked all their lives, their brief lives. Fed through the bars. Let out like animals, then locked in again. Without any hope of escape or release, in the clutches of those who wield the power of life and death over them. Slaves, bonded slaves, who will never emerge into the light. If ever they come out of those depths they will be blinded. I at least can go back to my home in Panadura. Even if only to die there. With my children around me, someone to press my feet, bring me a sip of water, wash my clothes for me.

Someday if I have made enough money I will take a few days off my job. Rest, bathe, spend time with the children, listen to their stories of school. What a relief it is to sleep the whole night without disturbance. For three whole years I have been doing this job. I am now used to it. There are worse kinds of drudgery than this. And sometimes I can afford to give my children more comforts than an ordinary wage earner can—jam and butter, apples, a small bunch of grapes, biscuits, toys, clothes. Or Somi takes the children to Galle Face Green where they can run about, breathe the fresh air of the ocean, fly kites, eat roasted kadalai, ice cream or hot godamba roti from the carts with their brilliant petromax lights.

In my own childhood I had few treats. My father had left my mother for another woman. My mother worked as a servant in houses, going early to work in the morning, coming back in the evening. Sometimes she would forego her mid-day meal and bring her packet of rice to be shared among us. Or she would do *kuli* work on the roads, on building sites where she had to carry loads of rubble and sand on her head. Another man came into our house. He didn't leave me alone. He would creep up to my mat. One night he clasped his hand over my mouth and raped me. Blood was everywhere on my clothes. What could I do? My mother was too scared to intervene. I kept awake at night. Night after night. I was afraid to close my eyes. But he would come. My mother was helpless. I couldn't continue going to school. She couldn't afford the money for books or school uniforms. I married Somi when I was sixteen just to escape that man and the poverty. At last now I have a home of my own. Everything in it is from my earnings—the furniture, the TV, the bed, dressing table, almirah.

I usually go to First Cross Street. Always near this particular hotel. Rooms can be rented out to women like us who take our clients there. They make easy money out of us. We pay Rs 150 for a few hours. On that particular night I was with my husband. A three wheeler drew up. There was a man peering out of it. I noticed the colour of his shirt. It was chocolate brown. His sarong was blue. With checks. The neon light from the hotel cast its reflection on his clothes. He beckoned me towards the three wheeler. I felt a sudden sense of fear. I didn't want to leave Somi and get into the vehicle, to be taken away somewhere alone, to be even murdered. Somi should always be within reach. Somi himself went up to the man and spoke to him. The man stepped out of the three wheeler and asked me to accompany him to the hotel. He seemed to know his way around here.

At the entrance to the hotel there were four men whom I recognized. The man went to them and began speaking. They were Ratne, *Podimahattaya*, Sene and Suduputha. Suduputha is the hotel servant. I went up the stairs by myself to the room I was accustomed to using. The walls were stained with damp, the plaster was peeling off like scabs. White paint scratched and scraped off revealed the hidden coat of blue beneath the surface. Most of these hotels are really old buildings. No one gives the insides a new coat of paint. I think some of these buildings are over a hundred years old. The walls are so thick that you cannot hear a scream or cry if anything were to happen. I'm not the only woman who comes here. There are plenty of habituals like myself. This part of the city teems with people. Some of them, indeed many of them, are pleasure seekers. Pleasure seeking, survival, trade and barter, everything goes on here. There are shops, boutiques, night *kades*, *apana shalawas*, hotels—not the posh hotels with red carpets, subdued lighting, crystal chandeliers and air-conditioned rooms. Beautifully furnished. Room service. Oh, the same things go on everywhere but at a different price. Here the rooms smell of sweat. The walls are grimy. The mattress sags. Dusty unswept floors bear the imprint of many feet . . . .

I kept waiting for the man to come up. To get it over and done with. Collect my money and go in search of the next client. Time was passing. He didn't come up. Suduputha came and told me to leave the hotel. I went down the stairs. There was no sign of the man in the chocolate brown shirt and the blue sarong. While I was coming down the steps of the hotel I saw the man in the inner section. Ratne and *Podimahattaya* were speaking to him. There was a heated argument going on between them. I didn't stop to find out the reason. For me it was a waste of time. I joined Somi and went off. I had still to earn my money. The night was young.

The next morning I heard that a man was lying dead on the pavement outside the Siripura hotel, the hotel I had visited. The encounter of course had come to nothing. Somi and I walked along till we came to the body. A crowd had gathered. The dead man was lying on the pavement, flies already buzzing about him. He was wearing a chocolate brown shirt and a blue sarong. His clothes were soaked in blood. There were large patches the colour of rust, still damp. I had had nothing to do with him so I felt nothing—no grief, no sense of loss. I hadn't taken his money either. If I had, I might have felt differently. I may have given some of it for charity, to some poor beggar. To help this unknown man in his next birth. This was his karma. Who knows what evil deeds he had done in the past to meet with such a violent death. He had been stabbed all over his body.

Somi and I went to the police station to give evidence. That was the least we could do for him, for this stranger whom somehow I had met in this vast ocean of *samsara*. At the police station we were asked many questions. Questions about my life. We had to attend court proceedings too. On the day we were present I recognized some of the men I had seen in the hotel. They were the suspects in the case. The lawyer interrogated me first.

'How often do you go to the hotel?'

'Often. For the last three years I have gone regularly there.'

'How frequently did you go?'

'About three times a day. With different men.'

'So, for the last three years you went to the hotel three times daily?'

'Sometimes I don't work. I keep away for different reasons but now I have started again to come to the hotel.'

Somi also had to give evidence.

'Where are you employed?'

'I have no job.'

'No other means of subsistence then?'

'No sir, I can't get employment. I have to live on what my wife earns.'

'Were you in the vicinity of First Cross Street at any hour on that day?'

'Yes, we were. At about twelve-thirty that night.'

'Did anyone invite your wife to go to the hotel?'

'A man who arrived in a three wheeler called my wife to accompany him. She said, "I'm afraid. Who knows what kind of man this is. You go and speak to him and see for yourself." I went up to the vehicle and spoke to the man. He asked me whether the woman was willing to go with him to the hotel. He said he knew that they would give a room there. He asked me how much I would have to pay my wife. I answered, one hundred and fifty rupees for my wife and another one hundred and fifty for the room. He agreed, and entered the hotel with my wife.'

'Where were you?'

'I stood outside waiting for her to finish her work and come back.'

'Did you notice anything in particular about the man?'

'Yes, sir, he was wearing a chocolate brown shirt and a blue sarong.'

'How long did you wait outside?'

'Not very long. A few minutes later . . . .'

'How many minutes later?'

'About five minutes later.'

'Yes?'

'My wife came out and told me that the man had been arguing with the employees of the hotel. Sudu, one of them, had asked her to leave the place.'

'What were they arguing about?'

'I think it was about getting the same room he had previously used.'

'Why was he so anxious about getting the same room?'

373

'Perhaps the others cost more.'

'What happened next?'

'There were sounds of an altercation going on. Raised voices, angry words . . . a violent argument . . . the sound of blows.'

'And then?'

'I peeped through the entrance and saw Ratne and *Podimahattaya* going into a room of the hotel. The man in the chocolate brown shirt and blue sarong was not to be seen.'

'Did you hear anything?'

'Yes, sir. I heard a voice shouting out '*Mahatthayo*, please let me go.' Later on I met my wife. It was about 1.15 a.m. She was tired. We decided to have a cup of tea and we came back to the same hotel. I heard one of the men giving some orders about bringing something immediately. I couldn't quite catch the words.'

'I take it you heard the words.'

'Sir, I . . .'

'Could it have been the weapon that was used on the man? A sword? A club?'

'It may have been sir. The next day I identified the man with whom my wife had gone to the hotel. I remembered him well by the colours of his shirt and sarong. Chocolate brown and blue.'

'Do you know how he died?'

'Yes, he was stabbed many times over in various parts of his body.'

That was the evidence that my husband gave. I myself am fortunate to be still alive. I may have been involved too had I been near by. I wonder whether anyone came forward to claim his body. Whether his body was taken back to his village to be buried by his people or whether he had come to the city and lost all connection with his kith and kin. Perhaps he will be buried at state expense. If no family member has claimed his body there will be no *pansakula* ceremonies. No funeral orations. Who will set fire to the funeral pyre after walking round it three times? Is his death a tragedy to anyone? And who would give *dana* for him? We are all the nameless people. I am one of the women in the case. I wonder who the other was. The man who was murdered was a trader from Maliban Street. Traders. So are we, in a way, though we trade in different commodities, our flesh consumed by the fires of lust. In the end we are all consumed by our actions and deeds over which we have no control. I am now more conscious of life, of death. What will my next birth be like? We must all suffer, endure our karma. I might have been able to save him if he had come with me. This thought nags my mind. If only he had not got involved in a violent argument. But perhaps his time had come. His death could not then have been deferred. A *sirri-sirri* bag had lain beside him. Two apples had rolled out of it. They were already going bad. I had fanned away a blue-bottle buzzing near my face. I had to continue my *samsaric* journey. I had still to earn my rest.

Fear: Meditations in a Camp

Upani Yati Loko Addhuvo'ti

(*Life in any world is unstable*—The Dhammuddesa)

I SAT ALONE on the porch. Cold with fear. A motor cycle stopped at the gate. I rushed to see who had arrived. Two priests from the Methodist Church, Reverend Harold and Reverend Artie, had come in search of us, to find out whether we were safe. The crowds had gathered at Padmasiri's *petti kade*, the small boutique of packing-case wood where men generally gathered to smoke a bidi or cigarette, the women and children to buy bread or buns or quartered bars of soap when they went down to the river to bathe. But this was in the past, the innocuous past. Now there was a great hubbub there. The two priests had been intercepted and interrogated.

'Are you one of them? A *Demala*?' they had asked. Reverend Harold was dark complexioned.

'Can you pronounce *baldhiya*?' had been the next question. Linguistic racism. Tamils were thought to say *valdhiya*.

Reverend Harold had a sense of humour. 'I can pronounce anything. I can recite all the Sanskrit slokas if you want to hear them. The *Dammudesa* in Pali too. Listen . . .' he began to recite the summaries of the teachings of the Buddha:

> *Upani yati loko addhuvo'ti.*
> *Attano loko anabhissaro'ti.*
> *Assako loko, sabbam pahaya gamani yan'ti.*
> *Uno loko atitto tanhadaso'ti.*
> *(Life in any world is unstable, it is swept away*
> *Life in any world has no shelter and no protector*
> *Life in any world has nothing of its own, it has*
>   *to leave all and pass on*
> *Life in any world is incomplete, is insatiate and*
>   *the slave of craving)*

In a light-hearted mood after his first witty rejoinder, the crowds gave ear to him in all seriousness and let him pass.

I opened the gate for the two priests with a sense of great relief. We prayed together for the safety and protection of the innocent victims, who were embroiled in the chaos and confusion of racial violence that was raging through the country after the landmine explosion in the North where thirteen soldiers had been ambushed and blown up.

'It is not safe for you to spend the night here,'

Reverend Harold told me.

'Where are we to go? The camps are not yet ready. If we were to take refuge with friends, they too would be in danger for harbouring us. We have to think of a solution.'

The priests prepared to go in search of the other scattered members of their flock who were in the same predicament as ourselves. Guru and the children were still in hiding. I walked through the open gate into the boutique. Into the very midst of the mob. Some of the young men were still restive, with Molotov cocktails in their hands. I was exhausted, drained of strength, yet I had to know what was going on. I did not know where Guru and my daughters had taken refuge. I was alone. I felt invisible. It was important at this point not to retreat. I stood around and listened.

One young man spoke out aloud.

'We ourselves will go to the North and fight. We are patriots. We will fight for our Motherland. We are not looters. We will not take even the ball of chilli that is left behind on the grinding stone. We only want to fight for our country against those terrorists, the Tigers. They ambushed our soldiers and killed them with landmines. What are we doing here? Let them send us there, to the North.'

Another young man gesticulated towards the houses on the hill. Middle-class houses. Stable bastions, solidly built to withstand yet another century of havoc.

'We too are victims. Aren't we also the deprived? Look at all these people living around here. Look at their lifestyles. All hi-fi people. They flaunt their wealth. Some of them will not allow us to pluck a single araliya flower to take to the temple on Poya day . . .'

'Or even a *kurumbu* or *thambili* off their coconut trees when we are sick.'

Hands gestured not merely in the direction of the burning Tamil house, our neighbour's house, but also in the direction of the Sinhala houses with their curtained shuttered windows, locked doors and bright, newly painted walls.

At that moment a police jeep drew up. Two policemen got off. They were armed.

'What is this crowd doing here?' they asked peremptorily.

'Go back to your homes peaceably,' they urged.

The crowd was too angry, too excited and worked up to pay heed. The policemen were ignored. There was an angry buzz. The policemen could not persuade them to disperse. The crowd knew that the policemen had no authority to open fire on them.

An army jeep now roared along the road. The officers and their men jumped out, swung their leather belts and rifles at the crowd and they all went shrieking back into the village. The women's voices were shrill, their protests vehement.

I moved quietly away from the periphery of the men, back to my home. I realized that we could not remain here. The words of the leader of the mob reverberated in my mind: 'We will return tonight.' I could not remain with that fear haunting me and keeping me tense and wakeful, listening to the footsteps that would move towards my destruction.

The dishes of food were still on the dining table, the food half-eaten. It had been our last meal together before Guru and the children fled. The rice had grown cold on the platter.

Guru and the girls finally came down from the hill where they had been hiding, in the houses of Sinhala friends. They had been compassionate people.

Mrs Kotalawella, who was in her eighties, and spent most of her time meditating, doing *bhavana*, had consoled the girls: 'These people who are doing these acts, who cause you so much pain and sorrow, are not even conscious of their terrible deeds . . .'

We decided to spend a few nights in my brother's office. When the camps were ready, we would seek refuge there . . .

We prepared to leave our home. None of us had the heart to clear the table. We made a few bundles of clothes and sheets. We had to travel light on this unknown journey. The path of endurance had begun. We had to tread it as best we could.

Alternate Journeys

We were being driven along Davie Road in the car of a friend. On either side lay stretches of green paddy fields bathed in golden light. Beyond the fields, the roofs and the walls of the houses of traditional dancers of the village could be glimpsed. I had seen great dancers like Ukkuwa and Guneya in days gone by, dancers who deserved to be immortalized for their knowledge and skills. They had lived in this village of Nittawela through which we were now passing in our fearful journey. I had seen these men performing the *vannams*, the classical dance compositions of the Kandyan period. Each man knew all eighteen of the *vannams*. Their supple bodies were able, even in old age, to translate every movement, every subtle nuance of the gods, of man, bird and beast into dance. They knew the *vannams* of the deer, the peacock, the eagle, the elephant, the tortoise and the monkey. They simulated the exploits of warriors and kings in their dance. They enacted the wars of the Dewas, chanted eulogies to the God

Sakra, sang of the adventures of Prince Siddhartha's horse, Kantaka. They sang praises to Lord Buddha. Their dances paid homage to all nature, all living things which surrounded them in the countryside.

I too was familiar with this world which we had shared. But where were those virtuoso dancers now whom I had seen dancing in the light cast by flaming torches, who had transported me into another world where I had felt more at home? Many of them were no longer alive. Their shrill nasal voices chanting incantatory verses which accompanied each gesture, are only echoes in my mind. I did not understand the words but it was enough to feel that ancient past still retained in the blood as those sinewy arms encircled with heavy silver bracelets flashed in the torch flares. Old men who had many years ago been taken to Europe, to Germany, to perform in Hagenbeck's circus.

In those cold, snow and ice-bound winter months they had shivered in their hotel rooms, huddled together, home sick and lonely. They were billed as the Wild Men of Ceylon. No one in Germany had seen such dances before. The parabolic trance-like curves of the hands lifted about their bodies, the ankles heavy with silver anklets, their *ves* head dresses shimmering with the wildly shaken silver bo leaves; the tossed tassels swing like plume-tails about their faces. What unaccustomed food had they eaten, what strange western attire had they worn on the streets or Berlin? These men were taken along on a sailing ship in the early years of the century by that European impresario, together with wild animals, trapped in tropical and equatorial forests, in their wooden crates buried in the hold of the ship.

The Kandyan dancers—with their elaborate, ritualistic movements, their ancient incantatory chanting, accompanied by the resonant throbbing of their drums—mingling with trapeze artistes, bare-backed lady riders in frou-frou skirts, clowns and animal trainers. Ukkuwa, one of the old dancers who still wore his white hair in a knot at the nape of his neck and trained young novices in a Roman Catholic school, used to say how cigarettes and money were tossed onto the stage by the audience in the German music hall and circus tents. The dancers, exhibited like wild, exotic other-world beings, rushed onto the stage to collect coins that were flung at them by the audience. Those drums had beaten out rhythms to create a thrilling sense of excitement in the breasts of the Aryans wrapped in their fur-lined winter coats, thick woollen scarves and mufflers, leather gloves, and Homburg hats set firmly on their heads. The smoke from their cigars and pipes hung in thick blue-grey spirals in the fuggy air. This was entertainment for them, wild beasts tamed under the whip and wild men leaping up and whirling in their convoluted movements.

The dancers had been sick to the gills on those ocean liners, staggering about on deck, their skins damp with sea-spray. Then disembarking at some foreign port, Hamburg, perhaps, their ears ringing with sounds of an unfamiliar patois, they were taken along those grey streets with the huge crates of animals and circus paraphernalia, the tamed beasts already docile with years of training, sedated and half suffocated by their own foetid droppings, soggy straw and remnants of bone.

The men had returned to this village with their memories. They had survived. The drums were heard once more and their sounds travelled through the still air of quiet nights when the rituals of dance and exorcism continued until daybreak and early cockcrow. Their arms stretched like antlers, curved upwards and swung like elephant trunks in that ritual forest as they danced the *vannams*. The miraculous blood awakened, swirled with their rhythms, reviving them, giving them back their ancient dignity. To me, passing by those tranquil fields, time was a suspended image, devoid of all animation, static against the violence and turbulence of my imaginings.

The threshing floor, the *kamatha*, stood like a small island beyond the sea of green paddy fields. It was here that the buffaloes treaded the grain; where the unhusked paddy was winnowed, its chaff flying in the wind, where the straw bales, rounded and piled with their fresh, wild natural fragrance of sun, wind and air, stood monolithic and everlasting in their endless and continuing cycles of creation. A deserted *kamatha* wrapped in an unnatural silence. I remembered those nights when the harvest had been gathered in and the grain was being threshed, the strong, nasal halloos of the farmers impelling their circling buffaloes tied to their yokes. Year in year out those cries had comforted me at nightfall.

The village receded into the past with our passage. Davy Road. The early Kandyan wars of 1803. Unwelcome colonial excursions were part of the exercise of those times, albeit into inhospitable territory. Major Davy after whom this road was named was one of the few survivors of that disastrous expedition to Kandy. After the massacre at Watapologa he had made his way along this road, 'half-dead of his wounds'. He survived and together with Captains Rumley and Humphreys was made prisoner in Kandy.

The two captains died soon after they were imprisoned. Major Davy himself did not live long after the imprisonment. Suffering from ill-health he was brought to Kandy from Dumbara in 1810. He expired in Malabar Street soon afterwards.

We all make alternate journeys for our survival.

Endless Night

The first night away from home was spent in the office room of my brother, Fidelis.

The desks were covered with hooded typewriters and files. We settled in, into the uncertainty of concealment, hiding our voices and bodies away from the glare of discovery. Of revelation. Here, we would spend the night. Perhaps several nights. There were two beds. Fidelis would sleep on one of them. His sleep would be sound and dreamless for he would never be one of the hunted ones. On the other bed my husband Guru and I would try to sleep. But it would never be sleep. Our bodies were cold. Nervous. Excitation and fear shuddered through our gelid veins. I lay floating in a nimbus of aqueous light. Luminous threads of water snarled my limbs into a web. Thoughts stabbed my mind.

The river flows through the valley. I would sit and gaze at the fires from the torches searing the dark water. Darker because of the piled shadows from overhanging trees. Clumps of bamboo. Coconut palm. The *chulu* light with fire-ends of dry coconut fronds would search out the fish even in darkness. The moon with its fragmented face, a torn *attana* flower, trumpet-throated. Dismembered petals tossed on the river currents. The darkness was violent.

The children slept on newspapers spread on the cement floor. I paced up and down, up and down. So the centuries are traversed. So the ship heaves through the ocean.

It began to rain. The windowpanes were blurred, blotting out the tiresome trail of images. Beyond the street, beyond the row of shops and houses and the railway line, was the cemetery. Shapes of death haunted me, gaunt shadows hovering about those marble monuments. My parents, grandparents, uncles, aunts, cousins, a young eight-year-old brother were all buried here. 'I have heard the sod fall, tumbling into that dark hole. Seen the coffins being lowered. The wreaths pile up on the mounds of earth. My tears tasted like salt on my lips. I wiped my damp cheeks.'

The children, as I turned to look at them, moved restlessly in their half sleep. The fear of that day, that endless afternoon, still disturbed them.

I thought of the diary of Anne Frank. Hidden with her family in an attic, writing day after day, recording the details of that fear-filled life, alert for the sound of footsteps nearing the hiding place—until she was taken away.

How long would we have to remain here? Would we be discovered? Taken away? From under the table my daughter watched my pacing feet. My limbs must have seemed disassociated from the rest of my body, like the *boru-kakul* man walking on wooden stilts. The night was endless. I did not want to wake my brother but each time I woke up to take a drink of water from the earthenware goglet, each time the water gushed out, I felt that the whole world was awake and listening.

Next door, in the timber shop, voices murmured throughout the night. They sounded conspiratorial. Menacing. Would those men sense our presence here and search us out? The thought was disturbing. I crouched on the bed like an animal. My whole body was cold. Limp. Clammy. This was the first time I had spent a night in an office room. In hiding. In the little pantry there was a loaf of bread roughly sliced. A tin of fish. Gazing at it all I recollected the parable of the loaves and the fish. Pages opened in my mind.

Then Jesus lifted up His eye and seeing a great multitude coming toward Him, he said to Philip, 'Where shall we buy bread, that these may eat?'

One of His disciples, Andrew, Simon Peter's brother, said to Him, 'There is a lad here who has five barley loaves and two small fish, but what are they among so many?'

Then Jesus took the loaves and when He had given thanks He distributed them to the disciples, and the disciples to those sitting down, and likewise the fish, as much as they wanted . . .

Morning arrived. The street was dead. Silent. We had moved through surreal time to reach here. A few vans overcrowded with passengers drove fast, at a desperate-seeming pace, to reach who knows where.

There was the sound of a jeep coming to a halt. It stopped at the gate. Footsteps came up the stairs. Measured footsteps. A knock on the door.

'Answer it. Answer it.'

'It's Colonel Upatissa.'

Colonel Upatissa. Small in stature. Dapper. In khaki uniform. Strange harbinger of news from the outside world. He was a University man and in that fact found a kinship with me. He was armed to the teeth. Our protector.

He sat before me. Twirled his revolver before our faces. I was mesmerized by its hypnotic movement.

He spoke of his student days on the campus. I thought back on the past. Even that sequestered world had its dangers: strikes, hartals, the police roaring along the tree lined roads, the air above blazing with flame-red flamboyant blossoms. They came in a phalanx on their heavy motorcycles in the darkness of the night. They entered the halls in a solid, threatening body. I was returning to my Hall of Residence when I heard the sound of rushing feet, batons falling on bodies. The whack and thud against yielding walls of flesh. I paused in the road. Yet it was not a sense of fear that stalled my feet. I waited and watched. Those were moments of history. Those were the beginnings. The portents of what would follow. One day, in a future not yet envisaged, dismembered bodies, headless torsoes, severed heads would be carefully, architecturally arranged in the pattern of the *cakka*, the Wheel of Truth, around the ornamental pool. The heads of the insurgents. The *Dhamma-cakka* of death. The Halls of Residence would be overflowing with refugees. I would be an inmate in one of them. Now, at this moment, going back in time I pushed the vessel of my body through the current. I passed, as a shade would, unnoticed. Unharmed.

The next day, in the pillared portico of the Arts Faculty building, Gehan, the President of the Students Union made his speeches to the students who crowded round him. He told us to keep calm. That solutions would be found. The turbulent crowd dispersed. So many still stood at the gate, watching. If it opened, who would rush in?

I was a fair choice for editing the University Magazine. I was approached by two cliques—the Left Wing group and the Roman Catholic, Legion of Mary, Catholic Student Body.

'We'll see you get the post. You have to support us,' the leader of the Left groupers told me.

I had given my word to the Catholic Group. I would not retract. What were the implications of belonging to either side?

The Union elections were held in a lecture room in the Arts Faculty. I was defeated. The Left was triumphant. The Left-wingers were more powerful than the Roman Catholic minority. I was left alone. The newly elected editor was applauded. A victory. Politics. Religion. Myself caught between two divisive forces. Where were all my supporters? There were none to be seen. All the Catholics were at Mass, praying and receiving Holy Communion. There was no one to escort the defeated back on that long, lonely road. I bent my head, accepted my fate and began to walk, past the avenue of trees, the flower beds of canna lilies, the ornamental park with its cascading bougainvillaea, the arched canopy of flowering trees, back to the Hall. There was no one to console me. I went back to my room, and began to read Ovid: *Opprime, dum nova sunt, subiti mala semina morbi, i procul, et longas carpere perge vias* (You may not like long walks; but they are an excellent cure for a sick mind.)

The road that stretched before me was endless.

Chariots of Wrath

All time is a reconstruction of events. We re-live each moment and seek out the meaning of our individual existence in a past that becomes the present and leads to the many-pathed future with its tortuous and winding routes, sometimes without thought of any destination.

We drove endlessly through empty streets. In the

police van the men with their guns were silent. Were the guns for our protection? A few police patrols stood at strategic points outside closed shops and buildings, holding revolvers and guns.

'Where are you taking us?' I asked.

'We will take you where you have to go,' answered one of the policemen.

Smoke spiralled up from gutted buildings. Where were all the people? Where were they hiding? Curfew kept them off the streets.

The police van hurtled through streets that had been familiar to me since childhood. The Kandy lake with the Queen's bathing pavilion which housed the Kandy Public Library full of English novels; the fountain with its cherubs; the Dalada Maligawa where I would take my children at the hour of pooja, at six o'clock in the evening, and the sounds of woodwind instruments and drums, the *horanawa* and *tammattama*, resounded from the stone pillars against which the men stood, filled our bodies which would bear the echoes for a long time. I would also take the children to the island in the middle of the lake where as a young girl I had watched the firework display on Independence Day in 1947; the Queen's Hotel where the big dances were held during the *Perahera* and New Years Eve and Easter; the big colonial shops of the past, Whiteaway and Laidlaw, Cargills and Millers. Every landmark was recognizable. But the connections were now awry.

The van reached the bottom of the hill opposite the police station. It then drove up the winding road until it reached the school building. It was one of the leading girls' schools in Kandy.

We clambered off the vehicle with our roughly knotted bundles of clothes. We had had neither the time nor the inclination to pack our things in suitcases. All we had with us were a few sheets hurriedly picked up, a few changes of clothing, a towel or two bundled in.

The foyer of the building teemed with hordes of humanity. The stairway was choc-a-bloc too. Streams of men, women and children of all ages, the younger ones carried in arms, climbed up and down the stairway. They had arrived before us and were trying to settle in. Their faces were anonymous but the same reasons that brought us here were responsible for bringing them too. Refuge. I felt a sense of relief being with this mass of people. The choking fear, the suffocation of threatening feelings, the sleeplessness that racked me began to evaporate lightly, like chill sweatdrops. My limbs were numb. All of us, my husband, myself and our children carried our individual bundles in our hands.

We stood before a desk at which sat two uniformed men with guns resting beside them. We began to utter the statistics required of us. Names. Ages. Number of family. Addresses. Our names and addresses on the electoral lists had originally marked us out, had brought the mob to our gates.

We felt the press of bodies against ours. Why were we in such a hurry to give information about ourselves? What would happen to all the data, the endless compilations that filled these enormous ledgers? They were the tomb's of the refugee. They would become historical records of each life. The bare, factual details that would remain in the archives of memory, worthy of preservation. No one was singled out for the unique distinction of being an individual. We were, after all, in the same boat. Among the crowds we would later on discover friends, acquaintances, familiar faces but at the moment each one was intent only on his, hers and the safety of family. We had reached an oasis. That was all that mattered. We had fled from the individual territory of fear. To rest, here. Even if indefinitely.

We walked up the crowded stairway through a forced passage of moving bodies along the corridors until we reached a classroom that was less crowded than the others. There was no friendly welcome. We stopped at the entrance. A group of youthful theological students were gathered in the corridor.

'Why are you here?' I asked them.

'Reverend Julian felt we would be safer here. The Theological College is too close to the village. Threatening messages reached us,' Mather told us. 'We shall remain here until the troubles are over'.

'We too were threatened,' I said. My voice had an edge to it. The tension still remained with me.

'Look at us,' I continued. 'Look at us. Forced to flee. They came for my husband. None of us felt safe, not after the mobs stood at our gate. We had nowhere else to go.'

The students stood calmly around, leaning against the parapet wall. A man with his forehead bandaged, paced restlessly up and down. The dressing on his wound needed to be changed.

We entered the classroom. Our presence was an intrusion. There was no welcome for us here. A group of young women, nurses from a Christian Medical Centre had taken up their abode. Chairs were arranged like a stockade to give them privacy. Their clothes, taken out of bags and suitcases, were spread on the backs of chairs.

They did not bother to look at us or ask after our welfare. They had placed loaves of bread and packets of butter on the school desks. They sat around eating the slices of bread which one of them cut from the loaves and carefully buttered. There was no offer of even a slice for the children.

Notwithstanding, I gave a sigh of relief. I could suspend thinking for the time being at least. Safety or danger had ceased to matter. If something was to happen there was nothing that could stop it. It would affect all of us. We were now beyond anxiety or panic. Yet, I could not help thinking that these young women were selfish. They had been brought here to the camp and deposited by their medical superintendent and his wife, both doctors. Their manner was one of collective coldness and indifference towards us. I went up to them and said, 'We too are here to share this space.' The chairs were moved reluctantly and with bad grace.

We deposited our bundles on the floor. We had brought some sheets of newspaper which we spread out for our four bodies. We sat on the floor, our backs to the half wall. There was no tomorrow. Only this hour in which we existed like tiny specks of iridescence within a fragile bubble that would soon be pricked and vanish, leaving no trace of our existence.

Windows existed. They were pointers to the outside world which we had left behind. For how long would we have to remain within this camp? Already there were barriers within it. People seemed to adjust to them. The nurses appeared not to want us here. This was their new map with their own borders and frontiers yet necessity drove me to make inroads into their carefully constructed defences.

For the moment I had abandoned the dangers of the outside world. The confrontation with threats and with death. Being beaten up, hacked or burned to death were our fears. There were other dangers too which my daughters sensed. I had never felt

392

such a sense of danger before. Never had to run away, acknowledge such a sense of defeat.

What mattered most here was life, even if it was to be lived in all this squalor where you would creep like an animal into a lair and feel your pelt prickling with instinctive fear. Civilization meant nothing here. Philosophies were absent. So was political theorizing. You delved deep into the hitherto undiscovered springs of your primeval psyche to find the source of pure and absolute energy. Or else there was a new defeatism you had to accept. You had to succumb to the strength of brute force; allow your flesh to cringe. At all costs, this must never happen.

My lips, pale, parched and dry, scabs on the wound of my face. I could no longer recognize the self that placed value on the conventions of refinement and decorum, those ideal if contrived states of mind of society. Then, in what now appeared to be a distant age, the animal within was kept at bay, hedged in by its own paradoxes. The volatile nature, with its great, leaping impulses, eager to devour the day with its appetite for life, was trammelled, confined. Who could envisage that such things would come to pass; that the body which once flashed silver and fishlike in its evanescent and fragile beauty, within the swift-flowing stream or in the light-glittering waterfall, would lie gasping on the rock. Those past beliefs belonged to the artifice of self-deception. What conventions held here? The philosophy of self-preservation? Strategies of survival?

Now it was the sweat of fear, the grime of the unwashed body and the snarled, uncombed hair tangled about the shoulders, the shabby rags of the refugee covering us like old, worn out skin, that transformed us. Our nature changed too. But we could not remain like this for long. We opened our eyes and looked around at the others, became conscious of their voices. We listened in silence but began to realize that very soon we must answer in the same measure the endless questions.

I longed for a cup of tea. I went down in search of something to drink. I did not even have a cup or tumbler or bowl to drink water from. The two men in uniform had their hands full coping with the streams of refugees who kept coming in as the buses unloaded them. In civil life the two men were teachers, quite unused to handling firearms. One man had a glass of plain tea for himself. He shared it with us.

In the quadrangle of the school, huge aluminium cauldrons of rice and sambara were being cooked. The cooking would take time. Everything had to be rushed to the spot—the rice, coconut, vegetables; the cooking utensils, the fuel. The whole building was overcrowded already but no one was unruly. There was a passivity in the acceptance of an inevitable fate. We had to respect each others right to a few inches or feet of space even if we had to sit upright or crouched up. We sat for the most part on the floor.

I returned to the schoolroom. The blackboard stared me in the face blankly. What message could I leave behind on its surface for those who would return if and when lessons were resumed?

I was drawn to the windows. The grey smoke spiralled in the air. The flamboyant trees seemed on fire with their flame-red blossoms.

No, we were by no means safe here, in the heart of the town. We were exposed and vulnerable and yet where else could we have gone? This was the first camp for refugees to be set up in the city. With the crowds coming in we would soon have to move.

This was the labyrinth, the maze, tunnelling into the brain. This was purgatory and the underworld. The patient puppets sat, lining the corridors, backs to the wall. Only the children continued to wail in hunger. We were left to comprehend the dark spaces of the soul. Hands stretched out for bread. There was little else to place in them. The apathy of sitting for interminable hours; the acceptance of a condition against which there could be no aggressive protest. Being herded together like animals in the close, confined space, shoulder to shoulder, created an intimacy among the passive sufferers. Each one of us had travelled into the nowhere clime of timelessness generated by escape and displacement. Each man, each woman had entered into the individual conflict, extending it within the larger conflict that lay outside these walls. We had already shed much that was once thought indispensable to a happy life. The few belongings we brought with us were only symbolic of some vague sense of continuity that we hoped would take us out of the tunnel and into the dazzling light that awaited us at the entrance. From then onwards we had to seek a new identity.

The act of eating became a significant event, of breaking bread with our bare hands, hands that had clasped and unknotted themselves a thousand times in some gesture or another, hands that now lifted a cup to the lips to take a sip of plain tea or water. All these gestures were individual acts of survival. The eyes of each man, each woman were desperate windows of darkness locked in within themselves. The apocalyptic vision of the tree with its flaming thrust of flowers or its crown of thorns burned in my eyeballs. The cross was ever with us. The windows, when they were briefly opened, embodied visions of both hope and despair.

Nothing must be made easy. Or else the act of penance, for here one took on the role of the penitent for the collective guilt of humanity, would count for nothing.

Those nurses who were bent only on their close and intimate act of survival, who resented the intrusion of even a fellow-sufferer, were safeguarding territory. From them one could not hope for any act of self sacrifice out of purely voluntary self abnegation. With ill grace they had shifted and shortened their piece of newly won space. Demographic maps were being set up in this classroom. Neighbours in newly formed human settlements need not necessarily be overfriendly.

I settled down once more upon the floor, stretching out full length and pillowing my head on my crossed hands. Here, in this camp, we would not endanger our friends by seeking shelter with them, but they would search us out. The messages hoping for our safety would reach us in good time.

In this camp one must discard and reject whatever might hinder us in the most profound discoveries we hoped to make about ourselves and our relationships with those whom we had cast our lot with. Even those who were closest to us. We had also to bear with a pain too horrific and elemental, buried in the recesses of mind and memory; to unearth it and lay it bare and naked on the parched plain with its single tree and crown of thorns. The heart, poor thing, was still alive.

We were beginning to learn what sweat and grime were as our clothes clung to our bodies. There was no necessity to change our skins. Others too had grown accustomed to the sight. We lived in full public view of everybody, sleeping, eating, talking, moving around, visiting each other's newly established territories. Queues were necessary. They formed everywhere, for food, for toilets. I was living in one set of clothes. There were no screens behind which one could change.

That first agonized cry on our entrance to the camp—'See what they have done to us'—was stilled. They, because there were no names to attach to those myriad faces of strangers, had made us fugitives. The hunted. We were wandering in the wilderness. Yet we were still alive. My husband, Guru, my children, lived and breathed even in this climate of fear and terror. What would that act of annihilation have accomplished anyway? As I looked upon the despair of others I realized that there was only one way to come back to life. Self pity had to be exorcised for all time. Self questioning takes place . . . then there will be room for reconciliation.

Refugees: Old Man, Old Woman

They sat where you asked them to, leaning against the walls. They curled up on mats, embryos in sleep. Some cursed and grumbled. Others kept silent. A baby, four days old, slept beside its mother. The father? Lost somewhere, perhaps dead or perhaps he had deserted mother and child. No one questioned. No one knew or cared. The young mother still groaned, she hadn't got over the rigours of labour and child birth. She asked for rags, old clothes to cover herself and her child with.

There was a young boy, sick, fevered, stretched out on the ground. He tossed and turned in delirium.

Buses came in, disgorged their loads, emptied their entrails of human bundles. Old men, women and children with bowls and plates stood in queues lining the stairways and passages for food.

A man, awake night after night, unsutured wounds on his head stuck together with plaster, paced the crowded corridors endlessly.

An old woman stood in the centre of the courtyard, a white cotton saree wrapped about her body, her earlobes empty of *thodu*. She stood still, entranced. There was no *thali* round her neck. She saw nothing, recognized no one in the crowd of refugees.

The silent throngs moved on. Coiling snakes emptying their poison sacs.

I stood before the old woman. We faced each other. 'Have you eaten?' I asked.

She did not answer.

A young woman came up to us and led her away. The old woman followed quietly. It was not important to her in which direction she was taken. Outside or inside—there was no guarantee of safety anywhere. The town was burning, burning. New fires broke out before the old ones died down, or were put out.

On a blackboard resting on the floor, an old man sat silently. We placed in his hands a veshti and a shirt. He could not understand our gesture.

'They are not mine,' he said.

'Take them, they are for you.'

He thanked us, prayed for us. We moved away, there were others who needed our ministrations.

I could not forget him. When we moved on to the next camp I thought of him—the old man, white-haired, bespectacled, drinking a bowl of hot milk. Was he still there, I wondered, in a corner by himself, patient, resigned to his fate? The old not clamouring for food and drink, not importuning like the others who stretched out their hands for everything . . .

I too held out a plate, stretching out both hands

for rice from the great cauldron. Would it still my hunger too?

Night

It was icy cold in the room although the windows were closed. The wind blew down from the hills, across the courtyard of the school, over the half walls and into the classroom which was our place of refuge. The cement floor chilled the body through the thin sheet spread on it which crumpled up with every movement of the limbs. Familiarity and anonymity existed side by side in this rectangular space. I stared at a blank wall with its locked windows. The view would never be the same again. The classrooms had half walls that opened out onto endless corridors. The rooms were adjacent to each other. The past and the present reconstructed themselves in these rooms through dreams, through vain and futile hopes. I remembered the house of cards I used to build in my childhood. Rooms, corridors, mazes, storey after storey balancing on the most fragile of foundations, would collapse. I would watch the collapse of my edifice, so carefully constructed, with dismay, but nothing deterred me and I would begin again. But that house of cards had no inhabitants. No one was buried beneath the debris. Here, in these crowded rooms, a vast and silent breathing heaved and rippled through the fugitive bodies heaped about, huddled together in room after room.

There was no space to spread our limbs. We slept shoulder to shoulder. My husband and my children lay beside me. Our being together, our touching, was security. We were enveloped in shrouds, our bodies swathed in winding sheets. Death was not a faraway thought. For those who had the capacity to sleep, to drown in this ocean of sleep, oblivion was a blessing, a refuge for tortured people. When darkness fell, the rhythms of time took over our bodies. We composed our limbs to slumber. There was no raving or ranting.

No one pleaded for pity. Safety for our lives, especially for our children, was the main concern. Yet I myself could not fall asleep. I was alert for sounds, for every movement, every footstep. Anyone could walk in and do his will with us. There were only two men to provide security for the thousands of us who were in here. This was a prison although we could have, if we disregarded our safety, walked out. But walk out where? Into danger. The outside world was not the same world we were accustomed to. Even a look, a word, could stab us. But our wounds went deeper. We bore with us for life a bruised and tattered psyche. So we became voluntary prisoners. The thought of prison food was bitter. The bread crumbled in our hands. We felt penitential. Readied ourselves for confession. I raked my mind for signs of guilt. What made me either an enemy or a stranger in the country of my birth?

At my feet lay a heavy-bodied old woman wrapped in a cotton saree. She slept in the foetal position, her bare feet sticking out from the edge of the cloth. She was completely abandoned to sleep. Snores erupted from her nostrils which were pierced with *mukukutthi*. They emerged as deep growls as of some predator in this jungle. What nightmarish dreams would be engendered by this experience? I tossed about. My eyeballs burned. My eyelids would not close. The beams of the searchlight from the huge trees in the compound of the police station illuminated this inferno. I thought of an ancient copy in my father's library of Dante's *The Inferno* with its illustrations of sombre shrouded figures by Doré. Should I also have uttered the words 'Abandon all hope, you who enter here'? I travelled through the bowels of that underworld in my mind. I could not dwell here forever.

I wanted to shake the old woman awake. I sighed loudly. I cried out in despair: 'Let me sleep, please, please you are keeping me awake. You won't let me close my eyes even for a minute. So loud, your snores. So loud. How can anyone else sleep?' I sat up, touched her body. Whispered again, 'I want to sleep.' But she was impervious to my pleading. Was I trying to restore a semblance of normality to my life? Sleep is synonymous with peace. Neither could exist here.

Others too must have been awake here but they were still. The windows were locked fast—but glass shatters so easily. A red glow appeared like a nimbus on its surface. The city was burning. Flamboyants were in bloom, a mass of red blossoms flamed through the branches. Our bodies lay prone on the cement floor. Our territory was marked out by the limiting stretch of bodies, ours and those of others. We needed so little space now. For the rest of my life, I thought, I will demarcate the amount of space my body will need wherever I live and I will tell myself, 'This is sufficient for you. This is all you need. Content yourself with this, then your mind can walk continents.'

Privacy was absent here. The acts of human bodies that demand the privacies of locked doors now became public. No intimacies were possible. The rough darns, the tears and rents on the sheets and crumpled newspapers were like welts against our bodies.

Every act was exposed. Our needs became common knowledge. Even defecation.

We established kinship with the perennial presence of the bluebottle that circled round our garbage.

The Offering

That evening we were alert, watchful, with intimations of an imminent attack on the camp coming in. From what direction would we be assailed? We were vulnerable, without defences, in the heart of the city. As dusk fell, searchlights fixed on the trees in the compound of the police station flung their beams, slicing the dark with their powerful arcs. We imagined we heard stealthy sounds and gazed fearfully at the ruffling leaves of the sunflower bushes on the high bank. Were the attackers hidden there? The nameless ones?

Tense. Fear made the skin crawl with beads of moisture, crepitating like beetles. Our eyes were fixed on the dark sunflower bushes, the ala-kola and ferns. The upper road ran above its dense walls.

One of the men guarding the camp took his torch and clambered cautiously up, flashing his light among the darkened trees and undergrowth.

Hands, innumerable hands, clutched the parapet, eyes fixed on that moving point. Fear. Fear choked us. Clothes clung, wet with perspiration, to our limbs. Our lips were parched and dry. We had no arms to defend ourselves. Our relief was great when no attackers were discovered. We went into the classroom to prepare for the night.

The room was now crowded with families as the refugees kept pouring in. In one corner a young woman sat alone. She had been brought and deposited here by her Sinhala husband and mother-in-law. She was very quiet and silent, isolated among the family groups.

In another room an altercation took place. A young couple, newly married had, a rubber mattress brought in to make themselves comfortable. But a good night's sleep in a refugee camp was unthinkable.

Voices rose.

'No, you cannot bring a mattress in here. There's not enough room for us to even stretch our limbs. Can't you see that we are sitting against the wall?'

'Lie on the floor like us. No one should expect special treatment here. We're all in the same boat. We'll suffer and endure everything together.'

'Take that mattress away. Take it away. Can't you see that even the children and the old people have to sleep on the floor?'

'Where do you think you are? Why don't you go to a hotel?'

'What, you expect home comforts here? Beds, pillows, sheets, blankets? And someone to bring you coffee to your bedside at break of day?'

'Give that mattress to that old couple over there. What if they die of pneumonia?'

'Shame on you. Young people like you. Selfish, selfish . . . .'

The mattress was taken away. The couple satisfied themselves with whatever space was allotted to them.

Footsteps, voices, sounded in the corridor. There was the clank of a big container being hauled along. We went outside to see what was happening. Some men stood with huge buckets of hot milk.

'I'm Douglas', one of the men said. 'We have come from one of the Buddhist societies with milk for you all.'

'Milk for us?' someone muttered. The voices were rebellious.

'We? Drink their milk after being chased from our homes?'

'What's the use of milk when we have lost our homes, our possessions—and others their lives?'

'Guru,' I whispered, 'Should we not go forward and accept this gesture of kindness?'

'Dangerous, dangerous,' I heard a voice at my ear. 'What if . . .'

'What if the milk has poison in it?'

'Are you prepared, Guru, to take the risk?' I whispered.

My husband stepped forward. He held out a bowl. The milk filled it. He took the first sip, passed it to me, then to the children. The others came out of the school rooms cautiously. Milk for the children and for the old. They held out bowls, empty jam bottles, mugs. And then when these were full, went back silently to their rooms.

We could not turn our backs on any tentative offering of peace.

Dreams of Fear and Terror

Dreams were continual. They happened every night.

I stood on the edge of the balcony, peering over. The staircase was no longer there. I was about to take a step. A yawning gap of darkness lay before me. I was in a ruined house. Everything around me was gutted, the wood still smouldering. Doors torn off their hinges leaned crazily awry. Splintered glass was strewn everywhere. I wanted to climb down from that upper storey. To escape. To that end I had walked alone, rapidly and stealthily, to reach the stairway but the landing was shrouded in darkness and till I tried to take the first step I had not seen the emptiness before me. I looked up and shuddered.

The roof had caved in. The windows were black holes. Only the walls still remained . . .

Startled out of sleep, I sat up suddenly in bed, then half fell to a side. I felt suffocated, drowning in darkness. Someone clutched my arm and pulled me up. Uttered my name. It struck my ears like a bullet.

'Am I safe?' I mumbled incoherently.

Dreams of fear and terror have never left me.

The year is 1977. Six years ago. I am in another room, in another house. I prepare to sleep. Stretch out my limbs. Stones clatter on the roof. I spring up from the bed, look wildly around me. The darkness spins round and round. I am caught up in its vortex. I fall into a vacuum of darkness shot with prisms of pointillist colour. Falling into space. Plummeting down into the Icarean sea.

There is no staircase.

The doors are locked and barred in a different house. The walls are charred. The fire has eaten into the wood. I look down into the pit. I almost step into its darkness. I try to push aside its dense mass, searching for a door through which I can escape.

The dream is constantly with me.

'Why am I alone?'

I am always alone in these dreams. Have the others escaped? Is it only at night that the fear trickles like chill sweat in my armpits? The nape of my neck is drenched with sweat. I lift the hair off it. Wet strands.

I am walking on splinters of glittering glass. The moon is up. It is the house of a neighbour. Giant hands have slammed the walls together. The doors are jammed. Broken furniture is shoved about. I pick up a book from the floor. It is a birthday present we have given the man, the householder. All his books are flung about on the floor. I turn the pages over.

405

Images of a country through the eyes of strangers from another continent. Experiences of missionaries, poets, sailors, priests . . .

I find myself running along passages and corridors. Pursued by someone who is faceless. Perhaps by many. They are always hunting me. I look for the open door at the end of the passage. It never appears. I never reach it. But I keep running. I want to stop but I cannot. I am exhausted. If I stop running it will be the end. Do I want to see the faces of those who pursue me? No, never. I only feel their presence. I cannot understand why they want to pursue me. Why are they my enemies? I do not know.

Memories . . . .

The forest surrounded the burning city. It was night. The trees grew tall, thickly leaved, close. The ancient rites of deflowering the virgin took place here, stealthily and deceptively in the dark. Reptiles rustled in the steep fern banks. The trails were concealed in shadow. Men came searching for lost cattle which had wandered away from the tether. Deep within the sanctuary there was a cave in which a Buddhist monk had lived for years. This was the forest hermitage. In the very heart of it there was a dark, bottomless pool. No one knew how many drowned creatures lay in its deepest depths. It was easy to lose your way here alone with the animals, the reptiles, the disturbed birds who flew above the tops of the trees in a flurry of wings.

The enemy had always been here. Sometimes there was a face. Once I had sat on a fallen tree trunk sketching the foliage and the trees, watching the butterflies swirl past me. Suddenly the man had appeared.

'What are you doing here?' he had asked fiercely

coming towards me. I had backed away from him, fled through the forest, through tortuous and winding paths, stubbing my toes against rocks and roots of trees, my sandals slipping off my feet, until I came to the entrance of the sanctuary. I had escaped that time but gasped with shock as I reached my home and flung myself on the bed. I grew hot with fever, delirious.

The nightmares never end. My feet keep pounding along passages and corridors. They are always just behind me, their hot breath fanning my neck. The pursuit is endless. Sometimes they are almost upon me, yet I dare not turn to confront them. I cannot afford to lose time. The dream never reveals those faces. I am always fleeing away from them. I wake up. I feel relief.

'I am safe. I have not been caught.'

But the face of the man at my gate is one I can never forget. The terror and fear of the new dreams continue from the mirror that holds his image.

Another memory . . .

It was the month of July 1983. The houses were burning. Everywhere. In the city of Colombo the child of one of my friends was cowering behind the huge settee in the drawing room with her parents and her grandmother. Through the windows they could see hundreds of people with flaring torches which reddened the sky. Smoke billowed in the air. Houses burst into flames. Human torches were set alight. The doors were battered in, the walls smashed.

'Will they find us?' the child asked. They prayed not to be discovered. 'Will they find us?' the child repeated.

When her mother told me the story I thought back on my childhood in that small provincial township. I remembered standing on the steps of one of the railway bungalows looking out on the Corpus Christi procession. The women were dressed in white clothes, white shoes and stockings, white tulle veils, singing hymns and carrying candles in their hands as they set out from the Roman Catholic church. Protecting hands shielded the flames that burned so brightly.

Now the crowds in this city bore their own processional torches. They searched out the houses that belonged to the Tamil families. Burning flames swept through the air. There was nowhere to hide.

The lights were put out in the big house, the gates were barred. The child looked fearfully at the reddened sky. She heard the crackling of the flames.

'Will they find us?' She was filled with terror.

I put down the louvres in our bedroom. They were at the gate. Hundreds of them. The leader of the mob was squat, heavily built. His voice was hoarse. He was muscular, a young man, perhaps in his late twenties, his sarong tucked up at the waist. There was only one reason why they should have been there. I knew it. At last it had happened to us. They had found us out. The names and addresses from the electoral list. I was afraid, not for myself, because I was not the quarry, but for my husband and my daughters.

'I am an animal. My fur prickles, my pelt slides with ice and drips on the ground. Fear. We are cornered.'

The leader's face, his body, remained suspended forever in my memory. I searched all the portrait galleries of time, of the world, to remember where and when I had seen that face before. Perhaps it was a face I had encountered in the street, in the market place, carrying heavy loads off the lorries packed with carcasses of cattle, goats, vegetables, fruits, crates of fish. A man for the moment with power in his hands, the power to mete out life or death. He was the awful judge of man's guilt. The Avenger for those thirteen deaths. Had such thoughts occurred to him before? Had he set out to right the world and clear the road for the uncorrupted? At his elbow stood the invisible manipulator who pushed him out onto the roads with the rock, the crowbar, the burning brand in his hands and then after his ruinous task was done he would be dismissed.

It was a sunny morning. The air was bathed in light. Even a shadow was clear-cut on the brown earth. The purple and magenta bougainvillaea thrust out thorny arms which twined round the mango tree. The mangoes had just been plucked, the gunny sacks filled with the fruit and carried into the house to await ripening. Sweet as nectar, those mangoes, the flesh orange red, the juice thick and golden.

Had I not seen that face anywhere before? From which lair, from which covert had he crept out?

My brother had gone before me and stood at the gate. He spoke in calm, persuasive tones.

'*Puthé*, son,' he said, 'go from here peacefully.'

Fidelis, my brother, was barebodied. The light fell on his skin which looked transparent. He continued talking to the leader as if he had resumed a conversation that had already gone some way.

'Listen, *Puthé*, the man you search for is not here. Please go away. I myself am in the army.'

'It is not you whom we want. We want that man. Where is the Demala? We want to go inside and get him. Open the gate. We will fall down at your feet and worship you, but if that man is here let us have him. It's him we want.'

My brother had been a Major in the Volunteer Force and had faced the Emergency of 1958. Yet he was a gentle intellectual, an Honours graduate in Western Classics from the University. I remembered him translating passages from Virgil's *Aenid*. He knew all the battlefields of the past as well as of the present.

Arma virumque cano. The words kept ringing, a bell tolling in my head. The tones of those half forgotten lines were sonorous and dirge-like. They were lines that I myself had once learned. The clash of arms was now closer in my ears.

'The man is not here. I tell you, he isn't. Believe me. It is not a lie. The man and his daughters have fled for safety, seeking sanctuary outside their home, in someone else's house, running desperately up the bank through the back door.'

My husband had had to crawl flat on his belly beneath the barbed wire. He was hidden away in a locked room of Sinhala friends. They placed a bible in his hands. He began reading the psalm:

> The Lord is my shepherd I shall not want
> He maketh me to lie down in green pastures
> He redeemeth my soul

Below the house, at our gate, on the road rose the shrill cries of the mobs and the people of the village. The house next to ours was going up in flames.

I stood beside my brother in the garden. Mudiyanse, who had been plucking mangoes and cutting grass, came up behind us flourishing the sharp bladed *dekathe*. He was known in the village as the mad one, the *pissu miniha*. He too was an outsider but one who in spite of being mocked and taunted had learned survival.

'Be careful,' he warned the mob, 'there is a man-eating dog here.'

'You keep quiet,' the leader shouted and picked up a big rock. He aimed it at Mudiyanse.

I stretched out my arms to protect him.

'No, no, do not hurt him. He is a harmless man.'

The villagers were lined up on the bank with their arms folded. They were watching the spectacle, innocent bystanders.

I could not remain silent. I called out to those who knew me in that village.

'Come, come and help us,' I appealed.

It was only Sarath, one of the brothers in the family that owned the boutique and bakery from which we bought our supplies of groceries and bread, who came out onto the road and spoke.

'Leave these people alone, go on your way.'

He was a man respected among the villagers, belonging to an old and well-established family.

Yes, it was only Sarath who spoke on our behalf. The watchers and the observers were those who had plucked *thambili* from our trees and araliya flowers for their temple offerings. They were silent. The mobs came in waves, from all directions with their crowbars and petrol bombs. We could not withstand them for much longer. I looked at some of the young men in the eye.

'Haven't I taught some of you when you were in school? Weren't you my students? How can you think of harming us?'

Suddenly the leader confronted me and lifted a threatening fist at me.

'We will come back tonight,' he said. The long phalanx began to turn and snake down the road.

The man had made an assignation with me. He knew we were vulnerable there. The territory we inhabited was now hostile. There was no one to protect us when darkness came. I felt as if my body was made of glass. Of a transparent, brittle substance. This stranger had smashed it with a stone. My flesh splintered and covered the earth with prismatic points of light. There was nothing now between myself and the outside world. Behind me was the sound of shattering glass, of doors being battered in, of the asbestos roof of my neighbours house crackling as it flamed with the Molotov cocktails thrown on it. The villagers streamed into my garden. The flames enveloped the entire house.

'Shall we pour a bucket of water to douse the flames?' Gunadasa asked in a joking manner.

I walked with the men, women and children of the village upto the hibiscus hedge that separated our two houses.

'What is the meaning of a Dharmishta Society?' I asked no one in particular.

'Keep your mouth shut,' my brother whispered fiercely.

The mobs had come from three different directions and had converged on the house. My neighbours had escaped in the nick of time. Where could they have gone?

One of the neighbours had telephoned the police, the army headquarters. A jeep came towards the house at a furious speed.

'What are you doing on the road, the curfew is on, don't you know you'll be shot?' the army lieutenant shouted at me. I had gone across the road with a bag full of my manuscripts to Yvette's house.

'Keep these poems safely for me. This is all that is of value at the moment,' I had told Yvette.

Refugees—As We Move On

It was for food or clothes they stretched out their hands, held out their children, always standing in those long endless queues. What did we put in their hands? A biscuit, a slice of bread, a plate of rice. Old clothes, a cup of milk, plain tea, sugar. Bottles, mugs, bowls were replenished. They were soon emptied. The residue lined the bottom of the vessel or the rim.

Buckets of milk, wood fires burning, old blackboard frames thrown in, waiting for cauldrons of water to boil, clothes wrung out lying on the grass to dry. Stench from excreta and urine, disinfectant sprinkled everywhere. Was it to destroy vermin? Yet we emerged like human insects, creeping out of corners. There was still some spark of light left in us although our spines were broken, our wings clipped.

A bluebottle buzzed over a mound of faecal matter. It zoomed, settling on another pile, travelling perhaps to some other camp.

We would meet it sooner or later as we moved on.

Prospero's Island

Sensitivity, not greed, were our demarcations in the camp. Our possessions were few, whittled down to the small piles of belongings stacked behind our backs to prop ourselves and avoid the chill of the cement wall. Sometimes we lay supine on the floor and gazed upwards at the ceiling where a single spider spun its web undisturbed to trap its prey. The bluebottle flew perilously close.

Existence was nomadic. But without herds. I had often wondered what I would do in a prison cell. How would I adjust the mind or the physicality of my body within a confined space? This had led to

413

endless ruminations: I would read the Bible from cover to cover; and a translation of the *Tripitaka*; the Vedic hymns; Virgil's *Eclogues*; and I would need paper, unlimited sheets of paper and pens, then I would voyage on the ocean of my life.

How long to stay here then? Who knew. Tentatively, until it was safe to go outside. Till such time, the necessity to sustain ourselves. Food and drink. The time for the arrival of food was uncertain. We pressed our hands against the craving within us and let the hours pass. But water? I was thirsty. As a child I would stand on the back verandah of our home in Kadugannawa looking up at the low tiled roof of the kitchen and store room upon which my father placed ripe pineapples to be impregnated with the night dews. He considered them to be an antidote to malaria. I remember . . . I would hold that brimming glass of water and drink slowly, sip by sip, and then my teeth, both new teeth and milk teeth, would scrunch the rim of the tumbler, explore and discover how brittle, how fragile this new substance—glass—was against the teeth, the tongue. My lips would bleed. My tongue graze. And then, at the dining table my father would slide his finger along the edge of water-filled tumblers to make music. Strange music which had no notations, which sounded, now that I let it travel through my mind and senses, as if from Prospero's island. Magical airs that rose from the sea, the wind, the trees.

Two young girls, volunteers from St. John's Ambulance, were lurking around.

'Water?' I asked them. 'Water please, I am thirsty.'

They looked at each other blankly.

'Water? But from where?' they said.

'I am so thirsty.' In my childhood home, pots and kettles of water were boiled and then cooled in earthenware goblets—*gurulethu*—their smooth, cool surfaces incised with fern-like designs in white.

Eventually, the two girls brought me water. I had first to search for a container. An empty bottle was precious here. Water had reached me—from what classical Elysian spring?

Ozymandias

Now the resolution had to emerge out of the fatality of our experience. To resolve our conflicts. Whether to succumb to total despair and clang the gates shut on life or to emerge into the day, however dark and murky. The resolution to resume life. To summon the will to live. This was a refugee camp. How then did we, who had spent all our lives in a house, a home, make this new decision that this camp would be our habitation for who knew what length of time? This decision was crucial to life. Whether to want to continue living or not. If the decision was to be a personal one and the choice lay before us like a basket of fruit, we could have stretched out our hands and grasped that which we imagined would sustain us. The fruits had been plucked by other hands. They were still fresh, full of nectar and juice. The colour and sheen had not yet faded from their skins. Black ants still crawled at a split lip, a honey sweet contusion. Soon the fruit would wither, the skin blacken. But before that happened, we had a choice, before the basket was whisked away and its contents spilt onto the garbage heap. I chose to pick out a fruit, crush it between my palms, share out the segments with my family. The tongue, the palate, could still savour its ripeness. But my hand must not hover too long over it . . . . I took what I wanted and pushed the basket in the direction of my neighbour.

I also became conscious of the blackboard that stared me in the face. The greater part of my life had been spent in classrooms. I had felt so much at home in them, adapted myself to their four walls. Sat first of all with the infants. Weren't we then on the side of the angels? And then, later, much later, sat in my own little territory with the blackboard and chalk at hand to make each significant sign that would be another pointer to all the mysteries of the universe. The blackboard had so much power then. I used that power as it had once been used on me. Lessons to be taught. Lessons to be learned. Voices pontificating or being persuasive. Voices as instruments—dulcimers, harmonious or discordant. The blackboard was blank. It had no message for me or for the others. There were no rewards for the faithful followers, for the interpreters of creeds and dogmas. In my mind, abstractions opened out like a delicate fan of Chinese silk held together by a fragile frame of sandalwood. Would it dispel the foetid air breathed from smoke and fire and slaughter? I walked across a stage where I confronted those moralities I once believed in. They now bore visages which grimaced and leered at me. They were apparelled in motley garbs. The abstractions were now personifications. I contended with their reality. The first figure that loomed up before me was of giant despair. I grappled with those gaunt arms that stretched and swung towards me. I pushed with my puny strength but was not strong enough to hurl it into the pit. I asked myself, in those endless hours of silent interrogation, on how many previous occasions I had felt the palpable presence of fear and despair? Only in those enactments on the stage. Only in allegories. Now I must relinquish a name. I became Everyman, Everywoman.

What then was the practicality of becoming and surviving as a non-person? One's needs had to create a space, even minimal, that would accommodate the physical body. A staked out territory with invisible walls. One erased from one's face all expression of humanity. One turned to stone. And stone could be assailed with only certain weapons. It did not burn like flesh. Nor did it bleed or weep. One would also learn from the lessons of history, from the presumption and arrogance of Ozymandias. A walk in that desert, among the lonely stretches of sand in which only colossal ruins of that 'king of kings' remain, would serve to humble the living witness. One would learn to live within the limitations imposed on oneself so as not to impinge on the territory of others. So, one would lay out with as much precision as possible, the sheets of newspaper or the single cotton sheet on the measured square feet of one's abode. It would become not merely the reprieve from the battlefield but a striving to attain nirvana, that desired world of non-being.

Here, one would try to overcome all sense perceptions, remove all those thorns that tore the flesh, seek the Absolute Truth, that 'extinction of desire, extinction of hatred, extinction of illusion'. This was the Buddha's definition of Asamkhata. 'Truth is. Nirvana is.' It is also the cessation of *dukkha*. Here, in this camp, within its narrowest confines, it was perhaps possible to take the path that would lead to the end of all illusion, craving, pain and sorrow.